THE
PROMISE

ALSO BY CASEY KELLEHER

THE
PROMISE

CASEY
KELLEHER

bookouture

Published by Bookouture
An imprint of StoryFire Ltd.
23 Sussex Road, Ickenham, UB10 8PN
United Kingdom
www.bookouture.com

ISBN: 978-1-78681-135-6
eBook ISBN: 978-1-78681-134-9

This book is a work of fiction. Names, characters, businesses,
organizations, places and events other than those clearly in the
public domain, are either the product of the author's imagination
or are used fictitiously. Any resemblance to actual persons, living or
dead, events or locales is entirely coincidental.

For Margaret Cooper – Nan.
Grief does not change you, it reveals you...
and you are one of the strongest women I know

x

In loving memory of Brian Cooper
Rest In Peace Grandad xx

PROLOGUE

Standing in the middle of the room, she began to sway.

Her legs suddenly weakened as the room began to spin violently, twisting her around and around until she felt as if she could barely stand.

She felt dizzy. Sick.

How had this happened?

How had she let this happen?

Her body started to tremble as it threatened to give way and collapse on the bedroom floor.

She was determined to stay upright, to stay focused.

She had to, even though her heart was pounding wildly. It echoed inside her head. Whooshing. The noise deafening.

The shouting stopped.

Now, a blood-curdling, terrifying screech.

Suddenly, she realised…

It was her!

She was screaming.

Pouring out of her uncontrollably.

It was as if she was outside her own body. Floating in mid-air.

She could see the looks of shock and horror on their faces. The tears in their eyes.

She looked down – saw what they could see…

A jagged spray of deep red splattered across the front of her clothes.

A flash of silver held in her hand, knuckles white, fingers still gripping the weapon's handle…

A pool of dark liquid around her feet.

Blood.

So much blood.

CHAPTER ONE

'See, I told you that Gary would come up trumps for us, didn't I!'

Ashleen Jacobs smiled at Javine Turner as the two girls made their way up the front steps of Mayfair's most exclusive nightclub – Liberties. Entering through the main doors, they pushed their way through the throng and headed towards the bar.

'Wow, this place is heaving tonight,' Ashleen shouted above the shrill music that screeched out across the club as she ordered them both a glass of wine. She was still beaming from the fact that she'd managed to get them in tonight, pleased that Gary, the doorman, had kept his word and put them both on the guest list. Of course, he'd only agreed to do it after he managed to blag himself a blow job for his efforts, though Ashleen decided to keep that little nugget of information to herself. She'd got them through the club doors and that was all that mattered. The five minutes of jaw ache had been worth every second judging by the grin adorning Javine Turner's face. Now she just hoped the rest of her little plan paid off tonight too.

'Yeah, it's all right, isn't it?' Javine said, nodding her head approvingly, for a change, as she scanned the nightclub. The place was packed out. The atmosphere electric, buzzing. 'Mayfair is the place to be. It feels a thousand miles away from the clubs in Brixton, that's for sure.'

Ashleen was right. It was heaving, and it certainly seemed to cater for a wealthy calibre of club goers; the only problem was: Javine couldn't help but notice that it seemed to be mainly female bodies in here tonight. Wall to wall girls, all in little packs. Probably all here for the same reason she was. To bag themselves someone rich and famous.

Up until Gary had lifted up the red ropes outside the club's main doors and ushered the two girls inside as if they were VIPs, Javine had been convinced that Ashleen had just been spinning her another one of her many lines. Since moving into Ashleen's tiny flat in Brixton a few weeks ago, Javine was learning fast that every other word out of Ashleen's mouth seemed to be either an outright fib, or far-fetched exaggeration. Her new flatmate just couldn't help herself. Either she was just eager to impress Javine, or the girl was a compulsive liar – Javine had no idea which. Tonight, however, Ashleen had come up smelling of roses, so Javine had to give credit where credit was due.

Though, looking around the place, it seemed Ashleen had been wrong about the club's clientele.

'Where are all the Premier League football players? There doesn't seem to be much in the way of decent talent.' Screwing her face up as she scanned the club in search of Ashleen's promise that it would be swarming with mega-rich footballers and wealthy Eastern Europeans, Javine couldn't help but feel more than a bit disappointed. She'd taken the girl on her word that they could scout for decent men here. Men with money. Real money. She'd been depending on it, in fact, having just spent her last two hundred pounds on having her hair and nails done especially for the occasion. She'd figured tonight would be a good investment, and she was counting on it paying off. Big time. Only, now they were here, apart from the doormen and bar staff, the only other men were a bunch of old blokes in suits with about as much money in their wallets as they had sex appeal.

Seeing Javine's sudden flicker of disappointment, Ashleen rolled her eyes.

There really was no pleasing some people.

'It's still early, Javine, here get this down you.' Handing Javine a glass of Chardonnay, Ashleen hoped her flatmate would lighten up a little.

Liberties was one of the best clubs this side of the river: far more upmarket than the usual haunts that girls their age normally frequented. This place was exclusive, kitted out with purple leather booths, LED dance floor and one of London's top DJs.

Javine didn't know it yet, but Ashleen had just the right guy lined up for her to get her newly manicured greedy little claws into; all they had to do was wait. In the meantime, Ashleen intended to make the most of their night out.

'If you fancy a little starter before the main course arrives, we could always blag a few drinks off those guys?' Ashleen said, pointing over to where three men were sitting in the main VIP booth. She was just as skint as Javine; the two glasses of wine she'd just bought had taken the last of her cash. Until later tonight, anyway. 'They might not stretch to a bottle of Cristal, but I bet we could wangle a bottle of Dom at least.'

'Who? Those three middle-aged suits?' Javine followed Ashleen's gaze, wrinkling her nose at her friend's suggestion. 'We're skint, babe, not desperate.'

'I think you'll find that they are one and the same, babe.' Ashleen grinned as she and Javine watched a gaggle of bikini-clad waitresses strutting over to the VIP booth laden with jeroboams of champagne, and bottles of vodka lit with sparklers, as a crowd of girls all danced around in front of their booth. 'If we don't make a play for them, they ain't going to be short on offers. Beggars can't be choosers, huh? Besides, look how many bottles of booze they've just ordered. They've clearly got some money.'

'Nah, they ain't got real money.' Javine shook her head, cringing as she watched the men jump up on the seats. Throwing themselves about as they danced without rhythm, they drunkenly passed the champagne around, each taking their turn to glug it straight from the bottle.

They were lapping up all the interest from the hordes of scantily clad desperados gyrating in front of them.

'How did you work that one out?' Ashleen said, wondering what Javine could see that she was clearly missing.

'They're too flash. They're trying too hard. Tonight's just a novelty to them. Trust me, they haven't got the kind of money that funds this lifestyle for longer than one night. I bet you anything you like that those blokes are going to wake up tomorrow crying into their economy box of cornflakes as they tot up how much money they pissed away while they were off their faces in here tonight,' Javine said knowingly, pursing her lips. She might only be seventeen but if there were two things she was already an expert in, no thanks to her good-for-nothing ponce of a mother, it was how to read men and how to spot money. Real money. Her mother had been setting her up with so-called 'sugar daddies' from the age of thirteen. Pimping her out to rich older men while she just sat on her old fat arse and counted up all the money that her beautiful daughter made for her.

Javine had made that bitch a fortune over the years, until she'd copped onto herself that her mother was just using Javine for her own gain.

That's why she had run away from home in the end.

Angry at her mother, she'd decided that if she was going to have men paw at her for money, then she was going to be the only one earning out of it. She was going to keep every penny that she worked her arse off for. Fuck giving it all to her greedy mother.

These men were nothing more than a farce. They didn't fool her for a second, though their little charade seemed to be working on some of the other girls who didn't look like they knew any better.

It was all just a game. Pretty girls and greedy men.

Well, Javine was ready to up her game. She was done with teasing and tantalising men for a few quid and the promise of a designer handbag. She wanted the real deal. Someone who would set her up for a good few years to come. Someone who was willing to pay the premium that she knew she was worth.

That was the only way she'd make it on her own.

She was completely skint. The little money she'd received from the last bloke she'd managed to snare had all but run out now. The cash was all gone.

Ashleen had been more than understanding about Javine being behind on her rent, but it had been almost three weeks, and Javine still hadn't managed to land on her feet yet. That's why Ashleen had offered to bring her here tonight, so that she could help her meet someone decent, with real money.

Shaking her head as she continued to watch the gaggle of girls in front of her with fascination, Javine couldn't help but laugh. These girls were complete amateurs. Dancing around the men provocatively as they all fought to outdo each other. They all looked so obvious, so needy.

'Well, at least if someone half decent does walk in here it won't be much of a contest,' Javine sneered, eyeing up the clones of girls with their dodgy bleached hair and their fake-looking breast implants and matching fake overfilled trout pouts. It was like a freak show.

'Well, you may be skint but you're certainly not lacking in self-confidence!' Ashleen muttered under her breath.

Ignoring Ashleen's comment, Javine flicked her long, jet-black hair over her shoulders before pulling out her compact mirror and eyeing her reflection approvingly.

Ashleen was just jealous. Most girls were. Javine was used to it. She was well aware how stunning she was. Of the effect that she had on men. The desire that they felt towards her. Women, on the other hand, normally despised her. They say beauty is a curse and a blessing, to Javine it was just a blessing. She didn't give two shits what people thought about her.

According to her mother, Javine owed her exquisite looks to her biological father, whoever he was. The man wasn't stupid either, it seemed; he'd upped and legged it just before Javine was born, clearly making his escape while he still could. His only contribution to her life had been the inheritance of his strong Iranian gene pool. Javine was blessed with the typical Persian features of her father's birth country. A smooth, tanned complexion and large cat-like, chocolate-brown eyes. She had his height too, apparently; six foot tall without heels, and a neat, perfect size eight figure.

It was just as well she'd got something out of the man before he'd abandoned her; if she'd only had her mother's traits to fall back on, she'd be nothing more than a fat, plain Jane with a humongous arse.

The only physical trait that Javine seemed to have inherited from her mother had been the woman's huge bosoms, which only added to Javine's appeal. Of course, Javine always dressed to accentuate her incredible figure by wearing tiny, skin-tight dresses that emphasised her large full breasts and impossible tiny waistline.

Her conniving mother had been more about her brains than her looks. She'd used her own child; pimped Javine out the minute she'd started puberty. The woman was heartless.

Still, at least it hadn't all been in vain. Javine was tough. She was going to be just fine. She'd make sure of it.

Looking down at her empty glass, she saw she needed another drink. Maybe Ashleen was right. If nothing else, these men could be the warm-up act at least.

'You know what, you're right. We may as well go and ponce a few drinks while we're waiting for someone better to come along,' Javine said, plonking her glass down on the table next to them.

Ashleen smiled, about to follow. Turning to walk over to where the men were sitting, Ashleen stopped, gripping Javine's arm.

'Hold your horses, girlie,' she said with a grin, nodding over. The two girls watched as the club's management approached the booth. Behind them, two men were standing. Judging by their stern expressions they were clearly annoyed that these men were in their seats.

Javine viewed with interest as the management team asked the group of suits to vacate the booth. Insisting the men move to one further away, they started to collect the bottles from the table as the two men behind them stared. Their presence in the club was gaining them everyone's attention.

While they looked seriously pissed off at being asked to move, the suits looked like they knew not to argue about the fact either. They moved without another word, as if they were too scared to even dare dispute it.

That alone spiked Javine's interest.

'What was that all about? Who are they?' she asked, confused, as she eyed the two men who had now taken up residence in the empty booth. They were older, probably in their mid-thirties, she guessed. The shorter man was white, stocky. He glared. Nothing special about him. It was the taller black guy that had caught Javine's eye. Dressed down, in trousers and a crisp white shirt teamed with an expensive-looking leather jacket, he looked sleek, understated. He had impeccable taste too, as, seconds later, he scanned the club and instantly locked eyes with her.

'That, Javine Turner, is your golden ticket, mate.' Ashleen smiled, glad that her work here was almost done. Three weeks she'd been lumbered with Miss Hoity-Toity; the girl had been seriously doing her head in. Well, in a few minutes she would be off her hands for good. Of course, despite how much the girl clearly rated herself, Javine Turner was too dumb to know any better.

'That's Delray Anderton. The bloke is minted. He owns an escort agency,' Ashleen said, spinning the well-rehearsed line that she'd used a hundred times before on as many other brainless bimbos as she'd happened upon. 'He's bloody picky about who he takes on, though. The bloke makes an absolute fortune. If you want me to introduce you, I can, but there's no guarantees that it will lead to anything.' She could almost see the cogs turning inside Javine Turner's tiny little brain.

She had dangled the carrot, and Javine was ready to take a bite. Fuck, sometimes Ashleen just loved her job. She'd already sent Delray a few screenshots of Javine, and he was keen to meet her. Apparently Javine was just what he was looking for.

'You wanna come and say hi?' Ashleen said, knowing full well what the answer was going to be.

'Er, yeah. You bet,' Javine said, as she stuck her chest out and plastered the biggest smile on her face, keen to make a lasting first impression.

Ashleen led her across to the booth where Delray was waiting for his next delivery.

Javine Turner thought that she was up for playing ball with the big boys; well, now was her chance to put her money where her mouth was. The poor bitch was so taken with the idea of being introduced to a successful, wealthy man like Delray Anderton that she didn't even realise how much this was all going to cost her.

And it would cost her.

Delray Anderton was a ruthless, nasty bastard and Javine Turner was about to be taught one of life's most valuable lessons. The girl was about to do a deal with the devil himself.

Nothing in this life came free. In fact, knowing Delray, Javine Turner was about to find out first-hand that some things could cost very dearly indeed.

CHAPTER TWO

She squeezed her eyes shut tight, but it was no use. Georgie Parker couldn't sleep.

Not with her younger sister, Marnie, pressed up against her, jabbing her sharp elbows and knees into Georgie's ribs as she wriggled about fretfully in her sleep.

Georgie lifted up her sister's arm from where Marnie had draped it over her chest, and placed it back down at her sister's side. In doing so, she felt the clamminess of her sister's skin. Wet, sticky to the touch.

Full of dread, Georgie screwed up her mouth, becoming apprehensive as she reached down and felt around the mattress they were lying on, relieved to feel that it was dry and her sister hadn't wet herself again. There was nothing worse than realising that she'd been sleeping in a pool of her sister's wee, and the last thing she wanted to do right now was strip the bed and her sister bare.

Last time, not wanting to wake their mother for fear of getting told off, they'd ended up having to sleep on the damp mattress with no covers.

Marnie rarely slept in her own bed any more; plagued with night terrors, she preferred to sleep with Georgie.

Georgie didn't really mind, if she was honest. Especially on the nights that their mother hadn't been able to afford to top up the Gas Card, and the house was freezing cold.

She and Marnie would both snuggle up together under the covers, and take comfort in each other's body heat as they lay in the darkness together telling silly stories.

The only downside was Marnie's bed-wetting.

Still, Georgie was grateful that tonight that wasn't the case. Her sister was just hot; burning up, her perspiring skin sticking to Georgie's. Georgie wondered if perhaps she was coming down with something.

Throwing the covers off them in a bid to try to cool Marnie down a bit, she twisted herself away from her sister's tangled limbs towards the edge of the bed.

She stared over at Marnie's empty bed. Just a few feet away, abandoned.

She could try to sneak into it, but she knew Marnie would wake almost instantly, be distraught that Georgie had left her.

Closing her eyes once again, hoping that sleep would soon come, Georgie counted to fifty.

It didn't work.

She was wide awake now, forced to listen to the sound of her mother's bed as it continued to bang rhythmically against the bedroom wall. Over and over again. Georgie pulled the bed sheets up over her ears in an attempt to try to block out the noise, but it was no use.

Her mother's loud, exaggerated moans were making Georgie feel physically sick but as she flinched, her movement woke Marnie.

Sitting up in the bed next to her sister, Marnie wiped her eyes as she stared around the room. Still sleepy.

'Is it morning time?' she mumbled, her eyes seeking out the thin slither of a streetlight that crept in through the tiny gap in the curtains and reflected brightly on the bedroom wall.

Outside, it was still dark. Marnie hated the dark.

'I don't want to get up yet; I'm still tired.'

'Good, lie back down. It's still night-time,' Georgie whispered, pushing back the strands of hair that were stuck to the side of her sister's face, encased with dried snot. 'Go back to sleep.'

Lying back down obediently, Marnie did what she was told, and Georgie pulled the covers back up around them.

They were both wide awake now, lying side by side in the darkness. Both forced to listen to the noises: the bed butting against the wall; the grunts from their mother; the groans from one of their mother's 'friends'.

'Are they doing the sexing again, Georgie?' Marnie whispered, her voice tinged with fear as she slipped her hand into Georgie's.

Georgie bristled.

Marnie was only five.

She knew just how scared her sister was. Georgie had been that way too once. She was older now, twelve. She understood more, but that didn't make it any better. She hated that this was their reality. That their mother had to do those things with men in order for them to have any money.

Most of the time, Georgie tried to ignore her mother's chosen vocation. She tried to block out the sound of her mother's so-called 'friends', i.e. the men that frequented the house at night, but Marnie was getting older now. She was starting to ask questions about it – and just hearing her little sister say the words out loud made Georgie feel hot with shame.

'Cover your ears, it will be over soon.' Unable to keep the irritation out of her voice, Georgie just wanted it to stop too.

Those noises brought forth images of her mother doing disgusting things with the men her and 'Auntie Mandy' brought back here.

'Sexing doesn't sound very nice. Does it, Georgie? It sounds like Mummy's friend is hurted himself?' Squeezing Georgie's hand tightly, Marnie's voice sounded quiet, faint. She was clearly as uncomfortable with the noises as Georgie. 'Is he trying to put his seed in her again?'

'Who told you about seeds?' Georgie turned to her younger sister, shocked that she would know about such things. She was seven years older than Marnie, and when she'd been Marnie's age she'd been oblivious to everything around her.

'Some of the other kids at school told me. They said about their mums and dads sexing each other so they can have a baby brother or a sister. Does Mummy want one of her friends to give us a brother or a sister?'

'No,' Georgie said, tensing up. 'You didn't tell them anything, did you? About our mother?' she asked.

Marnie shook her head firmly. She wasn't really sure what she wasn't allowed to tell people, but she hadn't told anyone anything. 'I just listened, Georgie. I didn't tell, I promise.'

'Good. The other kids wouldn't understand, Marnie. They'll just say nasty things and Mummy will get in big trouble.'

'Do you want a brother, Georgie?'

'No, I don't,' Georgie replied; then, not wanting to continue the conversation, added: 'Shh now, Marnie, just go back to sleep, yeah?'

There was silence. Until another loud series of moans echoed through the walls.

'He sounds like a big grunty pig.' Marnie giggled nervously.

Georgie giggled too.

Marnie was right.

'He does, doesn't he? A grunty fat pig like this.' Nuzzling her nose into her sister's neck, Georgie tried to make light of the situation. 'Oink, Oink.'

Her efforts caused Marnie to burst out laughing.

'Here!' Georgie said, quickly grabbing the corner of the duvet. 'Stick that in your gob, so they can't hear us.'

Pushing the material into their mouths, the girls stifled their laughter as they heard one final loud groan. The loudest one of all.

Then, silence once more.

Georgie waited, still unable to completely relax. She knew how quickly the mood could change in their house. Especially with her mother's friends here.

Sometimes Georgie would hear her mother roar with laughter and chat noisily, then the bed squeaking would start all over again. Other times, her mother would fight and argue.

Tonight, much to Georgie's despair, it was the latter.

Her mother started squawking. Bellowing loudly, she was shouting at the man she was with.

The girls winced as they heard the thud of something heavy being flung at the wall. Her mother had clearly missed her target as the man roared with laughter. The sound was nasty, mocking.

The bedroom door was launched open. Their mum and the man were both out on the landing now, right outside Georgie and Marnie's bedroom door.

'You're a piss-taking bastard, Benny. Next week? I can't wait until then for the money,' their mother screeched indignantly as she tried to drag Benny back up the stairs so he couldn't leave.

The girls could hear the scuffle.

'Why are they fighting?' Marnie whispered, confused at how quickly the atmosphere had changed.

Georgie didn't answer. Instead, she wrapped her arm around her sister, again pulling the covers up around them both, just as their bedroom door suddenly burst open. The girls screamed with fright.

The sight of a half-naked man stumbling into the room and landing in a heap in the middle of their bedroom floor caused both Georgie and Marnie to scoot backwards, pressing themselves up against the wall behind them.

'For fuck sake, Jos, you nearly took my head clean off,' the man bellowed.

Taking one look at his black silhouette lit up by the yellow hallway light behind him, Marnie became hysterical.

'The Bogeyman, Georgie. It's the Bogeyman.'

Marnie was up on her feet, scurrying to seek refuge behind her sister in a complete blind panic. She began crying inconsolably.

The man on the floor clambered to his feet, looking shocked at the realisation there were children in the house.

'Who the fuck are these?' Benny Taylor looked incredulously at Georgie and Marnie, then back to where their mother stood in the doorway wrapping her dressing gown around her naked body.

'You've got kids?'

Benny's face was twisted, contorted with both confusion and disgust as he took in the two little faces staring back at him.

Seeing the obvious judgement in his eyes, Josie Parker immediately got on the defensive.

'My kids are none of your fucking business. You got what you came for; now pay me what you owe me and do one, Benny.'

Josie was riled. The cheek of some men. Morals of a bleeding alley cat, yet they couldn't help but look down their nose at her. Benny had already outstayed his welcome here, anyway, by trying to pull a fast one. There was no way she was going to let him get away with bad-mouthing her as well.

'Oh, I'm going, don't you worry,' Benny said, turning back to look at the girls once more. The shock on their faces, their eyes wide with fear, it was like a slap in the face for him. Dragging his T-shirt on hurriedly, trying to at least cover himself up a little, he felt suddenly very dirty.

He couldn't even bear to think about what he and Josie had just been up to in the very next bedroom. The things he'd made her do, all the noises they'd been making, and the entire time these two kids had been in the very next room?

'What sort of a mother carries on like that with her kids just a few feet away?' Benny sneered.

'Oh, do me a favour, Benny. Like you give two shits.' Josie rolled her eyes, bored with Benny's antics. 'First, you try to underpay me; now you're trying to make out that you're some kind of holier than thou fucking saint. I didn't hear you complaining five minutes ago though, did I?'

'Five minutes ago, I didn't know there were two little kids listening to us. You should be fucking ashamed of yourself. You're fucking sick in the head. I ain't paying you shit, Josie.'

'You'll pay me what I'm owed,' Josie screeched, still fuelled with alcohol from earlier in the evening; her temper finally getting the better of her. Benny was using the girls as his get-out clause. Well, Josie wasn't having that. Launching herself at the man, she didn't seem to know or care that her dressing gown had come undone, exposing her bare breast as she lumped Benny repeatedly around the head with her closed fists.

He did his best to put his arms up above his head in a bid to protect himself, but he soon realised that he was no match for Josie Parker. The woman was a first-class lunatic. As mad as they came.

Raining punches at him, she caught him with a sharp hook in the eye.

Benny stepped back, clenching his face, anger surging within him now at the woman's attack.

'You are a fucking nutter, Josie. How the fuck am I going to explain a black eye to my wife?' he bellowed.

Up until this day, Benny had never laid his hands on a woman but, right now, he could happily wrap his hands around Josie Parker's throat and cheerfully throttle the woman.

'Mummy?' Marnie's voice called out, wrenching Benny's seething mind back down to reality.

Turning to look at the two little girls in the bed again, he shook his head, as he allowed his gaze to sweep across the filthy room that the two children were sleeping in.

His eyes resting on the greasy chip papers that lay discarded, scrunched at his feet on the floor. Strips of wallpaper hung from the damp, mouldy bedroom walls. Small chunks torn off in places. Probably by the girls. Something to do locked away in here, bored out of their minds while their mother entertained strange men in the next room.

The acrid smell that lingered in the air was what hit him the hardest. His eyes watering at the bitter stench of piss, like that of a public urinal.

Benny thought about his own two children, tucked away, safe, at home in their beds. The sudden pang of guilt consuming him as he thought about his wife. She did his head in, his old girl, but one thing he couldn't dispute was that she was a good mother, his missus. She lived for their kids. Forever fussing over them both, making sure they had nice clean clothes to wear, a decent bit of food in their bellies.

His wife was twice the woman Josie Parker was.

What the fuck was he doing here?

'Fuck this!' he said at last.

Grabbing the twenty pound note from his pocket, he launched the money at her.

'Here, fucking have it,' he spat. 'That's all you're getting from me. Buy your kids something nice with it. They deserve that and a lot more with you as their mother, poor little fuckers.'

Benny shot Josie one final look of contempt before he stormed out of the room, slamming the front door so hard as he left that he nearly took it off its hinges.

The house was silent then, but going by the thunderous look on their mother's face, the drama wasn't over yet.

Josie was still seething; angry with Benny for taking the royal piss out of her, and angry that the girls had just cost her most of a night's earn.

'Why aren't you two asleep?' she screeched. 'Can't you, for just once, do as you're bloody told? Why do you feel the need to make my life so bloody difficult?'

'Sorry,' Georgie said, meekly, though she wasn't sorry one bit.

It was all Josie's noise-making that had kept them both awake in the first place; only, Georgie knew it was pointless to argue with her mother when she was in one of her moods.

The best thing to do was simply apologise, even if she didn't mean it.

Their mother had been worse than usual lately with her mood swings, and Georgie knew why.

She was using again.

Georgie had walked in on her mother sticking a needle in her arm just a few days earlier. Not only that, but she was drinking heavily too. Georgie had been praying it was just a one-off, a mistake, but she knew the signs well. She'd lived through it once before.

Her mother had been clean for months. She'd been keeping on top of the housework, and getting Marnie to school on time. Things had been better. But now that she was using again, it would be all downhill. Georgie knew it.

'Sorry?' Josie was incredulous, the sarcasm evident in her voice as she slurred her words. She was drunk. Unreasonable. There was no arguing with the woman. 'Oh well, that's okay then, isn't it? If you're sorry. Makes it all all right that. Never mind that you both cost me most of my money tonight.'

Josie was stopped mid-sentence by a loud ping as the house was suddenly plunged into complete darkness.

'Oh that's just fucking great. Now we've got no lekky either,' Josie wailed, fighting the urge to cry at the electricity cutting out. The emergency funds on the electric key had barely lasted them two days.

'Can anything else go wrong tonight?' Shoving the twenty pound note into her dressing-gown pocket, she was beyond pissed off. She'd been counting on Benny's money tonight so that she could go see Billy Stackhouse tomorrow. Just thinking about scoring some gear from Billy tomorrow had been the only thing that had been keeping her going.

Josie needed a hit. Something stronger than just a drink to tide her over for a while.

Though she wouldn't be getting that now.

She'd have to sort out the bloody electricity.

'Go to bloody sleep,' she screeched. Tears stinging her eyes. She slammed the girls' bedroom door shut and stomped back off to her bedroom to cry herself to sleep.

Marnie started crying then too. Big, racking sobs that made her whole body shake.

She was scared, and rightly so. They'd both seen this before. Their mother in her moods.

She was getting sick again. Just like last time.

Georgie knew the signs well. The mood swings, the crying. Her mother was spiralling out of control again.

Pulling her sister in close to her, Georgie cradled her protectively in her arms.

'It's okay, Marnie, don't cry. Please,' she soothed. 'Whatever happens, I'm going to look after you, Marnie. It's going to be all right.'

'Promise, Georgie?' Marnie said, her crying subsiding at the reassurance of her sister's words.

'I promise,' she whispered as she felt Marnie relax, as Marnie nestled into her. Her breathing slower now, calm, as she started to fall asleep.

Georgie kissed her sister on the top of her head.

She meant what she said.

She was going to look after Marnie no matter what.

CHAPTER THREE

'Mummy! I need a wee!' Hopping up and down as they walked around the Co-op, Marnie's constant whining was really starting to get right on Josie's nerves.

'I told you to go before we came out, didn't I? You're just going to have to wait now, Marnie. It's tough luck!'

Eyeing the bottles of wine that lined the shelf, Josie grabbed the cheapest one there and shoved it in her shopping basket.

Walking around to the cereal aisle, she knew she was close to losing it.

Her head was pounding.

She'd stupidly thought that she was on top of it all, that she could handle a few hits again without getting addicted – but her body was craving another fix. She was clucking.

Josie remembered the signs well, how her body reacted when the heroin left her system.

She was annoyed at herself for getting sucked in once again. She'd been clean for almost two months. Two fucking long, tedious months.

She'd only wanted the occasional hit. Something to take her mind off all the mundane shit that she had to deal with in her life, but the heroin had somehow managed to get its unforgiving claws into her.

Today's comedown only clarified that; it was brutal. Every inch of her ached; the pain excruciating.

She'd woken up shivering this morning, covered in a veil of sweat.

It didn't help that she was completely skint either.

She knew she needed something to take the edge off or she'd never last the day, and for now that something was going to have to be a bottle of Lambrusco. Hopefully, she could stretch to a packet of fags too, because, for now, that was all she could afford.

Turning the corner, Josie scanned the boxes of breakfast cereal, looking for Weetabix, knowing full well that Marnie would refuse to eat anything else.

'Mummy, I'm going to wee myself,' Marnie squawked, cupping her hand over the crotch of her leggings.

'Five more minutes, Marn. Just hang on,' Josie promised.

'But I can't hold it!' Marnie cried, her face going bright red.

'Well, you're going to have to.' Holding Marnie roughly by the wrist, Josie rolled her eyes as she made her way over to the young lad behind the till.

'You haven't got a toilet this one can use, have you?' Josie asked, distracted, as she looked over the young boy's shoulder and tried to work out which cigarettes she could afford.

'We have, yes, but I'm afraid members of the public are not allowed to use it. We don't allow anyone out the back. Health and Safety,' the boy said giving a look of sympathy to the child that was hopping from one foot to the other.

'Can't you just make an exception? She's desperate,' Josie said, irritated.

'Sorry, it's strictly off limits. There's the public toilets at the other end of the parade?' he suggested.

Josie looked down at her daughter.

'Do you hear that, Marnie. This boy's got a toilet but he won't let you use it.' She spoke tartly. 'What a jobsworth!'

Not sure how to reply, the boy looked mortified as he began scanning the contents of Josie's basket.

'Oh, here we go!' Josie said as a new customer walked in.

Of all the people for her to bump into at this early hour of the morning, Javine Turner was the last person she wanted to see.

Javine hadn't lived around these parts very long, but already she'd managed to get most of the local girls' backs up, Josie included. Strutting around the place like she was God's gift to mankind as she looked down her nose at them.

Everyone around here seemed to know the smug little cow's fate better than she did. Swanning around, thinking she was Delray Anderton's new girl. Hanging off the man as if she was surgically attached to him. Javine Turner had no idea what she'd signed up for. Delray was just using her like he did with all of them.

Josie knew it herself, first-hand.

Javine might be flavour of the month for now, but it wouldn't last. Delray would soon have her out on the earn just like the rest of his girls.

Watching as Javine tottered over towards the magazine stand, Josie felt suddenly self-conscious. Javine looked like a million dollars, dressed up in a tiny mini-dress, her ample boobs spilling out of her top.

Josie looked a right state in comparison; she hadn't even bothered to brush her hair since she'd rolled out of bed this morning. She was still wearing yesterday's clothes too: a pair of tatty-looking skinny jeans and a baggy old T-shirt. Instantly irritated that she hadn't made more of an effort, Josie pursed her lips as she watched Javine bend over to get a magazine from the rack.

At least she had her dignity, unlike Javine, who was now displaying everything she had on offer to anyone who cared to look.

The girl was the epitome of everything that Josie hated about young girls of today.

Walking about half-naked, they were classless.

Tacky.

Turning back to the boy behind the counter, who was clearly enjoying copping an eyeful, Josie said, harshly: 'What do you reckon then, eggs and bacon, or muesli?'

He blushed, not understanding the question, clearly embarrassed that he'd been caught staring at one of the customers.

'Oh, sorry, I thought you were trying to catch a glimpse of what that skank had for breakfast?' Josie said sarcastically, enjoying the discomfort she was causing him. 'I wouldn't bet on it being much. The girl looks like an anorexic whippet.'

'I'm sorry. Do I know you?' Javine interrupted with a fake smile as she joined the queue behind Josie.

'No, love, but I know all about you. You're Delray's new girl.' Josie wrinkled her nose, pretending to look uninterested in Javine's small talk. 'I've heard all about you.'

'Is that so? Well, whoever you think you are, there's no chance of anyone ever mistaking you for being an anorexic whippet, is there? Though you look like you might have eaten a few.' Javine shot the older woman a smug grin; then, scanning the contents of Josie's basket she added: 'Ooh, Lambrusco and Weetabix. Breakfast of champions!'

'Why don't you just fuck off!' Josie muttered under her breath. She wasn't in the mood for this shit today. The way that she was feeling, it wasn't going to take much to start World War Three.

Delray had surpassed himself this time with this one. Javine really did think that she was something else altogether. Strutting around Brixton as if she had two fannies or something.

Josie was more than capable of wiping the floor with the likes of Javine Turner. The girl needed to watch her mouth.

Ignoring the threat in Josie's tone, Javine smirked.

'What's so funny?' Josie glared at her.

'I've seen you around, haven't I?' Javine shot Josie a smug grin as she realised who this woman was. 'Delray pointed you out to me.'

Javine smirked, remembering the afternoon they'd driven past Josie. Delray had told her that Josie Parker was some old tart that he used to know. Javine remembered feeling shocked that someone like Delray would even contemplate being associated with a woman of Josie's calibre. As Delray had said, though, everyone was capable of making mistakes, and now Javine had the pleasure of meeting Josie first hand, she couldn't agree with the man more.

'I bet he did.' Turning back to the boy at the counter, Josie ignored the girl. The last thing she wanted to do was start discussing Delray. He wasn't worth the oxygen.

'Can I get you anything else?' the boy behind the counter asked.

Josie guessed he was sensing the building tension between his only two customers.

'Can you stick a fiver on the electric key, and I'll have a pack of Benson's too. Just ten.' She needed a fag now more than ever.

'That will be £16.10, please.'

Josie nodded. Reaching into her pocket, she felt around for her money.

Nothing. Checking both pockets, she started to panic.

It wasn't there.

She searched the floor around her, just in case it had fallen out.

'Sorry, I had a twenty pound note, I must have dropped it somewhere,' she said as she dug around desperately in the bottom of her handbag, totting up the loose change she found, well aware that the smug bitch behind her would be loving this.

'Mummy, I can't hold it in any more.' Marnie was still harping on at her. Jumping up and down on the spot.

'Cross your legs,' Josie said gritting her teeth. She wasn't in the mood for all this shit today; she just wanted to get out of here, get home and have a large glass of wine and smoke herself stupid.

Trying to steady her now shaking hand as she counted the pile of loose change in her palm under the scrutiny of the shopkeeper and Javine, Josie could see that she didn't have enough.

Mortified, she realised she was going to have to put something back.

She wasn't going to forfeit her wine.

'Forget about the fags.' Josie stared at the boy behind the counter.

Keeping his expression neutral, the boy refunded the cigarettes.

'Actually, you'll have to refund the electric too,' Josie said, her face burning with humiliation as the boy behind the counter made a song and dance over the fact that he had to issue a refund on the electricity key.

Another night without any electric was going to be a royal pain in the arse, but right now, Josie couldn't bear to think about anything other than the intense yearning for something to take the edge off. It was consuming her entire mind and body. She'd just have to light some candles tonight, she justified to herself. The girls could have Weetabix for dinner again. That's all the girls bloody wanted to eat half the time anyway.

Sighing loudly, the boy behind the counter continued tapping in some numbers to his machine before pushing the bag containing the wine and cereal towards her.

'That will be £6.10 then, please.'

Looking down at her hand, eyeing four pound coins and a few silvers, the rest were all coppers.

'Mummy.' Marnie was crying now.

'Fuck's sake, Marnie, will you just wait,' Josie said, totting up the money, irritated that she still didn't have enough.

'Mummy.'

Trying to get her mother's attention, Marnie grabbed at Josie's hand, scattering the pile of coins.

Josie was down on her hands and knees, grabbing at the money as it rolled across the shop floor.

'Jesus! Delray said you were a mess!' Javine's voice boomed above her.

Josie smarted. Got back up on her feet.

'Oh, is that so? What else did your so-called boyfriend tell you?' She could feel the shop assistant's eyes on them as this jumped-up little trollop tried to get the better of her. But Josie wasn't having it.

'He's told me loads, actually.' Javine shrugged. She couldn't help but feel sorry for the child with Josie as her mother. 'You want to watch yourself, love.'

Josie shook her head, annoyed at the girl's blatant cockiness. 'Oh yeah, and why's that then?'

Javine grinned. 'Delray won't be happy if he hears that you were talking to me like this, that's all.'

Javine was loving every moment as she stared at Josie insolently, trying to gauge her reaction. Knowing full well that she was winding her up.

'Don't think yourself so important, love. I'm sure Delray wouldn't give two shits about the way people around here speak to you. He'll be doing it himself before too long when the novelty has worn off,' Josie spat, hoping to wipe the conceited look clean off the girl's face.

This was the kind of girl that Delray was employing these days for his so-called 'escort' business: bimbos who thought they were above everyone else around here.

Well, Josie had been on Delray's payroll from the beginning when he'd had his girls walk the street to earn their money. He was nothing more than a pimp, and Javine was nothing more than his next earn. Only, it seemed that Delray had managed to convince this stupid bitch that their relationship was something more than that.

Josie couldn't believe girls still fell for that kind of shit, but then, Javine wasn't much more than a kid, really. Young and dumb: just Delray's type.

'Oh, I think you'll find that Delray would be very interested indeed about how people treat me,' Javine sneered.

'Oh, whatever, Javine. You're ten a penny, love. Just another young bird he's shagging for now. He'll have you out flashing your clout for him soon; you just wait and see.'

'That's where you're wrong, Josie. Me and Delray are serious.' Javine's eyes gleamed triumphantly, and Josie couldn't help but laugh.

''Course you are, love. What's it been? Three weeks?' she sneered knowingly. 'What's he done? Made space for your knickers in one of his drawers in that shitty flat of his? Though, judging by the state of what I just saw when you bent over, you won't be needing much room – seeing as you don't seem to own any.'

'Oh, haven't you heard? He's just moved into one of those swanky apartments over at the Albert Embankment. You know, the posh ones overlooking the river.' Watching the surprise on Josie's face, Javine continued. 'The place cost him a bomb. Twenty-four-hour concierge service. Security on the main door. The penthouse, of course. You know what he's like. He insists on only the best. Well, at least these days he does.' She knew she was treading a thin line discussing Delray's business with the likes of her, especially as Delray had specifically told her not to discuss anything with anyone. He liked to keep his private life exactly that, but Javine just couldn't help herself. Josie was talking down to her as if she was nothing, as if she was just some stupid little girl.

Well, she was much more than that, and it was about time people around here realised it too.

'I've moved in with him.' Flashing the pile of interior design and home magazines that she'd just picked up off the news stand, Javine smirked.

'Mummy! Mummy!'

'What, Marnie?' Josie shouted as she looked down to where Marnie stood, her daughter's feet surrounded by a puddle of dark yellow piss. Her pink leggings soaked through.

'For fuck sake, Marnie!' Josie shut her eyes in despair.

'Oh dear. Looks like someone's had a little accident,' Javine quipped as she stepped forward and tossed two twenty pound notes on the counter.

Flashing the young shop assistant her most flirtatious smile, Javine was in her element. 'Here! Take whatever she's having out of that and let her keep the change. The old cow looks like she needs all the help she can get,' she said as she tiptoed her pointy black stilettos around the puddle of urine and marched from the shop, victorious.

Furious, Josie made a grab for the bag of shopping on the counter, shoving the bottle of wine that had been removed back inside.

The look on the boy's face behind the tills told her everything she needed to know.

Javine Turner had just made Josie look like a prize prat.

Desperate to restore at least some of her dignity, Josie held the boy's gaze.

'Here, seeing as you're so shit-hot on your health and bloody safety, you can clean that piss up,' she told him before grabbing Marnie tightly by her hand and marching out of the shop.

The quicker she got home and poured herself a glass of wine the better.

CHAPTER FOUR

'You're going to end up rubbing a hole in those,' Mandy Johnson quipped as she watched Davey Lewis continuing to wipe the imaginary dust from bottles on the optics behind him. 'You do know that you've already cleaned that same bottle three times while I've been stood here like a lemon waiting for a drink?' Mandy knew full well that Davey had seen her standing there; she'd clocked him looking at her in the mirror.

He was avoiding her, secretly hoping that Rita the barmaid would serve her instead; only, his plan hadn't worked. Rita had her head buried in a magazine at the opposite end of the bar, so Davey had been left with no choice but to finally acknowledge her.

Pretending not to notice the frosty reception she was getting, Mandy persevered with the small talk. 'You expecting a visit from bleeding royalty or something?' Smiling as she leant up against the bar, Mandy stuck her chest out a little bit more, making sure that Davey copped an eyeful of her more than ample cleavage as he poured out the drinks.

But Davey didn't even glance in her direction.

Now Mandy knew something wasn't right. Normally the sight of her well-endowed chest was more than enough to put a smile on the man's face; at least, it had done the last couple of nights. Tonight though, it seemed like a whole other story. Davey Lewis had barely acknowledged her existence.

'Oh sorry, Mandy, didn't see you standing there. I just thought I'd give the place a once-over, you know.' Davey shrugged, still not meeting her eyes.

Davey, cleaning – just for the sake of it? Who was the bloke kidding? The Old Bell pub was a typical South London boozer, slap bang in the heart of Brixton, complete with permanently sticky tabletops, beer sodden carpets and a pool table that was missing half its balls. As the pub's landlord, Davey had never seemed to bother about the state of the place. Until now.

'Two Chardonnays, was it?' he asked, already turning his back on her to get fresh glasses.

Mandy persevered. 'Yeah, cheers. Think me and Jos will just have one more before we call it a night,' she said, wondering if perhaps she was just being a bit paranoid. Maybe Davey just had things on his mind. He had mentioned to her numerous times over the past few weeks that the pub was haemorrhaging money left, right and centre. Maybe the man just had a lot on his plate.

'Saturday night ain't what it used to be, eh? This place is dead now thanks to all those fancy wine bars opening in the high street,' Mandy said, clocking the small handful of locals dotted about the pub – most of them looking as thoroughly miserable as this place felt. If it wasn't for the fact that she and Josie had already been barred from most of the pubs here in Brixton, they'd be at one of the wine bars too, in all honestly. Still, Mandy wasn't going to voice that to Davey.

Unlike all the other landlords around here, Davey had always turned a blind eye to the women's business dealings. They could speak to and meet up with anyone they wanted; as long as they weren't doing their business on his premises, Davey didn't mind one bit. Especially seeing as he didn't exactly have a stream of punters coming through the door.

Besides, it wasn't that bad, really, if you were partial to the shoddy selection of prawn cocktail crisps and old-man bitters.

Realising that Davey still wasn't engaging in conversation with her, Mandy decided to take the bull by the horns.

'Are you sure you're okay, Davey? Only, you really don't seem yourself tonight, mate?'

'Everything's fine, Mandy,' he said unconvincingly; his tone sharp, dismissive. He cursed as he placed the two glasses down on the bar in front of Mandy and one of them slipped from his grip. He caught it before it rolled on to the floor and smashed but soaked himself in the process.

Something was definitely up.

'I'm free later,' Mandy said, hoping that, whatever it was, Davey would feel that he could confide in her. She and Davey had got themselves into a bit of a routine lately. If Mandy had a slow night, she'd come here for a nightcap and, nine times out of ten, she'd end up having a lock-in, just the two of them.

She was starting to enjoy their little nightly ritual.

Davey would pour them both a nice brandy and they'd sit and talk for hours, putting the world to rights, laughing and joking with the ease of lifelong friends.

Tonight though, Davey was acting cagey, different somehow.

'I can't tonight, Mandy. I'm sorry.'

'What about tomorrow then?' Mandy said warily, testing him. Determined to get to the bottom of whatever was bothering her friend.

'Tomorrow's no good either, I'm afraid…' His voice was thick with regret as he glanced out towards the back; his body language shifty, nervous.

Mandy shook her head as the penny finally dropped.

'She's back, isn't she?'

The forlorn expression on Davey's face confirmed what she already knew.

Mel Lewis, Davey's fruit loop of a wife had come skulking back to him with her tail between her legs, no doubt, and Davey, being the soft touch that he was, had taken her back.

'Go on, then, what was her excuse this time? Let me guess: She realised that she'd made a mistake. She didn't know what she had been thinking.'

Mandy rolled her eyes as Davey flinched.

Bingo.

She should have known. Typical fucking Mel and her melodramatics as per usual. The silly old cow didn't know she was born, walking out on a man like Davey. The woman treated him like a doormat that she could stomp all over whenever the fancy took her – and the worst part about it all was that Davey seemed to let her. The number of times Mel had pulled a disappearing act on the bloke, Davey must have been blind, dumb and stupid to even consider giving her another chance.

The latest one she'd buggered off with had been one of the Polish drivers that delivered the kegs of beer to the pub, a bloke half her age.

'So what was it then? Love's young dream just didn't work out, eh? The grass wasn't as green as she thought it was going to be? What did she do? Step in some dog shit while she was over there?'

Davey baulked once again. Mandy was speaking the truth and they both knew it.

'She just turned up here this morning, Mandy. She said she missed me. That she couldn't be without me.' Shaking his head in wonderment, he knew he sounded ridiculous as he repeated the clichés that Mel had come out with earlier. Somehow, they'd sounded so genuine. Or maybe he was only hearing what he wanted to hear. He still wasn't sure himself if he was honest.

'Maybe this time she's finally seen sense, eh?'

Mandy screwed up her mouth, wondering who Davey was trying to convince. She would bet her life on the fact that the only reason the gobby cow had come back was because the fella she'd shacked up with had finally cottoned on to what a psycho Mel was.

It galled Mandy no end, but Davey had clearly made his choice – having taken Mel back again – so who was she to cause a drama?

'Well, you know what, Davey, I really hope it all works out for you. I really do,' she said, unable to hide the disappointment in her voice as she got her purse out of her handbag.

'Look, I know you probably think I'm mad to even entertain the idea of giving her another chance, but I've got to give it a fair go, haven't I? She is my wife—'

'You don't need to explain yourself to me.' Holding her hand up, Mandy stopped Davey mid-sentence. She knew him well enough by now to know that, of course, he would give his wife another chance. Unlike most of the scumbags around here, Davey was a decent man, forgiving. Too fucking good for a woman of Mel's type, that was for sure. Though Mandy decided to keep that little nugget to herself for now. 'Your business is none of mine.'

'Ah, I'm so glad that you're okay about it. I thought that you might, well, you know. I thought it might cause a bit of aggro.' Davey smiled, the relief written all over his face. 'You and me, we're just mates, aren't we?' he said, willing Mandy to go along with him, even though they both knew that wasn't the truth.

They had become much more than just friends the past few weeks. They cared about each other, or, at least, Mandy thought that they did.

She could kick herself. She knew better than to let her guard down, better than to trust a man. This was a painful lesson. Mel

Lewis had swanned back in here again, and within seconds Davey had dropped Mandy quicker than a hot turd.

'Yeah, Davey. We're just mates,' she said, her head held high.

Picking up the two glasses, Mandy turned on her heel and made her way back over to where Josie was sitting at the table waiting for her.

'Uh oh! What's wrong?' Josie could tell by her friend's face that something was up. She could read her like an open book. Mandy had done nothing but harp on about seeing Davey tonight, and now that she was here at the pub they'd hardly said two words to each other, and Mandy had a face on her like a slapped arse. 'I know that look, Mandy. What's Romeo said to you?'

Mandy shrugged, handing Josie her glass.

'Guess who's come crawling back out of her hole?' Mandy said, still fuming from Davey's rejection. 'His mardy cow of a wife. Turned up here this morning.'

'What, and he just took her back again?' Josie rolled her eyes.

Men. They really were fickle. Josie had honestly thought that Davey had come to his senses this time but, clearly, they'd both been wrong about that.

'What is it with fucking men, huh? Selfish bastards the lot of them. All they think about is themselves,' Josie said wistfully as she downed her glass of wine in one. She had enough on her own plate today without Davey pissing her off too.

'It's my own fault,' Mandy quipped. 'I should never have got involved with him in the first place. He's married. I knew that from the start.'

Mandy felt stupid. She'd broken her golden rule. Never get emotionally involved. She'd done quite well with it up until now: she was a cold, heartless cow, never allowing herself to let her guard down, never allowing herself to get hurt. But she'd thought that Davey was different. He treated her as an equal, with respect.

'That man must be a right bloody soft touch, swallowing his knob and letting that one waltz back in after she was swanning about with a bloke young enough to be her son. The woman's had more pricks than a second-hand dartboard since she married Davey; she's making the man look a right laughing stock.'

Mandy was rambling. The combination of Davey's blatant rejection mixed with the cheap acidic wine she'd just downed had put her in a thoroughly shitty mood.

'You really liked him, didn't you?' Josie said, surprised by the genuine hurt that she could hear in Mandy's words.

'Liked him?' Mandy shook her head, determined to save face. She wouldn't allow herself to get all sentimental over a man. Not even a man as decent and kind as Davey Lewis.

'Nah, I just feel sorry for the bloke that's all. I mean, I must have, what else was I thinking, huh? He's not exactly the catch of the century, is he? His hairline is so far back, even a archaeologist would have trouble finding it.' Mandy laughed at her own wit, but when Josie didn't join in, she couldn't help but feel a pang of momentary guilt at slagging Davey off.

She shook her head.

'Why is it girls like us never seem to cut a break, Jos? We ain't that bad, are we?'

Josie looked down at her empty glass, twisting the stem with her fingers. She was starting to wonder the very same herself.

'Fuck knows, Mandy. You're asking the wrong person if its reassurance you're looking for. Trust me, I've had the day from hell…' she said – about to tell Mandy about her run-in with Javine Turner that morning, and the latest gossip about Delray, when Mandy tapped her arm, interrupting her.

'Looks like our prayers have just been answered, Jos.'

Hearing a loud racket behind them, Mandy eyed the two handsome younger men as they stumbled in through the pub doors and staggered over towards the bar, talking and laughing animatedly, clearly both having a good time. They were good-looking fuckers and both smartly dressed. Mandy guessed they were in their late twenties. A bit younger than the clients Josie and Mandy usually pulled in, but the fact they'd both had a skinful told Mandy that she and Josie would be in good stead.

'Looks like our luck might have just changed.' Mandy grinned, then realised that Josie didn't look as keen. The girl was still staring at the main door, looking through the glass at the shadowy figure outside.

'Hello, earth to Josie. Did you hear me? Those two might be potential customers if we play our cards right. Maybe tonight hasn't been a waste of time after all, eh?'

'Yeah maybe…' Josie said vaguely. 'Is that Billy Stackhouse out there do you reckon?' Josie squinted, trying to get a closer look at the man smoking on the footpath outside.

'I think so.' Mandy narrowed her eyes, scrutinising her friend. 'Why? You after him about something?'

Mandy's words were loaded. The last person Josie needed to run into tonight was Billy Stackhouse.

'Oh, no. I just thought I recognised him, that's all,' Josie lied, unconvincingly.

Mandy eyed her friend, suspicious. 'What did you see, Jos? A fucking long brown tail and a pair of goofy fucking teeth? He's a fucking rat, Josie. You need to stay the fuck away from him.'

Josie nodded.

'You haven't been seeing him again, have you? After last time?' Mandy said, sick of pussyfooting around the fact that Josie had been acting more than a little off lately.

''Course not.' Josie was unable to look her friend in the eye. 'I ain't bloody stupid, Mand. I just saw someone through the glass, and asked a question; no need to get all on your horse about it, mate.'

Mandy nodded, knowing that if she wasn't careful she'd say something she'd regret.

'Sorry, love. It's just I worry about you. You know?' she said, seriously. Hating herself for doubting her friend, but she'd had to ask. She'd been here before. With Josie lying to her, and keeping secrets. She couldn't go through it all again. 'You just seem to be in a better place lately. I wouldn't want you to jeopardise that. Especially not for the likes of Billy Stackhouse. The bloke is a parasite, Jos.'

'I promise you, Mand, hand on my heart,' Josie said, looking her friend in the eyes and seeing genuine concern. 'There's nothing to worry about. I was just making conversation, that was all.'

Mandy nodded, though she still wasn't entirely convinced. But she knew she didn't have much of a choice other than to take Josie's word for it. All she could do was look out for her friend. What the girl did was down to her.

'What do you say then?' Mandy said, changing the subject.

'About what?' Josie shook her head, confused.

'About Tom Hardy and Jason Statham over there. You up for it? I reckon if I work my magic on them we could still get an earn tonight.'

'I dunno, Mand; for starters they look too bloody young for us…' Staring over towards the two men, Josie raised her eyes warily. 'And not being funny, but they probably have women throwing themselves at their feet. We might not be their type.'

'What are you trying to say?' Mandy quipped. 'That me and you are fat and old and bloody well past it? Speak for yourself, girly. Have you seen the time? There's no such thing as an ugly woman at closing time. As long as their shot glasses are as strong as their beer goggles we'll be quids in. You wait and see.' Mandy was full of confidence. 'We can call it an education. The poor fuckers won't know what hit them.'

Her eyes flickered over to where Davey stood, and she felt a pang of anger towards the man.

'Unless you've got something better to do, of course?' She eyed Josie, knowing full well that the girl was just as skint as she was.

'Go on, then. Let me just go to the loo, yeah. I need to sort myself out. I'll meet you over there.'

'Don't worry, Jos, leave the negotiating to me. I'll have them eating from the palm of my hand, you'll see.' Mandy grinned, pleased that she'd managed to get her mate on board.

Getting up, she made her way over towards the bar.

So far, tonight had been a complete non-starter. They'd earned fuck all money and she was almost twenty-five quid down from the booze she'd bought.

These blokes were their last-ditch attempt at not having to go home empty-handed once again.

Besides, they offered her a much bigger incentive than money. Mandy reminded herself about all that crap Davey had told her about giving it another go with his slapper of a wife.

Two could play at that game.

She was going to have great pleasure in pulling these blokes right under Davey's nose.

Hell hath no fury like a woman scorned, and all that.

CHAPTER FIVE

Billy Stackhouse leant up against the wall outside the Old Bell pub, a cigarette dangling from the corner of his mouth. He grinned to himself as he counted out the pile of money in his hand.

Tonight had been a lucrative evening. A very lucrative evening indeed. Changing his supplier recently had turned out to be a right touch. They'd come up trumps for him. Not for the punters, though, but then ignorance was bliss. Those fuckers didn't care what they were shoving up their nose or into their veins, as long as they got their hit.

Which was just as well, seeing as the new shipments his supplier had been bringing in was cut with so much dodgy shit, even Billy himself wouldn't go near it. Not unless he wanted his flesh to wither off and die – that's how much levamisole they were putting in the product these days.

The punters didn't give a shit. As long as they got their high, they were completely ignorant to the fact that they were snorting cattle de-wormer. The heroin was even worse. The usual laundry detergent and rat poison used to cut the gear had been replaced now by fentanyl, a synthetic opioid considered to be up to fifty times more potent than heroin. To the suppliers, the punters were just a means to an end – and the craziest thing of all was the junkies couldn't get enough of it.

Ignorant to what they were shooting into their veins, they just wanted the high. Billy knew that there was nothing on the market that came anywhere close to the level of hit in the gear he was supplying.

It really was a win-win for all involved. Unless some divvy fucker OD'd, of course – but even then, it was another waster dealt with. No loss, really.

Billy had made a good earn for himself tonight, pulling in just under nine hundred pounds with minimum effort on his part. The punters were coming to him now in their droves. If business continued like this he was going to be laughing.

He no longer touched the shit himself, not now he knew the potential risks involved. These days he was too busy reaping the rewards of his new-found fortunes. Money was his new drug, and Billy Stackhouse was addicted.

Debating whether or not he could be bothered going into the pub to have a well-earned celebratory pint or go home and have an early night, Billy grinned to himself as he saw Josie Parker tottering unsteadily around the corner in her trademark red high heels. The woman was clearly half-cut.

He knew exactly what she wanted, but there was no way that Billy was going to make it easy for the girl, not when he had the upper hand.

'You all right, Jos?' Tucking his money back down inside the pocket of his jeans, Billy smiled, his eyes roaming Josie's impossibly thin figure. Dressed in a tight leather skirt that hung loosely off her bony hips, he scanned the red lace top; her skimpy bra underneath leaving very little to the imagination.

'You're looking lovely this evening, doll.' Billy smirked to himself. He was lying, of course. Josie looked dog rough, but it wouldn't be in his interests to say as much.

That was why he was as successful as he was; because Billy Stackhouse knew to lay on the charm as and when he needed to. He was a master at playing people.

'Couldn't nick a puff of your fag could I, Billy?' Josie smiled, looking flattered at the compliment.

Billy stared down at the floor, trying to hide his distaste at the smear of bright red lipstick covering her two front teeth.

'Here, have this. I'm feeling flush!' He smiled, passing her a brand new cigarette from his pack and lighting it for her. Even from a few feet away, he could smell the alcohol fumes radiating off the woman, mixed with the bitter stench of body odour.

Fuck knows how the woman makes a living by selling her body, she bloody stinks.

Taking a deep puff of the fag, Josie inhaled the smoke down into her lungs before breathing it out, her eyes watching the white cloud of smoke as it hit the night air, disintegrating before her very eyes.

The wine had hit her more than she realised. She was drunk.

She'd hoped that the alcohol would have taken her mind off her cravings, but it seemed to do the complete opposite and make her want some gear even more.

'You had a busy night?' Billy said with a smirk, knowing full well that the likes of Josie Parker wouldn't know a busy night any more if her life depended on it.

She was the bottom of the barrel these days, compared to her competition.

The girls around here seemed to be getting younger and younger. Prettier too. Skimpy clothes, and faces full of make-up. Josie could no longer keep up.

'It's been a bit slow, but you know, it's not payday yet, is it? Everyone's skint.' Josie shrugged, making light of the situation.

Billy nodded, guessing, rightly, that when Josie said slow, what the delusional cow really meant was that her night had been dead. She might fancy herself as a lady of the night, but the truth was she was showing her age, and even under a cloak of darkness out here on the streets, Josie would be hard pushed to generate any kind of real business. She didn't even look like she'd combed her hair today let alone had a bath.

'I was hoping that I might bump into you,' Josie said, as she rooted around in her handbag for her mobile phone and then pretended to send a text message, despite the fact that her phone had run out of credit almost two days before. She was buying time, making out the encounter was a casual one; she didn't really have an ulterior motive as she gauged what kind of mood Billy was in.

'Is that so?' Billy feigned surprise.

She wanted something; it was written all over her greedy, desperate-looking face. And he knew exactly what it was that she wanted from him.

'And how can I help you?'

Billy rubbed his chin, staring at Josie with amusement.

Josie Parker had been a feisty little bird in her heyday, with her petite figure, and her long mane of white-blonde hair. She'd had a gob on her that was capable of making sailors blush, but somehow, because she'd been so stunning, she'd been able to pull it off.

Now, though, it just made her look cheap and nasty. It was a shame, really, what life could do to a person. How it could wear you down. Still, Josie was the one that chose this life. Working the streets, the drugs, the drink. The woman was a train wreck waiting to happen, but what did he care? If it lined his pockets, then, fuck it, who was he to quibble?

'You couldn't sort me out a wrap on tick, could you? Just until tomorrow. I've got a job lined up later… I'm good for it.'

Billy screwed his mouth up as if debating his answer. He'd known all along that she would come back for more. Once a smackhead, always a smackhead. It was people like Josie that kept Billy Stackhouse well in pocket. Just one hit, she'd said, when she'd scored from him the other day. Just something to keep the edge off. But here she was again, weak, already consumed by the power heroin had over her. She was a slave to it, just like they all were. That was exactly what Billy had been counting on. Supply and demand, that was what it was about in this business.

People like Josie kept his little empire ticking along nicely. No matter how long they'd been clean; no matter how hard they'd resisted the pull of the drug, the addiction was always there, bubbling away underneath the surface, ready to rear its ugly head at the person's lowest ebb.

'I know I still owe you some money, Billy, and I'll get it for you. You know I'm good for it,' Josie said; suddenly, all her dignity gone as she openly begged Billy to sort her out.

He scanned the street, cautiously, to make sure that no one was watching them.

'No one' being Delray Anderton, Josie's pimp. If Delray caught Billy supplying any of his girls again, Billy knew that he would be in deep shit. It wasn't worth the aggro, he figured, but then, Josie wasn't really one of Delray's main girls any more. Word on the street was Delray had moved on to much bigger and more lucrative things.

'Please, Billy,' Josie said, as she threw the cigarette down on the floor, stamping it out with the toe of her shoe. 'I'll have the money for you tomorrow, and in the meantime, I'm sure we can work something out.'

Her eyes flickered to the dark alleyway that ran the length of the side of the pub.

She didn't need to say anything else; Billy knew exactly what the woman was offering him.

He shook his head, pretending to be taken aback by her offer.

'I dunno, Jos,' he said, well aware how to play the game.

He could see the pure want in Josie's eyes. The desperation that lingered there. The poor bitch was probably still trying to convince herself that she wasn't back under the trance of the drug, that she was still in the early stages of her love affair with it, that it was all under control – but Billy could see that she was way past that stage now.

Still buzzing from tonight's successful earn, it would be a shame to call it a night so early and go home on his tod when Josie Parker seemed so eager to put a smile on his face.

'One wrap.'

He started making his way up the alleyway; Josie eagerly following behind as if it was him doing her the favour.

The woman might be a munter, but it was nothing closing his eyes and thinking of England wouldn't solve.

As the saying went, you don't stare at the mantel while you're poking the fire.

Billy grinned once more as he relished the perks of his job.

'Just this once mind, Josie; don't let it become a habit. So you better make this worth my while.'

'Jesus fucking Christ, Jos, look at the state of you!' Mandy stared down at her friend in disbelief. The woman had only been out of her sight for twenty minutes. How the hell she'd got herself into this state Mandy couldn't quite fathom.

Josie was sitting on the pavement, slumped against the pub garden wall. Her legs sprawled out in front of her; her head lolling to one side.

'You're wasted?' Mandy exclaimed, shaking her head. Josie'd had pretty much the same amount of wine as she'd had. It couldn't be just the drink. She'd seen this all before. Suspicious, she scanned the length of the alleyway, remembering that Billy Stackhouse had been hanging around earlier.

'What the fuck have you done, Jos? Have you taken something?' she said, unable to hide the disappointment in her tone. She'd seen this all before. She knew the signs. Mandy had witnessed every heartbreaking gruelling minute of it first-hand. Josie lying and stealing, brought down lower than low as she had tried to get her hands on the gear in any way possible. Then there was the cold turkey. The sweats, the pain. The agony Josie had endured until she'd finally moved on to methadone.

It had taken Josie months to get completely clean, and she was two months on: the longest amount of time she'd been off the gear since she'd had Marnie.

Now she was back where she started. Back on her knees in the gutter once more.

Hearing her friend's voice, Josie lifted up her head, forcing her eyes open.

She was back in the land of the living. Back down to earth with a crash, after being so enthralled in the euphoric rush of the brown she'd smoked just ten minutes earlier. It pained her how the oblivion she craved never lasted long enough. The heaviness of her limbs, the warmth that had wrapped itself so tightly around her body, making her feel invincible, always seemed to leave just as quickly as it arrived. That bastard Billy had made her work for it, but he'd been right. It had been so worth it.

There was nothing on this earth that compared.

'I haven't taken anything,' she lied. She was glad that Billy Stackhouse had got what he wanted from her and was now nowhere to be seen. At least there was a small chance she could still blag her way out of this. The last thing she needed was Mandy breathing down her neck and lecturing her.

Josie tried to sound convincing but she didn't look it. Staring at Mandy, her pupils gave her away. Minuscule like pinpoints;

the evidence was there for all to see. Still, she continued with the charade regardless, determined not to be caught out.

'It's that cheap wine that Davey sells. That stuff is lethal. It's like rocket fuel. It probably doesn't help that I haven't eaten anything today either. I just felt a bit queasy so I came out here for some air.' Placing her hand down on the cold concrete floor she tried to stand, wobbly on her feet, using the wall behind her as leverage.

'Air?' Mandy rolled her eyes. She didn't know who Josie thought she was kidding, but she sure as hell wasn't falling for the spiel.

'What the hell am I supposed to do with you now, huh? Those two fellas are well keen to come back. I promised them a good time; yet, here you are barely able to stand up. You look about as much use right now as a bacon sarnie in a fucking mosque.' Mandy gripped Josie by her arms and dragged the unsteady woman up on to her feet.

'I'm fine,' Josie said shrugging her friend from her.

Mandy glanced down the road to where Dean and Jason were standing, eagerly awaiting her and Josie's return. A taxi pulled up next to them.

Mandy bit her lip, unsure if the blokes going back with them was such a good idea now.

She needed the money, they both did, but with the state Josie had somehow managed to get herself into, the chances of that were becoming slimmer to none.

'Shall I cancel them? Tell them something's come up?' Mandy said, unable to keep the annoyance from her voice. 'Christ, Josie, I've spent the past twenty minutes working my charm on those two; it was all for nothing. I could have really done with the cash, Jos.'

'Don't cancel,' Josie said, thinking about the money.

Mandy was right. Work was so thin on the ground lately there was no way they could turn down what little came their way. She was just going to have to pull herself together.

'I'll be all right in a few minutes, honest. Come on.' Linking Mandy's arm, Josie walked down towards the waiting taxi, determined to see the job through. Not only because she didn't want to let her mate down but also because she knew she'd been lucky catching Billy in such a generous mood tonight. But he wouldn't be so accommodating next time she asked for a handout. Billy wouldn't give her anything else on tick until she paid up what she owed. That was the way he worked, especially now that he had her right where he wanted her.

Despite Josie's best efforts, the heroin had won, again. Like the monster it was, it had snuck up on her, catching her unawares before locking its grip and pulling her back in once more.

She was going to need all the money she could get from now on.

CHAPTER SIX

Pulling up in the Mercedes just outside the main doors of Selfridges on Oxford Street, Lenny Oldham gestured to Javine Turner to get her arse in gear.

'Get in,' he shouted, aware that he'd stopped on a double yellow line. The road behind him was heaving, gridlocked with traffic, and the last thing he needed today was a parking ticket from some jobsworth of a traffic warden.

Javine was doing his head in.

Lenny had driven the demanding little cow halfway across London. Westfield, Harrods, now Selfridges. Surely there was only so much shopping a woman could do?

'Any chance of a hand? I can't carry all this lot on my own.'

Javine pouted, unprepared to carry the bags any further, even if it was just a few feet. Delray paid Lenny to be his right-hand man. To chauffeur him around and, by extension, to chauffeur Javine around too. He was staff. The least he could do was help her out.

Gritting his teeth, Lenny jumped out of the motor, well and truly narked now. He'd had enough of this prissy little tart barking orders at him. He worked for Delray, not Javine. Though right at this particular moment in time it wouldn't be in his interests to voice that. For now, he was just going to have to suck it up and try to bite his tongue.

He hoped that Delray knew what he was doing.

Lenny had seen Delray with many different girls over the years; they were all the same. Money-grabbing whores. But Javine Turner was a whole other level of demanding.

Knowing Delray, he would get bored of the girl sooner or later. He always did. But so far, this one had stuck it out longer than Lenny had anticipated, though that was only down to the fact that the conniving little bitch was busy playing games, stringing Delray along. The girl was making out she was some kind of born-again virgin, though who she thought she was kidding, Lenny had no idea.

'Get in!' Lenny said as he grabbed the pile of bags and shoved them inside the boot. Then he turned back to face Javine, who was now standing expectantly beside the passenger door.

'Are you fucking having a laugh?' Lenny shook his head in wonderment as he realised Javine was waiting for him to open the door for her.

This tart really was taking the piss. Lenny's temper finally got the better of him, but the only thing that stopped him was hearing the bus that had pulled in behind the car beeping its horn. Further up the road, a traffic warden was making his way swiftly towards them.

'Fuck sake,' Lenny muttered. Grabbing the door handle, he ushered Javine into the car before slamming the door behind her and running back around to the driver's side. He pulled away in a rage.

'I take it you're done for the day?' Lenny glared at Javine through the rear-view mirror.

Javine wrinkled her nose up.

'Actually, I'm a bit hungry. Can you take a right on to Wardour Street? I saw a bakery on our way up here earlier doing little cupcakes. I might get some for Delray.' Javine was oblivious to the glare that Lenny was shooting her. 'I'm bloody starving too. Shopping doesn't half take it out of you.'

Staring down at her phone, Javine was miffed to see that Ashleen still hadn't answered her calls or text messages. She'd called the girl at least a dozen times a day. All she wanted was to check on Dolce and Gabbana, her two little fur babies, but Javine hadn't heard from the girl since the night she'd met Delray at the club, three weeks ago.

She grinned to herself. It had all been a bit of a whirlwind, how things had worked out. Delray seemed besotted with her. He must be: he'd done nothing but ply her with presents and money. Like today, for example, sending her off on a shopping trip to buy whatever she liked. No expense spared.

Javine had hit the jackpot.

She'd known it the second she'd laid eyes on the man. Never one to pass up a golden opportunity, Javine had grabbed it with both hands. She'd gone back to Delray's apartment on the very first night, and had yet to leave. She had standards, though. She hadn't let him have his wicked way with her yet. She was making him wait.

Tonight, though, that was all about to change. Javine knew it was time to up the stakes.

She was going to give Delray the best night of his life. Once she was through with him, the man wouldn't want to live without her.

Then she'd bring the conversation of her dogs up again.

That had been the only downside to this little arrangement. Delray had point-blank refused to let Javine bring her dogs to the apartment, and knowing Ashleen, the girl would be doing her nut being stuck at home with them.

That's why Javine was surprised Ashleen hadn't picked the phone up to her yet. She thought the girl would be screwing.

'Ah! You've just driven past it. Pull over here.' Looking up from her phone, Javine screeched at Lenny, her voice high-pitched with indignation that he couldn't just do one simple thing. 'Pull over.'

Lenny had a face on him like thunder; his dislike for her obvious by the way he was staring right through her. Quite frankly, Javine didn't care.

This was another conversation that they'd need to have once she was a little more established with Delray. She'd be having words with him about old Lenny here.

'I'll have to walk,' Javine tutted, realising the shop was now a good hundred yards up the road and, in her high heels, it wasn't going to bode well. Her feet were already killing her from the mileage she'd done around the stores today.

'You'll have to wait here for me.' Javine pursed her lips, irritated.

Lenny didn't respond.

Instead, he pulled into the side road and switched the engine off, keeping his anger contained until Javine got out of the car and stomped up the road in a huff.

Once she'd gone, Lenny lost it, smashing his fists into the steering wheel. Still, hopefully he wouldn't have to put up with the stupid cow for that much longer. Delray always got bored with his new toys sooner or later, and this time, Lenny was actually waiting with bated breath.

Javine was doing his nut in.

The sooner the girl got a reality check the better.

CHAPTER SEVEN

Jason Hunter was hammered.

He must be. How else had he managed to let his best mate, Dean, talk him into coming back to this shithole?

The little that he'd seen so far of this dingy flat was disgusting and, as for the smell, the place stank. Old and musty, just like the furniture that was dotted around the room. Jason followed the trail of half-finished mugs of coffee that had been left abandoned on the carpet alongside the overflowing ashtrays strewn with hundreds of stale dog-ends.

This place was a fucking mess, as was the old slapper currently straddling his lap and fiddling awkwardly with his fly.

'How do you want me?' Trying her hardest now to sound alluring, Josie Parker sounded as bored as Jason.

How did he want her? He just wanted this bird to get the fuck off him, that's how he wanted her – and preferably as far away from him as possible.

He was so pissed that he could barely talk, let alone get his todger up, but the state of the woman straddling him wasn't helping the situation one bit.

This was all Dean's fault. So much for being his best mate.

The bloke had set him up.

Knowing Dean, he'd probably had this all planned from the very start of the evening.

Dean had been the one to persuade him to go out for a few jars down the Old Bell in the first place; Jason hadn't even been that bothered, if he was honest. Dean though, never one to give in without a fight, had insisted, saying that they needed to celebrate the birth of Jason's newborn son.

'Wet the baby's head,' he'd said.

Only now it seemed the baby's head wasn't the only thing Dean wanted to get wet tonight.

Jason had no recollections of exactly how or when they seemed to have managed to pick up these two old slappers, but now the dawning reality of what he was about to do was kicking in.

What the fuck was he thinking?

'Hey, lover-boy! Wakey-wakey. I said, how do you want me?' Watching Jason as he stared into space, Josie was trying to appear sexy; only, her efforts seemed to have the opposite effect on the bloke.

Jason winced.

The woman was coarse; her husky voice making her sound like she smoked about eighty fags a day, which, judging by her potently stale breath, was probably the case.

'How about from behind?' he suggested, flipping her around so that he didn't have to look at her crooked smile and her yellowed teeth.

The dimly lit taxi they'd all been in earlier had been kind to her, but now he was able to get a good look at her in better lighting, he could see that she was at least a decade older than him, and the sight of her draped over his lap now, her white, slack skin of her belly hanging over the top of her tight black knickers, was a sobering vision indeed.

He couldn't go through with this. Not even in this drunken, paralytic state. He'd lost count of how much he'd drunk tonight.

Dean had just kept lining them up. Ten pints maybe? He must have had a right old skinful to have even considered coming back here with this old trout.

He searched his mind to find an excuse to get up and leave, but knew it wasn't going to be an easy feat. He could already hear Dean out in the kitchen, loudly banging away with his bird. Christ knows how he'd managed to get it up; the bird he was shagging hadn't been much better than this one. A right pair of old dogs; though, by the sounds of all the giggling and groaning, it didn't sound like that was stopping Dean from getting his end away. But then, Dean did always like to get his money's worth.

Jason, on the other hand, was losing his boner quicker than he was losing his nerve.

'Oh, is that how you like it? From behind? You naughty boy!' Josie murmured now as she bent over purposely to give Jason the full view of her arse as she grabbed her glass from beside the blaring loudspeaker next to them. Downing the dregs of her wine, she started grinding up and down on his thighs, hoping that she was not only doing a good enough job of hiding the fact that she was now on a comedown, but that she was also succeeding in getting him in the mood.

Jason recoiled. Just the sight of Josie's white arse bobbing up and down on top of him was too much. Closing his eyes, he thought about his young girlfriend back home.

If Shelly could see him right now she would fucking slaughter him.

What the fuck had he been thinking?

His Shelly was a stunner; she'd knock spots off this old bint. Petite at five foot nothing, Shelly had lovely long blonde hair and piercing blue eyes. A tidy little figure on her too, even after giving birth to little Brandon, their firstborn son, just a few weeks ago.

And here he was risking it all, for this?

He was overcome with guilt.

Fucking Dean! He could brain him for getting him into this mess tonight.

Knowing Dean, he would be loving every minute of this; that's how the sick fucker's mind worked. He'd be revelling in having a sidekick for the night, purely for the fact that it meant he wasn't the only one doing the dirty on his missus. Jason's participation would be all the justification the man needed to help ease his conscience.

Dean didn't possess a moral compass; the man fucked anything in a skirt. Jason wasn't like that.

Until now.

He'd been with his Shelly for almost two years, and in that time, he'd never even so much as looked at another woman.

'I can't do this… I'm sorry.' Caught by his sudden pang of conscience, Jason pushed Josie away from him.

This wasn't right. He wasn't a cheat. He couldn't do this to Shelly.

'Hey! Relax.' Landing on the floor with a bang, Josie scrambled to her knees. 'It's okay. Chill.' She tried to sound understanding, but already she could see that she had her work cut out for her tonight.

Mandy and her fella were busy going at it like hammer and tongs in the kitchen; it was just Josie's luck to get stuck with Mr Frigid.

The bloke wasn't just playing hard to get. He seemed genuinely nervous.

Josie figured she knew exactly why too. She had seen it a million times before.

This was his first time with a prostitute.

All he needed was a bit of gentle persuasion. Someone to take control of the situation, and get him going.

'Listen, if you're not up for it, we don't have to have sex, but they seem to be pretty busy in there,' she said, softly. 'How about I just give you a little massage, huh? There's nothing wrong with that, is there?'

Smiling sweetly, Josie firmly pushed Jason back in against the seat with one hand; at the same time, quickly slipping her other hand down inside the front of his jeans.

'I dunno…'

Jason tried to shrug her off, but his cock betrayed his protests: responding instantly to Josie's expert touch.

'Just close your eyes and relax. You seem awfully tense…' Josie whispered soothingly, smiling to herself, triumphant, as Jason finally leaned back in the chair, allowing her to continue what she'd started.

Thinking about the money that she was going to get, Josie quickly tugged down Jason's jeans before he got any ideas about changing his mind.

'You're not doing anything wrong. I'm a fully qualified masseuse you know…' she lied, knowing full well that she was back in control. Just a little bit more coaxing from her and there would be no going back.

'I dunno…' Jason protested, but he was rock hard now. His body was physically fighting against his brain.

He had to admit, despite the bird looking a bit rough around the edges, she certainly knew what she was doing with her hands.

He and Shelly hadn't had sex for almost two months. She'd complained that she was too fat to have sex with him. Since the birth, it hadn't been much better either.

She'd already told him that he wouldn't be getting inside her knickers again until she'd got back into shape and lost a bit of the baby weight. Jason had thought Shelly was just being silly; the girl didn't have anything to worry about. Even if she had put on a few pounds, she always looked perfect to him, but he knew not to push his feisty girlfriend into doing anything she didn't want to do.

He could be waiting months until she let him sleep with her again. He didn't even realise how much he was gagging for it until now. The massage felt so good.

This bird was right; it wasn't really cheating, not if he didn't even fancy the woman.

It was more of a service. A massage. A bit of TLC – and Christ knows how much Jason had needed some of that lately.

What Shelly didn't know wouldn't hurt her, would it?

Closing his eyes, he groaned loudly as Josie replaced her firm hand with the warmth of her mouth.

All thoughts of Shelly were suddenly pushed to the back of his mind.

Feeling Jason relax properly now, Josie took her cue. Ignoring the discomfort of her chafed knees on the rough floor, she gave Jason all she had.

She could tell by the way that his body was responding to her touch that he wouldn't take long.

She was glad.

On a massive comedown from the gear, she was starting to feel a bit queasy.

It didn't help that Jason was thrusting at her now. Shoving himself further down her throat. Groaning loudly, completely oblivious to her struggling.

He was almost there.

She needed to focus.

A few more minutes and it would all be over. Her job would be done for the night.

She'd have made her money.

Only now, the room was spinning. The walls were creeping in on her. She swallowed down the watery bile that threatened at the back of her throat. Her sudden overwhelming urge to be sick was interrupted by Jason's rough hands as he grabbed at her hair.

He was holding her head tightly now, guiding her up and down to match his own rhythm. He gave one final long grunt, and Josie didn't stand a chance. Gagging, she threw up all over him.

Mid-climax.

'WHAT THE FUCK?'

The acidic stench that filled the room caused Jason to retch too as he stared down at the woman, at himself covered in vomit, while his body continued to shudder.

'What the hell are you doing?' Disgusted, he winced, launching her off him. The shock and anger of what had just happened caused him to use more force than he realised.

Josie toppled backwards. Losing her balance, she fell, her head cracking loudly against the corner of the coffee table, the wooden table legs crashing down under the force of her weight.

She was out cold, a trickle of blood running from the cut on her forehead, a trail of vomit down the front of her exposed flesh.

'What the fucking hell have you done to her?'

On hearing the commotion, Mandy was in the room, half-naked, dragging her dress back over her body. She took in the scene before her.

'What did I do to her? Look what the fucking bitch has done to me…' Suddenly defensive. 'She yacked up all over me… while I was… while my cock was…' Jason couldn't finish his sentence, mortified, as he stood with his jeans still down around his ankles, and vomit dripping from his legs.

Grabbing the tatty-looking throw from the sofa, he started to wipe the sick from his skin, his face twisting in disgust at the sour smell.

'Ah mate, this is just fucking comedy gold. Wait until I tell the lads at footie about this.' Pulling up his jeans, Dean couldn't help but roar with laughter at his friend's predicament. 'This is like something from one of those Carry On films. Here, I've got to get a photo.' Grabbing his mobile phone ready to get a picture of Jason in all his glory, Dean didn't expect the sudden blow as Jason whacked the phone straight out of his hand.

'This is all your fucking fault, Dean. We should never have come back here. You fucking caused all of this.'

'Oh, come on, Jason! I didn't force you to stick your dick in her gob, did I?' Dean held his hands up, feigning innocence.

He'd never seen his friend look so angry. The bloke looked like he was going to burst into tears. Which only made the whole thing funnier as far as Dean was concerned.

Listening to the two men talking amongst themselves, Mandy didn't have a clue what the fuck was going on in here, but she could see that Josie was hurt. Going by the state of her face she possibly needed stitches too.

'Josie? Can you hear me, babe? Are you okay?'

Slowly Josie opened her eyes, instinctively raising her hand towards the gash on her head. She could feel the warm trickle of blood running down her forehead.

She tried to sit up, but the room started spinning. The sharp bang to her head, mixed with the alcohol and gear still in her blood, making her feel dizzy.

'Don't move,' Mandy said, watching Josie struggling. She realised that her friend was really hurt.

She knew the drill. If a punter kicked off, no matter what the circumstances, you didn't hang around to ask questions. Picking up her mobile, while Dean and Jason continued to argue amongst themselves, she tapped in a text message to Delray Anderton and pressed send.

Mandy looked down at Josie. Sprawled out on the floor, she tried to pull herself up but she couldn't move. The woman was going to get an absolute bollocking, but there was nothing that

Mandy could do about it. Her priority was to let Delray know that one of his girls had been assaulted. Otherwise, it would be her head on the chopping block.

'Trust you to get landed with the munter though!' Dean had tears rolling down his cheeks, his amusement undeterred by Jason's foul mood and sudden sense-of-humour bypass. This was hands down one of the funniest things he'd ever seen. 'I'm surprised you weren't the one that threw up, judging by the state of her. I didn't think you'd actually go through with it. The bird's a skank mate.'

'Oi! Why don't you watch your mouth.' Zoning back in on the two men's conversation, Mandy glared at them, incensed at the audacity of the man behind her. 'Have some respect. You've really bloody hurt her.'

'Oh, have a laugh! Look at the state of her. The woman's fucking slaughtered. She probably just fell over; she wasn't that steady on her feet as we walked up to the flat if I remember rightly.' Dean looked at Jason, expecting him to back him up. 'Is that what happened, Jas, did the divvy cow fall?'

'I only gave her a shove, just to get her off me. I'm covered in puke. I didn't mean for her to bang her head.'

Dean rolled his eyes. All Jason had to do was play along. It was his word against hers, and the bird was clearly off her face. Now he was holding his hands up, admitting he'd assaulted her.

What a muppet. The bloke had so much to learn.

'Look, unless you both want trouble, I suggest you pay up and get the fuck out of here,' Mandy said, hoping the men would just pay what they owed and leave.

Dean shook his head, ever one to spot an opportunity.

'There's no way we're paying. Are you having a bubble darling?'

They'd got what they'd come here for; well, he had, anyway, but if these women thought that he was going to pay for what had essentially been the worst fuck he'd ever had, they could both do one.

'You need to pay,' Mandy said.

She needed to have some cash ready for when Delray got here. Maybe that would soften the blow. Though he'd only have to take one look at Josie to clock the score. He was going to be fuming, no matter what.

Not only that, but Mandy didn't take kindly to punters trying to rip her off. Especially ones as cocksure as this one. She'd worked her arse off tonight. She deserved her money.

'Just pay her, Dean, then we can get the fuck out of here.' Jason was starting to feel impatient, yanking his jeans back up. He'd wiped away most of the sick, but a damp patch remained on the legs. All he wanted to do was get the fuck out of here.

'Pay her? Nah, these two ain't getting shit from me,' Dean said with a grin. 'I'd rather spend my money on a doner kebab and a taxi home.' He was thoroughly enjoying rubbing Mandy's face in the fact that she wasn't getting paid.

'Well, don't say I didn't give you fair warning.'

Hearing the key in the door, Mandy suddenly paled. Anticipating Delray's reaction when he clocked them all. She almost felt sorry for these two twats.

Almost, but not quite.

She'd given them a chance, but they had refused her; both too stupid to do the right thing.

They'd have to deal with Delray Anderton directly now – and they only had themselves to blame.

Mandy's only priority right now was Josie.

Aware that Georgie and Marnie were in bed, she prayed that the two girls didn't come in and see their mother.

Josie looked awful, a trail of blood trickling down her face. Mandy was convinced that her friend needed an ambulance; only, it would be Delray that would be calling the shots now.

CHAPTER EIGHT

'This had better be fucking good!'

Entering the room, Delray wrinkled his face in disgust as the putrid stench of vomit hit him.

His eyes went straight to Josie who was now conscious but sprawled out on the floor, blood trickling from the cut on her head, her legs splattered with vomit.

Glancing suspiciously over towards the two men in the room, Delray was glad that his mere presence had instantly rendered them both completely silent. It made life easier if these fuckers knew exactly who they were dealing with. It helped that his reputation proceeded him; everyone around these parts was more than aware of who Delray Anderton was.

'Is one of you useless looking cunts going to tell me what the fuck has been going on here then or what?' Delray addressed his question towards the two men standing awkwardly in front of him, then he looked at Mandy.

'She was out cold for a few seconds, but I think she's okay.' Seeing the stony look on Delray's face, Mandy instantly regretted texting him and telling him that Josie had been assaulted.

These two brain-dead fuckers should have listened to her in the first place. This could all have been avoided. But Dean and Jason wouldn't be going anywhere now.

'It was an accident… it's not what it looks like.' Sensing their impending danger, Jason looked to Dean. But Dean appeared to have lost his bollocks suddenly, staring back at Jason blankly, his eyes suddenly full of panic. Jason had heard that Delray Anderton had that effect on people, and now realised it was true; especially when he was standing in front of them both, gripping the metal baseball bat tightly in his fist. Up until this moment, Jason had thought that his night couldn't get any worse, but somehow it just had.

Anderton. THE Delray Anderton.

'And what exactly does it look like?' Delray said, a thunderous expression fixed to his face. There would be no placating the man with flippant excuses. Delray was out for blood. ''Cos from where I'm standing, I'm going to hazard a guess that one of my girls is hurt and one of you morons fucking well hurt her.'

Jason shook his head profusely.

'She… Josie…' Pointing his trembling finger over towards where Josie lay, Jason was determined to explain things to Delray in the hope of calming down the situation. 'She yacked her guts up all over me. In the middle of, well, you know…' Jason felt his cheeks burn with shame as Delray glared at him, void of emotion. 'She's wasted. She fell. Whacked her head on the table. It was an accident.' Realising the severity of the situation, Jason was babbling. 'She was sick everywhere. I just wanted her to get off me. I didn't know she was going to fall so hard. I just tried to get her away from me.'

'So you pushed her?' Delray asked, cutting the man dead, mid-sentence.

He lifted the bat up above his head, ready to strike. Accident or not, anyone laying so much as a finger in the wrong way on any of Delray's girls was blatantly disrespectful, and Delray was left with no choice but to rectify it.

'I didn't mean to. Please, it was an accident.'

Ignoring Jason's pleas, Delray didn't hesitate. Slamming the bat down towards Jason's head, he put the full force of his mammoth weight behind the swing.

Jason tried to jump out of the way but, consumed by fear, his reflexes were too slow.

The bat slammed into his shin with colossal strength.

A sickening crack filled the air as Jason's tibia shattered.

The noise was nothing compared with the horrific sound that Jason made next. Howling in agony like a wounded animal as the pain ripped through him, he collapsed on to the floor in a mangled heap.

He was crying now. Uncontrollably, unashamedly. As he looked up at Dean, searching his friend's face for help, he could see that Dean looked just as terrified as he was. Dean was no use; frozen with fear in the middle of the room, his eyes were wide with shock at the scene unfolding before him.

Delray lifted the bat again.

'Please, no more!' Jason was cowering on the floor, wrapping his arms around his head to protect himself as Delray loomed over him for a second time, ready to strike once more.

Losing control of his bladder, Jason pissed himself.

'Tell him, Dean,' he sobbed. 'Tell him it wasn't my fault.'

Finally, Dean spoke up. 'Look, mate, please, he's telling you the truth. It was an accident. This bird was off her face when we met up with them. Probably on crack or something. She weren't right. Jason's telling you the truth. He didn't mean to hurt her.'

Dean was begging.

He could see a jagged outline of bone protruding through the material of Jason's jeans. Tonight couldn't get any worse, so he figured he might as well just be honest with Delray. 'She's off her fucking face, mate. The woman can't even stand up.'

Delray looked over at Josie again. Still slumped on the floor, she was heaving. Bringing up the rest of the contents of her stomach on to the carpet.

She hadn't dared to make eye contact with him since he'd arrived.

'I think she's been drugged!' Mandy lied, knowing full well that Josie was going to land herself in trouble for the mess she was in. 'I've been with her all night, Delray. I matched her glass for glass. Someone must have slipped something in her drink when she wasn't looking.' Mandy looked at Dean, defiance in her eyes. This would teach the cocky little prick to act like he was so above her, picking and choosing whether or not he would pay for her services.

'Oh fuck off!' Raising his eyes in disbelief, Dean realised that Mandy was trying to drop him and Jason well and truly in the shit. 'She wasn't even with you in the pub. You found her down the alleyway out the back. Even the fucking cab driver would vouch for that. She might be fucked up on something but it ain't got fuck all to do with either of us.'

'My leg!' Jason cried out in agony, grunting loudly through the sheer force of the pain that swept through him.

Mandy continued, her conscience almost getting the better of her until she remembered that, if these blokes didn't cop it tonight, then Josie would.

'How do you explain not paying, then? You got what you wanted, so why do you think you can waltz out of here without settling up?'

Delray looked at Dean as the man stared down at Jason, writhing in pain on the floor. Delray frowned. 'Unless you want to end up like your little friend here, then you need to pay up what you owe,' he said, digging the bloodied bat down into the carpet as he held out his free hand for the money.

Taking one look at his friend, broken and crumpled on the floor, Dean didn't need to be told twice, although he was far from happy.

'They should be paying us; it was more of a chore than a pleasure, trust me—'

Delray had heard enough.

Grabbing Dean roughly by his bollocks, he hoisted the man off the ground.

Dean screamed in agony as a hot white pain jolted through him like nothing he'd ever experienced before, immobilising him instantly.

'Enough of your fucking lip. Pay up.'

Delray twisted Dean's balls even harder then, to cause maximum suffering.

The pain was intense; Dean almost passed out.

'Okay, okay.' Fumbling for his wallet, Dean didn't even bother to count out the money. Instead, he just shoved a handful of notes into Delray's free hand; relief spreading through him as Delray finally released his grip and dropped him down on to the floor.

'Now, get your mate and get the fuck out of here. I don't want to see either of you two pricks around here again. Do you get me?'

Dean nodded, grateful that their ordeal was over. Hoisting Jason up from the floor, ignoring his friend's obvious groans of pain, Dean hobbled out of the flat as quickly as he could move, dragging Jason alongside him.

'Jesus. Look at the state of her.' Mandy was focused on Josie now.

The woman was still being sick. She looked almost ghostly, her skin so pale that she almost looked translucent. Her eyes were smudged with black, huge circles under her eyes.

'Thanks for that, Delray. I'm sorry to call you out so late, but I figured you'd want to know we had trouble.' Seeing one of the ten pound notes on the floor that Delray must have dropped, Mandy picked it up, and handed it to him, trying her hardest to keep Delray sweet. She knew that he wasn't buying any of her bullshit though. They both did.

Snatching the ten pound note from her grip, Delray's hand remained firmly on Mandy's as he squeezed her fingers tightly, making her cry out in pain.

'Have I got cunt written across my forehead?' Delray bellowed.

Tears sprung to her eyes as Mandy shook her head.

Delray didn't stop squeezing, gripping Mandy's fingers tighter with each spoken word. 'Then don't treat me like one.'

'I'm not, Delray, I promise.'

'What the fuck has she taken?'

Mandy shook her head frantically.

Josie was gagging again, unable to speak up for herself, while Mandy was trying as hard as she could to smooth the situation over.

'Nothing. I swear. We only had a couple of drinks. She didn't leave my sight. That's why I thought someone must have spiked her drink. There's no way that she could have got like this otherwise.'

Delray squeezed even harder, causing Mandy to scream out as she felt her bones breaking under his strength. Still, he didn't stop.

'I said, do not treat me like a cunt!' Delray was raging once more.

'I'm not, I promise.' Mandy was crying now. 'I'm telling the truth. We had a few glasses of wine. Please, Delray, you're hurting me. I honestly don't know if she's taken anything. Please, I'm telling the truth.'

Seeing how adamant the woman was, Delray let Mandy go. Had to give her kudos for not giving in and grassing on her mate; he knew he wouldn't get a single word out of Mandy where her friend was concerned. The pair of them were thick as thieves.

Mandy was trying to save Josie's arse, Delray was almost sure of it, but he didn't have time for the melodramatics. Instead he counted out the money.

'Where's the rest of it?' he said glaring at Mandy once more.

'That's it. He just gave it to you,' she said meekly, knowing full well what Delray was implying. He meant the rest of the money they'd made tonight.

He wanted his cut.

'It was a quiet night, Delray. That's all we got.'

'This is all the pair of you are worth.' Delray shook his head. The incomprehension of these woman was just unbelievable. 'Is it any wonder that neither of you are capable of bringing in a decent earn? Open your fucking eyes, Mandy. Take a look around you. Look at the fucking state of you both.'

Delray kept his voice neutral, which somehow made him sound even more sinister.

'Please, Delray, tonight was a one-off. It won't happen again. I know you don't believe me but Josie's genuinely sick. Maybe she wasn't drugged. Maybe it's a bug?' Mandy was clutching at straws, desperately trying to talk her way out of the situation; only, Delray didn't have the patience or the energy to deal with this shit tonight.

His beef was with Josie, not Mandy. He'd deal with her personally.

Tucking the money inside his jacket pocket, he nodded his head towards where Josie was still slumped, looking sorry for herself.

'When she's in a fit state to listen, tell her I'll be paying her a visit first thing tomorrow morning.' He glared at Mandy. 'In the meantime, I suggest you get this fucking mess cleaned up,' Delray spat before storming out into the hallway, ready to leave.

He stopped dead in his tracks as he saw Georgie and Marnie huddled together on the edge of the bed inside one of the doorways. Georgie had her arm wrapped protectively around her younger sister, who had clearly been crying.

Delray wondered how much they'd heard. By the scared looks on their faces, it was clear they'd heard everything.

Unsettled now, caught off guard, Delray looked annoyed.

'What are the pair of you doing sneaking around? You should be in bed. Go on, hop it.'

Shooting Delray a wary look, Georgie did what she was told and took Marnie back to bed.

Delray shook his head once more. Poor little fuckers, having Josie Parker as their mother. They must have seen some right sights in their short little lives.

'Fucking women!' Delray muttered to himself as he stepped back out into the cool night air.

Josie and Mandy were a different breed altogether. They were done in this game. Their careers were long over.

Unlike the delectable Javine Turner.

Getting in his car, Delray turned the key in the ignition and finally grinned to himself at the thought of her awaiting his return. He would deal with those two wasters tomorrow.

Tonight, he had much better things to focus his attention on.

CHAPTER NINE

'Mummy?' Marnie called from the doorway, tiptoeing into the room. The curtains were still drawn and, so far, her mother hadn't stirred from the bed.

Her mummy was getting sick again.

Marnie didn't like it.

She didn't want her mummy to be angry and shouting all the time, and even worse, crying.

She'd been better for so long, but it was all happening again, and all Marnie wanted to do was make her mummy well.

'I made you a cup of tea,' she whispered through the darkness, uncertain if her mother was even awake. She could just about see the rise and fall of her mother's body underneath the covers.

Marnie had heard her throwing up all night after Delray had left.

Aunty Mandy had put her mum to bed, and tried to clean up some of the sick, but the place still stank. The smell was even worse here in her mother's room with the windows all shut. Wrinkling her nose to weaken the acrid stench, Marnie could barely breathe.

Stepping carefully across the room, she looked down at the floor as she made her way around the bed avoiding the piles of clothes that were scattered across the bedroom floor.

She'd filled the cup too much.

The liquid was slopping out all over the sides, dripping down her legs and all over her mummy's carpet.

Luckily it wasn't that hot. Marnie had only used water from the tap in the kitchen sink to make it; Georgie said she wasn't allowed to use the kettle, in case she burned herself.

'Mummy,' Marnie whispered once more, reaching her mother's side of the bed now. She looked down at the mop of her mother's tangled blonde hair, saw the pool of dribble on the pillow she was lying on. 'Are you awaked? I made you some tea, Mummy, so that you would get bettered.' Balancing the mug carefully with one hand, she reached out and touched her mother lightly on her shoulder with the other.

'Mummy?'

The cold chill of Marnie's hands woke Josie with a start.

Still half asleep, she moaned out loud at being woken up, lashing out with her arm to tell Marnie to go away; her hand catching the mug, bringing it down on top of her.

Soaking her and the bed in the process.

Josie screeched, thoroughly fucked off at Marnie for being so bloody clumsy.

'For fuck sake, Marnie!' Josie said, leaping from the bed and dragging the blankets off the mattress.

'What are you playing at? I was a-bloody-sleep!'

Marnie's bottom lip trembled, upset that her good intentions had been ruined, that her mother was mad at her.

She didn't mean to make her mummy mad.

'I've been up all night sick, Marn, the least you could do is leave me be. Where's Georgie?'

'She's pouring out some cereal for me. Will you still take me to school?'

'You'll have to ask Georgie. I'm in no fit state this morning.' Josie's head was banging.

She felt like death warmed up. Whatever Billy Stackhouse had given her last night had sent her off her head. She was having the worst comedown ever.

Wincing, she suddenly remembered all the drama from the previous night.

Delray had been here. That poor bloke's leg when he'd broken it with the bat.

Before she left last night, Mandy had told her that Delray would be having a word with her today.

'I can't find my uniform.' Marnie said, trying her hardest to be a brave girl and not to cry. She didn't want to make her mummy angrier.

Closing her eyes tightly, Josie took a long exaggerated breath.

She'd meant to wash the girls' uniforms but she'd completely forgot. She wondered if she should salvage them out of the wash basket, and spray a bit of air freshener on them, but she couldn't be arsed.

'Just stay here today. Don't go in. Tell Georgie to whack the telly on for you! Go on.'

Josie watched as the girl left the room, visibly upset now, rolling her eyes in dismay. Marnie must be the only kid in the world that looked sad about not going to school.

Staring at the tea-sodden bed, the covers strewn all over the place, Josie scowled.

As if her morning couldn't get any worse.

Still, maybe Marnie's little early morning wake-up call had done her a favour.

If Delray was paying her a visit, anything was possible. Josie would need to get her shit together before he got here.

CHAPTER TEN

'Thanks, Delray! I love him!' Squealing with excitement as Delray Anderton handed her the biggest, fluffiest bear she'd ever seen, Marnie Parker wrapped her arms around her new teddy. She thought she might never let it go.

'That thing's almost bigger than you.' Delray couldn't help but laugh as Marnie hugged the bear tightly to her chest. He could barely see the kid now, just two little feet sticking out the bottom, a mop of short, dark curly hair at the top. 'Go on then, what are you going to call him?'

Marnie held the bear up, deep in thought for a few seconds as she carefully scrutinised the bear's face. Then, wrinkling her nose, she decided.

'I'm going to call him Mr Snowflakes. 'Cos he's all white and snowy looking.'

'Mr Snowflakes?' Delray joked. 'Well, bang goes that poor little fucker's street cred then!'

'Mr Snowflakes. Mr Snowflakes!' Singing loudly now, Marnie kissed the bear on its nose, giggling to herself as she swung her new gift excitedly around the kitchen.

Catching a wary look from Josie as she stood with her back up against the sink, Delray grinned cockily. 'Twenty quid well spent, eh?'

'If you say so. Though I could think of better things to spend money on. Like food and electricity.' Turning around, Josie flicked her fag ash on top of the pile of unwashed crockery in the sink.

She'd been on tenterhooks all morning waiting for Delray to turn up here and start throwing his weight around. Now he was here though, the man seemed preoccupied in playing Mr Nice Guy.

Josie knew what he was doing though. Not only was he buttering up the kids, trying to make up to them for what they'd heard last night, he was trying to make her sweat it out for longer too.

Which she was.

On a heavy comedown after last night, her paranoia had well and truly kicked in. Things had got way out of hand. Delray had broken some poor bastard's legs and, worse than that, Georgie and Marnie had listened to the entire thing.

It had been Josie that had been the one left to pick up all the pieces. She had a gash on her head, and a hangover from hell, and yet she'd still been the one who spent the night comforting Marnie as the kid had cried her eyes out with another one of her night terrors.

The child had been traumatised at the thought of Delray beating the living shit out of a man in the middle of her front room. She hadn't slept a wink all night, and that meant Josie hadn't either.

Marnie's night terrors had been bad enough before all of this happened. Now though, they would be worse than ever.

Josie took another drag of her cigarette.

Delray was up to his usual tricks today; she could read the man like a book. He was busy executing his 'clean-up operation'.

Josie knew he didn't give two shits about the girls. He was just making sure that they didn't tell their teachers or blab their mouths off if the Old Bill came crawling around here.

Which, of course, they wouldn't.

Those two blokes last night didn't have the bollocks to go up against someone like Delray and send the filth round here.

Delray would never take his chances on that, though. So, here he was dishing out crappy toys as if he was Father bleeding Christmas.

Still, maybe Delray was actually on to something for once. Marnie was clearly easy to appease, Josie thought, staring at her daughter as Marnie continued to spin around the kitchen.

'You love Mr Snowflakes, don't you, Marnie?' Delray smirked, winking at Josie, smug in the knowledge that his job here was done.

Marnie seemed a lot happier now she had her present; it was just a shame the same couldn't be said of her older sister.

He looked over to where Georgie was lingering in the kitchen doorway, hands buried deep in her pockets, her gaze low to the floor – Delray was well aware that the girl had barely even acknowledged his presence in the house this morning, let alone her new teddy bear.

'You not going to say thank you too then, Georgie?' Delray said, noting the sullen expression on the child's face.

Georgie shrugged.

'I'm a bit old for teddies, ain't I!' Watching her younger sister prance around the kitchen, squealing excitedly, spinning her teddy bear around in circles, Georgie rolled her eyes as if making her point. 'Teddies are for kids, and I ain't a kid no more.'

'Oi, what have I told you about manners, Georgie? Watch your bleeding mouth!' Josie interrupted, even though a part of her revelled in her daughter's stand-offish comments to Delray.

She was actually glad that her eldest wasn't as easily fobbed off as Delray would have liked. Unlike most females in this part of London, Georgie wasn't falling for Delray's charm. Her eldest daughter was smarter than Josie gave her credit.

Still, this wasn't the time or the place for backchat. Josie knew Delray only too well.

He'd smile at you one minute and turn on you the next without a second's warning. After the state Josie had gotten herself into last night, Delray was already on the warpath. The last thing she needed was Georgie riling him up even more than he was already. Especially seeing as it was going to be her head on the chopping block today.

'You know better than to speak like that, Georgie. Delray's brought you a gift. Now, what do you say?'

'Thanks.' Catching her mother's warning look, Georgie shrugged but made no attempt to retrieve the gift from where it lay discarded on the table. 'What?' she said as her mother continued to glare at her. 'Just because everyone else around here bows down to him, doesn't mean I have to as well,' she said, making her feelings perfectly clear. 'He always does this. Bring us stupid toys the day after you've got really drunk, or someone's beaten you up. It doesn't make it all better, you know.'

'Georgie!' Josie warned.

If Georgie wasn't careful she'd have a lot more to worry about than being given 'stupid toys'.

'Leave it, Jos.' Delray's eyes twinkled in amusement.

Georgie Parker was a chip off the old block, it seemed. Josie has been exactly the same in her younger days. Argumentative, defiant, stubborn as hell. Shit, she was still like it now. The woman could start a row in an empty room if the mood took her.

Anyone else talking back to Delray like Georgie would have earned themselves a clip around the ear, but Delray found Georgie highly amusing. 'She's right, she ain't a little kid any more. She's all grown up.'

Suddenly it was like seeing the child with new eyes. She was pretty, but looked nothing like Josie. Both the girls had darker skin for a start, not like Josie's pasty-white complexion. They had long dark hair too, chocolate brown, matching their eyes.

'I tell you what, Jos, it ain't going to be much longer and you're going to have some trouble on your hands with that one. What is she now? She must be eleven, huh? With a bit of slap on her she could easily pass for fifteen. She's gonna have every young scrote this side of the river trying their luck with her. You could cash in on that, you know.'

Delray grinned at Josie, seeing the anger in her eyes at his suggestion.

He was winding her up, purposely trying to piss her off.

'I'm twelve.' Georgie corrected him, her cheeks reddening as she realised what Delray had just implied. 'And I ain't interested in boys. I've seen enough sad excuses of men in this house over the years to put me off for life.'

Josie held her breath, horrified at the child's blatant insult to Delray.

For a second, the room was completely silent. Even Marnie had stopped spinning around the place like a demented fairy.

Josie stared at Delray, trying to read his reaction. To her surprise, he started to roar with laughter.

Josie couldn't help but laugh then too.

'Jesus Christ, Georgie! You ain't half got a gob on you!'

As much as her daughter drove her around the bend with her mouthiness sometimes, at least she said it how it was, and she didn't seem to give a shit who she was up against either. Anderton included it seemed. For a second, Josie almost felt proud of her daughter. Only for a second, though, until she reminded herself who they were dealing with here. Georgie needed to remember her manners, otherwise Delray might remind her of them.

'Oi, madam. Delray was only paying you a compliment! God, you can't half be a right narky cow sometimes, do you know that.' Raising her eyes to the ceiling, Josie tried to make light of Georgie's comment. As funny as Josie had thought it was, Georgie was going to cause bloody murder in a minute if she didn't rein herself in.

'Don't worry, Josie. I'm used to trappy women and, let's face it, with you as their mother, it was inevitable that they'd inherit your big gob, wasn't it?' Delray grinned. 'Luckily, that's where the similarities seem to end. This one's got her head screwed on. Fuck knows how. She's obviously seen what she doesn't want to turn into by looking at you.'

Josie was offended again at Delray making his snide digs. Using the kids as ammunition against her.

Sensing the tension between her mother and Delray, Georgie knew that there was a row brewing. Especially after all the dramas that had gone on here last night.

'Come on, Marnie, let's take our new bears to our room, yeah?' she said, eager to get Marnie out of the way.

'Yay!' Marnie squealed, completely oblivious to the underlining hostility in the room. She was delighted that her sister wanted to play with her and, grabbing Georgie's bear, was happily led from the room.

Delray took a seat at the kitchen table. Now that the girls were dealt with and out of the way, he didn't want to waste any more time in getting straight back down to business.

'So, go on then,' he said, finally, 'what the fuck was all that about last night, and don't spin me any bullshit lines, Josie. I had enough of that from Mandy. I want to know the truth.'

Josie shrugged and, knowing that she had landed herself well and truly in the shit last night after her actions, leant back against the sink and lit herself another cigarette.

'I fucked up, Delray. Okay.' Holding her hands up, she knew that Delray wouldn't tolerate any form of deceit. She had already crossed the line with him as it was. 'I had a really fucking bad day yesterday. I guess I just got a bit carried away with the drink.

It won't happen again, trust me. If it makes you feel any better, I'm really suffering. I've got the mother of all hangovers today. My head's pounding.'

Eyeing the gash on her forehead from where she had fallen, and her sickly pale skin, Delray could clearly see how rough Josie looked but, in his opinion, she wasn't suffering nearly half as much as she should be. Not after the way she showed herself up last night.

'You're a right fucking mess, Josie,' he said, disgusted, as he took in the greasy mop of hair that was stuck to her scalp. Josie hadn't even showered this morning. Her clothes were creased and dirty as if she'd picked up discarded clothes from the floor, which, knowing Josie, she probably had.

'It looks more than just a hangover, if you ask me.' Delray glared at her. His eyes boring into her. Steely. Cold.

He was making Josie nervous.

'I feel like I'm dying, Delray, but, honest to God, this is the worst hangover I've ever had. I know I shouldn't drink on the job, but I thought we were done for the night. I didn't know Mandy was going to pick those two blokes up at closing time. I was already half gone. She said something about someone spiking my drink? Who knows, eh? There's a lot of chancers about.'

Delray pursed his lips and nodded, as if understanding Josie's predicament.

'So someone slipped you a roofie, eh?'

Josie nodded and visibly relaxed at Delray's words, breathing a sigh of relief that she had somehow managed to talk him around. Their little chat was going better than she had anticipated. She had royally fucked up, she knew that, but the last thing she needed right now was Delray reading her the riot act.

'Having your drink spiked, eh? That's pretty fucked up,' Delray said.

'It was pretty terrifying.' Josie nodded in agreement.

Delray was glaring at her. Looking right through her as if he could see all her secrets.

She'd read this all wrong.

The conversation wasn't going well at all. Delray was just fucking with her. Letting her dig herself a deeper hole, and when the time was right he was going to bury her in it.

Trying her hardest to keep her composure, Josie could feel her heart hammering inside her chest.

'There's some sick fuckers out there. Those blokes didn't seem the type, eh? But I guess you just never can tell!'

Delray twisted his lips as he took in the dark circles around the woman's eyes; her pupils still tiny as she stood there gnawing on the inside of her cheek between her words.

She was shaking too. Every time she brought her cigarette up to her lips, she fought to keep her jittery hand still. This was more than just the drink.

Delray had known it the second he'd clapped eyes on her last night. Sprawled out on the lounge floor, fucked off her face, as high as a proverbial kite.

'You know, Jos, I like to think I'm a fair man,' he said, sounding bored. 'I gave you the chance to come clean. To be honest with me… but, as always, Josie, you're too fucking stupid to comply.'

Launching himself off the chair, Delray grabbed her roughly by her throat and pushed her backwards, causing her to shriek in agony as her back arched awkwardly over the sink behind her.

'Do I look fucking stupid, Jos? Huh? Do I look like I was born fucking yesterday?'

Taking the cigarette that was still gripped between her fingers, Delray flung it into the sink amongst the pile of dirty crockery before grabbing Josie tightly by her arms. 'You've been smoking smack again, haven't you?'

He shook his head. Disgusted.

'Didn't you do enough damage to yourself last time, Josie? Is it any wonder why you're losing business left, right and centre? Why work is "so slow". No one wants to fuck a skaghead, Josie! Especially not one that smells and looks as bad as you.' Delray was raging now. Shaking his head as he glared at her, he could smell the pungent stench of her body odour. Her sour breath.

She had let herself go to shit, and now to top it off she was back on heroin.

Delray was fuming. He'd been giving the woman a free pass for ages. Months. Josie was a fucking liability at the best of times, but even more so when she was back on gear. It was no wonder punters were avoiding her like the plague.

'It's not how it looks, Delray. I ain't using, not properly. I'm just chipping,' Josie tried to explain.

'Chipping?' Delray was incredulous.

'Yeah, just dipping in now and again. Having a small hit once in a while to tide me over. I've got it under control this time. I know what I'm doing.'

'I know what fucking chipping means, Josie; I wasn't born fucking yesterday. You are fucking deluded if you think you've got this under control. That's the trouble with you skagheads, you lot lie so much that you even manage to convince yourselves of your own bullshit.' He was no longer in the mood to listen to the woman's spiel. 'Who the fuck's been supplying you?' he bellowed, twisting Josie's wrist angrily.

Whoever it was must be either fucking brave or fucking stupid to think that it was okay to sell heroin to one of his girls. Especially after the beating he'd dished out on the last parasite that had served up to Josie.

'You're hurting me, Delray.'

'Tell me who fucking supplied you.'

As he twisted her arm right around now, Josie screeched, scared he was going to snap her wrist.

'All right, Delray, I'll tell you. It was Billy. Billy Stackhouse.'

Delray shrugged her away. 'Are you fucking having a laugh? That fucking ponce.'

He was incensed.

Billy Stackhouse was the one that had got Josie hooked in the first place. Delray had handed out a beating to him that time too. Stackhouse was already on a warning for supplying Delray's girls; though, clearly, a warning wasn't incentive enough for him.

Delray would deal with the fucker later; first, he needed to sort out this mess in front of him.

'Chipping? Behave? You're well and truly gone, Josie. Look at the state of you. Bet you'd love a hit now, wouldn't you?'

Josie couldn't argue with that. She was clucking today, badly. All she'd been able to think about was how she was going to be able to get her hands on some money so that she could go pay Billy the money she owed him, and have enough left over for another score.

Delray had seen Josie in some states over the years, but he'd never seen her look as downtrodden as she did now.

Looking around the flat, at the squalor, he shook his head in disgust. The sink was full of dirty crockery; the dustbin overflowing; a thick trail of dirt and grime on every surface.

'And you're bringing punters back here? Fuck me, Josie! This place is a shit-tip. A fucking health and safety hazard. I'd be surprised if it isn't infested with cockroaches and rats. Mind you, even they probably have higher standards than you.'

Years ago, when Josie was starting out, she had been one of his main earners. Not any more. The woman standing before him was barely recognisable. Unhygienic, and looking at least a decade older than her years, Josie was a mess. Working under his name, too? Under his protection. He couldn't have this.

Sitting back down at the kitchen table, Delray drummed his fingers loudly against the wood. The truth was, he'd been carrying Josie for years. The woman had been past her sell-by date long ago, but Delray had thrown her a lifeline, not that the ungrateful cow had ever appreciated it. He'd allowed her to keep working for him. Earning money for as long as she possibly could. It had done him a favour too, for a while, to have extra income coming in, but he wouldn't be cutting the woman any more slack. That went for Mandy, too. The pair of them were losing him business, costing him his reputation at a time when Delray was trying to make a real name for himself.

'I'm cutting you loose, Josie. You and Mandy. You're both out.'

'What?' Josie shook her head, certain that Delray wouldn't really do that to her; he couldn't. He was just angry. 'You can't do that to me, Delray. What about the girls? How am I going to afford to feed them, eh? To keep this roof over their heads. I'm boracic. I haven't got a penny to my name.'

'You should have thought about your girls before you started pumping your veins full of that shit then, shouldn't you, Jos!'

'I should have thought about them?' Josie laughed, a crazy maniacal sound gurgling at the back of her throat. She was shaking violently. Not because of the hangover or the gear, but because of the anger that surged inside her. The barefaced cheek of Delray Anderton. Telling her to think about her own kids, as if that wasn't what she did her every waking minute.

'How dare you! I do everything for my girls. *Everything*.'

'Do you, Jos? 'Cos looking around the place, I find that highly fucking unlikely, girl.'

Making his point Delray dragged at the kitchen cupboard handles, almost pulling the doors off as he spoke. 'Do you see that? Fucking empty. This is what you're giving your girls, Josie. Sweet fuck all by the looks of it. You're already struggling to bring any money in, and now the little you do get is going to be used so you can get off your face. So spare me the fucking sob story, will you!'

'Sob story?' Josie shook her head. 'This isn't a sob story, Delray. This is my fucking life. A life that clearly you know fuck all about, seeing as you're so busy living it up in your fancy fucking new apartment with that little tramp, Javine Turner.' Glad that she suddenly had his full attention now, her eyes were blazing. 'You do know that she's only seventeen, don't you? Barely much older than my Georgie! She's just a kid, Delray. Not that you care, eh?' Delray wouldn't give a shit how old the girl was. As long as she was legal, that little snippet of information wouldn't make the slightest difference to the man.

'Who the fuck do you think you are chatting shit about my business, huh?' Delray shouted, pissed off that Josie seemed to know all of his concerns.

'Me? You need to have a word with that Javine! That's what kids do, Delray. They run their mouths off.' Josie shook her head in anger. 'All this time you've been making out that you're still living in that dingy little flat in Lambeth and, really, you've gone up in the world, haven't you, Delray. How's that, eh? How is it that I'm the one lying on my back for strangers to make ends meet and you're the one living it up in some poncy apartment on the Albert Embankment?'

Josie knew she was crossing the line but she no longer cared. She'd held her tongue for years for fear of Delray punishing her and, suddenly, she realised with clarity that she had been being punished all along. Delray had used her. Like he did with all 'his girls'. Now he was done, he was spitting her out like she was nothing.

'You've taken everything from me, do you know that, Delray? You've fucking destroyed me. From the first day I ever met you all you did was fill my head with bullshit. Coming around here, holding your hand out for my money that I earned—'

'That's enough.' Delray slammed his fist down on the table, his patience wearing thin. He'd heard enough of Josie's mouth. Fighting to regain his composure, he could feel the vein in the left side of his forehead throbbing. He clenched his fists tightly at his sides. It was taking every last bit of control that he had inside of him not to react, not to launch his chunky fist into Josie's face and knock her crooked yellowed teeth down the back of her throat.

'I don't owe you shit, Josie. Not even for old times' sake.' Grabbing his keys off the table, Delray walked towards the back door. 'You're out, Josie. You and Mandy. If I find out that either of you are so much as thinking about touting for business in a twenty-mile radius of here, I promise you now it will be the last thing either of you ever do.'

Slamming the door behind him, his word, as always, was final.

CHAPTER ELEVEN

Staring down into his pint with vague amusement, Billy Stackhouse laughed in the face of the pitiful man standing next to him at the bar.

Tony Daley was nothing more than one of life's wasters. A leech. Traits that Billy normally depended on when building his long list of clientele. Usually, the more needy and desperate the punters were the better; only, today those same qualities weren't standing Tony Daley in good stead at all. The man was begging. It was pitiful to listen to him pleading so desperately for a bit of gear on tick. The sound of his whiney fucking voice was starting to grate on Billy, making him want to jump off his bar stool and smack the fucker around the head with it, just for his blatant fucking piss-taking.

The only thing that stopped him was the fact that Tony Daley had his little kid in tow. The man wasn't as stupid as he made himself out to be. What sort of a parasite would hide behind his three-year-old son?

Billy took a deep breath. Aware of the child, Billy was trying his absolute hardest to rein in his temper. Despite what most people around these parts thought about him, he wasn't a complete arsehole. He wasn't about to start toe-punting people in front of their kids, no matter how much money they owed him.

'You must be having a fucking giraffe, Tony!' Billy snarled as Tony continued to try his luck tapping him up for yet another score. Tony hadn't even paid for the last three times that he'd weighed him in.

'You already owe me a monkey, and now you're asking me to give you another bag of gear on tick? What do I look like, eh? Your fairy fucking Godmother? You've got bollocks mate, I'll give you that.'

Shaking his head in utter disbelief at the gall of the man in front of him, Billy couldn't disguise the venom in his voice. Tony Daley was nothing more than a useless ponce. One of life's freeloaders, sponging off the social for every benefit the bloke could get his hands on. Tony Daley hadn't done a single day's honest graft in his life. He didn't give a shit who he fucked over as long as he got a hit. His only hope of doing that, according to him, was to beg – only, Billy had other ideas.

'You all right, mate?' Billy said, eyeing the kid that stood at Tony's side.

The kid didn't need to be dragged round to dives like this pub while his dad tried to score. What hope did he have with Tony for a father?

'Look at the state of your boy, Tony! What are you playing at?'

The boy was filthy, still dressed in his pyjamas despite the fact that it had just gone midday. His little blue pyjama bottoms stopped way above his ankles. They looked at least two sizes too small.

'Fuck me, Tony, ain't you got more important things to spend your money on, mate! Like some decent clobber for your kid. He looks like a fucking street rat.'

Billy ruffled the hair of the little boy, trying to ease the fear on the kid's face. It wasn't the boy's fault that his dad was a complete fucking numpty.

'Why don't you go home, Tony. Give your boy a nice hot bath. Get some grub inside him.' Billy shook his head then as he was reminded why he hated smackheads so much.

They lost sight of themselves.

That's what the drug did to them. It stripped them bare. Of their morals, their dignity. By the time it was done with them, there was nothing left. Just an empty shell that didn't give a flying fuck who they needed to cunt off in the process, as long as they got their gear.

Wives, kids, grandparents. No one was sacred. No one mattered. Only them and their selfish, twisted obsession of getting high.

That's what had attracted Billy to dealing in the first place. It was such a lucrative business. All it took was a couple of times and the punters were hooked on the gear, and he had a loyal customer for life.

The money was good, but Billy had grown to despise his customers.

'Have some fucking respect for yourself, mate, and for your kid, yeah? You're a fucking embarrassment, Tony, do you know that!' Billy spoke through gritted teeth, but he could see that his insult hadn't even touched the man. 'Even your boy looks fucking mortified to be seen out with you.'

Tony didn't blink an eye at the insult. Instead, he shamelessly persevered.

'Please, Bill. All I want is enough to get me through the next couple of days. I promise I'll get you your money.'

Billy stared over towards the barmaid, Rita Gregory, who'd been hovering around the optics nearby, pretending to restock one of the bottles. Billy knew that the bird was just having a nosey, so he gave her something worth listening to.

'I'd love to help you, Tony. Only, you've already put me in a bit of a predicament, ain't you?'

Tony shook his head, pretending he didn't know what Billy was talking about.

'Oh, what's the matter? You suffering with memory loss as well as being a complete and utter twat. Do you not remember sending your old dear out to the door to feed me a load of bullshit about not knowing where you were when I popped round for my money the other day? Bit convenient, don't you think? You doing a vanishing act the day you're due to pay up what you owe me.'

Billy knew when he was being played; he had known it when old Mrs Daley had stood at her front door and barefaced lied to him; no doubt the gutless piece of shit had hidden himself away down behind the sofa, whispering silent prayers to himself that Billy wouldn't come into the house looking for him.

Seeing him now, it was obvious Tony had believed that Billy had actually swallowed the story.

But Billy was too shrewd for that.

He'd heard just about every excuse known to mankind over the years. Skagheads were the worst kind of liars. They were desperate, and desperate people always showed their true colours, eventually.

Billy had chosen to walk away, deciding to play the long game, knowing full well that Tony would come looking for him eventually.

And, as predicted, the fucker had.

That was the beauty of this game. You didn't have to go looking for smackheads, because they always came looking for you. Crawling all over you like cockroaches when they needed their next hit.

'I wasn't dodging you, Billy, I swear. I had to go away for a bit to sort some stuff out. I told her to tell you that I'd be getting your money. She mustn't have heard me properly. She's getting on a bit, my old dear; she sometimes gets her facts wrong; there must have been some kind of a communication problem.'

'A communication problem? Is that so?' Billy nodded, and saw Tony physically relax next to him as he thought he was in the clear. That he could blame the fact that he was a gutless piece of shit on his elderly mother.

'So you'll sort me out?' Tony said.

'Oh, I'm going to sort you out, mate, yeah. Consider it done.'

Tony visibly relaxed, relief written all over his face.

'I'll give you until Friday to get me my money. No later, do you hear me?' Billy said sternly.

'Whatever you want, Bill.' Tony nodded his head, eager to get his gear now and get going.

'I'm glad we're finally on the same page, Tony,' Billy sneered, the malice to his tone suddenly apparent as he continued: 'Because I want every penny that you owe me and a ton on top.'

Tony shook his head, confused.

'That's six hundred quid,' Billy said, speaking slowly so that the idiot in front of him could understand what he was saying.

'But I thought you were happy with me paying you in instalments?'

'Oh yeah, I was.' Billy nodded 'Only, you broke that little arrangement, didn't you, by trying to pull a fast one on me and not paying up. So you're going to have to cough up the full amount now. I want every single penny that you owe me.'

Tony nodded, reluctantly.

There was no way he was going to be able to find that kind of money but, right now, he was willing to agree to anything that Billy Stackhouse demanded. As long as it meant that he would get his gear. He was so close now that he could almost taste it.

'I'll have it. I swear.'

'Good.' Billy smiled now; picked up his pint and took a sip. 'See you Friday then.'

'What about my gear? You said you were going to sort me out?' Tony asked, confused as Billy turned back to the bar.

'Oh, I'm sorry, there must be some kind of confusion. Another one of those little "communication problems". Fucking awful things they are, ain't they?' Billy grinned, smug that he possessed the kind of power that could make or break the man in front of him. 'When I said I'd sort you out, what I meant was: if you haven't got my money together in two days' time, with a ton on top, then I'm going to come around your house and, in front of this poor little sod here, and your old dear, I'm going to break both of your fucking arms and legs. How's that sound for sorting you out?'

Tony stared at Billy, dumbfounded. He looked down at the floor, knowing from Billy's tone that there would be no changing the man's mind.

Billy was sick of the sight of him. 'Go on, then. Fuck off out of it. Your ugly mug is putting me right off my lovely cold pint.'

Billy watched as Tony turned to leave.

'Oi, numb-fucking-skull!' He pointed down to where the little boy was still standing next to his barstool. 'You forgetting something?' Watching as Tony walked back and picked up his son, Billy shook his head in dismay before downing the rest of his pint.

'Can you believe the fucking audacity of some people, eh?' he said, knowing that Rita had been listening to every word, and had seen Billy get the better of the man.

Rita shook her head in agreement, but kept her own counsel as she took Billy's glass from him.

'You want another one, Billy?' Refilling it before he had a chance to refuse. 'There you go: it's on the house.'

'Thanks, darling.' Billy smiled. Rita didn't normally give him the time of day, but he'd obviously impressed the woman by putting that low life firmly in his place.

He wasn't stupid. He knew what was going on here.

The old bird had the hots for him.

It was hilarious.

Rita Gregory wasn't really Billy's type. He liked his women younger. But lately he hadn't really had much in the way of offers, if he was totally honest, other than the quickie with that skaghead Josie the other night, and that was hardly the stuff dreams were made of.

Taking in the sight of Rita now, she wasn't too bad as older birds went. Dressed in a pair of ill-fitting jeans and grey baggy T-shirt she was a bit frumpy-looking, compared to the usual sorts that Billy managed to get a leg-over. Rita had a face on her that could make an onion cry, in all honesty, but she had a rack on her to die for, and by the way she was lingering around him, Billy reckoned that she was well up for it. One thing he did like was a keen bird.

'Some people really are a joke, ain't they,' he said, carried away being the big I am. 'Letting something like smack fuck everything up for them…'

'You're right there, Billy. Some people really are a joke.'

Hearing the main doors go behind him, Billy ignored it, too distracted by Rita.

She sounded suddenly off with him. Maybe he was reading it wrong but it was as if her entire demeanour had suddenly changed.

'The real scumbags are the dealers, though,' Rita snarled. She was glad that she didn't need to listen to the constant barrage of crap that Billy Stackhouse was spewing now the cavalry had arrived. 'People like you that feed people their poison and then sit back and watch as their lives fall to pieces around them.'

The venom in Rita's words stopped Billy in his tracks.

'You what?' He laughed nervously, thinking that maybe he'd misheard her. One minute the old cow was giving him free drinks, the next she's mugging him off?

Only, he hadn't misheard anything.

Hearing a noise directly behind him, Billy turned, clocking the sight of Delray Anderton and his sidekick, Lenny Oldham.

'All right, lads,' Billy said, determined not to lose face as he realised he'd been set up. That the conniving bitch behind the bar had been acting on Delray's orders. She must have given Delray the heads-up that he was here. Now the free drink suddenly made sense.

'As it happens, Billy, I ain't all right. No.' Delray screwed his face up in distaste as he pulled up a bar stool right next to Billy and sat down: so close that the two men were almost touching.

Picking up Billy's pint from the table, Delray took a large mouthful, all the while glaring at Billy, before he finally put the drink back down again.

'I hear you've been giving one of my girls gear again?'

Billy tried to keep a straight face. Bloody Josie Parker. She'd sworn blind that she wouldn't let it get back to Delray that Billy had sorted her out. What was it with these bloody women and their big mouths?

'Delray! Mate! I'm just doing my job; if the girls want a bit of gear, who am I to say no? I'm just trying to earn my way, mate. I don't mean you any malice.' Billy knew that he was out of his depth. If Delray Anderton and Lenny Oldham had come looking for him, then he had already dug his own grave. It was too late for excuses.

'Billy. "Mate",' Delray replied, 'me and you have already had words about this, haven't we? I told you not to give Josie any more gear. I warned you what would happen if you did, didn't I!'

Delray was staring at Billy like he was nothing more than shit on his shoes. Vermin.

Which, of course, was exactly what the man was.

Delray might be into a lot of dodgy shit, but drugs were a mug's game. He'd leave them for the likes of Billy here.

'She begged me, Delray. I told her that I couldn't do business with her, but she wouldn't drop it. She kept hassling me. She was desperate.'

Billy didn't mention just how desperate and persuasive Josie had been. He didn't think Delray would appreciate hearing any of the graphic details… unless the silly old tart had opened her mouth about that too.

'Clearly a friendly warning ain't good enough for you though, is it, Billy-boy? Such a shame.'

'Is Davey still down at the cash and carry?' Delray directed his question to Rita as the woman shrugged her coat on, getting ready to make herself scarce.

Rita nodded her head. 'Yeah, he'll be a good while yet,' she said, knowing that was exactly what Delray wanted to hear. 'Mel's gone with him.'

Delray nodded, glancing at Lenny to sort Rita out with some cash, he added: 'Go on you, shoot off. Lenny will show you out.'

Rita didn't need to be asked twice. Grabbing her handbag, she swiftly made her way over to the pub's main doors, smug in the knowledge that not only had she just earned herself a few more brownie points and an extra bit of cash by helping out Delray, but she'd also managed to shaft Billy Stackhouse in the process.

She hated scum like Billy. They were the lowest of the low as far as she was concerned. It was about time someone taught the man a lesson that he wouldn't be forgetting in a hurry.

Billy sat and watched as the bitch strutted out of the pub and Lenny Oldham bolted the door behind her.

He took a final sip of his pint; he figured he was going to need it.

He cursed Josie Parker. The quick fumble he'd had with her the other night had not been worth any amount of aggro, certainly not of this magnitude.

His ego had got the better of him. He'd started to think he was invincible. Only now it was really dawning on him that he had fucked up.

Delray Anderton wouldn't be letting him off easily.

CHAPTER TWELVE

'You can't have eaten your sandwiches already?'

Josie stared at her two daughters questioningly. She'd sent them both into the kitchen not even five minutes ago and already they were back, slouched on the end of the bed, both looking gormless as they stared at her reflection in the mirror, watching Josie attempt to do her make-up.

She wasn't in the mood for this evening, in all honesty, but she had to make herself look at least half decent.

'We don't have any butter so I just did jam for Marnie,' Georgie said, twisting a lock of long brown hair around her finger like she always did when she was irritated. 'Only, Marnie won't eat it; she doesn't like jam, and the bread's gone stale. We've got nothing else to eat.'

'They were 'scusting!' Marnie pouted. She held Mr Snowflakes tightly as her bottom lip trembled and her eyes, red and blotchy, threatened tears once more. 'I only like chocolate spread or Weetabix, but Georgie said there's nothing else to eat, and I'm hungry.' Feeling sorry for herself, Marnie started to cry.

Josie rubbed her temples. Today had been a long day.

Now Delray had outed her she was beyond skint.

Georgie was right. The cupboards were bare, and Josie had lost count of the number of tantrums that she'd endured over the past few days. Still, hopefully, that would all change very soon.

She was counting on tonight, and the last thing she needed was Marnie having another meltdown.

'Jesus Christ, Marnie. It's a sandwich, not the end of the world. You'd think I asked you to eat dog poo the way you're acting.' Rolling her eyes, Josie knew that her youngest daughter's picky eating habits were down to her. Lack of money and pure laziness had made the option of chocolate spread sandwiches and bowls of Weetabix a staple food in their household. Only now, Josie had made a rod for her own back, it seemed, as she couldn't get Marnie to eat anything else.

'What about the microwave dinners that are on the kitchen side?' Georgie said knowing that her mother was saving them for 'her friend' Trevor tonight.

Her mum was acting as if the bloke was royalty.

She'd even done some housework today. Nothing too miraculous. Just a few dishes and spraying a bit of air freshener around the place, but even so, she was definitely making more of an effort than usual.

'You won't like them; they've got mushrooms in,' Josie said as she watched Georgie screw her face up in distaste just as she knew she would.

'And they're for you and Trevor?' Georgie said, raising her eyebrows as she exchanged a knowing look with her younger sister.

'Yes, actually, they are,' Josie said as she leant in towards the mirror, carefully applying another coat of mascara to her upper eyelashes. 'Only, whatever you do, don't bleeding tell him that his dinner has come out of a packet, will you? I want him to think that I made it all myself. In fact, you two don't bleeding tell him anything. I want you both out of the way tonight. Stay in your room.'

Georgie shrugged. She didn't care for any of the men her mother brought back here, so why her mum thought she'd suddenly have an interest in this one, Georgie had no idea.

Josie turned her attention back to her reflection in the mirror. Wincing, as she spotted yet another newly formed line stretching out across her forehead, she shook her head.

'Thank Christ for make-up and candlelight, eh! Jesus. Look at the state of me.' Staring at her tired-looking face, Josie felt suddenly depressed. She looked like shit tonight.

She'd like to blame motherhood for accelerating her ageing skin, but she knew that it was years of drink and drugs that had done it to her.

Her addictions had sucked the life out of her. Drained her. Even now, it was all she could think about.

She wasn't really in the mood for seeing Trevor tonight.

The man was hard work; he wasn't like her other punters.

She suspected that he'd had a bit of a thing for her. Of course, he always tried to play it down, but Josie could tell that he really liked her. She'd seen him when she was out, following her around like a love-struck puppy. For a while she had almost convinced herself that he was some kind of stalker, but as she had got to know him better she knew that he was harmless enough really. He just had a few odd ways about him.

Even stranger, the man didn't want to have sex with her.

Josie had thought it was beyond weird, at first. How he'd booked in his appointments every Tuesday like clockwork and then insisted that all they did was lie on the bed together. Fully clothed. He'd never laid a finger on her.

It was all very odd, but what did Josie care? She did fuck all with the man and still got paid.

He was probably just shy; a fifty-year-old virgin or something.

Still, he seemed very keen about coming around tonight. He hadn't sounded very happy when Josie had told him about having to cancel her clients.

She'd found herself telling him the truth: that a couple of nights ago Delray had told her she wasn't allowed to work any more.

Trevor had sounded as gutted as she felt about the whole thing. Ten minutes later he'd phoned her back and said that he had something he wanted to discuss with her.

Staring up at the clock now, Josie contemplated cancelling on the man, but she knew that it was too late. Besides, she needed the money.

Smothering a thick layer of tanned foundation all over her face, she took her time applying her favourite lipstick: pillar-box red, her trusty old faithful. Pouting now, it did the trick. The vibrant colour seemed to take the emphasis away from her drawn, tired face.

'That will have to do.' She sighed.

Behind her, the girls burst into fits of laughter.

'What's so bleeding funny?' Josie asked, suddenly paranoid that they were taking the piss out of the state of her face.

'Georgie said—' Marnie started to repeat what her older sister had said, but was stopped mid-sentence as Georgie pinched her arm hard to quieten her.

'Oww!' Marnie squealed, her face contorting with pain.

'Georgie, get off her now,' Josie berated her, trying to restore normality before she set her sister off on one of her epic tantrums.

Georgie let go of Marnie's arm.

'Georgie said that you're going to sex Trevor so you can buy us some Weetabix.'

The girls squealed with laughter again.

Josie, however, didn't.

Biting her lip, she stared over towards Georgie.

It galled her that the girls thought this was funny. That her having to make a living was seen as nothing but a joke. Everyone around her seemed to be looking down their noses at her lately; apparently, even her kids.

'That mouth of yours is going to land you in some serious trouble one day, Georgie,' Josie warned her eldest daughter. Then turning to her youngest, she added: 'Ignore her, Marnie, your sister doesn't know shit.'

'I know all about Trevor, though,' Georgie said, glaring at her mother, her words loaded.

'Oh, is that so? And what is it exactly that you think you know then, huh?' Josie challenged.

Georgie pursed her lips.

She wanted to say that she knew everything. About the parties that her mother and Mandy had when Georgie and Marnie were supposed to be asleep. About the men she brought home most nights. About the sexing that they could hear through the thin bedroom walls.

Georgie could feel the words lingering on the tip of her tongue, but she wasn't brave enough to say them.

Marnie did though.

'Georgie says that Trevor is a weirdo…' Marnie chimed in, unaware of the building tension in the room between mother and daughter. 'We don't like him, do we, Georgie?'

'Georgie! You need to stop teaching your sister bad manners. Trevor's not weird; he just has his own ways of doing things's all.'

Exasperated, Josie didn't have the energy for another argument with the child, not tonight.

She barely had the energy for Trevor, if she was honest.

'Enough with your bleeding comments. You want to get me in trouble do you, Georgie? Going around saying shit like that. If the police hear those lies, you know what they'll do? They'll take me away.' Josie glared at Georgie: Georgie thought she knew everything. 'You know what will happen if they take me away, don't you? They'll take you away too. You'll end up in one of those horrible children's homes,' she threatened.

'Well, at least they'll have food there,' Georgie quipped, not letting her mother's empty threats scare her.

Josie was starting to lose her rag, fast. She felt like she'd spent the past few days doing nothing but justify herself.

She was a good mum.

It might not seem like it at times, but everything she'd ever done she'd done for them. Now though, she had everyone throwing her efforts back in her face.

She'd already had Mandy screaming down the phone at her, fuming that Delray had decided to cut them both loose – all because of Josie's actions. She didn't need the kids chipping in too.

She'd had enough.

'I've worked my arse off to try to keep this roof over our heads.' Josie was on one now. Though she'd lost count of the amount of times she'd had this argument with Georgie. 'To put food on the table, to pay all the bills,' she said, unable to keep the hurt from her voice as she spoke.

'Well, you clearly ain't trying hard enough, are you, Mum? We haven't got no food, and the electricity is always running out.'

'You cheeky little cow,' Josie screeched, gobsmacked. She didn't know what had got into Georgie lately but the girl seemed determined to push her over the edge.

Well, she wasn't having it. Georgie needed to learn some manners: have some respect. Josie had done nothing but try to provide for the girls, and this was all that she got back in return.

Standing up, Josie grabbed hold of Georgie by her arm and then, for good measure she grabbed hold of Marnie too.

'Right, that's it. Both of you can have an early night.' Grabbing the two girls by their arms, Josie marched them both out of her room, and towards their bedroom. Flinging open their bedroom door, she shoved the pair of them inside.

'Get your arses into bed.'

They realised that they'd pushed their mother too far this time; Josie was screeching at them like a banshee now. Georgie and Marnie didn't dare answer back. Instead, they both nodded obediently.

'I don't want to hear another peep from either of you again tonight, do you hear me!'

Without waiting for their reply, Josie pulled the door shut behind her as she left the room. She leant up against the door frame, exasperated.

Shutting her eyes, she took a slow deep breath just as she heard the doorbell chime.

Trevor was here.

Georgie had been spot on about Trevor: he was a bit weird. He'd even given her the creeps a bit sometimes but, right now, he was Josie's only option, and she wasn't going to let her girls fuck it all up for her.

Plastering on a fake smile, Josie fixed her hair in the mirror, before making her way to the front door.

CHAPTER THIRTEEN

'How's that for you, baby?' Purring as she straddled her new boyfriend, Javine Turner smiled to herself, basking in the fact that for three whole weeks she had been driving Delray Anderton wild with desire for her.

She'd been purposely holding out on him. Saving herself until she thought that the time was right, so that Delray would think she was a good wholesome girl that didn't just give herself to anyone.

Delray had fallen for it too. Hook, line and sinker.

He'd let her move in with him and told her that there was no pressure, though she could tell that his patience was starting to wear thin lately.

He'd been a bit short-tempered with her. Not his usual attentive self.

Still, she'd put that down to the strain of running the little empire he had going on here.

'That's good, baby!' Delray's voice was barely audible, face down in the pillow as he enjoyed Javine's massage techniques.

Javine smiled, Delray was a beast of a man, but currently surrendered to her between her silky smooth thighs; proving that even beasts could be tamed eventually. By the time Javine had worked her magic on him, Delray would be nothing more than a pussycat, eating out of the palm of her well-manicured hand.

'Is there anything that you can't do?'

'Well, that's for me to know and you to find out,' Javine teased.

She knew how to play the game.

Men like Delray needed the chase. Otherwise, what was the point? Delray could have any woman he wanted, especially in the industry that he worked in, and Javine didn't want to be just any woman.

She wanted to be so much more than that.

She wanted Delray to want her, to crave her physically, like a drug.

Tonight was finally the night. It was time for Javine to show Delray exactly what she could offer him.

Delray Anderton – the catch of the fucking century. Javine smiled to herself now as she leant in and pushed her breasts against Delray's back. Whispering gently in his ear as she applied more pressure, she teased: 'Do you want me to go a little deeper?'

'You go as deep as you like, girl.'

She could hear the urgency in his voice, the lust for her.

Pouring some more essential oil into her hands, Javine slid her palms the length of Delray's spine, working all the knots out of his muscles as she went.

She smiled to herself as she recalled the look on his face when he'd come home tonight and found her waiting at his dining table, wearing nothing but her white lacy Agent Provocateur underwear that he'd bought her, and a pair of six inch Louboutin's. Just a few of the many expensive gifts that he'd plied her with since she'd moved in with him.

She'd looked a vision, and she'd seen the lust that he had for her reflected in his eyes. How he had wanted to take her right then and there on top of the glass table top.

She had enjoyed making him wait.

Though, truth be told she had waited so long that she was actually gagging for Delray to fuck her now more than he was wanting it.

She felt like one of the luckiest girls in the world. Here, with Delray, in this fancy apartment.

Delray was one of the most notorious faces in London. The man was at the top of his game. He wasn't just ruthless when it came to making money, he was smart too. Javine could see the drive in him, the determination. He didn't give a fuck who he had to trample over to get what he wanted and that's what Javine liked about him the most.

They were kindred spirits.

She wanted this lifestyle as much as he did, and she was determined to get it. Permanently.

Delray didn't quite know it yet, but he had finally met his match.

Glancing out of the large balcony doors spanning the width of Delray's penthouse apartment, Javine cast her gaze out across the breathtaking panoramic views of the Thames – the warm dazzling lights of the Houses of Parliament. Compared to the shabby little flat that Javine had shared with Ashleen over in Brixton, Delray's was a completely different world: a world that Javine had spent a lifetime longing to be a part of.

'How about you turn over and let me work the front of you,' she teased now as Delray turned over on to his back.

Still smarting from his earlier conversation with Josie, Delray had been planning on having a few words with Javine about the fact she'd been running her mouth off around half of London. Though he'd been a little more than pleasantly surprised to come home tonight to find the girl waiting for him with a few plans of her own. He figured, under the circumstances, that for now, he'd let it go; he'd deal with it later.

Much later, the way tonight was panning out.

Straddling Delray once more, Javine took her time, relishing the effect she was having on him. Caressing Delray's bulging arms, she glided her fingers down across his rock hard stomach.

That wasn't the only part of him that was rock hard.

She could feel him pressing into her.

Something in her stirred now too as she realised that she wanted him just as much as he wanted her.

Taking him in her hand, she guided him inside of her.

Delray let a loud groan escape from his mouth.

Javine grinned. He was hers now.

Insatiable, he moved into her, hungry, urgent.

Normally, Javine just moaned and groaned in all the right places, so that she seemed like she was enjoying herself: tonight, she didn't have to put up any pretence.

She was enjoying fucking Delray.

Hooking up with this man had more perks than just the money.

Reaching his peak now, Javine could feel Delray was quickly on the brink of losing control.

Panting heavily, her heart raced as she matched his breath.

'Go on, baby!' she urged, as she ground herself down around him – harder – faster.

Closing her eyes she threw her head back as they both climaxed together, visualising the beautiful diamond Cartier engagement ring she'd seen in Selfridges earlier that day.

A huge sparkling rock set in a thick platinum band.

She'd made a point of sending a picture of it to Delray, letting him know in no uncertain terms what her intentions were.

She wanted this – to be here with Delray – to be part of this life.

It would be hers soon, she had no doubt about that and that thought alone made her squeal out loudly with ecstasy.

CHAPTER FOURTEEN

'Well this smells gorgeous, Josie.' Already digging into his dinner, Trevor Pearson looked across the table to where she sat, her food untouched as she waited for him to take the first mouthful. 'A proper home-cooked dinner. Lovely! What did you say this is again? Beef what?'

'Beef Stroganoff.' Josie wished she hadn't bothered to pass the food off as her own as she secretly prayed that Trevor didn't ask her for the recipe. Apart from the obvious ingredient of beef, she hadn't a clue what else was in it. She'd discarded the packaging as soon as she'd read how many minutes the food needed to be nuked.

'Does it taste all right? Only, I think I might have overdone it with the salt.'

'It tastes more than all right, Josie. You're a good cook,' Trevor said as he began greedily shovelling mouthfuls of the steaming hot food into his mouth. Better than the sloppy takeaways he'd been gorging himself with. It wasn't the same sitting in his flat every night and eating on his tod either. 'I could get used to this. It makes a nice change.'

This was exactly what he was after. Being here with Josie and her two girls. He wasn't quite sure how to broach the subject so he just decided to say it outright.

'Which brings me to the little idea I had.' He put down his knife and fork and looked at Josie seriously.

She was all ears now. When she'd told him she would no longer be working, Trevor hadn't taken the news very well. He'd seemed so disappointed, begging her to keep their Tuesday night arrangement, even though Josie had explained that she couldn't do it. She thought the mention of Delray would be enough to make Trevor see sense, but even that hadn't put him off. Somehow, she'd let him rope her into making dinner so that they could discuss things properly.

The least she could do was hear him out, and, of course, she was going to be paid for her time, so bunging a ready meal in the microwave wasn't a complete hardship.

'I know you say that you can't work any more, because of Delray, but what if me and you had some sort of private arrange-ment going?'

'What do you mean?' Josie shrugged, unsure what Trevor meant about a 'private arrangement'.

'How about we become an item?' he said.

Taking a sip of her drink, Josie almost choked.

This was the last conversation Josie had ever envisaged when Trevor had said he had something to run by her. She was utterly speechless.

'Sorry, my drink went down the wrong way.' Seeing the hurt on Trevor's face at her reaction, she started coughing loudly. 'Well, as lovely as that offer sounds Trev—'

'Hear me out,' he said holding his hand up to stop Josie mid-sentence. 'We won't really be "together" together, if that makes sense – we'll just make it look like we are.'

Josie shook her head, totally bemused. If she was being completely honest, she was confused as to why pretending to be in a relationship with Trevor was going to be of any benefit to her.

Trevor persevered.

'It will be a business arrangement just between us. If Delray gets wind of anything, then we say it's legit. We're a couple; making a go of it. How would he know anything else?'

Josie was quiet. Though she still couldn't for the life of her fathom how this would work out.

'Say I come around… what? Three nights a week? And, in return, you will cook me a nice home-made dinner. Maybe do a bit of washing for me. To all intents and purposes, we'll look and act like a couple.'

Josie was trying not to laugh. This was simply absurd. Madness.

'And, of course, you'll let me stay over.' Trevor said now, placing his final card on the table.

'Overnight?'

Trevor nodded.

'Oh, I don't know about that Trevor…' Josie didn't know what to say. She could see that Trevor was deadly serious about his offer, but she'd never let a punter stay here at the flat before.

It had always just been her and the girls. The three of them.

She wasn't sure that she could manage with Trevor being a fixture here too, even if it was just three nights a week.

'I mean, it's a lovely idea and all that but I really don't think—'

'I'll pay you £600 a month,' Trevor added, making sure that Josie was clear on exactly how serious he was.

Suddenly Josie was taking him very seriously indeed.

He'd already told her how he'd been left a large inheritance from his parents who had passed away. The mortgage on his flat was all paid off. The bills were all being managed. Everything was in order, and yet something very big was missing from Trevor's life. That's why he'd first got in contact with her in the first place.

'What's in it for you?' Josie asked suspiciously, knowing full well that in the months she'd been seeing him, Trevor had not once made any kind of move on her.

It wasn't like the man was getting his share of hot, passionate sex in return for his money.

Trevor looked down at the table. Picking at the edges of the tablecloth with his fingers.

'It's a lonely life, Josie, on my own in the flat,' Trevor said, sincerely. 'You, and your girls. You're like a little ready-made family. I guess, for me, it's more about company. You know. A nice home-made dinner, some good conversation.'

Josie nodded. That made sense, she thought. Trevor being lonely.

There was no crime in wanting a bit of company.

Josie had been familiar with loneliness herself over the years. Having to carry the weight of looking after and providing for her girls solely on her own shoulders. Life could be a real bastard like that, and six hundred pounds a month would be the answer to her prayers right now.

It was complete and utter madness, but, in a weird way, Trevor had a point: it might just work. If it meant that she could still earn her wedge and, at the same time, she could keep Delray Anderton as far away from her as possible, then maybe it was the perfect solution to both their problems.

'So we make out we're a couple? You and me?'

Trevor nodded.

'And what about my girls? I mean, they live here too,' Josie said, as an afterthought. Georgie would probably kick up a right stink, but Marnie would be okay about it. Josie was sure.

'They're not an issue to me, Josie. Like I said, you're a family. Nothing needs to change.'

Josie nodded, deep in thought.

She was already spending the money in her head before she'd even earned it. Gulping down her glass of wine in one, she thought that, somehow, it just made sense. She was currently up shit creek without so much as a broken paddle, and Trevor was offering to bail her out.

She'd be a fool not to grab the opportunity with both hands.

Nodding, she grinned at Trevor as she held up her glass to toast their newly formed business arrangement.

'Okay, let's give it a go,' she said. 'To us!'

Beggars couldn't be choosers, after all; besides, where was the harm?

It was about time Josie Parker caught a lucky break.

CHAPTER FIFTEEN

Hearing his phone ring, Delray Anderton rolled over and tutted loudly, irritated by the unexpected distraction that had drawn him out of his sleep.

He must have dozed off. Javine had completely knackered him out earlier. The girl was better than he'd expected. She certainly knew what she was doing between the sheets, and together with her tight, toned body and her perky luscious tits, the girl was like a walking, talking wet dream come true.

Delray was smitten.

He always picked his girls well.

Now though, draped across the bed in all her naked glory, with her arms locked around his, she was starting to get on his nerves. She was too clingy. Delray fucking hated that.

Shrugging the girl away from him, he grabbed his phone from the bedside cabinet.

'Tiffany? What's up?' He was instantly vexed at being disturbed at this late hour. Whatever she was calling for it had better be good.

Earlier in the evening Lenny had dropped the girl off at the Mayfair Park Hotel to one of Delray's most important customers. Richard Epping was a copper, and Delray was making sure that the bloke was being properly looked after by sending his pick of the girls.

'Tiffany?' he said, screwing his face up as the girl sobbed down the phone at him.

'What the fuck's going on? What's happened?'

'I'm locked in this bloke's en suite, Delray. You need to come and get me. He's off his head. He's shoved that much coke up his nostrils that he doesn't know what day of the week it is. He started choking me, and when I managed to get away he started getting really rough with me. I'm bleeding…' Tiffany spoke through her sobs.

Delray rubbed his head, fuming with the fact that the greedy pig he was trying to butter up had the cheek to take advantage of his generous gift to him tonight. He could hear shouting in the background. A loud banging sound as Tiffany continued to cry.

'What the fuck is that?'

'He's trying to break the door down, Delray!' Tiffany sounded scared now, and rightly so, the bloke sounded like a total nutjob.

'Fuck sake! Okay, just hang on, yeah? I'll be there as quick as I can.'

Putting the phone down, Delray dragged the covers from his body, wondering, briefly, if he could just send Lenny to sort it out.

Richard Epping was a first-class prick. The bloke clearly couldn't handle a few lines. Delray had cut him a favour tonight sending him Tiffany free of charge. It was supposed to be a symbol of their new-found friendship. To seal the little arrangement they now had going that Richard Epping would oversee any problems that arose should Delray ever need a pig in his pocket. Only, the cheeky fucker sounded liked he'd gone too fucking far.

It was nothing a few slaps wouldn't sort out; but he'd have to deal with this himself, personally.

The man sounded like he needed a little lesson in learning some fucking respect.

Delray sat up and swung his legs off the side of the bed.

On the plus side, he thought, this might just give him that extra bit of leverage over the cunt… having the knowledge that he'd tried to rape and beat a helpless, young girl. If you looked hard enough, there was always a bright side.

'What's up, baby?' Javine purred.

'I'm going to have to shoot out. I've got some shit I need to deal with.'

'But it's three o'clock in the morning! Surely whatever it is can wait.' Pulling herself up on to her elbows, she didn't bother hiding her incredulity.

'It's business,' Delray replied curtly, not offering any further explanation as he shrugged on his crisp white shirt. 'My business.'

His eyes flashed her a warning. Instantly het up by Javine's whiney voice, he didn't take kindly to being told what he could and couldn't do. Delray never answered to anyone, especially not a woman, and he wasn't going to start now; only, Javine was too angry or too thick to read the signals.

Persisting, the girl continued to pout: 'Can't it just wait until the morning?' Crawling across the bed, her pert bare arse sticking up into the air, she was trying her hardest to look sultry.

She was testing him. If he wanted her badly enough, he'd stay at home with her. Fuck the business; that could wait.

Grabbing at Delray's boxer shorts as he tried to buckle up his trousers, she playfully scraped her long painted nails across his navel.

'Come on, baby, we got our own business to attend to. You're not going to just leave me here, are you?'

Stepping back, Delray didn't bother to answer her.

Javine could look as fucking doe-eyed as she pleased, but business was business, and no woman – no matter how good a fuck she was – was going to get in the way of how he ran things around here. He hadn't got to where he was today by listening to some whiney fucking bird chirping non-stop in his ears that was for sure.

Watching as Delray tugged on his trousers and reached for his car keys, Javine copped the major hump now. They'd just spent the past hour and a half making love, and now Delray was going to up and leave her as if she was nothing more than some quick, convenient fuck?

'Oh well, that's just charming, isn't it?' she huffed.

Though it wasn't just Delray she was annoyed with now: she was pissed off at herself too. Maybe she'd given in and slept with him too soon? Maybe she should have held out just that little bit longer. She thought that he'd be besotted with her by now, well and truly under her spell, but instead, all of a sudden, he was just treating her as if she was an inconvenience. Just some girl that he happened to have shagged.

Well, Javine wasn't having it. If she let Delray walk all over her now, then there'd be no going back. He'd for ever act like he was the one in control, that he didn't need to answer to her, and she wasn't prepared to put up with it.

'Fine!' she said dramatically. Jumping out of the bed she stomped across the room. 'Well, you go about your business and I'll go about mine too,' she said, sounding like a sulky little child as she threw open the wardrobe doors in search of something warm to wear.

She could feel Delray's eyes on her. Burning into her. Probably taking in the view of her spectacular arse. Good! Let him look. She wasn't going to let him treat her like some kind of plaything. Like she could just be used as and when he wanted her and then tossed aside.

'Business?' Delray asked, sounding almost amused. 'What business do you need to attend to?'

Javine smiled to herself triumphantly. Glad that she'd finally got Delray's attention now that she'd hinted about leaving.

'I'm going to go home and see my babies. I'm sure Dolce and Gabbana will be missing their mummy.' Pouting, Javine pulled a plain black dress over her head. 'Especially seeing as you won't let me bring them here…'

Javine was on a roll. If this was going to be their first official argument, then she intended to make it count. She was going to tip the odds in her favour. She was still pissed off over the fact that Delray had point-blank refused to let her bring her doggies here when she'd moved in with him, that she'd been forced to leave them behind with Ashleen.

Once Delray had apologised to her for ditching her tonight and they'd made up, she was going to insist on him bringing her dogs to her.

In truth, she was desperate to see her two little rascals. A full-scale tantrum couldn't have been timed any better, in all honesty; it meant not only that she'd get to see them, but she might also be able to talk Delray into letting her bring them back with her when the man finally came around grovelling. Which he most certainly would, she was sure of it.

'Stop with the melodramatics, Javine,' Delray said, clenching his fist, close to losing his rag.

'Says the man that's swanning off out in the middle of the night…'

Delray was across the room.

Javine smiled, believing that he was going to wrap his arms around her, tell her that he wouldn't leave.

Instead, he was on her in seconds.

By the time Javine registered the grave mistake she'd just made talking to Delray so disrespectfully, it was too late.

'Do you know what, Javine, I've had enough of listening to your whiney fucking voice.' Grabbing her by a clump of hair, Delray dragged her across the room, launching her backwards on to the bed.

Screaming at the searing pain in her scalp, Javine tried to prise Delray's hand from her hair, but he only yanked it harder, ripping a huge chunk of it out.

'What the fuck are you doing?' Javine screeched, unable to believe what Delray was doing to her.

'You don't get to tell me shit. Do you get me?' Delray bellowed now.

'Please, Delray, get off me—'

'Are you still telling me what to do?' Delray sneered.

Javine stopped talking.

Delray let go; then, grabbing her roughly by her chin, he squeezed his fingers into her skin, hard.

'See this mouth of yours, Javine, it's going to land you in a lot of trouble. Telling *me* what to do! Telling every other fucker all about my business. What the fuck do you think you're playing at discussing me with the likes of Josie Parker, huh? You need to learn when to keep your trap shut.'

'You're hurting me.' Javine tried to talk. 'I'm sorry. I didn't think it would matter. She was being mean to me, looking at me like I was a piece of shit. I just wanted her to give me a bit of respect now we're together.' Javine fought to keep her voice neutral so that she wouldn't antagonise him any further, but her tears betrayed her.

'Together?' Delray sneered, squeezing her face tighter. Javine could barely answer. 'Are you having a laugh? If I wanted to be with someone, I'd go for someone with a bit more class than a little money-grabbing whore like you.'

Javine stared back at Delray, his words hitting her as if they were a sharp, jagged punch to her gut.

'I don't understand…' she was spluttering her words out as Delray maintained his strong grip.

It was as if suddenly she was seeing Delray for the first time, like his mask had slipped.

His eyes flashing with anger, he glared right through her as if she was nothing.

She realised that she didn't know him at all.

'You really fancy yourself as something special, don't you?' Delray leaned in to her – so close to her face that Javine winced. She could feel Delray's hot breath on her cheek; the spittle from his lips, spraying her when he spoke. 'Girls like you are ten a fucking penny, darling! I've had your card marked since the day we met, Javine. Only a stuck-up little bint like you would have been too blind to see it.'

Javine was shocked. Up until that moment, he'd been the perfect boyfriend. He'd treated her like a princess. Now, she didn't know what to think, what to believe. This had all been an act, some kind of a sick ploy, and she'd stupidly fallen for it. She knew without doubt that this was the real Delray Anderton staring back at her now.

Cruel, vicious. Unrelenting.

Delray laughed. He was thoroughly enjoying the look of shock on her face: the confusion that was there.

This was the part that he loved the most.

The moment of reckoning.

All this time, Javine Turner thought that she was the one in control when, really, she had been playing directly into Delray's hands.

Women were so fucking stupid.

Delray had ideally wanted a few more weeks to work on the girl. He wanted to see if he could get her to agree to the little plans that he had in store for her by getting her onside. Some girls were like that: they fell for him, and agreed to do anything he asked, regardless of what it was.

Only, Delray knew Javine wasn't quite there yet. The girl wasn't driven by love; that wasn't why she was here. She was driven by greed. Lapping up his fortunes as if she had a God-given right to them. The silly cow had forced him to play his hand sooner than he would have liked, so now she was going to have to learn the hard way. With force.

'You know your problem, Javine, you're too far up yourself.'

The bitch still didn't have a clue. She was completely brainless, but then, that was one of the reasons that Delray had picked her in the first place.

'If you weren't so vain and self-obsessed, Javine, and you looked up from your little hand mirror once in a while, you might have seen what was going on around you.' He screwed his face up. 'You did make me laugh, though, with all that virtuous nun routine. Making me wait three weeks until you finally gave in and let me shag you. I mean, come on, sweetheart, you and me both know that your snatch has seen more fingerprints than Scotland Yard.' Delray shook his head disapprovingly. It was a shame that he had to go out; he was really starting to enjoy himself. He loosened his grip.

Javine didn't understand what the hell was going on. She just knew that she needed to try to calm the man down, for her own sake if anything. She just wanted to rewind tonight, make everything go back to the way it was. Back to when Delray had been nice to her.

'I'm sorry, Delray,' she said, meekly. A stream of tears trickling down her face, snot running from her nose, Javine was trying her hardest to make him realise she was complying. She hated herself for sounding so weak, but she was terrified now and she didn't know what else she could say or do.

She was sorry; she just no longer knew what she was sorry for. Sorry that she'd fallen for this lunatic's facade. Sorry that she was here alone with him in his apartment. Sorry that she'd been stupid enough to get herself into this mess in the first place.

'I'm sorry for sounding like I was telling you what to do. I won't do it again, Delray. Can we just forget tonight ever happened? We can go back to bed, cuddle up?'

'Hello, is there anyone in there?' Jabbing Javine hard in the side of her head with his forefinger, Delray mocked her now. 'Fuck me, you really are thicker than shit. Cuddle up? I test out the merchandise, Javine, I don't fucking cuddle up with it afterwards.'

Merchandise.

Delray's words rang loudly in her ears.

Javine felt sick.

Delray shook his head. 'Nothing in this life is free, Javine. You think you can just open your legs once in a while and this is the sort of lifestyle that you'll get from it? That's called being a whore, love, and if you're happy to act like one, then I'm very happy to treat you like one.'

Javine's face paled. Seeing the car keys in Delray's hands, her eyes flickered over towards the doorway behind him.

Delray grinned.

'Don't you be getting any silly ideas now, Javine.' Wagging his finger, Delray let her know that he was still one step ahead of her.

'I'll be asking Lenny to look after you while I'm gone. Lovely man, is Lenny. I know you don't think so, seeing as you spent the best part of the past three weeks talking down to the bloke like he was some kind of personal fucking lackey. Talking to him as if he was some kind of a twat while he drove you here, there and every-fucking-where as if he was your own personal chauffeur.' Delray couldn't help but chuckle to himself. 'Old Lenny's got a heart of gold, but you get on the wrong side of him – which, in case you're wondering, you did – then he can be a right fucking ruthless bastard.' Delray's eyes glistened with amusement. 'Fuck me, Javine. Even I wouldn't have the barefaced fucking cheek to talk down to Lenny the way you have these past few weeks.'

Throwing open the bedroom door, Delray stomped down the hallway towards Lenny's room to fetch him.

Hearing them talking, Javine scanned the room, panicking, as she looked for a way out. Even if she snuck out of the large bedroom doors that led to the balcony of his penthouse apartment, there was nowhere for her to go.

The only way out was past Delray, but there was no chance of that: Delray was already walking back towards her. Lenny walking behind him.

Javine's heart sank.

'Lenny said he'd only be too happy to keep a close eye on you, Javine. That's nice of him, isn't it?'

Seeing the look that exchanged between the two men, Javine couldn't suppress the pathetic sob that escaped her mouth.

Which only seemed to amuse Delray further.

'Don't let her fool you into thinking that she is all sweet and innocent.' Delray patted his friend on the shoulder. 'She likes it rough mate; the rougher the better.'

Smirking now, Delray grabbed another fistful of Javine's hair. Pulling her head back, he leant in towards her once more, his mouth almost touching hers as he got off on the pain he was inflicting.

'Don't you make the mistake of telling me what I can or can't do ever again, do I make myself clear?' Delray spoke quietly. His tone menacing.

Javine tried her hardest to nod, but her head felt like it was in a vice. She could barely move.

'What was that?' Delray tugged harder.

'I won't,' Javine spluttered, choking on her own sobs.

Delray smiled, but he was a tiny bit disappointed, if he was honest. He thought Javine would have had a bit more fight in her than this. Thought she was going to give them both a run for their money.

'Good!' Bending down, Delray kissed her full on the lips, enjoying the power that he had over her as she flinched when he forced his tongue into her mouth.

Done with her for now, Delray let go, letting her fall backwards on to the bed.

Javine was nothing more than a quivering wreck.

Oh yes, he was going to have a lot of fun breaking this one.

By the time he and Lenny had finished with the girl, Javine Turner wasn't going to know what the fuck had hit her.

CHAPTER SIXTEEN

Wiping her hands down the front of her jeans, Josie stood back and admired her handiwork.

The dish she'd prepared didn't look bad at all; in fact, for once, she was actually impressed with herself. Her culinary skills were limited, to say the very least. She'd never made a shepherd's pie from scratch before. Smiling to herself as she placed the dish in the oven, she knew that she'd done well today.

She hoped that Trevor would see that she was really trying to make an effort. So far, their little arrangement hadn't been anywhere near as bad as Josie had anticipated. Trevor had his funny little ways but she'd known that before she'd agreed to let him stay over. Not only was it a bit odd in the bedroom, with him still insisting on just lying next to her fully clothed, but he was a complete control freak when it came to the flat, too.

He'd told her that he couldn't stay here if she left the place in such a mess. She needed to get the place tidied up. To start making an effort. It had galled her to be pulled up on having to clean her own home, but Trevor held all the money, therefore, he owned all the power. Josie was in no position to argue with the man, and the last thing she wanted to do was piss him off.

She'd made a deal, and she needed to stick to her side of the bargain.

Hence tonight's humble offering of shepherd's pie. Even Trevor would be hard-pushed to find fault with tonight's dinner, and that man seemed to find fault with just about everything. Trevor Pearson, as odd as he seemed, did not miss a trick. The bloke had eyes on him like a hawk.

Scraping the bottom of the saucepan, Josie eyed the huge lump of mash potato that she had left over. Even though there was food in the cupboards now, she couldn't abide wastefulness. It physically pained her to throw away any kind of food. Probably because they never had any food in this house.

She'd keep it, she decided, bending down to search inside the cupboard for a small dish to store it in.

'Bloody typical,' she exclaimed as she saw the bowl that she wanted was right at the back of the cupboard. Stuck underneath a large pile of dishes.

Stretching her arm inside as far as it would go, she twisting herself around, contorting her body.

Almost.

Spanning her fingers out as wide as they could go, she could almost touch it. She just needed to lean in that little bit more. Stretch her arm as far as it would go.

'Shit!'

Catching the top of an old blue vase she squeezed her eyes shut as it toppled over. She waited for the sound of the glass breaking.

Only, it didn't. Opening her eyes, she saw that it had just landed on its side at the bottom of the cupboard, and rolled towards her. She felt relieved. The last thing she needed right now was broken glass all over the place when Trevor was due to turn up here at any moment.

She wanted everything to be perfect. Just so.

She'd already spoken to the girls, who, since Trevor had started coming around, had gone into permanent sulk mode. They were to be on their best behaviour tonight.

Standing the vase upright, she heard a clang against the glass: something loose, rattling inside. Reaching her hand in, she felt the familiar rectangular flat shape at the bottom.

Her mobile phone?

Josie stared at it for a moment in complete disbelief. She'd kill those two bloody kids of hers. Her phone had been missing for well over a week. She knew it had been them, the pair of stroppy little brats, even though they'd swore blind that they hadn't taken it. To think they had just sat there and stared at her gormlessly as she'd dragged the house apart looking for the bloody thing too. She'd convinced herself that she must have lost it when she was drunk, and all this time those two ungrateful children of hers had been laughing at her behind her back.

She knew why they'd done it, too. The pair of them were on a mission to cause her as much grief as humanly possible. Sulking because suddenly Trevor was constantly hanging around. They'd done it to teach her a lesson.

Josie Parker shook her head. She hadn't realised her two daughters could be that manipulating. For now, Trevor was sticking around whether they liked it or not. The man was a guest in this house, and the girls needed to make him feel welcome. She wouldn't let them fuck it up for her.

She couldn't; she was depending on Trevor's money now. If the girls didn't like it, then tough luck. Josie Parker was going to rein the girls in – and sooner rather than later.

She thought of Mandy.

Josie hadn't heard from her friend for weeks. Not since the blow up with Delray. It wasn't just that, though, Josie thought, knowing that she was kidding herself really. Mandy would have been devastated to learn that her friend was back on the gear again.

Josie had let her down. She'd let herself down too; she knew it.

She could have gone to see Mandy herself; only, Josie didn't think she could manage the fall-out from it all.

And she still wasn't feeling properly like herself. Groggy, her head fuzzy. She couldn't put her finger on it. It was like living under a thick black cloud of depression; the darkness consuming her. She didn't remember feeling like this the last time she had withdrawn from the gear.

Last time had been one massive brutal shock to her system. Stopping the heroin, then gradually introducing methadone. Last time she hadn't had to do it all on her own; she'd had Mandy at her side, holding her hand every step of the way. Even when she'd been forced to show Josie some tough love and lock her in her bedroom for three days whilst she went cold turkey, she'd endured the screaming and shouting, the barrage of abuse as Josie had tried to break down the door to get out. To get away from her demons. From the night sweats and shivers that consumed her like waves, washing over her viciously in quick succession.

Mandy had helped take care of the girls for her, too, that week; seeing them both off to school; making sure that they weren't too scared of their crazed mother locked away in her room.

And how had Josie repaid her? By fucking up their earn with Delray and then keeping herself to herself the last few weeks.

Fingering the black screen, Josie wondered if she should just call her. Make amends.

It would be good to hear her voice.

Convinced that the battery would be flat, Josie pressed the button – pleased to see the screen light up moments later. The phone instantly bleeped as a series of messages flashed up on the screen. Nine text messages, and eight missed calls. A voicemail message too.

All of them from Mandy.

Josie held back her tears. Mandy had been trying to get in touch with her after all.

Dialling the number, Josie felt full of emotion on hearing her friend at the other end of the phone.

'Mandy it's me,' Josie said, almost bursting into tears, overjoyed that her friend had actually answered her call.

'I know it's you. Your name shows up as the caller ID,' Mandy replied tartly, her voice deadpan.

'Oh, Mandy, it's so good to hear your voice, babe. I've missed you so much,' Josie said, letting the tears roll down her cheeks. She didn't care how pathetic she sounded.

Mandy didn't answer.

'Are you still there?' Josie said, checking that the screen hadn't gone black, that the battery hadn't ran out.

'Yes, I'm still here.'

'I'm sorry for everything, Mandy. Really I am. For what happened with Delray, for lying to you about being back on the gear. I'm not on it now. I swear to you, on Georgie and Marnie's lives.'

Mandy tutted at that, her disapproval clear. She had seen and heard it all before. Josie was wasting her breath.

'And what about all the shitty messages you sent me?' Mandy said now, feeling her temper get the better of her. 'You sorry about those too, are you? Don't tell me you didn't mean a word of them?'

'What messages?'

'Let me enlighten you shall I. Let's see. First there were the ones saying that I was to leave you alone. That I wasn't to make any kind of contact with you. Then when I tried to reply, you started sending me the nasty ones. Calling me names and stuff. Saying that I dragged you down. That you wanted to better your life and the only way you could do that was by cutting all ties with me. The cheek of it, Josie.' Mandy was unable to disguise the hurt in her voice. 'Just because you've shacked up with one of your punters, don't mean you can pretend you're something you're not, Josie Parker. You're no better than the rest of us.'

'But… I didn't send you any messages,' Josie said, confused.

'It's probably the smack, Josie; it's made your brain deteriorate,' Mandy said, sarcastically. 'Go on, then, why you calling me now all of a sudden, huh?' Mandy was smarting. 'Has the novelty with you and your fancy man worn off already?'

'It's not like that, Mandy. Me and Trevor, we're not together—'

'Ohh, I bloody knew it. As soon as it all fell to pieces, you'd come running back to me. Well, you know what, Josie, you can stick our friendship up your arse, sideways!'

Holding the phone to her ear, Josie fought back her tears as Mandy's angry voice was replaced by the phone's bleeping.

Then she heard the key in the front door.

Trevor was back already. Earlier than she had expected.

Josie panicked.

Hurrying, she bent down and quickly stuffed the phone back inside the vase, pushing it as far towards the back of the cupboard as she could reach, before jumping to her feet again, just as Trevor walked in the kitchen behind her.

'Oh, I didn't hear you come in,' Josie swept her fringe out of her eyes as she tried to compose herself. Her heart pounding.

Something wasn't right. She knew it.

What Mandy had said about those messages? It didn't add up.

'What's up with you?' he asked, noting the red rims around her watery eyes. 'You look like you've been crying?'

'Oh, I was just chopping up some onions.' She had no intention of telling him that she'd found her mobile phone.

Suddenly, it all made sense. The little mentions of Mandy here and there; the times that Trevor had put the woman down, told Josie that she was better off without her. Trevor had hidden her phone. He'd sent Mandy those text messages, Josie was sure of it. But why?

'Is that so?' Trevor said, not convinced, his eyes going to the cupboard behind her.

Desperate to try to pacify him, so that he wouldn't probe her further, Josie started cleaning the kitchen worktops. She didn't want to draw any attention to the fact that she was on to him. That she'd caught him out. Playing games with her life. Lying to her. Controlling her. Instead, she did what she did best. She plastered on a big, fake smile.

'I've made us all dinner. Shepherd's pie,' she said. 'It's all home-made.'

'That will be what that black smoke is then.' Trevor nodded towards the cooker.

'Shit!'

Grabbing a tea towel, Josie pulled the piping hot dish out of the oven. The potato was black. Burnt to a cinder.

'A bit distracted, were you?' Trevor's eyes were boring into Josie's.

'I was just cleaning up, you know. I must have lost track of time,' Josie said, her voice small as she tried to disguise the quiver.

Trevor nodded once more. His eyes resting on the smears of mashed potato on the worktops; the dirty dishes in the sink.

He was annoyed now, Josie knew how much he hated liars.

Yet, here she was, lying straight to his face.

CHAPTER SEVENTEEN

Looking out across the panoramic view from his penthouse apartment, Delray Anderton smiled as Lenny handed him a glass of whisky.

'Cheers, mate!' he said, taking a large swig; the heat of the alcohol seeping through him.

Lenny grinned.

He was a sick fucker, Lenny. With a penchant for violent sex. Taking out all his aggression on Javine earlier had been a much-needed release for him. He had wanted to teach that jumped-up little cow a lesson since she first started talking down her nose at him as if he was nothing more than the hired help. Still, for Delray's sake, Lenny'd known he had no choice but to play along. He bided his time, knowing full well how Delray worked.

His boss had big plans for Javine, and this was all part of it. Making her think that she was something unique, that Delray was crazy about her. Delray didn't mean any of it. To him this was just all part of the game.

Javine had obviously rubbed him up the wrong way, though, and Lenny could see how. The bitch really did think she was something special.

Delray had played his hand quickly this time though. Normally he let this little charade play out until the girl was besotted. Devoted to Delray, she'd hang off his every word; it was a work of art to see it in motion. To see these girls go from happy, loved-up little wannabes to pathetic, needy neurotic messes.

'So what next then?' Lenny asked, watching Delray closely to gauge the man's mood. 'Did you speak to our client?'

If that little bitch in there thought what Lenny and Delray had just done to her was bad, she had no idea about the sick fuckers they had lined up for her next.

Delray screwed his mouth up, shrugging.

'He said he'll take her for now, but he wanted someone younger.'

Lenny nodded. He'd guessed that might be the case. Delray's newest business associate, a wealthy Arab called Hamza Nagi, had a penchant for younger girls. Much younger girls.

Delray had been adamant that Javine would fit the bill being only seventeen but Lenny had known better. Javine didn't fit the criteria at all. She might be seventeen but with her curvy figure and sexual experience she was more of a woman than most a decade older than her. Hamza Nagi wanted sweet and innocent, and Javine Turner was neither of those things.

'We could tone her down a bit. Dress her in something young. Make sure she's got no make-up on,' Delray said, knowing full well that he was clutching at straws. 'I don't know! Short of sticking the girl in a school uniform and fucking pigtails with bows, there's no way he'd be happy. She's too busty. She might be young, but she's got the body of a fucking porn star. He ain't into that.'

Delray looked out across the Thames. Staring out at the flickering lights of the city as he pondered what he could do. He was irritated that, so far, he hadn't been able to come up with the goods for his new client. The meet was scheduled for next week and, so far, Javine was the closest thing that Delray had managed to get to offer the man. Delray had wanted to impress, to show him that he was good for the order.

The money for this arrangement would be life-changing.

Even with everything he had, Delray had to physically pinch himself in order to believe how far he'd come. Living here in this plush apartment. Looking out over the Albert Embankment. He shared the building with lawyers, architects and the like. Some of London's highest-paid professionals. He was literally living it up with the rest of London's elite.

Fuck it, he was the elite. He was the one in the penthouse lording it up over the lot of them fuckers. Not bad for a boy that had been dragged up in Lambeth, that was for sure; but, as always, Delray wanted more, and he knew that he could have it too.

To think he'd started pimping out a couple of street walkers and now he had all this: the three brothels; a high-class escort agency: business was booming. He'd made an absolute mint. Clawed himself up from the bottom by all means necessary in order to get what he wanted.

But now he had it, he wanted more. This deal with Hamza Nagi was a real game changer. He stood to make a fortune. Only, the fucker was very specific on his requirements. Even if he stuck Javine in a school uniform the girl still wouldn't look demure.

Delray had been hoping to come up with the goods. Personally, Delray thought the man was a first-class nonce. Ordering young girls, children, was sickening even to Delray. But this wasn't personal: this was strictly business, like always, and Delray always took business extremely seriously – especially when he stood to make an absolute killing.

Thousands for every order completed. Minimal leg work, minimal fuss, all he had to do was keep old Hamza happy by supplying the sick fucker's demand; the money would speak for itself after that.

Delray rubbed his head irritably.

'Who fucking knows, huh! We still got a week before he flies here to England. Hopefully by then we will have sourced something a little more to the man's taste.' Delray shrugged. 'He's agreed to take Javine off our hands though, so that's one problem dealt with.'

Lenny nodded. Downing his whisky, he grinned to himself. The jumped-up little bitch was in for a real shock. Like Delray said, they still had just over a week to sort something else out for their new contact.

Anything could happen between now and then.

CHAPTER EIGHTEEN

'Mind out the way, girls, this dish is roasting.' Leaning in between her two daughters, Josie dropped the steaming hot oven dish down in the middle of the kitchen table, cursing as the heat ate through the tea towel and burnt her fingers.

'What's that supposed to be?' Georgie asked, aware of the brewing tension in the room between her mother and Trevor.

She didn't care. She didn't like Trevor and she didn't want him here. She wanted him to know it too. Everything about him made her feel on edge. From his funny combed-over hair, to his stumpy little square teeth. The man was strange-looking, and he had mean eyes.

'What does it look like!' Josie quipped through gritted teeth.

She'd already warned Georgie to behave this evening. To try to be more welcoming to Trevor. Clearly, Georgie had no intention of taking heed of her mother's warning. The girl was well and truly pushing her luck.

'Well, to be fair, Josie, going by the state of it, it could be a dog-shit casserole for all we know.' Eyeing the black charcoal crust that vaguely resembled mashed potato, Trevor prodded his knife into the top of the cremated food.

'It's shepherd's pie. I must have had the oven up too high. But I've managed to scrape most of the black bits off, so eat up girls.'

Sensing the stilted atmosphere in the room, Josie was trying her hardest to keep the mood of the house neutral; though, already that was proving an impossible task.

Trevor was in one of his funny moods again. He'd barely said anything this evening, but instead, he'd silently made his presence felt. Staring around the room with that stern look on his face. His beady little eyes looking right through them all. He was pissed off, and Josie knew why.

It was the same reason the dinner was ruined.

Josie had found her mobile phone. She'd caught him out.

She still hadn't been able to get her head around what was going on. Why would Trevor take her phone and then lie to her when she asked him if he'd seen it? What could he possibly gain from it?

She knew that Trevor didn't like Mandy; he'd already said as much to her at every given opportunity. He thought that Mandy was a bad influence, that the woman dragged Josie down to her level. It hadn't occurred to him that Josie and Mandy were two of the same.

In Trevor's mind, Josie wasn't like that. Not now, anyway, not now she had him around the place.

What was bothering her the most was what Mandy had said. How she'd been sent nasty messages. Telling her to stay away, that she wasn't wanted.

It was almost as if Trevor had been trying to alienate Josie. Some sort of control thing.

A bit like when they were in bed together and he insisted that he would just lie there and watch her fall asleep. Josie had waited for him to make his move but, even now, after all these weeks, Trevor still hadn't touched her.

It was odd, that was for sure, and Josie was starting to have reservations now about their little arrangement. But she was stuck. Penniless.

'I'm not eating this,' Marnie said, breaking Josie's train of thought.

The child mimicked the look of disgust on her sister's face, screwing her nose up at the food in front of her.

'Oh, just eat it, Marnie. Stop being a drama queen,' Josie warned, staring at her youngest daughter.

It was one thing Georgie getting stroppy, Josie was used to that, but she hadn't expected Marnie to follow suit.

The pair of them were at it: sulking because they hadn't got their own way, they'd ignored her warnings and seemed determined to bring the mood down in the flat once again.

Desperate to try to defuse the situation, Josie dolloped a smaller portion of food on to Marnie's plate, hoping it would pacify the child.

'I don't like shepherd's pie. It's yuk, and I can still see the burnie bits. . .' Pushing her plate away, Marnie stared sulkily at her mother. 'Why can't I have some Weetabix like I normally have?'

'You've never had shepherd's pie, not like this one. It took me all afternoon to make it. Why don't you just try it? You never know you might like it.'

Josie gave Marnie a small, tight-lipped smile, hoping that, for once, she would just do as she was told.

But Marnie shook her head. Point-blank refusing to even try one mouthful.

Marnie had been exhausting this week. Josie suspected that the child was rebelling against Trevor being here.

So far, her night terrors had worsened, and she'd become quieter and withdrawn. The only time Josie saw Marnie now was when she coaxed her out from her bedroom and forced her to come to dinner.

Georgie was the same, the pair of them, as always, thick as thieves. If one was off, the other would be off too. It was always the same. They were determined to let Trevor know that he wasn't welcome around here.

'Think about all those poor starving children in Africa, huh? Here you are complaining when those poor children don't have anything.'

'Stick my dinner in an envelope and send it to them then, 'cos I'm not eating it.' Close to tears now, Marnie threw down her cutlery in a strop.

Trevor intervened.

It was the first time he'd spoken to the girls directly since he'd started coming around, but he felt he couldn't help but have his say.

'The way you talk to your mother is appalling.' Trevor pointed his finger at Marnie. Jabbing it in the air in front of him.

Marnie didn't even look at Trevor. Instead, she folded her arms across her chest and glared down at the table defiantly.

Trevor glared at the child. Unwilling to back down, he bellowed loudly.

'*Eat!*'

Everyone at the table jumped with fright. Georgie looked at Marnie first, then at her mother. Trevor's outburst had shocked them all.

Marnie too.

'I don't want to eat it,' Marnie said as her bottom lip began to tremble and tears cascaded down her cheeks. 'I don't want him here. Make him go away.'

Sensing the thunderous look on Trevor's face, Georgie tried to calm the situation, coaxing her sister into doing as she was told before she got herself in trouble.

'Come on, Marnie, it's not too bad. Just take a big mouthful and swallow it down quickly…' Georgie said. Picking up her sister's fork, Georgie loaded it up with food, and offered it to her.

Marnie, in the throes of an epic tantrum, smacked the fork out of Georgie's hand, sending the food flying and landing all over the table.

Trevor slammed down his cutlery too. Annoyed at Georgie poking her nose in.

'Stop mollycoddling your sister!' he demanded. 'Marnie, do as you're told and eat your dinner.'

Marnie shook her head, refusing point-blank to even look at the man.

Georgie spoke up. 'You can't make her eat it…' She knew that Marnie could be just as stubborn as Trevor. The more that the man told her to eat, the more Marnie would refuse.

'You what?' His eyes glistened.

'I said, you can't physically make her. You don't have anything to do with us. You're not her dad.'

'Just leave it, Trevor, please…' Sensing that the conversation was getting out of hand, Josie tried to placate him, but her words only seemed to have the opposite effect.

'Leave it? Is that what you would do, is it, Josie? Just let these two fucking kids run riot? No wonder the pair of them don't do anything they're fucking told. It's about time someone around here taught them both some bloody manners.'

Up on his feet, Trevor leant over the table, shooing Georgie away from her sister as he set about bellowing at Marnie. 'Do what your mother said, and bloody well eat it.'

Despite the tears rolling down her cheeks, and her bottom lip trembling, Marnie shook her head stubbornly.

The smack came out of nowhere.

Trevor's hand caught Marnie off guard as she felt a fierce slap to the side of her face.

The force of the whack propelled her clean off her chair. Marnie landed with a thump on the cold kitchen floor. She started bawling hysterically, both from the sting of the blow and the fact that she was aware that everyone's eyes were now on her.

A sea of faces, all wearing shocked expressions.

Georgie was the first to move.

Seeing her sister hurt and crying, instinctively, she jumped down to Marnie's aid.

'You're okay, Marnie,' she said as she crouched down on the floor beside her and hugged her tightly. 'It's okay.'

Only, it wasn't okay. Not really. None of it was okay at all.

Georgie could see the raised outline of Trevor's handprint emblazoned in red on her sister's cheek. She was also aware that, so far, her mother hadn't moved an inch from where she was sitting at the table.

She hadn't said a word.

She was just going to sit there and let Trevor smack them.

Georgie glared at her mother.

'Aren't you going to say something?' Georgie was waiting for her to start screaming and shouting, to throw Trevor out. Only, her mother didn't do anything at all.

Lately, she didn't do anything except pander after Trevor.

That was when she was able to drag herself from her bed. Constantly tired, and yawning. Complaining that she felt ill.

Georgie had wondered if it was the drugs again. The ones that her mother pushed into her veins with a needle, but she knew that her mother hadn't left the house and, apart from Trevor, no one came around any more. Not Mandy, not Delray, not any of her mother's so-called friends.

'Mum! Say something!' Georgie said, losing her patience.

'Get up, Marnie, and finish your food,' she said simply.

'Not to her, to him. To that bastard there.' Pointing at Trevor, Georgie saw red. If her mother wasn't going to stick up for Marnie, then it was down to her to do something. 'Don't you ever touch my sister again.'

'And what you going to do about it?' Trevor stuck his bottom lip out, mocking the child as he strolled over to the kitchen side and poured Josie another glass of his home-made wine that he insisted she drink. Walking back to the table he stepped over Marnie as if she was invisible before handing Josie the glass.

It was the final insult.

'I mean it. If you touch her again, you'll be sorry.'

Trevor came close to Georgie. Leaning down, his face almost touching hers.

Bracing herself for Trevor's reaction, Georgie flinched as Trevor leaned in further.

The last thing Georgie expected to hear was Trevor roaring with laughter, but that's exactly what he did.

'Jesus, Josie, this one's got some fire, ain't she!' Trevor had tears running down his face then; he was laughing so hard he could hardly breathe. Trevor could see that the child was a lot like her mother. Brash, opinionated, short-tempered.

Georgie's face went red. Humiliated that Trevor was laughing at her, that he wasn't taking her seriously, Georgie felt suddenly helpless.

She looked at her mother for some support, but Josie kept her head down.

'Mum?' Georgie's voice was small as she waited for her to answer. To do something.

'You heard Trevor. That's enough now. I want you both sitting back up at the table and eating your dinner. No more arguments.'

Georgie stared at her mother in disbelief.

'Come on, Marn, get up. Let's just eat it, yeah?' Georgie leant down and hoisted Marnie back up on to her feet.

Marnie didn't argue. This time she did as she was told. Sitting back down at the kitchen table, wiping her snotty face with the back of her hand, she picked up her fork and took a mouthful of food.

'That's better.' Trevor grinned smugly as he sat back down at the table and looked over to Josie. 'See. I told you what the girls need is a firmer hand. Bet you're glad I'm here now, ain't you?'

Picking up his fork, Trevor ate a huge mouthful of food before taking a long swig of his beer. Sitting back in his chair, he watched as Josie and the girls continued eating their meal in silence.

Finally, his authority had been noted.

It was exactly what this household needed, a firm hand, and Trevor Pearson was just the man to instil it.

CHAPTER NINETEEN

Lifting her head from the pillow as soon as Lenny had left the room, Javine eyed the bedroom door.

She'd been pretending to be asleep when he'd come in so she didn't have to look at the man. Hoping that if he thought she was asleep he'd leave her alone.

He had.

Staring at the tray down on the floor. A cheese sandwich and an apple. Then she looked back at the door. He hadn't locked it behind him. She was sure of it.

Dragging herself up out of bed, Javine felt like shit. She could smell her own body odour. Her staleness. She needed a shower.

The room was tiny. Claustrophobic. With no window to look out, it was making her feel disorientated.

Pressing her ear up against the door, she listened intently. She couldn't hear any voices outside; there was no TV on either. She wondered whether, perhaps, Lenny had left her food and then gone out. Though he wouldn't be stupid enough to leave the door unlocked, would he? Pulling the handle down, she realised he had as she opened it just a sliver.

Enough to peer out across the large open-plan living space.

The lounge, the kitchen. Empty.

Eyeing the row of doors along the hallway, the bedrooms and cloakroom, Javine wondered if perhaps Lenny had only gone into one of those rooms.

What if he had? He might hear her trying to flee. She couldn't just stay here, though; she needed to at least try.

Taking her chance, her only chance, Javine grabbed the sheet from the bed and wrapped it around her body. Running as fast as she could, her feet bare, cold against the ceramic floor tiles, she made it as far as the front door.

Her heart was hammering inside her chest. As she went for the lock, her hands trembled so much that she could barely turn the handle.

Somehow, she managed it.

Pulling the heavy front door open, she eyed the lift right in front of her. All she had to do was press a button. If she could make it downstairs she could tell the concierge to get help. To call the police.

Javine felt like crying with relief.

It was short-lived.

'Javine, what a pleasant surprise,' Lenny said as he stepped out from the corner where he'd clearly been waiting and glanced down at his watch. 'Four and a half minutes. Not bad. Nice that you dressed for the occasion too.' Lenny grinned, eyeing the sheet that Javine had tied around herself.

Javine was confused; she didn't understand.

Then she realised she'd just been had – again. This was just another one of Lenny's headfucks. He was playing his stupid little games, deliberately letting her think that she could make her escape.

'Tut tut, Javine. What do you think happens to girls that can't do as they're told, huh? You were supposed to stay put, weren't you? Trying to do a runner? That's not very clever, is it?'

Javine shook her head.

'I'm afraid you're going to have to be taught another lesson, Javine.'

She wished to God that she'd stayed in the bedroom, as Lenny held open the front door and marched her back to her makeshift prison.

Lenny, left to his own devices, was far more sadistic than Delray could even dream about, and Javine had just played right into his hands.

CHAPTER TWENTY

'Drink some more of the wine,' Trevor said, as he topped up her glass, smiling all the while, as if his earlier outburst against Marnie had never happened.

'Of course,' Josie said obediently. Placing her fork back down, she did as she was told for fear of upsetting the volatile Trevor once again.

Picking up her glass she sipped at the wine, forcing herself to swallow the bitter, acidic liquid that burned her throat with every mouthful.

'Nice?'

Josie nodded.

She couldn't tell Trevor that the stuff tasted disgusting, not when he'd made such a big deal about how he brewed the drink himself. How it was his own special recipe. As if he was some kind of wine connoisseur.

Josie had tasted enough wine in her life to be the real judge, and this stuff tasted like lukewarm piss. Still, the alcohol seemed to be taking the edge off her shock at Trevor's earlier outburst.

The sudden change had frightened her; he'd frightened the girls too.

Josie had seen the way that Georgie and Marnie had looked at her before they'd gone off to bed. How they'd eyed her miserably. The confusion on their faces as to why Josie was letting Trevor talk to them the way he was. That she'd allowed him to physically strike out at Marnie.

Josie couldn't understand it herself, if she was honest.

She couldn't understand much these days. Her head was fuzzy. He'd done something else earlier too.

What was it again? Oh, that was it. He'd taken her phone and hidden it from her. Or had that been Georgie and Marnie messing around and hiding it from her on purpose?

She thought of the messages to Mandy. The girls would never have sent them. It had to be Trevor, but why? What would he achieve by cutting Josie off from Mandy?

She should say something, do something; only, she couldn't because she didn't know what to say.

'Are you all right, Josie?' Trevor asked. His eyes boring into hers with intensity. 'You look a bit pale?'

Josie nodded. She could feel her heart hammering inside her chest. Palpitations, making her feel angsty, on edge. How the fuck had she let things get this far? Trevor had somehow wormed his way into their lives. He was acting as if they were a genuine item, as if he had some say in how Josie and the kids ran their lives. Controlling, manipulating; there was something else too, only Josie couldn't put her finger on it. She couldn't think straight. She hadn't been able to in days.

'I know you think I was being hard on Marnie earlier, Josie, but I was only doing it for her own good. For all of your own goods. There needs to be some discipline in the house. The children need to learn to do as they are told. Instilling a little fear into them would do them the world of good.'

Josie didn't respond. Quiet, she sat staring at him with that strange look on her face.

Trevor couldn't help but smile. His eyes twinkling with amusement.

'Are you okay, Josie?' he said. 'You look a bit off colour.'

Josie tried to nod, but she couldn't move her head. Opening her mouth to speak, her lips wouldn't part. Her voice was stuck, deep down inside her throat.

Trevor was talking, his words vague. She couldn't hear them properly, couldn't focus. It was as if he was speaking to her from afar, somewhere way off in the distance. The noise echoing around her.

Laughter?

Was Trevor laughing at her? Had she missed the joke?

Her throat was so dry, raspy. She needed a drink.

Trying to reach out for her glass again, she couldn't even get anywhere near to it, let alone grip it. She was paralysed. Her limbs suddenly rendered useless; her arms weighed down to the table.

Her mind – the only part of her that seemed to be alert, suddenly went into panic mode. Was she having a stroke? Or a heart attack? This is what it felt like. *Oh my God, she was going to die.* She'd suddenly lost all control of her body. She needed to get up, but she couldn't move. Her body was numb, stuck in the chair, redundant, as her legs betrayed her, buckling beneath her as she tried to move.

She could feel Trevor next to her. The overpowering scent of his musky aftershave making her feel nauseous.

He was holding her. Gripping her tightly in his arms. Wrenching her up on to her feet.

Her eyelids drooped involuntarily.

Then she felt a whoosh of air that swept against her cheeks. The rush of coolness as her hair swished back behind her.

She was moving? Trevor was guiding her through the doorway.

She was sick? He was helping her to the doctor? She'd be all right soon. Trevor would take her to a hospital. They'd fix this. Fix her.

Her eyes shot open for a few seconds, long enough that the stark bulb in the hallway startled her as they passed the front door. They weren't going outside?

Glimpsing down, she could see her feet as they clumsily padded along the threadbare carpet in the hallway.

Her feet touching the floor; only, she couldn't feel the ground beneath her.

She couldn't feel anything now, in fact. It was as if she was floating.

Drifting in and out of her body, suddenly weightless.

They reached another doorway.

Inside, Josie could smell the familiar sweet scent of her perfume all around her.

They were inside her bedroom.

Trevor was helping her into bed?

Suddenly, she wasn't sure that Trevor was helping her at all.

Fighting to keep her eyes open, refusing to give in to darkness, she tried to keep focused. Her eyes fixed on the stream of light on the wall. Gone in an instant as she heard Trevor close the door.

She could feel herself falling now. Backwards.

Sinking down on to her bed. The warmth of the duvet enveloping her body.

Trevor was close by; she could smell his sickly sour breath.

Turning her head, to avoid the stench, she fought to stay awake, to stay conscious.

She tried to speak, to cry out to the girls, but she couldn't.

Was he leaving her here to die? Alone in her bed?

She felt her eyes roll then, lost all of her vision as she finally gave in to the black void that awaited her.

Josie Parker gave herself up to oblivion.

CHAPTER TWENTY-ONE

Opening her eyes, Josie winced as the bright stream of daylight poured in through the gap in the curtains.

It was morning already?

Pulling the covers back up over her head to block out the light, she groaned. She was in her own bed. That was something, she supposed. Though she had no recollection of how she got here. Her head was pounding. She could barely lift it. She felt awful, disorientated. As if she was hungover from a three-day bender; only, Josie knew this morning that wasn't the case. She tried to think straight, tried to focus her memory on the previous evening, but she couldn't even do that. It was as if her brain was a puzzle and she was missing a huge vital piece of it. Something was up. She could feel it in her gut.

She tried to remember if she'd taken any of her meds. Some Xanax, or Valium. She took them every now and again to take the edge off. They helped with the comedowns and the cravings. They helped with her shit life in general, she thought. She hadn't taken any yesterday though? Or had she?

She must have. That must have been why she'd blacked out.

Trevor.

Forcing her brain to try to capture the last memory she had, Josie could visualise Trevor sitting at her kitchen table again. How he'd forced her to drink back her wine. She could still taste the bitter tang from the slimy coating on her tongue.

Licking her lips, feeling dehydrated, she reached over for the glass of water that had been placed by the side of her bed. Trevor must have left that for her too, before he'd gone back to his flat this morning.

Josie winced, trying so hard to remember the missing chunk of her life that her brain wouldn't allow her access to.

Swallowing down the mouthful of water gratefully, Josie still couldn't shake the feeling from her mind that something was up.

Something deep inside her, gnawing away, as if it needed to come up to the surface.

She felt edgy, anxious. But then maybe that was just the effects of the medication leaving her body.

Swallowing the bile in the back of her throat, Josie turned her head to look at the alarm clock beside her.

Shit.

It was almost midday. She'd slept half the day already.

She thought of the girls. Both waiting obediently in their bedrooms until she gave them permission to come out. They knew the rules. Josie didn't want them wandering around the house when she had clients here, and Trevor was no exception.

Leaving them this long would mean one thing. Marnie would have wet her bed again. Or the patch of carpet over in the corner of the room by the door. The child barely made it through the night, let alone half the day too.

Lately, Marnie had been getting worse. It was like she was doing it to her on purpose. The more Josie berated her, the more Marnie did it.

The girls' bedroom reeked of stale piss. Everything was saturated in the stuff. The carpets, the mattresses, the bedding. All of it ruined.

Josie didn't have the stomach for cleaning up piss again today. She'd have to get Georgie to clear it up for her. Though knowing

Georgie, the girl would only kick up a big fuss and start another argument.

No, Josie would just have to sort it out herself.

Just like she did with everything else in this house.

She was in a bad mood. Sighing, already agitated before she'd even placed one foot out of her bed yet.

Slinging the covers from her, Josie Parker finally dragged herself up out of bed. Unsteady on her feet, her head was banging. She felt like she'd been hit over the head with a sledge hammer, like she'd been drugged.

She paused by the doorway.

A revelation.

That was it. It must be. That cheap, acidic home-made wine Trevor had been making her drink every night he'd been here.

Trevor was drugging her. She was convinced of it.

CHAPTER TWENTY-TWO

Knocking at Mandy's front door, Josie scanned the street convinced that she was being watched.

She was being paranoid but, after last night, she had every right to be. Trevor had set her nerves on complete edge over the past few days with his sudden change of behaviour. It freaked her out, and the more that Josie thought about it, the more she was starting to believe that he'd really been drugging her. It was the only thing that made any sense. He'd harped on about the stuff as if he owned a fucking vineyard. He'd always poured two glasses out though, always made out that he was joining her but, thinking about it now, Josie had never seen Trevor actually drink any of the stuff himself.

Josie had needed to escape, to go and see her friend Mandy.

She'd know what to do.

Only, now she was here, she had no idea if Mandy would even give her the time of day let alone help her, and her fears were confirmed a few seconds later when Mandy opened the door. The cantankerous look on her face said it all.

'Oh, it's you!' Mandy said, clearly surprised to see Josie standing at her front door. 'Well there's something for small mercies; love's young dream clearly isn't doing you the world of good, you look bloody awful.'

'Thanks a bunch!' Josie said with a small smile. She'd missed Mandy's knack of being brutal whilst speaking the truth.

She'd left the house in a hurry, not even bothering to get dressed. Instead, she'd shoved a coat on over her pyjamas, and taken a rare opportunity to get out of the house, so that she would have a chance to speak to Mandy without Trevor getting wind of it. Mandy was right, she was a mess, but she didn't look half as bad as she was physically feeling; that was for sure.

'Can I come in?' Josie asked, hoping that her friend was in more of a forgiving mood than she had been a few days previously on the phone.

Scanning the path behind her, Josie just wanted to get in off the street, away from any prying eyes, away from the fear of Trevor finding out that she'd come here.

To her relief, Mandy nodded.

'Come on, then. You better come in. You'll have the neighbours all twitching their curtains standing there in that get-up,' Mandy said, stepping aside to let Josie in the house, before leading her through to the kitchen. 'You want a cuppa?'

Josie nodded, grateful that Mandy was at least prepared to hear her out now she was there.

'I'm so sorry, Mandy.' Standing awkwardly in Mandy's kitchen, Josie was close to tears. She knew that her apology sounded weak even to her own ears. She had so much to make up for she didn't even know where to start with it all. The last few weeks were the worst of her life. She felt like she was on the brink of losing her mind.

'Go on, then, tell me what you're sorry for, Josie? Just so we're clear…' Mandy said, not wanting to make it easy for her. 'Let's see, shall we? Sorry for going back on the gear and lying to my face after everything that I did for you the last time to help get you back on the straight and narrow? Sorry for making us both lose our earn with Delray? Shall I write you a bloody list, Josie?'

'For all of it,' Josie said, full of guilt, unable to hold back her tears. Mandy was the last person in the world she wanted to hurt. 'I'm so, so sorry.'

'If you're still on the gear then I don't want to know, Josie. So, for once in your life, don't come around here and start treating me like a mug,' Mandy said, tartly, scrutinising her friend's pale, gaunt face. Steely dark shadows under her eyes.

Josie still looked like she might be on drugs. That would explain the state of her. If she was, she could drink up her tea and leave. Mandy wanted no part of it.

'I swear to you on Georgie and Marnie's lives, I haven't touched any gear for weeks now. I promise.'

'Oh, on your kids' lives.' Mandy laughed. 'Oh well, that means you must be telling the truth then, eh Jos? Ain't like you haven't said all this before. Swearing on your kids, Jos? Come on. You're better than that. Look at you, you look like shit.'

Well aware of how it must appear, Josie completely understood why Mandy didn't trust her. She'd lied to her face. If they were really going to sort things out today, then Josie needed to be a hundred per cent honest.

'I think Trevor is drugging me, Mand,' Josie said through her sobs.

'Why would he do that?' Mandy narrowed her eyes in disbelief. Josie raised her eyes to meet hers.

'I don't even know where to begin with it all, Mandy. So much has been going on. I swear to you, on *my* life. On my soul. I'm clean. I haven't laid eyes on Billy since that night outside the pub.' Wiping her tears, Josie looked her in the eye, determined that Mandy believe her. 'I don't even know why I went back on it. I just wanted a break, you know. From all the shit. All the fucking endless struggle. I thought I could handle it, just the odd hit every now and again, but somehow it just sucked me back in.

I'm clean now though, I swear. I haven't touched the shit again and I won't. I swear to God.'

Mandy nodded. Josie sounded convincing, and her story added up about not seeing Billy Stackhouse. Rumour had it that man wouldn't be capable of serving himself a cup of coffee for some time, let alone serving up his poison to any of his punters. Delray and Lenny had done a right number on him by all accounts. A fractured skull, two broken legs, and a broken jaw – amongst other things. It couldn't have happened to a more deserving guy, Mandy figured at the time, hoping that the scummy bastard enjoyed eating hospital food, because that was all that would be on his menu for a good while yet.

'And Trevor? Why do you think he's been drugging you? That's just crazy. I thought you two were making a go of it?' Mandy was unable to keep the bitterness from her voice.

It still stung. In all her days, Mandy had never once thought that Josie would cast her aside for some bloke. She'd hurt Mandy so much, and as much as she wasn't quite ready to forgive she could see that Josie was in a real mess. Sober, bawling her eyes out. Mandy might be a lot of things, but heartless wasn't one of them. In all the years of their friendship, she could count on one hand how many times Josie had broken down. They'd been through so much, so much shit.

This wasn't Josie. Something was really up.

'Here, have a tissue,' she said, passing Josie a sheet of kitchen roll.

'I'm not shacked up with him. It was a business arrangement,' Josie said, trying to steady her breath. 'Only, it's all gone wrong, Mand. Trevor isn't who I thought he was. He's acting really odd. Skulking around the place all the time; always watching my every move…' Josie searched Mandy's face to see if she believed her. 'He was the one who stole my phone, Mand. He was the one that sent you all those messages telling you to stay away from me. He's a control freak. I think he wants me all to himself. It's like he's trying to cut me off from the rest of the world. I can't do anything without asking his permission. He doesn't know I'm here now; he'd go mad. He ain't right in the head, Mandy.'

'He's a bloke, Josie. None of them are "right in the head",' Mandy quipped, though she could see that Josie was visibly distressed. Handing her a cup of tea, Mandy watched as Josie put the cup to her mouth, her hand shaking.

'Jesus, Jos. He can't be that bad, can he? I mean, so he's a bit controlling. A lot of men are. They can be set in their ways is all. Maybe you're just not used to it. You've been on your own for so long, maybe it just takes some adjustment.'

'It's more than that though, Mandy,' Josie said, shaking her head, frustrated that Mandy didn't understand what she was trying to say. Shit, Josie couldn't understand it herself, in all honesty. 'The girls hate him. They won't even go in the same room as him. In fact, these days they barely step out of their bedrooms. Marnie's night terrors have been getting worse; she's wetting herself in the day now too, and Georgie is just so angry with me all the time. The other night Trevor smacked Marnie so hard that she fell off her chair, Mand, and do you know what I did? I did fuck all! My head's been wrecked. I can't even think straight.' Josie gulped. 'The only thing I can think of is that he's drugging me, Mandy. I'm not completely sure, but it's the only thing that makes sense. Last night, I was sitting at the kitchen table and he made me drink something that he'd brewed, some manky home-made wine. The next thing I knew was half an hour ago when I woke up in my bed. I don't even know how I got there.'

'But why would he drug you? What would he get out of that?' Mandy said, uncertain now.

Josie shrugged. That was exactly what she'd been asking herself all the way here.

Trevor Pearson sounded like a nutjob all right, a control freak at best, but why on earth would he be drugging Josie? He had her right where he wanted her by the sounds of it.

'This is going to sound a bit odd, but we haven't actually done anything yet. You know, in bed…' Josie confessed.

'What do you mean? You haven't had full intercourse?' Mandy frowned. Trevor had been seeing Josie regularly for weeks before the two of them had shacked up together. 'You've done other stuff though, right?'

Josie shook her head.

'We haven't done a thing.'

'But you've been seeing him for weeks? What are the pair of you doing, playing bleeding Monopoly?' Mandy raised her eyes questioningly.

'He's got some weird kind of fetish.' Josie came clean then. 'I knew about it before, before I told him he could stay over. It didn't really bother me then. He just likes to lie on the bed. That's it. I thought it was company, at first, or that maybe he was a bit nervous, you know, a virgin. But I've looked it up on the Internet and it's a genuine fetish. It's called Somnophilia. Have you heard of it?'

'Somna-what? It sounds more like a frickin' disease to me?'

Josie shook her head.

'It says on the website that that's how some people with the fetish get themselves off. By touching you and stuff when you're completely unresponsive. I think that's why he's been drugging me. It's all part of what gets him off. A power thing, I guess.'

'Sounds a bit creepy to me.' Mandy screwed up her face, unconvinced. 'So, you're saying that this Trevor literally pays you to keep your knickers on and just sleep?'

Seeing the look of disbelief on Mandy's face, Josie nodded.

'They call it Sleeping Beauty Syndrome.'

'Oh have a laugh, Jos, you're winding me up. Sleeping Beauty? With your bonce?' Mandy roared with laughter, but Josie didn't laugh.

She was deadly serious.

'I'm not fucking with you, Mandy. I'm genuinely scared. I think he's a bit of a nutjob. I think he might be a bit mentally unstable.'

Mandy looked thoughtful for a second. In the past, any problems they'd had Delray had sorted out for them. They'd paid him a premium for the privilege, of course, but he'd had his uses.

'How about Delray? I know you two have fallen out, but can't you just have a word with him? Maybe he will get rid of him for you? You know, for old times' sake. It's the least he could do for you really…'

Josie shook her head again. 'No, I can't go to him. He already warned me what would happen if I carried on working, I can't risk him finding out. Trust me, I know what he's like.'

In truth, the thought had crossed her mind, but she couldn't do it. Delray Anderton would be the last person she'd ever go to for help now.

Mandy didn't know what else to suggest.

'You're just going to have to end it with him then, Josie. Tell him it ain't working out and hope for the best.' Mandy was unsure what other advice she could offer her friend.

'He sounds like a proper fucking oddball. You'd never in a million years have contemplated putting up with this sort of shit from any man. The only reason he's got away with treating you like he has is because he's caught you at your lowest ebb. He's taken advantage of you. Get rid and pronto.'

'I know, I know.' Josie nodded in agreement. If she hadn't been so low with the drugs, and having no money, then Delray cutting her off too, she would never have even considered letting Trevor Pearson anywhere near her.

Everything had just spiralled out of control.

The kids, the house, the lack of money.

Josie didn't know where to begin with it all; it was such a mess.

'I'm going to be back at square one again, aren't I? I'm boracic lint. I don't know how I'm going to earn any money, not when I'm going to have to keep looking over my shoulder for Delray…'

'Where there's a will, my lovely, there's always a way!' Mandy said with a wink. Seeing the surprised look on her mate's face, she laughed. 'What? You think I've just been sitting here twiddling my thumbs these past few weeks? Reading my Kindle on my tod with only my kettle for company? I'm meeting someone tomorrow night. In a little bar over near Peckham. The place looks a bit studenty; not the sort of bar that would show up on Delray's radar.'

Josie raised her eyes, curiously.

'It's all kosher too. There's a site on the Internet called CougarCatcher.com. That's what they call us at our age, you know, Cougars or MILFS – you know: Mums I'd Like to Fuck.'

Josie nearly spat her tea out.

'I know what it means, Mand.' Josie bit her lip to stop herself smiling. Only Mandy could cheer her up when she was feeling this low.

'Can you believe it? There's actually a market out there especially for us. Apparently, women of our age are much more experienced. Who knew, huh? The toy boys love us. We're all the rage!' Mandy laughed. 'Fuck me, this bloke I'm meeting up with tomorrow ain't going to know what hit him though is he, Jos. Experience – I've done more screwing than Black & Decker.'

Mandy laughed before eyeing her friend seriously.

'It's a dating site technically, but this guy knows the score. He wants the full works, he even asked me if I had a friend that I could bring along for one of his mates too. I was going to ask Fat Karen from the pub, but I'd much rather if you did the job with me?'

'Oh no, Mandy. I couldn't. My head's wrecked as it is. I've got too much to sort out with Trevor before I can even think about doing a job,' Josie said, not keen on the idea of trying to act seductive again for two toy boys. Especially after what had happened the last time.

'It's as easy or as hard as you wanna make it, Jos,' Mandy said knowingly. 'Just tell Trevor to sling his hook. He might not like it, but really, what's he going to do about it? Like you say, it's a business arrangement. You're not a couple; you don't owe him anything.'

Josie nodded her head. While that may be very true, it wasn't as simple as that. But she couldn't explain it.

She wasn't certain Trevor would leave; that he'd take her ending their arrangement very well. In all honesty, she didn't know how he would react.

That made her nervous for some reason.

'It's all paid for by the client, Jos. Drinks, a bit of grub; I told him how much I'd want on top for any other services he required and he sounded good for it. Go on Jos, we could both do with a decent night out on the tiles,' Mandy said.

A night out on the town was just the remedy Josie needed to get her out of this slump she was in.

'Come on, I've missed you, Jos. I've felt like my right arm's been missing the last two weeks without you. What do you say, huh?'

Josie gave Mandy a small smile. When Mandy put it like that she couldn't help but agree with her. It was about time that she took some control of her life again. She had a family to look after.

Kids to support. Wincing as she thought back to Trevor hitting Marnie, Josie bit her lip. Trevor had crossed the line, and Josie couldn't – wouldn't – allow him that opportunity again.

'Go on then!' Josie grinned, feeling instantly lighter now that Mandy had helped clear her head.

She needed to sort this mess out once and for all. First, she'd get rid of Trevor, and then she'd get things back on track with her and Mandy.

For the first time in a long time, Josie actually felt like she was finally back in control.

CHAPTER TWENTY-THREE

Trevor Pearson bit his tongue.

He knew something had changed the minute he'd walked through Josie's front door this evening. He was sitting opposite where Josie was standing, hugging his overnight bag on his lap, still wearing his coat. Staring at Josie in complete and utter disbelief.

'I'm sorry, Trevor, we gave it a go, but it just isn't working. We need to call it a day.'

Trevor didn't speak. He'd fucked up. Hitting Marnie had been a step too far. He'd known it the second that it had happened. He'd thought he was bringing a bit of order to the household. A bit of control. Josie should be thanking him for teaching her children to have some respect and some manners, not ending their arrangement.

This was absurd.

He scrutinised the woman. She seemed different today, unfazed. Standing with her back to the kitchen sink, a cigarette in her hand. It was as if she'd somehow got her head together.

'I know you think I've been hard on you and the girls, Josie, but I was just trying to help,' he said, not knowing what else he could say.

He already knew there would be no persuading her. Her lines were all well-rehearsed, too, he realised. She was resolute.

'I'm sorry, Trevor,' Josie said with a shrug. Desperately wanting to let him down gently. She felt as if she was properly splitting up with him, as if she was ending a relationship.

That was how he was looking at it, too. That was half the problem. She had given Trevor an inch, and he'd taken a mile. Once he got his feet firmly under the table it was as if he'd forgotten this was all a business arrangement. That they simply had a mutual agreement. Trevor was just a means to an end. Her only way of making any money. Trevor, however, saw Josie as more than that – she thought. Somewhere in his warped mind, Josie was convinced that Trevor really believed they were a couple.

'I have to put me and the kids first, you know…'

Trevor didn't speak. He could feel the vein throbbing in his temple. His heart thudding inside his chest. His temper was raging, roaring. The heat of his blood was surging through his veins. He couldn't believe what he was hearing. After everything that he had done for this woman. He'd offered her so much, and now, it transpired, as Josie Parker threw it back so ungraciously in his face, she was nothing more than an ungrateful little bitch.

'The girls aren't happy. I'm not happy,' Josie said honestly. The tension in her voice almost palpable. 'I just think that for now we should call it a day.'

There – she'd said it. Taking a pull of her cigarette, she waited for his reaction. Trevor had already shown his true colours; she knew that there was a brutal temper hiding away inside. She was ready for him. If he wanted a row about this, then bring it on. Her head was much clearer today. Having Mandy for backup had helped her too. Her friend had been right. Josie'd had enough of pussyfooting around the man. This was her house and her kids. Trevor had no place here. Josie didn't even know what she'd been thinking agreeing to Trevor's idea in the first place. It was insane letting him move in here. With his odd little ways, his controlling, sneaky behaviour.

Josie had been ready to say all this to him too. Ready to tear strips off him about taking her mobile phone. About her suspicions about his drug-laced home-made wine.

But, as unpredictable as ever, Trevor wasn't giving her any cause for an argument. He was simply sitting there with his head down, nodding in agreement.

Finally he broke his silence. 'I understand. If that's what you want.' It took everything Trevor had to keep his voice neutral, controlled.

His heart was thumping, pounding so loudly that he could hear it in his ears.

He'd invested so much in Josie. Putting food on this woman's table. Paying her fucking bills for her – all the while having to endure a constant stream of the mind-numbing verbal diarrhoea she constantly spouted.

It had all been for nothing. A complete waste of his time. All that plotting and planning; all that waiting for the right time.

Now, because of Josie's selfishness, his plans had been scuppered.

Trevor couldn't believe the cheek of the woman. The pure gall.

How he had managed not to react, not to leap over the table and throttle her, he would never know, but somehow, he was still in control.

Focusing on his breathing, deep and slow, he was a master at pretending to be something that he wasn't. He'd spent a lifetime doing just that. Suppressing who he really was. Hiding behind his mask, and he had no intention of letting that slip now just because Josie Parker had decided to ruin everything that he had worked so hard to achieve.

He shouldn't have smacked Marnie. That's what this was all really about. Josie had been quiet ever since that night. Subdued, distant. As if she was deep in thought, not just absent-minded, vacant, like he'd hoped.

He'd thought that Josie would have respected him as the man of the household, but he realised that he had underestimated her. She wasn't capable of respecting him; she didn't even respect herself.

Trevor had stupidly shown his hand, exposed his true colours and because of that Josie was rejecting him.

She was rejecting *him*.

Well, there was no way that Trevor was going to let the bitch know how deeply that cut him.

He'd fucked up. Cursing himself now for not being more observant, and realising that Josie hadn't been quite as medicated as he had thought. He should have upped the dosage of his 'Special Brew'. Made sure the concoction of sleeping tablets and depressants was working its magic on her.

It'd been the perfect strength at first.

Knocking her out almost instantly.

She'd been a nervous wreck too, all anxious and jittery. The side effects as the drugs left her system made her depressed; that's what Trevor had been counting on.

He needed to get Josie dependent on him, to keep her in a drug-induced fog.

He hadn't factored on her building up a tolerance to the laced drink. He could kick himself for not being more vigilant.

He had still been in the process of his planning stages. He was all out of options. The only thing he could do to redeem himself right now was to go along with Josie's request. Make out that he was respecting her wishes.

He'd have to play the long game.

He would give her a few days on her own. Let her start questioning her decision. Once the bills started rolling in and Josie started to struggle, Trevor would try his luck once again.

'Well, it's a shame it's come to this, Josie, it really is,' Trevor said, getting to his feet. He could see the surprise mixed with confusion written all over Josie's face.

This was good. It meant she was doubting herself, questioning whether or not she was making the right choice. Which, of course, she wasn't; the dumb bitch was too blind to see that.

'Well, yes, it is a shame,' Josie said, realising he was leaving.

Now here they were: Trevor was up on his feet. Leaving without so much as a fuss, or argument.

'I'll see you around, Josie. You take care.'

Josie watched him go, until he closed the front door behind him, and she realised she'd been holding her breath.

She'd done it.

Mandy had been right all along. It really was as easy as this. Telling him straight and, like Mandy had said, if he didn't like it, there wasn't much he could do about it.

CHAPTER TWENTY-FOUR

'Jesus, Marnie! Would you stop bleedin' gawping at me like that. By the look on your face anyone would think I'm abandoning you or something. I'm only going to be out for a few hours.' Irritated at the sudden need to justify herself to her children, Josie wasn't prepared to put up with any of Marnie's whining tonight.

Marnie was getting worse and worse. She was acting like a nervous wreck.

For the sake of her own sanity, Josie needed this night out more than ever and no amount of Marnie begging and pleading for her to stay at home was going to work.

'What about him though? What if he comes back?' Flickering a glance over towards the front door. Marnie was petrified of Trevor. The poor kid didn't want to even be in the same room as the man since that night at dinner when he'd smacked her.

Josie sighed. Realising that she wasn't the only one that had had the week from hell, she knew that she should really cut the girls a bit of slack. It wasn't just her that'd had to endure the man's company; the girls had suffered it too. His presence in the house had affected them all so much more than she had realised.

'He's not coming back. I told him to leave.'

'But what if he doesn't listen to you? What if he still comes back?' Marnie said, sitting down on the bottom step in the hallway as her mother stared back at her through the reflection in the mirror, brushing her hair.

'Marnie, trust me. He's not coming back.'

Josie was confident of that. Trevor had surprised her, if she was honest. She'd expected an argument, at least, but instead the man had just accepted her decision quite humbly and gone without too much of a fuss.

Josie wondered if perhaps she'd misread the situation. Maybe he hadn't been drugging her at all. Maybe she had just been paranoid? She'd been self-medicating too, to soften the brutal comedown from heroin. Maybe that's what had made her feel groggy?

Trevor certainly had his odd ways about him. There was no denying that, and he should never have laid a hand on Marnie either. That had been bang out of order, but maybe Josie had been too abrupt with her resolve.

And maybe, she thought to herself with a smile, she needed her bleeding head testing.

Glancing at the clock, she needed to get a move on. Mandy would be here soon, and Josie was looking forward to going out and getting steaming drunk with her mate, especially after the last few weeks of shit she'd endured.

'He ain't coming back. I promise you. Why don't you and Georgie stick a DVD in the machine and chill. I'll only be out for a few hours. I promise.'

Marnie still didn't look convinced. Twisting a strand of hair around her finger, the child pouted, looking positively sorry for herself.

'Marn, please! I've been sat in front of that bloody telly every night this past couple of weeks. Smoking myself to death, bored out of my friggin' mind. This is just one night off. Please don't make it difficult for me.'

'But what about the Bogeyman?' Marnie's voice was barely audible now. A whisper. The child looked terrified even just saying the words.

Josie stopped what she was doing and stared over at her, feeling the surge of guilt spread through as she saw that Marnie was genuinely terrified.

She knew that it was all her fault. She'd been the one to put the stupid story into the girl's head in the first place. All those times when she hadn't been able to afford a babysitter, she had thought she was being clever by using stories about the Bogeyman to frighten the girls into staying in their beds at night while she went out working. She'd told them if they were naughty then the Bogeyman would come.

Marnie was obsessed that the Bogeyman was going to come into her bedroom at night and take her away. She wet the bed almost every night now, suffering with the most awful night terrors. Her so-called 'brainwave' had turned into Marnie's biggest phobia.

'The Bogeyman isn't going to come and get you, Marnie,' she sighed knowing full well that no matter how many times she'd backtracked and told Marnie that the Bogeyman wasn't even real, that she'd made him up, her daughter would never believe her.

She used a different tactic.

'You've been a good girl today, yeah?'

Marnie nodded. She had been good. She had tried so, so hard to be good every day.

'There you go, then. You're safe. He only comes if you've been really, really naughty, remember?'

Marnie nodded again.

Josie knew that she shouldn't feed on the girl's fears, but she also knew that the way the conversation had been going, she was about to have an epic meltdown on her hands, and right now all Josie wanted was a skinful of gin and tonic.

Thankfully, it seemed to do the trick. Marnie was quiet now; sucking her thumb, she continued to watch as Josie finished scrutinising her appearance in the mirror.

Josie had no idea why Marnie was so fixated on such things. She'd never had these kinds of problems with Georgie when she was younger. Instead, Georgie had gone the other way. It was now that she was older she'd turned into a stroppy little mare. She'd been driving Josie nuts lately too. Complaining that she was constantly tired, and fed up. Josie was sure that it was just Georgie going through the motions of being a typical pre-teen. The girl's hormones were probably raging. Josie sighed once more as she realised this was only the start of it all. She had many teenage years ahead of her for both of her girls and, if they were anything like she had been, she was going to have her work cut out for her. How the bloody hell had time flown so quickly? All these years, it was like she'd blinked and suddenly her firstborn was almost thirteen. Almost a teenager. No longer a little girl. It didn't bear thinking about.

'Go on, then, how do I look?' Josie said as she gave herself one final once-over before her friend arrived.

She wasn't sure if she fitted the stipulation of being a cougar by any means but, from what Mandy had told her, these two blokes they had arranged to meet tonight sounded dead keen. After ransacking her wardrobe for something to wear, she'd opted for a plain black skirt and a lacy camisole top. After washing her hair, and painting on a bit of make-up, she was starting to feel a bit like her old self again.

'You look very pretty, Mummy.' Marnie beamed. 'The prettiest mummy in the world.'

'I know what you're doing, Marnie, and it ain't going to work, love.' Josie eyed her youngest daughter suspiciously as she laughed.

The kid was a fast learner. 'You're trying to butter me up, aren't you? So that I stay at home. You don't miss a trick, do you?'

Marnie shot her mum a cheeky smile.

'Right, come on. Take your thumb out of your gob, and go and get some tissues and wipe your snotty nose, will ya!' Josie said, bringing the child back down to reality with a bump as she heard the knock at the door.

That would be Mandy. Bang on time as always.

Josie was looking forward to tonight. She'd missed her friend greatly the past few weeks. This was just what she needed: a good night, and the pair of them putting the world to rights.

'Right, Georgie,' Josie called out to where Georgie was curled up in the front room on the sofa. She'd been in there half the day, lounging about, her eyes glued to the telly.

'Remember what I said. I want you both in bed by nine o'clock. Do you hear me?'

Georgie grunted.

Josie rolled her eyes, knowing that was the only response she was likely to get.

'Right, Moosh. You remember what I said 'en all,' Josie said as she grabbed her handbag and planted a kiss on the top of Marnie's head. 'You be good, okay.'

Marnie nodded. 'I will, Mummy, I promise.'

Josie smiled.

Seconds later she was out the door, determined to let her hair down and have a bit of fun tonight with her best mate, her two children already forgotten.

CHAPTER TWENTY-FIVE

Josie was hammered.

Sitting in the corner of the tiny little booth in Southwark, Mandy hadn't been exaggerating when she'd said this place was 'studenty'. It would be, wouldn't it? Seeing as it was the student bar of Camberwell College of Arts.

Their dates had been real posh boys too. Andy and Jonathan. Nice lads – as it went. Way too eager to impress, the pair of them had gone back up to the bar for what must have been the tenth time tonight.

Josie and Mandy stood out like a pair of turds in a fruit bowl. Not that either of them gave a shit. They were too busy having fun. Showing all these stuck-up students how a night out on the lash was really done.

Already into their third bottle of wine, Josie was so glad that Mandy had persuaded her to come out tonight; she was thoroughly enjoying herself for once.

'I'm not kidding you, Jos, the state of the woman,' Mandy was slurring now. Their focus on the two men had long since dwindled.

They were so engrossed in their conversation that they'd forgotten the reason they were even here tonight.

Mandy and Josie were having a really good catch up as she filled her in on everything she'd missed. First topic of conversation was, of course, the delightful Mel Lewis.

'She's only gone and shacked up with some Rastafarian bloke over in Lambeth. Get this, they live in a Rasta temple, which turns out is some old run-down squat. According to Davey, the silly old cow reckons she's found her calling in life; though, trust me, going by the state of the ratty dreadlocks she's now got growing out of the top of her head, her calling isn't what she should have been looking for. She should have kept her eyes peeled for some decent shampoo.'

Mandy shook her head in wonderment. 'You couldn't make it up, Jos. Poor Davey. I mean, the woman's making a holy show out of him, isn't she? Running off with any fella that even looks at her twice.'

'What's Davey said about it all?' Josie couldn't help but feel sorry for the man. She'd always liked Davey. He certainly didn't deserve the shit that Mel Lewis served up to him on a regular basis. He was a genuinely nice man; the type of person that looked only for the good in everyone he met. He'd even seen the good in her. Josie had lost count of the times Davey'd helped her out over the years, never once asking or expecting anything in return. Davey didn't have an ulterior motive like most blokes around here did – making a point of collecting back favours from her in kind.

Davey wasn't like that; he was a gent through and through. Though, that was probably why Mel treated him the way she did. She mistook the man's kindness for weakness.

'Oh, you know Davey. Buries his head in the sand when it comes to that woman. He says they're done now for good; but then, he says that every time she does it, don't he? Before you know it, she's back again. Though, I don't know; this time he seems pretty adamant. Maybe he's learned his lesson. There's only so many times you can keep taking someone back, isn't there?'

Josie grinned. Mandy would never admit it, but she was smitten with Davey. It was written all over the woman's face.

'So, are you two back on then or what?'

'Well, I don't know about "back on" as such. We're just good mates, really. I just want to be there for him, you know.'

'Oh, I "know" all right.' Josie rolled her eyes and giggled. 'You just want to be there for him in his hour of need. Just as mates.'

'Oi you! It ain't like that.' Mandy grinned back, knowing full well that she didn't sound even the slightest bit convincing, not even to herself. 'I like him, really I do, but I don't want to keep playing second fiddle every time old yo-yo knickers buggers off with a bit of strange.' Mandy shrugged as if she'd put a lot of thought into her decision. Her tone serious.

'I'm going to wait for Davey to come to me this time; play hard to get.'

Josie eyed her friend suspiciously. 'Okay!' she said doubtfully. 'Then answer me this, truthfully, Mandy…' Her voice deadly serious as she looked into her friend's eyes, pausing dramatically for effect. 'The last time you went to see him, did you have your best knickers on?'

Judging by Mandy's giggle, Josie knew she was spot on.

'I bloody knew it. Hard to get? You just wanna be mates while you're wearing your best kecks! Come on, Mand, who you kidding?'

'Oh, bugger off you!' Mandy should have known that she could never get anything past Josie. The woman knew her better than she knew herself sometimes.

'Well, you know what they say. Always be prepared. You never know when the "opportunity" will arise. So to speak.' Mandy winked at her mate; seeing the men were walking back over with a tray laden with more drinks, she quickly added: 'Though given half the chance, I'd have him up against the wall quicker than the bloke could say pork scratchings.'

'You all right there, ladies?'

Jonathan and Andy sat down, wondering what was so funny as Mandy and Josie fell about laughing. The website had been right about one thing, instead of the usual boring mind games and pretentious shit that went part and parcel when it came to dating, Josie and Mandy at least knew how to have a laugh.

Placing the drinks down on the table, Andy looked at Jonathan and shrugged. The women were clearly wasted.

'The bar's stopped serving food,' Andy said warily as he placed the tray of shots down in the middle of the table, before picking up the packets of snacks in the middle. 'Thought you could do with something to munch on, though. What do you fancy, nuts or pork scratchings?'

'Oh, Mand is quite partial to a pork scratching, aren't you Mandy!'

Mandy and Josie were on the floor then, roaring with laughter at their private little joke, much to their dates' amusement. Almost spitting her drink out, Mandy blushed all the way down to her feet.

CHAPTER TWENTY-SIX

Opening her eyes, Marnie sat up and looked around her bedroom.

She must have fallen asleep. She hadn't meant to. She'd been waiting for Georgie to come to bed too, but her sister had wanted to stay up and watch another film.

Their mother had told her to be in bed by nine on the dot, and that's exactly what Marnie had made sure she'd done. Even though she was scared of being in this room all on her own, she'd forced herself to get into bed. Forced herself to lay down under the blankets as she waited for her mother to return. So that she could see that Marnie was being good. Just like she told her.

Only, she must have fallen fast asleep.

Her mother had lied to her. She'd promised that she'd only be a few hours. She'd been out most of the night. Much later than she said she'd be. Georgie had watched at least three films tonight in the time their mother had gone.

The television was still on, still blaring.

Marnie listened. She could hear her sister moving about. Walking around the flat, probably getting ready to come to bed. Marnie was glad. She hated being here in this room all by herself. Marnie wondered what Georgie was doing. She wanted to get out of bed and have a look, but she knew it was bad, and she didn't want to be a bad girl tonight. She wanted to be a good girl.

So she stayed where she was. Listening to the TV; the sound of someone creeping about the house.

She started to feel scared.

'Georgie?' Marnie said, her voice barely a whisper as it came out.

She already knew it wasn't Georgie. She'd heard this noise many times before.

'Please, no,' she whispered out loud to herself. Her heart thumping inside her chest now. Her body trembling with fear. Every one of her senses heightened as she waited for what she knew was to come.

Lying back down, she pulled the bed cover up over her head, knowing that there would be no escape.

Pressing her body down into the mattress, she prayed that maybe he wouldn't find her; only, he always did.

There was nowhere to run; nowhere to hide.

She heard the door creak.

He was here in the room. She could hear him breathing.

Feel him watching her, even under the shield she tried to make with her covers.

He was dragging something. Something big. Leaning it up against the bedroom door.

He was barricading her inside. She wouldn't be able to escape.

'Georgie?' Even as she tried to say the word she knew in her heart, in her soul, this wasn't her sister.

She couldn't even speak now; full of fear, her voice had simply vanished, betraying her.

She felt the whoosh of cold air as the blankets were lifted from her body.

Then she saw him.

Standing above her, looking down at her in her bed.

That icy-cold look in his eye, that twisted smirk on his face.

Her mother had lied to her. She'd said that if Marnie was good he wouldn't come for her.

But he had.

The Bogeyman had come for her.

She started to scream.

CHAPTER TWENTY-SEVEN

Squeezing his eyes shut as Josie worked her magic on him, Andy Lyons felt ecstasy building inside him. His mate, Jonathan, had been right. Older women were more experienced, more keen to comply. This one certainly was anyway.

Grabbing a fistful of Josie's hair, Andy tightened his grip as the anticipation built inside him. The feel of Josie's mouth around him, pleasuring him, was like nothing he'd ever experienced before.

He was ready to explode.

Not yet though.

Him and Jonathan had spent the night plying these two birds with alcohol, and the least they could do now was make sure they gave them their money's worth.

Enthralled with lust and excitement, Andy pulled Josie up from the floor, and spun her around. Grabbing at her breasts through her bra. Doughy. Full.

He was there. Caught up in the moment. Panting like a wild animal, his primal instinct kicked in.

Josie, surprised by Andy's sudden forcefulness, yanked her skirt up and bent over.

A sudden screech of surprise escaped from her lips as Andy plunged into her. Barely capable of one thrust, he let out a loud groan and collapsed with a shudder.

'Well, that was bleeding quick.' Josie grinned as she shook the man off her, and yanked her knickers back up, registering the disappointment on Andy's face that he hadn't been able to last longer.

'Don't worry, darling, it happens to the best of them.'

Josie tried not to laugh. Another perk of shagging a toy boy: these blokes didn't look capable of holding their pints, let alone their stamina. Maybe Mandy really was on to something here. Tonight had been the easiest money Josie had ever earned and, on top of that, she'd actually enjoyed herself too.

'Here, Jos? Are you done? I ain't interrupting, am I?' Mandy said, staggering towards where Josie and Andy had been doing the deed up against an old van in the back of the college car park.

'It's all right; me and Alan are all done.'

'It's Andy, actually.' Doing up his fly, Andy corrected her, insulted that the woman couldn't even remember his name.

'Andy. That's what I said.' Josie winked at Mandy. Then seeing the look on her friend's face she realised something was up. 'What is it Mandy, what's wrong?'

Mandy shook her head. 'I'm not sure, Jos. I got a phone call from your mobile. Only, when I answered it, it was your Georgie.'

'Oh bollocks. I must have left it at home,' Josie said as she opened her handbag and rummaged around, just to double-check.

'She sounded in a right state, Jos. Crying her eyes out. I couldn't get any sense out of her. I think you need to get home, mate.'

Josie nodded, then realised that Andy was still standing next to her, gawping at her like she had two heads growing out of her shoulders.

'What?'

'You've got kids?'

'So what if I have,' Josie said picking up on the judgement in his voice.

Andy screwed his face up.

'Oh, don't tell me you suddenly got a conscience, have you? You didn't seem to have any issues two minutes ago when your trousers were down around your ankles.'

Josie was bored. She'd got her money.

She needed to get home to see what the matter was with Georgie. Knowing her girls, Marnie had probably had another massive meltdown about something. The kid had been on the verge of tears before Josie had even left tonight.

'You told me you didn't have kids though.'

'Yeah, well, you told me that you had a big cock, didn't you? So I guess we're both even now, aren't we. You coming?' Josie said to Mandy as she saw a cab pulling up just across the road.

'I might pop over and see if Davey's still up,' Mandy said. 'Unless you want me to come back with you and check on the girls?'

Josie shook her head, knowing full well that Mandy was dying to get round to see Davey. It was all the woman had spoken about all evening.

'I'll call you tomorrow, babe,' she shouted as she ran across the road, flagging the taxi down before it drove off.

The quicker she got home and sorted the girls out the better.

CHAPTER TWENTY-EIGHT

The loud scream dragged Georgie out of her sleep.

Still tired, she stared over towards the television screen, disorientated, trying to figure out where the noise had come from.

Her film must have finished, now replaced by an old-fashioned cookery programme that dominated the screen. She must have fallen asleep, though she wasn't sure how long ago. Maybe she'd just imagined the noise? Or maybe she'd dreamt it?

She should go to bed; she'd been waiting up for their mother to get home. She'd said she'd only be a few hours, but then that could mean anything in their mother's book. The woman seemed to have no concept of time. Happy to come and go as she pleased. Georgie was used to being left to fend for herself and her little sister.

Yawning once more, Georgie decided that she wasn't going to bother waiting up. She'd go to bed. She was surprised her sister had gone ahead of her, if she was honest. Marnie normally hated being on her own, but her sister had been adamant that she needed to be in bed by nine. She'd said that Mummy had told her to be good while she was gone and, obsessing as always over the Bogeyman coming to get her, Marnie must have taken herself off to bed.

Georgie smiled.

Marnie was a little character. She drove her mad sometimes with the tantrums and the night terrors; the bed-wetting was the worst part for Georgie, but she still loved her all the same.

Georgie had barely made it as far as the lounge door before she heard another strange muted noise, like a muffled scream.

It was real, she realised, the noise that had woken her.

It sounded like Marnie. Another night terror?

They had been getting worse lately. Every night she'd been having them.

Georgie tried her best to help her sister, but nothing seemed to make them go away. They were affecting her in the day now too. Making Marnie anxious, nervous. It was like some kind of phobia she'd developed.

Making her way to their bedroom, Georgie prayed that Marnie hadn't wet the bed too. She could cope with the tears and the tantrums, but having to change all the bedding again would be a chore.

'Marnie?' she said curiously as she saw the bedroom door was closed. Marnie never closed the door; she was too frightened to be left in her room all on her own.

Turning the bedroom door handle, Georgie realised Marnie had locked it too.

How odd.

'Marnie?' Georgie said. Cautiously now, she rapped her knuckles against the wood. Waiting for her sister to reply.

Maybe Marnie was just playing some kind of a joke on her. Georgie wasn't sure, but something deep in her gut didn't feel right. Marnie would never lock the door.

'Marnie? Is Mum in there with you?' Georgie asked as she made her way towards the bedroom, her heartbeat thudding inside her chest.

Had her mum come home already? While she'd been sleeping? But then why didn't they answer her? They must be able to hear her banging at the door.

Georgie tried it again.

Twisting the door handle, she bounced her body weight against it as if to try to break the lock.

It wouldn't budge.

Leaning up against it now, Georgie could feel herself getting anxious. Something really wasn't right here.

'Marnie, can you hear me? Marnie, answer me?'

Georgie was getting angry. Shouting through the door she banged her hands against it repeatedly to get her sister's attention. When that didn't work, she pressed her ear up against it and listened.

She could hear the sound of heavy breathing. As if Marnie was suppressing her sobs. As if she was underneath her covers.

Or someone was holding something over her mouth.

'Marnie? It's me, Georgie. Open the door.'

Georgie was shouting now. Banging her fists as hard as she could.

Thumping her body off the wood repeatedly.

'If you don't open the door right now, Marnie... I mean it, Marnie. This isn't funny. Open the door.'

Silence. Nothing.

Then another noise. A low, deep whisper.

Georgie couldn't make it out.

It sounded like someone was in there with her.

The loud crash inside the room startled her. Something or someone had fallen? She heard a scuffle then. As if someone was scurrying across the carpet, only to be dragged backwards again.

Her sister's voice, screaming.

'Georgie. Help—'

What sounded like a loud slap.

Then silence once more.

Georgie was frantic, throwing herself at the door. Kicking it, hitting it, but nothing would make it budge.

'Marnie, it's all right, I'm going to help you.'

Running the length of the corridor, Georgie could barely think straight.

She didn't know what to do. She could run around to the neighbours' house and ask them to call the police. They would get here quicker than her mother would. They would know what to do. But then Georgie knew the rules.

You never, ever called the police.

Their mother had told them time and time again that the authorities wouldn't give a fuck about them, that they would take Georgie and Marnie away. Pigs, she called them.

Georgie scanned the kitchen, looking for something, anything, to help her break down the door.

Her eyes rested on her mother's phone on the kitchen table; her mother must have left it here. Grabbing the mobile, Georgie tapped in Mandy's name and listened as the phone started ringing. Wasting no time while she waited, Georgie dropped to her knees and started pulling apart the cupboard under the kitchen sink. By the time Mandy answered Georgie was sobbing inconsolably. Unable to comprehend what was happening, all she knew was that her sister was in danger, and she didn't know how to make it right.

For the first time in her life she was genuinely scared. Terrified, in fact.

Her words came out all jumbled. Stuttering, panicked, as if her mouth couldn't keep up with her brain.

'Mandy. Tell my mum she needs to come home right now. It's Marnie. He's come back. I can't get to her.'

Not hearing Mandy's reply, Georgie pulled the phone from her ear and stared at the black screen.

Shit!

The battery on the phone had died. She didn't even know if Mandy had heard anything she'd said. Georgie was going to have to do something, and fast. She couldn't wait for her mother to turn up here; it might be too late by then.

Pulling at the kitchen drawers she picked up a carving knife.

Chucking it back down – that wasn't going to help her, she needed something bigger. Something that would aid her in breaking the door down.

A saucepan? A Rolling pin? She needed something stronger. Something that wouldn't break on impact.

Sweeping all the contents from the cupboard out into a pile all over the kitchen floor, Georgie ducked her head down low, and climbed half inside, her arm reaching towards the back.

A hammer.

That would do; she was sure of it.

Grabbing it by the handle, Georgie ran as fast as she could back to the room, skidding on the cold kitchen tiles as she ran.

By the time she reached the bedroom door, she was exhausted, but she knew what she had to do. Making a run at the door, she swung the hammer up above her head and launched at it.

It made a loud thud, a tiny dent.

She wasn't strong enough.

Determined not to give up, Georgie continued to hit out repeatedly. Over and over again.

The wood began to weaken, splitting in places as the metal tool impacted.

She felt like she'd been hitting the door for ages and getting nowhere.

Hysterical, she could feel her tears pouring down her face now, blurring her vision. Her shoulder was aching, burning, but she had to keep trying.

She couldn't give up.

'What in the name of fuck is going on?' Josie said.

Walking in through the front door, the first thing she heard was the loud banging.

'What the fuck are you doing to the door, Georgie?' Josie said looking horrified as her daughter yanked out the hammer that was now wedged inside the wooden frame and sent small splinters of wood flying all over the hallway floor. Josie honestly didn't know whether to laugh or cry; she couldn't believe what she was seeing. Wondering if the girls had had a row, and Marnie had locked her out. The house was destroyed. 'Are you out of your fucking mind, Georgie? What on earth is going on?'

Just the sound of her mother's voice behind her was enough to tip Georgie over the edge.

She broke down, screaming.

'Help me, Mum. He's got her. He's locked them both in. He must have snuck in here while I was asleep. I can't get in. I've been trying to break the door down, but I can't get in.'

Josie walked the few steps towards Georgie as if in a trance.

She mustn't have heard her daughter right. Couldn't have.

Someone had Marnie?

There must be some sort of a mistake.

'What do you mean "he's got her"? Who's got her?' Josie asked, a sinking feeling in her stomach as the realisation struck her with such force she felt like she'd been punched. 'Trevor?' Her voice was almost a whisper now too.

Seeing Georgie nod her head, the terrified look on her face, Josie knew it was true.

Her legs turned to jelly, weakened at the thought that all this time Trevor had been drugging her. The fact he never wanted to have sex. The way he skulked around the house, watching, observing, with all his odd little ways.

It had never been about her.

He'd just wanted her silenced, immobilised, so that he could get to Marnie.

Her protective instincts kicking in, she'd never known anger like it as she grabbed the hammer from her daughter's grasp and began battering the door down with it. The sheer force of the blows making the door bounce off its hinges.

Creaking, the wood gave way, splitting the door open.

How could she not have known?

Marnie had told her so many times about the Bogeyman that was trying to get her. How she was scared he would come if she wasn't a good girl.

'Leave my daughter alone!' Josie was screeching like a woman possessed. Unable to control her body, her instincts took over, consuming her. She slammed so hard against the door that she almost snapped the wooden panel in two.

She was in.

There would be murders now.

CHAPTER TWENTY-NINE

'Get the fuck away from her. Now!' Josie screeched as she switched on the bedroom light. Her worst nightmares confirmed as Trevor Pearson stared back at her.

She'd expected him to look as guilty as hell. Caught red-handed in Marnie's bedroom with the door locked. Instead, he looked at her with disdain, a twisted smirk on his face.

'Marnie, are you okay? Did he hurt you, baby?'

Marnie shook her head.

Sitting up with the bedcovers pulled up around her, Josie could see just by the child's expression that she was traumatised by the night's events. She looked terrified. Like she'd seen a ghost. A monster.

The Bogeyman was standing in the middle of the bedroom.

'This is what this has all been about?' Josie said; her voice sounded strange, alien, even to her own ears. The fear of the man had left her now. Replaced with something else, something much more powerful.

Pure hate.

He didn't scare her. He disgusted her.

Sickened her to her core.

Trevor didn't move an inch. Like a wild animal caught in the headlights, his hand twitched at his side as his eyes dotted around the room. Yet still he stood there, perfectly still.

'You planned this all along, didn't you? Our little arrangement. It was never me you wanted, was it? You sick piece of shit.'

'What's this? The concerned mother?' Trevor laughed.

The sound rippling through Josie like another blow to her stomach.

He was laughing, actually laughing in her face.

'You and that Mandy. Always gallivanting around the town like the pair of slags that you are. You didn't care about these kids then, did you, Josie? You couldn't give a fuck about them.'

'You don't know anything about me, Trevor. You don't know jack shit.'

Josie was defensive. But he was right.

This was her fault too.

She'd let this man into her house, let him get near to her kids, despite her intuition telling her otherwise; her need for money had been much stronger.

What had she done. *What the fuck had she done?*

Her poor, poor Marnie.

Trevor stepped towards her. Unsure whether he was going to strike her, or whether he was making his way to the bedroom door in a bid to escape, Josie lifted the hammer once more. Her voice a clear warning.

'Move the fuck back. Move over, get the fuck away from my daughter.'

Her voice was steady. Eerily calm.

Only, Trevor wasn't listening to her.

He was still moving towards her.

He was trying to leave she realised. Like the coward that he was, he was looking for his escape.

Georgie could see it too; instinctively, the child stepped out, deliberately blocking his way.

She was no match for Trevor though.

Trevor grabbed her hard with both hands. Gripping her by her shoulders, he slammed Georgie into the wall.

There was a thud as her head hit the bricks behind her.

A sharp intake of breath as she slumped down to the floor, lifeless, like a rag doll.

'You bastard.' Josie spat. Dropping the hammer to the floor, she went to Georgie's aid.

'Georgie, are you okay?' she asked, seeing Georgie's eyes flick open, relieved that she hadn't lost consciousness.

The next thing she felt was Trevor's hands from behind her, wrapping themselves tightly around her throat.

He knew he wasn't going to get away with this. Josie wasn't just going to roll over and play dead for him. Not after what he had done. She was going to fight.

The man needed to pay, and the way Josie felt right now towards Trevor, she was capable of ripping the man's head clean off his shoulders with her bare hands.

Swinging her arm backwards, she clawed at his face, his throat, anything to try to get him to release his grip on her.

He was relentless.

Forcefully, he squeezed her throat even harder with both hands.

She couldn't breathe.

Trevor was too strong.

Spluttering, straining, she could feel her eyes bulging in her head. Her lungs screaming for air inside her chest. The rattling noise that crept up from the depths of her throat causing her to choke.

She couldn't die like this.

She couldn't let Trevor get away with this.

Reaching around on the floor for the hammer before she passed out… she couldn't find it. She swept her hand across the carpet.

Trevor didn't know what hit him when the blow came. A look of complete disbelief flitted across his face.

His invincibility shattered.

His eyes opened wide in horror as the metal hammer ripped through his skull.

Once. Twice. Until the sharp jagged claw caved in Trevor's skull. Embedded in his brain.

A strained strangled noise escaped from his throat as he gurgled on a mouthful of his own blood.

Then he slumped down on to the floor.

Blood.

So much blood.

The Bogeyman was dead.

CHAPTER THIRTY

'Here you go, girls. It's out of a machine so I can't guarantee that it will taste very nice, but it's better than the other choice on offer, which is mushy pea soup.' Handing the two little girls a cup of hot chocolate each, DI Ben Drayton was trying to cheer them up, but he knew it was no easy task after what they'd both witnessed tonight.

'Why are we here? Have we been bad too?' Marnie said, looking up at the policeman. 'Is this prison? Is our mummy here?'

DI Drayton shook his head, unable for a few seconds to find his voice. He was trying to stay professional, trying to keep control of his emotions, all the while battling the raw lump that had formed in the back of his throat as he stared at the two girls, both wrapped in the station's blankets, huddled together on the bench inside the police cell – as they stared back at him with fear in their eyes.

He'd seen a lot in his time as detective inspector of Brixton police station, and considered himself not easily unsettled, but the sight of these two children sitting in a police cell, after everything they'd both been through, didn't sit easy with him.

'Neither of you did anything wrong. Do you hear me? Nothing at all. None of this was any of your fault, okay?'

Marnie nodded, but he could see by her face that she didn't look convinced. He wasn't surprised either. The kids were sitting in one of the police cells, for God's sake. Of course they were going to feel like a pair of criminals. Who wouldn't in their shoes?

'Why are we here then?' Georgie asked, scanning the bare walls, the thick heavy metal door. Wrinkling her nose, unimpressed, as her eyes rested on the toilet cistern in the corner.

'We're just making some arrangements for you both, Georgie, with Children's Services. You haven't been bad. The station is a bit busy tonight; this is just a nice quiet place for you both to sit and wait.' DI Drayton knew that finding a placement for two kids at this time of night could sometimes prove nigh on impossible, but Children's Services needed to pull their finger out. The police station was no place for children, especially ones that were clearly traumatised from witnessing a horrific murder.

'Your caseworker is on the way here now; she won't be long. She'll be looking after you tonight.'

The policeman seemed kind, but Georgie didn't trust him one bit.

She didn't trust any of them.

So far everything her mother had told her about the police was true. They made out that they were going to help you, but then they just took you away.

So far, they'd taken their mother away.

Screaming and crying, Georgie had watched her mother being led away in handcuffs. Put in the back of a police car.

Now Georgie and Marnie were here at the police station too.

'It's going to be all right, okay,' DI Drayton said getting to his feet.

Georgie nodded. He was lying to her again. Trevor was dead. Her mother had been taken away, was going to be locked up in prison for murder. It was never going to be okay again.

'Our mummy is a good person. She only wants to minded us,' Marnie said through her stifled sobs.

DI Drayton nodded.

He could find no words to answer her. From what he'd seen of Josie Parker tonight the woman was anything but a good person. She'd been openly revelling in the fact that she'd just murdered a man in cold blood.

A gruesome murder, too.

He was an experienced detective, but even he'd recoiled at the sight of Trevor Pearson splayed out on the girls' bedroom floor, a claw hammer embedded in his battered skull. Splatters of brain tissue, blood and skull, splashed up the bedroom wall and all over the children's nightclothes.

The most harrowing part of it all had been the way that the perpetrator, Josie Parker, had shown no remorse. She'd been like a woman possessed when they'd arrived at the scene of the crime. A lunatic. Screeching to everyone who was listening that she was glad Trevor was dead. That she was glad that she'd killed him, and she'd do it all over again if she had the chance. Deranged, the woman had even spat a mouthful of phlegm at Trevor Pearson's corpse as the police had dragged her away.

Josie was a known heroin user and prostitute. The motive was still unclear, but judging on the amount of alcohol in her blood, DI Drayton was putting his money on it being a drunken domestic that had escalated.

'Right. I'm going to shut the door behind me now, okay, but I'm just going to be right outside this door. I won't be far. You both finish up your drinks.'

Closing the door, DI Drayton took a deep breath and shook his head sadly.

What a bloody night!

As bad as it had been, the worst for those two children in there was yet to come.

Who knew what hand fate had played them both now?

Foster care, children's homes. A murdering prostitute for a mother.

Georgie and Marnie Parker didn't stand a chance.

Josie Parker, a good woman? Please. Women like her should never have been able to have kids. She should have been sterilised at birth.

CHAPTER THIRTY-ONE

Lying on the massage couch of one of his most lucrative business premises in Soho, Delray Anderton was currently sampling the sensual delights of his newest member of staff: the delectable Layla.

The girl was just Delray's type; in fact, she was just about any bloke that had a pulse's type, he thought, taking in the sight of her lean, taut body as she strutted around the couch. His eyes spanning the length of her long, tanned legs that seemed to go on for miles, stopping only at the tiny black G-string that left very little to the imagination indeed.

He smiled to himself.

The girls he had working for him these days were something else altogether. They were the crème de la crème. Models, real natural or sometimes unnatural beauties.

Give this girl her dues though, Layla wasn't just a nice-looking pair of perky tits and arse, she knew how to give a good massage too. Pummelling the shit out of his back and shoulders with her wide range of moves, Delray didn't know whether to lie there and submit, or flip her over the couch and show her some of his own moves.

Hearing his phone go, he was irritated at the interruption. He never got a minute's peace lately. Business was certainly booming that was for sure. So much so that Delray was going to have to expand his workforce.

When Delray saw the caller ID he frowned. What did this bitch want? He had half a mind not to answer it, but his curiosity got the better of him.

Picking up the phone he rolled his eyes.

'What do you want?'

A few minutes later he put the phone down on the side and smiled to himself as Layla started to remove his boxer shorts.

Who'd have guessed? Josie Parker arrested. The crazy bitch had only gone and bludgeoned some poor bastard to death. Her boyfriend, apparently; though Delray would hazard a guess that the poor unfortunate bastard had been another one of her punters. Knowing Josie, she'd probably still been pulling work in on the sly.

He shook his head in disbelief, unable to get his head around it. He'd been right about her all along. The woman was off her fucking rocker. Probably off her face on smack. He was glad that he binned her off when he'd had the chance.

He didn't need his name involved in this shit.

Josie Parker was on her own now, and for a long fucking time too apparently. The crazy bitch was looking at years behind bars for what she'd done. You couldn't make this shit up.

He thought of Georgie and Marnie then, all on their own without their mother. Poor fuckers had been through the mill with that one looking out for them.

He grinned. Talk about cutting him a lucky break. Turns out his little deal with Hamza Nagi might just go ahead after all. What were the fucking chances of that?

It looked like he might need to make some use of Javine. He'd need her onside if his little plan was going to come together.

Fuck! He hoped that he hadn't pushed her too far already. He'd been enjoying playing his little games. Javine had had what he would determine as a major wake-up call. All that swanning around London thinking that Delray would buy her whatever she wanted, she hadn't even contemplated that he might want something back from her in return. That's how simple the girl was. Making out that she believed in love and happy ever after when all along all she'd wanted was his cold hard cash.

If he was going to make it up to the girl, get back in her good books, he was going to have to do something pretty drastic. Something that would make the divvy cow hang off his every word. After the week he'd just made Javine endure, it wasn't going to be an easy task, that was for sure. If anyone could do it though, Delray was certain it was him. He could charm the birds right out from the trees. To him, getting women to do what he wanted was a natural gift.

Smiling to himself at the thought of natural gifts, he knew exactly what he needed to do. He relaxed a little. For now, he could get back to the job in hand.

Or mouth as it would seem.

He could feel Layla caressing the inside of his thighs, the tickle of her hair as she gently made her way up his legs towards his groin.

Teasing him with her tongue, as she ran her sharp nails up his skin.

Pleasure and pain, instantaneously; Delray couldn't get enough.

The girl was keen, he'd give her that.

She'd worked every part of his back, easing his aches and pains. Soothing his muscles, now she was going to give him his long-awaited happy ending. After the phone call he'd just had, it turned out it was going to be a very happy ending indeed.

CHAPTER THIRTY-TWO

Making her way up the hallway, Rose Feltham held her breath as she noted the colourful felt-tip drawings scribbled in amongst the mass of black mould that spanned the entire length of the wall. The place was riddled with damp; the walls and ceilings all covered in mildew: no wonder it smelt so bad in here.

Basic living conditions; that's what the previous social worker had written on the Parker family assessment. But this flat was in abysmal condition, barely more habitable than an abandoned squat. If it had been down to Rose to carry out the family's last assessment she would have deemed the place unfit for a dog to reside in, let alone two children. Then, if it had been her that had dealt with the Parker family case in the first place, maybe none of this would ever have happened. Someone in their department had fucked up by not flagging a report in the system. Of course, no one would own up to it though. Whichever one of her lazy, delusional colleagues it had been on the last assessment, six months ago, they had failed to report what was really going on inside this house; their incompetence meant that Georgie and Marnie Parker had slipped underneath the radar. The Parker family hadn't had any form of supervision or home checks in months. It was simply madness. Especially, Rose thought, after she had read the case notes.

She'd been shocked at the extent of what she'd learned about Josie Parker: an accident waiting to happen. A repeat drug offender. A heroin addict, and a prostitute. She had several convictions against her name too, for Public Intoxication, Resisting Arrest and Assaulting a Police Officer. The notes on the file said that Josie had verbally assaulted a few of Rose's co-workers over the years too.

Clearly, after brutally murdering a man tonight, the woman had a temper on her. It annoyed Rose that the family hadn't been made more of a priority seeing as they were so vulnerable. Her department should have been ensuring that a follow-up appointment had been made; the Parkers should have had regular help and support on hand. There had been no emergency assessment. No aftercare, nothing.

Instead, their last caseworker had simply shoved the vague details of the last visit inside the family's folder, and the file had somehow mysteriously ended up down behind the filing cabinet.

Rose was making it her personal duty to do whatever she could to make it up to the two poor kids.

The press would have a field day once this story broke tomorrow. They'd make a point of publicly beating the department down, pinning the blame on Children's Services for failing to protect the children under their care.

The papers loved that, making an example of the flaws in the system, and the system was greatly flawed. The papers would be right too. Those poor children had been failed miserably by them all. The only real victims, other than the deceased, of course, were Georgie and Marnie Parker.

Lives had been ruined, destroyed – and why? All because someone in her department hadn't done their job properly and now it was down to Rose to pick up the pieces. Rose accepted the challenge humbly.

Already tonight she had fought tooth and nail with her department not to allow the girls to be separated. It had delayed getting them a placement in foster care, but she'd managed to get them into a children's home. A place called Rainbow House. That was something. At least for now. If she could keep them together, they would have some small comfort.

She'd come to their home to collect some of their belongings, as requested by one of the police officers currently taking care of the children.

The girls had asked for their pyjamas, and the youngest child had asked for her favourite teddy bear, Mr Snowflakes.

Reaching the end of the hall, Rose poked her head inside the first doorway – eying the unmade double bed that was strewn with washing. The air in the room the same as everywhere else in the flat: stale, musty. Dirty knickers cast aside on the floor. A mug of tea on the dresser; a thick film of mould settled on its surface.

Josie's room, she guessed. She shook her head. The woman clearly couldn't even look after herself, let alone two children. The saddest thing of all was that the state of the flat wasn't by any means a rarity. Rose had seen homes like this one a thousand times over. This was just the way some people lived. The harsh reality for many. Just another slum riddled with poverty and neglect. She didn't know how people did it – how they could live like this, with no electricity, no heating or hot water. The cupboards all bare. Perhaps they had no choice in the matter. This was all they had known. All they were capable of.

Making her way to the second bedroom, she pushed the bedroom door open and immediately covered her nose and mouth with her hand. The body had been moved now, the forensics had been and gone, but the smell in the room was still horrendous.

Rose had passed an officer on the front door who had told her that he was waiting for the crime scene cleaner to arrive; he had warned her about the amount of blood on the floor, but what he'd failed to mention was the strong stench of urine. It was so overpowering that it physically forced her to step backwards out of the room, as if trying to physically get away from it. Her eyes watered at the pure strength of the ammonia that hit her. Keeping her hand firmly in place, over her mouth, Rose stepped inside the room.

This was definitely it. Georgie and Marnie's bedroom. The sight of the place, the stench, made Rose want to weep. Looking around this hovel, she couldn't help but wonder what hope those two kids ever had with this as their only form of sanctuary.

The two beds in the room were filthy. The flimsy bedding on each one was saturated with yellow watery stains. The floor was worse. The carpet was sodden, making clear to Rose where the stench of urine was coming from.

Her eyes going straight to the large dark stain in the middle of the floor, she shuddered. This was the spot that Josie Parker had smashed the victim's skull wide open with a claw hammer. Right here in her daughter's bedroom in front of her two children.

The girls would need years of therapy to help them get over this. If they ever did.

Diverting her eyes away from the harrowing scene where the man had met his gruesome demise, Rose spotted the teddy bear tucked down between the bed and the wall.

The thing was filthy. Once fluffy and white, she imagined, now it was tinged with grey. Blackened by dust and dirt just like everything else here.

Stepping around the edges of the room, careful not to tread anywhere near the bloodstained floor, Rose pulled open a drawer in the dressing table, scanning the clothes inside. She just wanted to get out of here as quickly as she could.

Rooting through the chaos of clothes, all rammed into the small drawer, screwed up into balls – dresses, socks, jumpers – she pulled out a pair of purple fleece pyjamas dotted with yellow stars, and other stuff too; dried bits of food, a hole in the top, the tatty hem around the ankles, frayed.

She shoved the clothes back into the drawer. Her mind made up. She wasn't even going to run a request through via her department, fuck it. She was going to pop into the all-night supermarket down the road and grab the girls some new clothes. This one would be on her.

She couldn't bring the girls any of these rags; they were going to have a hard enough time settling into their new place of residence as it was.

She'd buy a new teddy bear too for the youngest one, Marnie.

Kicking the filthy teddy bear under the bed, she took one more look around the room before turning on her heel, and closing the door loudly behind her.

Rose Feltham was going to do right by the two girls, no matter what.

It was about time somebody did.

CHAPTER THIRTY-THREE

'I don't understand. Why do we have to come to a children's home?' Stepping into the bedroom behind Rose Feltham, Georgie folded her arms tightly across her chest, a permanent scowl fixed across her face. Her guard was well and truly up as she looked around the bedroom.

Two beds side by side and a small dresser in-between. No windows, she noted.

'I can look after Marnie myself. We could have stayed at home. We would have been fine on our own,' she said, making no excuses for the fact that she really didn't want to be here.

She wanted to be at home with Marnie and their mother too. Rewind time to before everything bad happened.

'You know you can't be at home on your own, Georgie. You're here because right now it's the safest place for you,' Rose said as she placed a hysterical Marnie down gently on one of the beds.

'Come on, Marnie, this place isn't that bad, really. I promise you. Isn't it nice that you at least get to stay with your sister?' Rose was at a loss how to soothe the child. Marnie had been crying inconsolably since she learned what was happening.

Georgie pouted, eyeing the woman with disdain; she watched as Rose tried but failed to calm her sister down. The woman clearly had no idea that once Marnie went off on one of her meltdowns there was nothing anyone could say or do to stop her. Only Georgie knew how to do that.

The social worker was just like DI Drayton, the policeman at the station. She was acting all nice to them but Georgie knew it wasn't real.

This was all part of their plan.

What did her mother always call them? That's it: Jobsworths and Do-gooders. She said they were always poking their noses in, always trying to pick faults and cause problems for people like them. It was all just talk. All these empty promises that Rose was making them. About doing everything in her power to make sure the girls were safe and looked after. It was just an act. A lie, to try to get the girls to talk. To confide in her.

Georgie knew better than that. She'd already told Marnie so too. They weren't to trust Rose no matter what she said, and Georgie had no intention of liking the lady either.

'Children's homes are nothing but dumps full of reject kids. This place is shit.'

Rose knew that Georgie was angry, that she was rebelling. For now she'd give her the benefit of the doubt, and let her off for her appalling manners. However, Mrs Reed, the House Manager, had other ideas.

'Er, that's enough thank you, Georgie. We don't use that kind of language around here,' Mrs Reed kept her tone light but stern. She'd had children in here from all walks of life, all kinds of situations. Most of them had endured the worst abuse and neglect she'd ever come across. Even so, she always started as she meant to go on. Firm but fair; these children needed some normality restored in their lives. They needed some common ground and here was as good as any place to start. 'I think that you'll find the children around here are lovely; they are no different to you and your sister. They just need that extra bit of support.'

'What? So I can't say shit?' Georgie quipped. 'What about fuck? Is that any better?'

Mrs Reed looked at Rose; they both knew exactly what was going on here.

Marnie was crying, screaming, clearly distraught. Georgie was showing her distress in another way. She was lashing out at them, trying to get a reaction. Seeing how far she could push them both. It was common practice for children to act this way. Mrs Reed had seen and heard it all a thousand times before.

Taking a deep breath before answering, her voice remained steady and calm, showing no reaction at all.

'No, Georgie. We don't use any words like that here either. Thank you.' Tight lipped, Mrs Reed refused to rise to Georgie's bait.

The child's language didn't surprise her in the slightest. In fact, more often these days Mrs Reed almost expected it. It was how a lot of parents seemed to communicate with their children.

Name-calling, put-downs, obscenities.

Georgie was seeing how long it took until the woman snapped.

Well, the child would have a long wait.

Mrs Reed had the patience of a saint when it came to looking after the children in her care. Twenty years she'd been doing this job and she'd yet to have a child come through her door who she hadn't been able to reach out and get through to.

Rose had already briefed her on what Georgie and Marnie had been through in the past twenty-four hours, and Mrs Reed felt nothing but compassion for them both.

'Stupid bitch,' Georgie muttered under her breath.

Worried that Georgie was going to continue giving Mrs Reed nothing but a mouthful of abuse, Rose shook her head in dismay.

'Georgie. Please. Mrs Reed has been very kind to give you and Marnie a place to stay here.' She shook her head at Georgie despairingly. 'If it wasn't for her, you and Marnie would have both had to go into separate foster homes. This was the only way that I could keep you both together. I know this is really hard for you, but all Mrs Reed and I are doing is trying to help you.'

Rose hated to sound so stern but she'd already fought tooth and nail to get Georgie and Marnie a placement together here at Rainbow House. The children's home was already full to capacity. Mrs Reed had thrown Rose a favour by making room for the girls and the last thing that Rose wanted was for Georgie to jeopardise their placement here the minute they'd walked in through the door.

Sensing the tension, Mrs Reed shrugged her shoulders nonchalantly. 'It's okay, Rose.' She nodded. 'Don't you be worrying about me. It's perfectly normal for the girls to feel anxious. They always do on the first night. I don't take this kind of talk personally. Water off a duck's back, my lovey!' She smiled at Georgie too. 'You'll be grand after a good night's sleep. I expect you're both exhausted too, aren't you?'

Mrs Reed's words of comfort only seemed to antagonise Marnie more.

She began wailing louder. 'I don't want to sleep here. I want my mummy. I don't want to be here. Take me home. Take me home,' she sobbed.

'It's okay, Marnie. It won't be for ever. Just get some sleep tonight, darling.' Rose hugged the girl tightly to her. 'Tomorrow we can sit down together and talk everything through. You're not on your own.'

'But I don't want to talk to you. I want to go home. I want my mummy.'

Marnie was kicking out. Working herself up into such a state, her whole body shook violently.

Rose was starting to look worried. Nothing she said or did was helping. The child had been like this for well over an hour – screaming so loud that her face was a shade of purple, her eyes bulging in her head.

'Do you know how much longer he's going to be?' Rose asked, hating seeing the poor child so distressed, so relentless. She'd hoped that she would have burned herself out in the car journey here, and slept, so that they didn't need to get the doctor in, but that clearly wasn't going to be the case.

Marnie hadn't let up. If anything, she was working herself up into more and more of a state.

'He's on his way. I'd say another five minutes or so.'

Eyeing the women dubiously, Georgie bristled. 'Who's on their way?'

The women were being guarded about something. Something about her and her sister.

Mrs Reed, seeing the angry look on Georgie's face, decided that it was only fair she was honest with the older child.

'It's nothing to worry about, Georgie. We've just asked the doctor to call in so that he can make sure you're both okay.' Mrs Reed tried to assure the girl.

'Why do we need to see a doctor? We're not sick.' Confused, Georgie shook her head.

Rose interrupted: 'He's just going to give Marnie some medicine to help her to sleep. She's had a nasty shock. You both have. The doctor just wants to check you're both okay.'

'But I don't want to see a doctor. I don't want to go sleep. Tell them, Georgie. They can't make me go to sleep. He'll get me.' Wailing loudly, she started thrashing about wildly in Rose's arms, trying to escape from her clutches. Rose was holding her tightly.

'Who'll get you? The doctor?' Rose looked at Georgie, confused. 'The doctor isn't going to hurt either of you. He wants to help too.'

'I can't go to sleep. That's when he'll come. The Bogeyman.'

Marnie was acting deranged. Flinging herself around in a wild rage, trying to break free from Rose's firm hold. Rose felt helpless. Seeing the child so frantic, she didn't know what else to do. She was worried that Marnie would fall on to the floor and hit her head. That she'd really hurt herself. She had no choice but to try to restrain her: pin her arms down to her sides to stop her from doing any serious damage to herself. Her actions made Georgie see red.

'Get your hands off of her, you bitch!'

She launched herself at the social worker. Her mother had been right all along. These people didn't want to help. They wanted to shut her and Marnie up. They wanted to lock them away. Just like her mother had said they would.

'Get your hands off my sister. You're hurting her.'

Georgie was grabbing at Rose. Hitting her with her fists; shouting at the top of her voice.

'Georgie, please, I'm trying to help you.' Trying her hardest to shield herself from Georgie's blows, Rose twisted her body away from her.

'Get off my sister.' Georgie didn't believe her. Raging, desperate to protect her sister, Georgie was out of control.

Mrs Reed had no choice but to step in too. Grabbing Georgie she pulled the girl backwards, locking her tightly in her arms.

Georgie was crying now. Tears of frustration running down her cheeks.

'Why can't you just leave us both alone? Let go of my sister.'

Mrs Reed held Georgie tightly, repeating firmly over and over in the child's ear: 'It's okay Georgie. We are not going to hurt you or your sister. We are here to help you. We just want to help you.'

It worked. Rose watched as, gradually – somehow, Mrs Reed's words of assurance sunk in. Georgie relaxed; the fight inside her diminishing.

Rose spoke softly, truthfully. Praying that she could get through to her.

'Georgie, we are on your side. I wish you would believe me. I'm going to do everything in my power to help you and Marnie. I just wish that you could trust me.'

'My sister doesn't need a doctor. She only needs me,' Georgie said. Her eyes flickering as she spoke.

'Okay.' Rose nodded. Wanting to show that she was listening. 'Do you think maybe you could calm her down? If you can, I'll tell the doctor that he isn't needed.'

Georgie nodded.

Mrs Reed let go and Georgie ran to her sister.

Wrapping her arms around her, she pulled Marnie in close.

'If you stop crying, Marnie, they won't make the doctor give you the medicine. I promise,' Georgie said, speaking through her sister's wretched sobs. 'Come on, lie down with me, yeah. We can sleep in the bed together.'

Georgie looked at Mrs Reed for reassurance, and Mrs Reed nodded.

'I'm here, Marnie. I won't leave you.'

Marnie's tears stopped almost instantly. 'Promise?' she asked Georgie.

Rose looked over to Mrs Reed and gave her a small smile, relieved as, finally, the two girls lay down in the bed together, settled and quiet, before the two women left the room.

Exhausted from crying, Marnie looked up at her sister, her voice almost a whisper. She asked again: 'Promise me, Georgie?'

Georgie nodded.

The fact that her mother was in prison, that she wouldn't be coming out any time soon, was finally starting to hit Georgie. She was all Marnie had in the world now, and Georgie had made a promise to her mother that she would protect her little sister. No matter what.

'Cross my heart. I promise.'

CHAPTER THIRTY-FOUR

Staring down at her bowl of cereal, Georgie swished the spoon about in the milk as she chased the cornflakes around the bowl; anything, so that she didn't have to make eye contact with the group of children sitting directly across from her at the breakfast table.

This place reminded her of school. The kids were already in their own little clique; she and Marnie were the newcomers and they were treating them both as such.

Taking a mouthful of food as the other kids all stared back, watching her and Marnie like hawks, Georgie self-consciously chewed her food. Ravenous, she ate slowly, refraining from taking the big hungry mouthfuls that she so wanted to. She hadn't eaten properly for days at home. Deep pangs of hunger made her hollow stomach growl loudly. Still, she wasn't going to give these kids the satisfaction of seeing that she was starving. She wasn't going to give them anything. Her time. Her conversation.

'Eat up, Marnie,' Georgie said to Marnie who sat silently beside her. A single piece of toast smothered in her favourite chocolate spread remained on the plate, untouched.

Marnie didn't answer; instead, she slipped her hand underneath the table, and grasped Georgie's hand tightly. Twisting her fingers around her sister's. Anxious and scared.

'Move around, Shaun James is here.'

There was a flurry of movement as the children all shuffled around the table, moving down a seat to make room for the large chunky boy that had just entered the room.

Georgie didn't move.

She stayed exactly where she was. Still holding her sister's hand, glad that the attention was finally off her and Marnie and that the children were now focusing on the boy that approached the table. She wondered why there seemed to be such a sense of panic and urgency suddenly, as if this boy was someone of importance. Raising her eyes out of curiosity, Georgie didn't think that he looked very important at all.

A couple of years older than her, maybe fifteen? She wasn't sure. He was huge though. His stomach protruding over the top of his jeans; even his chunky arms had rolls of fat hanging off them.

'Move it you bender.' Glaring at one of the kids who hadn't moved fast enough, Shaun James watched as the kid got up without arguing and scarpered, leaving him to take the seat at the head of the table.

He grinned, a cocksure smile on his face, then he sat back in the chair and sneered at everyone around him, pleased that his presence in the room was having the desired effect.

They all knew the score.

'Is that the last chocolate croissant?' Shaun directed his attention towards a girl called Annie.

Georgie watched as Annie, after spending the morning gossiping about her and Marnie and shooting them dirty looks, suddenly looked meek and pathetic.

Nodding her head; her cheeks reddening; she looked intimidated by the older boy.

'Give it here then, you greedy bitch.' Holding out his big chunky hand Shaun snatched the food from Annie's grasp before turning to the boy sitting the other side of him.

'I thought I told you to get my breakfast ready for me? Go on then, Corey, pour me out a drink.'

Corey did as he was told. Jumping up out of his seat without a second's hesitation, he poured Shaun a large glass of orange juice, and handed it to the expectant boy.

Shaun didn't bother saying thank you. He just drank the drink down in one, before stuffing his face with the croissant. Chomping the food loudly with his mouth wide open, he stared over at Georgie and Marnie.

'Are you the two fucking brats that woke everyone up last night?' He glared at them, his squinty, piggy eyes scrutinised the two girls.

Georgie didn't answer. She kept her head down; her gaze low, focusing on the food that adorned the huge table: a huge decorative glass bowl filled with a colourful selection of just about every fruit imaginable in the centre; next to it, a row of carefully aligned cereal packets; a huge plate of toast, pots of jams and spreads; the jug full of orange juice – anything but Shaun James. The boy was a nasty bully, and Georgie had taken an instant dislike to him.

'Oi, I'm talking to you!' Slamming his glass down on the table, Shaun slumped back in his chair as if was a king on his throne. He scowled as he watched her intently. Her head down; her hand clasped tightly around her spoon as she sat there perfectly still. Like a rabbit caught in the headlights.

She was scared of him. Just like everyone else sitting around the table. His reputation had clearly preceded him once again.

Shaun James grinned.

Annie spoke up, trying to redeem herself after Shaun had made her look like a prize prat in front of everyone.

'Yeah, they are. I heard Mrs Reed talking about them this morning.' Annie shot Georgie a smug grin, glad that the focus was off her for now. 'The youngest one's called Marnie; she pissed the bed in the middle of the night. I heard Mrs Reed on the phone telling her social worker that she had to strip her bed down at four o'clock this morning.' Annie screwed her face to show her disgust.

'What about her?' Shaun said, looking Georgie up and down with interest. The stuck-up little cow wouldn't return his eye contact.

'Her name's Georgie. Proper thinks she's something special,' Annie said spitefully, annoyed at the stir the girl had already created amongst the boys of the house. Annie had seen them all looking at this Georgie with sudden interest and it riled her that even dressed in crap clothes and her hair pulled back in a messy bun, Georgie Parker was way prettier than Annie would ever be.

Annie took a dislike to the girl on first sight.

'She's well fit,' Corey said right on cue, confirming what Annie had been secretly thinking. 'She ain't got no tits yet though.' He laughed.

Annie laughed at that too. That was something she supposed. At fourteen, Annie was lucky; her own boobs were more than ample. In fact, they were her best asset. Georgie Parker couldn't compete with that.

'Her chest looks like two paracetamols on a draining board.' Annie laughed too. 'Though looking at the state of her, they could actually be flea bites. They both look infested! Feral!'

All the children laughed, while Georgie shifted uncomfortably in her chair. Her eyes still focused on the table as the other children taunted her and her sister. Her cheeks burning violent red as they all laughed at their expense.

Pushing her breakfast bowl away from her, Georgie had lost her appetite.

'We should give them both nicknames,' Shaun piped in now, thoroughly in his element that the other kids had taken his lead, as always, and were putting the new girls in their place. 'The older one, I reckon she should be called Jugs.'

A cackle of laughter filled the air.

This was the power that Shaun held around here. He could make any of these little fuckers do anything that he liked, and no one would say shit to him, because they were all too scared.

Well, Georgie and Marnie Parker needed to fall in line too.

'Jugs really suits you!' he sneered.

Georgie held her temper. Aware that it wouldn't bode well for either her or her sister if she fought back, she decided to keep quiet for now. If Georgie didn't rise to the crap that this boy was spouting, he'd soon get bored.

Ignoring him, she focused on her sister instead.

The toast in front of her still untouched.

'Do you want some cereal, Marnie? There's some Weetabix? Or there's some fruit? You can have a banana?' Georgie whispered, worried about her sister. Marnie hadn't eaten a thing.

'Tell me what you want and I'll get it for you.'

Shaking her head, Marnie squeezed Georgie's hand tighter, not wanting her sister to let her go.

The big boy, Shaun, was still glaring at them. The other children were still watching them, too, all whispering and laughing at them. Marnie didn't want breakfast, and she didn't want to be here.

'I just want Mummy.' Her bottom lip trembled. Unable to stop herself, the tears came.

Locking her arms around her, Georgie hugged Marnie tightly. Not caring that everyone was looking at her. Not caring what any of them thought. All she cared about was her sister.

'It's okay, Marnie.'

'Oh, here we go. I want my mummy. Boo-hoo-hoo!' Putting on a high-pitched voice, Shaun was mocking them both. 'Well, I'm going to guess by the fact that you're here in this shitty children's home that your mummy doesn't want you – does she?' Smirking now, as his words had the desired effect.

Already beside herself, Marnie started sobbing so loudly that her entire body shook.

Georgie finally lost it. She couldn't let her sister get worked up again. Not after last night. The poor girl was on the verge of a breakdown.

'Our mum does want us,' Georgie snapped, angry as she heard the quiver in her voice. 'You don't know anything about us, so why don't you keep your big *fat* nose out of it.'

The other kids stifled their giggles.

No one ever spoke back to Shaun James like that.

'What did you just say, Jugs?' Pushing his chair back, Shaun James leant across the table, challenging Georgie.

She stared around the table at the sea of anxious faces all eagerly awaiting her reply. While she didn't fancy her chances going up against the likes of Shaun James, she knew she had no choice. He was gunning for her, and if she didn't stick up for herself now, herself and Marnie would end up as the boy's newest targets.

'I said: *Keep your big. Fat. Ugly. Nose out of my business.*'

'Ohh, listen to old Jugs here!' Shaun laughed, desperate to save face and hide his shock. No one spoke back to him. No one with half a brain anyway.

Georgie Parker didn't know who she was messing with.

'And what are you going to do about it, Jugs? You gunna set your little pissy-knickers sister on me?' Shaun sneered knowing full well that his words would get a rise from Georgie. He could see how protective she was. 'Eww I can smell her from here. Pissy-knickers-Parker. That's what we'll call her.'

The children all roared with laughter at that, right on cue, like a row of Shaun's little puppets.

Georgie could feel Marnie flinch beside her. That was all she needed. Shaun James could call her whatever the hell he wanted to, but she was not just going to sit here and say nothing while he terrorised her sister. Marnie had been through enough.

'Do not talk about my sister like that.' Georgie was glaring. Her fists clenched at her sides.

'Who?' Shaun said, raising his arms, feigning innocence. 'Oh, you mean about Pissy-knickers-Parker?'

Corey piped up then too: 'Pissy-knickers-Parker. Pissy-knickers-Parker.'

'That's it. Sing along, everyone!' Shaun commanded, until the room was loud with the chants.

Unable to control her temper any longer, Georgie stood up in such a rage that she knocked the jug of orange juice over. Leaning her hands on the table, she stared across at Shaun defiantly. One more word and she was going to scratch his ugly eyes out.

The other kids were all up on their feet too. Avoiding the spillage of orange juice as it dripped off the edge of the table, they all laughed in chorus. Only this time they were directing their attention at Shaun. Pointing at him as he stared down at his lap. His crutch covered in orange juice; the wet patch trickling down his legs.

'Look, Jugs made Shaun piss himself.' One boy giggled loudly.

Shaun shot the mouthy boy a death stare: it instantly silenced the boy and the other children nearest to him.

'You're going to pay for that!' Shaun was furious. His face red and blotchy; his hands clenched into fists at his sides as he realised that he was now the butt of some of the children's jokes.

'You and your little pissy-knickers-sister.'

Leaning forward he grabbed at Georgie's arm. Gripping her wrist with his fat chunky fingers, he pulled her towards him over the top of the table.

Georgie didn't even think twice about her actions. She had to fight back. To show this boy that she wasn't scared of him. Lurching forward with her free arm, she swung out. Catching Shaun unawares, her fist caught him hard in the face. There was a loud crack of her knuckles as they made contact with his nose, causing him to stumble backwards, cupping his nose to stem the flow of blood that was now streaming through his fingers.

Shaun looked momentarily startled. As if he literally didn't know what had just hit him.

The rest of the kids were shocked too. Rendered silent now. Every pair of eyes were staring from him to Georgie and back again, as they waited to see what was going to happen next.

He knew what they were all thinking though: Shaun James had just been beaten by a girl. Humiliated by her.

That's when he made a grab for Georgie's hair. Wrapping his blood-soaked hands around the bun on the top of her head, he pulled her down on to the floor.

He was on top of her now. The humongous weight of him pinning her slight frame. He raised his fist above his head, ready to punch her back, square in the face.

'I told you I was going to make you pay, you skanky little bitch.'

Waiting for the blow that was coming, Georgie flinched.

Opening her eyes suddenly as she felt the weight of him shift from her. A shrill voice in the room shouting: 'What in God's name is going on in here?'

It was Mrs Reed. She was dragging Shaun from her, shaking her head at him as she stared at the pandemonium in the room.

The children had been out of control. Chanting and screeching as they had watched on as Shaun James was physically assaulting one of the new girls. Mrs Reed was utterly disgusted.

'All of you return to your bedrooms immediately,' she bellowed, desperate to restore some normality once more into the house.

This was not how she ran things around here. She would not condone violence in any shape or form.

'What the hell are you playing at, Shaun?' her eyes flashed with fury. She'd lost count of the number of times that she'd had to deal with this child in the eighteen months that he'd resided here at the house, but his behaviour was becoming more and more volatile as the days went on. He was a law unto himself. Bullying and intimidating every child that walked in through the doors; girls included now, it seemed.

'She hit me,' Shaun spluttered.

The bitch had busted his nose. He was sure of it. It wouldn't stop bleeding. The pain so acute he had tears in his eyes.

He could see the other children staring at him as they all left the room, all drinking in his humiliation: most of them secretly glad that Shaun James had finally got his comeuppance.

'Who hit you?' Seeing the blood running down Shaun's face, dripping on to the floor, Mrs Reed could see that he was indeed hurt. That was a first. Normally it was him that inflicted the injuries around here.

'Her.' Shaun pointed towards Georgie. Though he didn't dare call her by the nickname that he'd given her now Mrs Reed was standing between them.

'Georgie, is this true?'

Georgie nodded. She wasn't sorry, and she didn't care what Mrs Reed said to her either; she wouldn't say she was. Not if her life depended on it.

'Well, that's not the way we behave around here. I want you and your sister to both go to your room and wait for me there.'

Georgie didn't argue. Only too happy to be sent off to her room. Away from these horrible kids; away from Shaun James. She grabbed her sister's hand and led her out of the room.

'Is that it?' Shaun had the hump. Mrs Reed had barely raised her voice at the girl.

Georgie should have been punished. She should have all of her privileges taken away from her. She should be sent to isolation. That's what Mrs Reed would have done if it was his fault. She'd have punished him dearly. Though somehow Georgie had managed to get away with it scot free.

'Don't you worry about her, Shaun, you just worry about yourself. Let me take a look at you.' She could see the tears glistening in the corner of the boy's eyes, from both pain and humiliation.

Biting the inside of her cheek to stop the small smile forming on her lips, Mrs Reed couldn't help herself. 'Wow, that must have really been one hell of a punch she gave you. I think your nose might be broken. We better get you down to the hospital and get you checked over.' She spoke loud enough so that Annie, who was hovering around nearby, could hear her.

Annie was one of the last to leave, trailing behind as always so that she could try to find out every last detail. Mrs Reed knew that she'd spread that last bit of news all over the house.

Not only would the children know that Shaun had been hit by a girl, but that he'd also been taken to hospital.

Served the little shit right. Shaun James was an out-and-out bully. An instigator of nearly every fight and argument that went on here at Rainbow House; yet, today, he'd finally met his match in the little slip of a girl called Georgie Parker. Who'd have thought it?

CHAPTER THIRTY-FIVE

Somewhere far off in the distance, Georgie could hear Marnie laughing. Giggling.

The sound of whispering filled her head, echoing inside her mind.

Still half asleep, enthralled in her dreams, Georgie kept her eyes closed, willing them not to end. Not to be woken.

She wanted them to go on for ever. To never stop.

She was back home with her mother, with Marnie. The house looked warmer in her dreams. A rich yellow. They were in their mother's bedroom. She and Marnie both perched on the end of their mother's bed, just like they often did when they watched their mother getting ready for one of her nights out. Only this time was different. They were so busy laughing and having fun that their mother had announced that she was going to stay at home with Georgie and Marnie instead. The three of them had spent the evening doing makeovers on each other. Their mother had drawn big black slug-like eyebrows on them all with an eyeliner pencil, and Marnie had giggled so much that she had tears streaming down her face.

Then their mother had taken her favourite lipstick. Bright pillar-box red, her trademark – and drawn a thick red circle around the outside of her mouth. Clown-like, she turned and gave the girls her biggest smile.

Laughing.

'Georgie… Georgie…'

Giggling and whispering again. In her dream? In the bedroom?

Unsure if the noise was in her dream or in the room, Georgie grumbled to herself in her sleep.

'Georgie, Georgie…'

Stirring, annoyed that her dream had been snatched from her, Georgie felt her sister clamber on to her bed beside her; the weight of Marnie making Georgie sink into the mattress and roll towards her.

Irritated, Georgie shuffled over to one side to make room for her, still refusing to open her eyes, refusing to be dragged away from the sweet escape of her slumber. She pretended that she hadn't noticed Marnie slipping underneath the bedcovers beside her and lying down.

In true Marnie style, that wasn't good enough.

Marnie wanted Georgie to wake up. To comfort her.

Fidgeting, the child dug her sharp pointy elbows and knees into Georgie as she shuffled around underneath the covers.

The whispering and giggling continued.

'Sshhh,' Georgie grumbled. 'Go back to sleep.'

Placing her arm around Marnie now in a bid to shut her sister up, Georgie was glad when her sister finally stopped moving about.

Snuggling into her sister's body, relishing her warmth, she was eager to get back to her dreams.

Back to their make-believe happy home with their mother.

She wrinkled her nose.

That smell?

Unfamiliar, musty. She could smell stale body odour. Sweat.

She froze.

Terror enveloped her as she realised that the person lying next to her, the person that Georgie had draped her arm around, wasn't Marnie.

Awake now, on high alert, Georgie's eyes flew open. Disorientated, surrounded by darkness. Her heart started thumping loudly as the whispering and giggling continued; this time, Georgie could hear it loud and clear. The hushed voices, the laughter.

'Shaun?'

His huge weight beside her in the bed.

Underneath her covers.

'What the hell are you doing?'

Engulfed with blind panic, Georgie knew she needed to get away. Pushing herself backwards, up the bed, she tried to move, to get up so that she could run.

Suddenly she was pulled back down on the mattress. A sweaty hand clamped tightly over her mouth.

Shaun's hand.

'Don't fucking move.' This came from Corey. Behind her at the head of her bed.

He was here too.

'Hold her down,' Shaun instructed.

Corey did as he was told.

Crouching over her, Corey dragged Georgie's arms up above her head; pinning her down by kneeling on both of her hands. Then, as Shaun moved his hand from Georgie's face, Corey replaced it instantly with his own.

Corey had a tight hold of her now.

Georgie couldn't move.

She tried to kick out with her legs, to unsteady Shaun, but he straddled her.

The heavy weight of him pinning her down to the mattress.

Unable to make a sound, her eyes flickered wide with terror as Shaun moved his hands under the covers.

Touching her. Laughing.

'I told you I was going to make you pay, didn't I, Jugs?' He sounded menacing, as if he was enjoying her fear. His chunky hands kneaded her thighs, squeezing her flesh roughly as he moved his hand higher.

Petrified at what the boy was going to do to her, Georgie felt sick. Hot bile burned through her. Maybe Shaun was just messing with her head. Just teaching her a lesson. He wouldn't do anything that bad to her if he had Corey here with him too? Would he? This was just a twisted little game to get her back for humiliating him earlier. For showing him up in front of the entire house.

Shaun tugged at her nightdress. Yanking it up.

Georgie realised to her horror that she was very wrong. Shaun was going to make her pay in the worst way possible. She thought about her mother, and all those disgusting sounds. Georgie felt nauseous.

Kicking out, as hard as she could, she wriggled around in the bed frantically in a bid to escape.

The boys just laughed, finding her panic amusing.

Georgie recognised another voice then too.

High-pitched laughter.

Annie.

Then she spoke sternly: 'Stop fucking squirming about Pissy-knickers or they'll do the same to you.'

Georgie could hear the muffled cries of her sister, as if she was being restrained too. Annie must be holding her; clamping her mouth shut so that her sister wouldn't be able to alert anyone about what Shaun was intending to do.

She tried to bite Corey's hand. Desperate to escape, to save her sister from these animals. Only, he was holding her too tightly; she couldn't get any leverage.

She was crying now. Hot tears poured down her cheeks. Helpless, weak there was nothing she could do. She was completely at Shaun's mercy.

'I told you I'd make you pay,' Shaun whispered in her ear as he climbed on top of her, pulling down her knickers.

His voice sounded thick, breathless with excitement. He was enjoying the fear that he was instilling in her.

The weight of him above her, crushing; she tried to move, to turn – anything to try to shake him off, but he was too big. Too strong.

Pinned down underneath him, the air burst out of her lungs. Crushing, heavy. She tried to breathe, to draw in some air, but she couldn't. Her chest was tight, wheezy.

Heady now, she thought that she might actually die. Trapped underneath the boy, unable to breathe.

There was another pain now too.

A sharp, hard pain that she'd never felt before.

Inside of her. Searing, so painful. It was as if it was ripping her in two.

Shaun was grunting on top of her.

The rolls of sweaty skin sticking to her body as he pressed himself against her.

It felt like for ever.

Corey and Annie were laughing. Egging him on.

'She ain't going to be so full of herself now, is she?' Annie said, satisfied that the new girl had got what she deserved.

Then they were laughing.

Corey and Annie both mimicking the grunting sounds that Shaun was making.

Still, Shaun didn't stop.

The noises only seemed to spur him on to hurt her even harder.

Staring up at him she could see the dark shadows under his eyes; the bandage across his nose where she'd hit him earlier. She sorely regretted doing that now.

Shutting her eyes in a desperate bid to shut Shaun out too, Georgie was in survival mode.

Concentrating only on her breathing, on the sound of her sister, she tried to make everything else that was happening to her disappear.

She zoned out.

Unsure of how long it had been, she registered the sound of Shaun making one final last grunt on top of her, before he stopped. Collapsing on her, crushing the last bit of air inside her lungs with his huge fat body.

She could feel the hot sticky sweat dripping from him. The foul stench of his bitter body odour would be engraved in her memory for ever.

Finally, he rolled off her and sat up.

'You liked that didn't you,' he smirked.

Georgie didn't answer. She didn't dare. She couldn't, even if she wanted to. Corey's knees were still pressing down on her palms; his hand still clamped over her mouth.

She just stared ahead, up towards the ceiling. Willing Shaun to leave now. For Corey to go with him.

'I said you liked that, didn't you?'

She knew he wouldn't go until he heard her say the words. So she nodded. Telling him what he wanted to hear. So that he would just go. So he wouldn't hurt her sister too.

'I can't hear you?' Shaun said; then nodding at Corey, the boy removed his hand from Georgie's mouth so that she could answer.

Only, when Georgie opened her mouth to speak, no sound came out.

Nothing.

Her throat was burning as she swallowed down the hot bile that threatened to escape.

Shaun grabbed her face. 'I want to hear you say it.'

'Yes. I liked it,' Georgie spat. Crying now, humiliated. She saw the amusement in Shaun's eyes staring back at her.

'If you tell anyone, I'm going to come back and I'm going to do exactly what I just did to you to your sister,' Shaun said with a wry smile.

'I won't tell.' Georgie knew he meant it. 'I promise, I won't tell.'

Shaun nodded, satisfied that Georgie was telling the truth; but just for added measure he said: 'Good, cause even if you did, Mrs Reed and that stupid social worker of yours don't give two shits about you. You know that, don't you?'

Shaun nodded over to Corey and Annie, and the three of them laughed: a private joke that Georgie was being left out of.

'We know all about your mother. We overheard Mrs Reed talking about her on the phone. A murderer and a prostitute. You're just like her – a little slag too.'

Georgie locked eyes with her sister across the room. Snotty, with tears running down her cheeks, and a look of confusion on her face. Too young to comprehend what had just happened to Georgie but she knew it was bad. That Shaun had hurt her sister.

'At least they're getting rid of this little whiney brat tomorrow,' Annie piped up, enjoying seeing Georgie's demise first hand. The girl wouldn't be so full of herself after tonight's little show that was for sure. 'Found a foster home for her, haven't they? But they couldn't find one for you.'

Finally, Annie let go of Marnie.

She ran across the room and flung herself into Georgie's arms. Hugging each other tightly, the two girls were locked in their embrace.

Annie grinned.

'Make the most of your time together. You probably won't see her again. You'll be stuck in here for good just like the rest of us rejects.'

They all left the room, closing the door behind them. Georgie could hear Shaun still laughing, smug in the knowledge that he'd taught Georgie Parker a lesson she wouldn't forget in a hurry.

Pulling Marnie in close to her now, Georgie Parker closed her eyes. Relieved that Shaun James had a least spared her sister from his brutal attack.

It was her only saving grace.

She could barely comprehend what the older boy had just done to her.

How he'd hurt her. Humiliated her.

Swallowing down the acrid bile that rose in the back of her throat Georgie embraced the numbness that swept over her as she fought back her tears.

She had to be strong for Marnie now, if no one else.

She knew that if she started crying now, she'd never be able to stop.

CHAPTER THIRTY-SIX

'I'm really sorry, Rose. I know it's not what you want to hear, but this isn't going to work out, I'm afraid. Following the incident this morning, I really think it's best that we find a more suitable arrangement for the Parker girls.' Mrs Reed spoke with regret, well aware that Georgie and Marnie Parker had already been through enough drama the past few days without her adding to it further by taking this action, but she didn't have any other choice. 'I can't condone any form of violence in the house, and seeing as we are already well over capacity…' she paused regretfully. 'I'm afraid it's the only viable decision left to make.'

'Is there any way that you could perhaps reconsider?' Rose asked, knowing that Mrs Reed couldn't, even if she wanted to. She was simply following protocol.

Mrs Reed shook her head.

'Look, I'd love to help you. Really, I would. I can see that Georgie and Marnie have been through so much, but I just can't. Whether or not the attack was provoked, is neither here nor there. Georgie Parker has barely been here twelve hours and already she's broken another resident's nose, and given him two black eyes in the process. There's no way that I could keep her here now. I just can't allow it.'

Mrs Reed knew that this now meant that Georgie and Marnie might be split up in order to find them some suitable accommodation, and she felt heart sorry for that, she really did, but she had a business to run here. Other children's welfares at stake. She couldn't risk any more incidents occurring.

'Look, trust me. Shaun James is troublesome, and the likelihood is that he instigated the attack. The boy is notorious for his intimidating behaviour. Maybe Georgie just snapped? She's been through a lot. I understand that. But I just don't think it would work out if we kept her here. Her and Shaun would be at loggerheads with each other and, right now, I just don't have the resources to deal with it. I'm understaffed as it is. I think that the girls would be better off being moved into longer-term foster care.'

Rose nodded. She'd been shocked when she'd first got the call from Mrs Reed informing her that Georgie had not only been involved in a physical fight, but that she'd also been the main assailant. Even more so when she'd found out that Georgie's adversary was a boy. An older, troubled boy at that.

'I know that placing Marnie won't be an issue. We have families lined up that could offer her a placement as early as tomorrow morning. It's Georgie that might be the issue, going on her recent behavioural issues that I'd have to declare to the foster families, and her age; teenagers can be harder to place. It might take me a few days to find her somewhere. Are you happy for her to remain here until then?' Rose asked, feeling physically sick at the thought of having to tell the girls that they were to be separated.

She had promised them that she would do everything in her power to keep them together. Now the decision was out of her hands. Georgie's actions this morning had forced this. There was nothing more that Rose could say or do on the matter.

'Two more days,' Mrs Reed said, finally. 'No more than that, though, and if Georgie causes any more trouble, then I'll have no choice but to ask you to remove her at the very first instance.'

'Thank you.' Rose relaxed slightly, relieved that at least Georgie could stay for now. She'd speak to her. Ensure that Georgie was aware of how serious the situation was. Make sure that she kept herself out of trouble.

'I know it's late, but do you think it would be okay if I went and spoke to the girls and let them know about the arrangements?' Rose figured that, at least if she told them tonight, the girls would have a chance to get their heads around the idea. They could have their last night together rather than being snatched away from each other in the morning when the first they'd hear of it was when she came to collect Marnie.

This was kinder, even though right now it really didn't feel that way.

'Of course.' Mrs Reed was up on her feet, and opening her office door. 'I'll walk you down to their room.'

Leading Rose down the corridor, past the dayroom, Mrs Reed knocked on the girls' bedroom door. Glancing over to Rose she offered her a small smile. She felt sorry for her. She could see that Rose genuinely cared: she looked anxious.

'I know it's tough, but you do have both the girls' best interests at heart. You're doing everything you can.' Mrs Reed smiled warmly. 'Sometimes we get so caught up with the job itself, with all of the dramas it entails, all of the paperwork, the formalities, that we forget the real reason that we chose to do this job in the first place. To make a difference. You will, Rose. They might not realise, at first, but you're doing your absolute best for them.' Mrs Reed placed a comforting hand on Rose's arm.

She nodded. Right now, she didn't feel like she'd done her very best. She felt like she'd lied to them. That she'd made them a promise that she hadn't been able to keep, and Georgie and Marnie deserved better than that.

They had enough people in their lives who had let them down without Rose adding herself to that long list.

Mrs Reed, on hearing no answer from the room, knocked one more time.

No answer.

Pressing down the handle, she pushed the door wide open.

The beds were made but the room was empty.

'Maybe they're in the dayroom.' Mrs Reed concluded; though, already, the alarm bells were ringing in her head. She remembered saying goodnight to the two girls earlier.

They'd gone to bed hours ago; she was sure of it.

The two women hurried now.

Down along the corridor to where they found Annie in the main sitting area, her feet up on the sofa watching the TV.

'Annie, have you seen the Parker girls? Georgie and Marnie?'

Annie shook her head. 'No why?' she said, feigning innocence, worried that Mrs Reed had found out what Shaun James did to Georgie. But she didn't get any more information from the women. Instead they carried on running through the house, checking every room as they called out Georgie and Marnie's names.

Though they both already knew – Georgie and Marnie Parker were long gone.

CHAPTER THIRTY-SEVEN

'Keep up, Marnie.'

Turning her head as she continued to run as fast as she could through the darkened streets, Georgie shouted at her sister who, much slower than her, was lagging far behind.

'I can't runned that fast. Wait for me, Georgie,' Marnie called out, struggling to breathe as she tried her hardest to keep up with her older sister's fast pace.

'Come on, we're nearly there, Marnie.' Out of breath now herself, Georgie's bare feet continued to pound against the cold rickety paving slabs beneath her. She winced as a sharp shooting pain ripped up through her ribcage.

A stitch.

She couldn't stop now though; they were almost there, almost at the pub. It was the only place that Georgie could think of to go.

She had to get away from the children's home. From Mrs Reed, Rose and Shaun.

Shaun.

She couldn't even begin to think about him and what he'd done to her. Not yet. For now, she just needed to get away. Get Marnie away. They could figure the rest out later.

'Ouch,' Georgie screamed out in agony as she felt the stab of something sharp crunching underneath the sole of her foot.

Looking down she could see the dark patch on her heel. Blood. Something had sliced through her skin. Hopping on one leg, she lifted her injured foot up to inspect it, brushing her bare skin so that she could free the debris that was firmly embedded in her flesh. Glass.

Ignoring the searing pain, Georgie pulled out a thin slither, and threw it down on the floor behind her – away from the footpath so that Marnie wouldn't step on it too, as she caught up now, close behind.

Continuing to run, it was starting to rain. Tiny droplets pattered down around her. Her nightdress wet through, sticking to her skin. Desperate to make a run from the children's home, she stupidly didn't think about getting dressed into anything warmer. She hadn't given a second's thought to the bitterly cold night air. She'd just wanted to escape. To get away.

Grabbing Marnie by the hand, they had both waited until the coast was clear.

Until Mrs Reed had been tucked away inside her office, and the rest of the children were in the dayroom watching the TV for the night. It had been the perfect opportunity to escape without being seen.

They'd snuck out through the kitchen door, out through the vast back garden, climbing over the padlocked back gate.

They'd been running for ages. Georgie hadn't realised just how far away the home was from where they lived. She'd got lost a few times too. London looked so different under a blanket of darkness – the long winding streets that somehow managed to merge into one. She'd only been able to gather her bearings when she'd reached Brixton High Street. She knew this part of London like the back of her hand.

They were almost there now. Reaching the alleyway that ran alongside the Old Bell pub Georgie could see the bright lights just up ahead, a warm glow of yellow beaming out from the pub's windows illuminating the alleyway. She could just about hear the

faint hum of music, too, from the jukebox. The noise dulled down
by the sirens that screamed off somewhere out in the distance. The
police? Or an ambulance? Georgie couldn't distinguish which.
The noise made her feel nervous. Anxious suddenly.

Maybe they should have stayed put. Georgie could have told
Mrs Reed what Shaun had done. Maybe Mrs Reed would have
called the police on Shaun. Had him taken away.

Georgie doubted it though.

Remembering Shaun's words.

A slag. Just like her mother. Even if she told, no one would
believe her.

Georgie knew he was right too.

Why would they believe her?

Georgie had felt scared tonight – not that she'd ever admit
that to her sister though. She needed to stay strong. Try to hold
herself together for the sake of Marnie.

Her sister needed her.

Reaching the pub door, Georgie called out once more. Frustrated, as she watched her sister running towards her – her pace
barely faster than walking.

'Come on, Marnie!' Georgie shouted. Her voice full of urgency.

She wanted to get inside before someone saw them. The
police might have been alerted to their disappearance by now.
They needed to keep out of sight. As Marnie got closer, Georgie
could see that her sister was sobbing. Big fat tears, rolling down
her cheeks.

'I'm sorry, Georgie, I tried to runned faster…'

Georgie felt guilty then.

'It's okay, we're here now. Come on.' Pushing the pub doors
open she ushered her younger sister inside, conscious of the small
cluster of customers that were sitting around the bar who turned
to stare at them.

People were whispering. Georgie could hear them.

They were gossiping about her and her sister – about their mum.

Wrapping her arm protectively around Marnie's shoulder, Georgie continued to lead her through the bar.

'Ey, I hope you two have got your ID on you!' one man sitting at the bar quipped, amused by the unusual sight of two small children walking into a pub on their own this late at night. 'I know what they say about girls looking older than their years these days, but you two definitely look underage to me.'

The man laughed as he caught Georgie's eye.

Georgie looked away from him, scanning the rest of the faces around her; she didn't recognise a single one.

'Davey?' Worried, suddenly, that maybe he wasn't here tonight. Georgie didn't know what she'd do if that was the case. 'Where's Davey?'

She was starting to panic.

Maybe they shouldn't have come here.

Maybe they should have stayed where they were.

'Are you girls okay?' Rita Gregory asked, standing behind the bar. She'd stopped serving the drinks. Looking at the state of them, they were clearly anything but okay. 'You won't find Davey down here. The man's called it a night. It's closing time in twenty minutes.' She eyed the children suspiciously. Her voice full of concern. 'What are you both doing out in the middle of the night anyway?'

'It's all right, Rita, I know these kids. They're Josie Parker's young ones. Who's supposed to be minding you?' The woman on the end of the bar leant down towards her.

Bristling at the woman's interrogation, Georgie didn't answer. She knew not to. Mary Sheelan was the local busybody. The woman practically lived in this pub. Propped up at the bar; poking her nose into everyone's business. Josie Parker had never liked

Mary, and as far as Mary was concerned the feeling was mutual. Georgie and Marnie had witnessed a fair few fights between their mother and Mary over the past few years. Georgie had no intentions of telling this woman anything.

Tonight, Mary was drunk, too, by the looks of it. Her face red and blotchy; the usual slur to her voice.

Even standing a few feet away, Georgie could smell the overpowering alcohol on the woman's soured breath.

'Your mother has a lot to answer for. Look at the state of you both, running about half naked.' Mary now eyed the child with disdain as Georgie purposely ignored her. She was only asking a few questions; there was no need to be so rude. Though what had she expected? The child had been raised by an ignorant trollop like Josie. Georgie clearly didn't know any better.

'I always said your mother was a wrongun. I was right too, wasn't I? Out whoring at all times of the day and night. A druggy too so the papers say. Doesn't surprise me one bit. She looked like she needed a good bath your mother. Dirty, inside and out.' Mary ran her eyes over the two girls as they both stood in silence. Their heads down. Mortified, as this woman humiliated them in front of everyone in the pub. 'You two little sods don't stand a hope in hell. You'll probably grow up to be just like her.' Mary Sheelan was off on one tonight.

Shrugging away the hand of a man sitting beside her as he told her to be quiet, Mary couldn't help herself. She was in her element now that Josie Parker had been locked away. Now, she could freely voice her opinion so that everyone in the pub could hear her, and there would be no repercussions.

'Still, she's in the right place now, isn't she, after what she did to Trevor, God rest his soul.' Mary's voice quivered at her last words.

Truth be known, she'd barely even known Trevor Pearson, but that hadn't stopped her from cashing in on the man's death. She'd been making out that they'd been close, that Trevor had been a kind man. That she'd miss him now that he'd gone. All the while, smiling and nodding graciously as she collected sympathy drinks from people around her who were stupid enough to fall for her farce and offer her their condolences.

'Don't talk about our mother,' Georgie warned. Unable to stand here and listen to another word that came out of the woman's mouth, she felt her anger building inside her. Her fists clenched at her sides. A heat surging through her.

Somehow, she managed to keep her voice calm and steady, though the warning was there for everyone in the pub to hear.

This woman was nothing more than a vicious drunk with a poisonous tongue, and Georgie would not let her sit there and talk about her mother like this.

'Ooh and who's going to stop me?' Mary sang, looking around with confidence at the handful of locals propped up at the bar alongside her. None of them brave enough, nor stupid enough, to start trouble with her. 'Everyone's talking about the woman. How could they not? She was wicked through and through.'

'If my mother was here now she'd wipe the floor with you.' Georgie saw the smile disappear from the woman's face, replaced with a twitch. The woman knew it was true.

Georgie herself had watched a few times when her mother had beaten the crap out of this woman for saying much less.

'Well, your mother isn't here, is she? She's been locked away with all the rest of the scum. Personally, I hope they throw away the bleeding key an' all.' Mary Sheelan laughed, delighted with the fact that the child could be so easily riled. 'Cut from the same cloth; you're just like her.'

Her words hit Georgie like a blow to her chest.

The same words that Shaun had used.

She spoke up. Loud. Not caring what anyone thought about her.

'My mother was right about you. You're nothing but a vicious old cunt,' Georgie spat, repeating her mother's favourite profanity. 'And just so you know, she's not in prison. Didn't you hear? The police made a mistake. They've let her out. She's on her way here now, actually, to pick us up. I expect she'll be dying to see you, especially when I tell her all the things you've been going around saying.' Georgie watched the colour drain from Mary's face.

Rendered silent, Mary Sheelan looked as white as a ghost.

She'd done nothing but slander Josie Parker the last few days, revelling in the fact that the woman was locked away behind bars. She felt a bit worried now, and rightly so.

Josie Parker had always been a force to be reckoned with. A right gobby cow she could be, with a bastard of a temper on her. Only, now she'd added murder to her résumé.

She'd bludgeoned a man to death. The papers said it was some drink-fuelled domestic.

The woman was clearly a lunatic.

The other people at the bar were all whispering amongst themselves, nudging each other.

'Come on, Marnie. Let's see if Davey is upstairs while we wait for Mummy.' Grabbing her sister's hand, Georgie continued to lead Marnie out the back.

Mary was right. People around here would talk shit about her mother, regardless, but at least now Georgie had given them something worth talking about.

CHAPTER THIRTY-EIGHT

Davey Lewis was in his element. He'd finally seen sense and told his Mel to sling her hook and, for the first time in months, he felt genuinely free to do as he pleased, and right now, what pleased him was rolling around naked in bed with his good friend, Mandy.

'Did you hear that?' Mandy said now, sticking her head out from underneath the covers. 'Sounded like someone calling you?'

Davey stopped what he was doing and strained to listen.

He could hear the blurred sound of voices floating up through the floor beneath him, general buzz of chatter from punters, music blaring out from the jukebox. A loud laugh. Nothing out of the ordinary.

'Nah, you probably just heard one of the locals; you know what they're like once they've had a drink in them. Probably trying to give the likes of Michael Bublé a run for his money, singing along badly to the juke box. Rita has it all in hand, I'm sure. That woman should be a bouncer not a barmaid!' Davey grinned. 'Now, where were we?' He winked, bowing his head back down underneath the covers. 'God I've missed you, Mandy,' he said, genuinely.

''Course I know you missed me, you daft bugger. How could you not? I'm the best thing you've ever had, mate, and don't you forget it.' She felt exactly the same. Her and Davey were like two peas in a pod. For the first time in her life, Mandy had met a man she could actually talk to. Like, really talk to, and more importantly Davey seemed to listen. She was determined to do whatever it took to make this work out. Even if it meant giving up her job. That's how serious she was about the man. She wasn't going to let anything fuck it up for them.

Davey pulled Mandy around so that she was on top of him. Throwing the covers off, revealing her ample breasts, Mandy almost got the shock of her life to see Georgie and Marnie Parker standing at the foot of the bed.

'Jesus Christ, you scared the bleeding life out of me!' she shrieked, covering up her naked body with the duvet.

Perplexed at Mandy's sudden outburst, Davey sat up too, pulling the covers over himself.

'Girls?' Davey narrowed his eyes. 'What are you doing here?'

Suddenly feeling awkward, exposed, talking to the young girls without his clothes on, Davey reached down for where he'd discarded them in a pile on the floor, and pulled his jeans on.

'What on earth is going on?' Mandy asked, shaking her head in confusion. She'd been gobsmacked when she'd heard that Josie had been arrested for murdering Trevor.

The first thing she'd done was rush around here to Davey, so that they could both try to work out what the hell had gone on, but neither of them had known what to think.

None of it made any sense.

Murder?

Josie Parker was capable of a lot of things, but murder?

'The police said you'd been taken into care.' Mandy stared from one girl to the next. 'Why are you here?' Both of them dripping wet, no shoes on their feet.

Hearing the shock in Mandy's voice, Davey tried the softer approach.

'All right, Mandy, I'm sure that the girls don't need an inter-rogation.' Crossing the room, dressed now, Davey could see the turmoil on their two little faces. They looked scared. Terrified, dressed only in their nightdresses, which were now soaked through. Their bare feet blackened from running through the streets. Georgie's foot covered in blood.

God only knew what these poor children had been through the past couple of days. Right now they didn't need a barrage of questions to add to their troubles. They needed someone to help them.

'Whatever's happened, girls, it will be all right. I promise,' Davey said now with conviction. 'Jesus, you both must be freezing. Look at you both, blue with the cold. Here.' Rummaging inside his wardrobe, Davey brought out two of his old cardigans, wrapping them around their shoulders. 'Let's get you two all warmed up, eh.'

Then looking at Georgie, Davey said: 'You want to tell me what's going on?'

Georgie could see the genuine concern in Davey's eyes. She knew that she'd been right to come here. Davey was kind. She liked him. He had always made a fuss of her and Marnie on the rare occasions that their mother had brought them into the pub. He made sure that they had a glass of lemonade, on the house, of course, and if he had them he'd give them a lollypop each too.

Georgie nodded. 'We ran away,' she said simply, no hint of apology in her voice as she spoke. 'They took us to a children's home, but then they said they were going to take Marnie away from me. They were going to put her in a foster home. So we ran away.'

'You ran away?' Mandy rolled her eyes. 'Oh that's just great. Well, we'll have Children's Services on the doorstep any minute then, won't we, and the police too.'

Mandy couldn't blame the girls though. In such a short space of time, Georgie and Marnie's lives had been turned inside out by the dramas that had unfolded around them.

'We're going to have to call the police, Davey, and let them know the girls are here,' Mandy said, not wanting them to bring any trouble to Davey's door. The man had enough on his plate with his nightmare of an ex, and this place, without harbouring runaways too.

Seeing the fear in the girls' eyes at the suggestion, the look that passed between them, Davey shook his head adamantly.

'Not yet, okay.' He shot a warning look to Mandy. 'Let's just get the girls settled first. How about I make us all a nice mug of hot chocolate, eh? I might even have some biscuits out the back too. How does that grab you?' He smiled, guessing that they were probably hungry as he took in their waiflike forms, how fragile they both appeared.

Davey's kindness was too much for Georgie. His soothing voice; his lovely smiling eyes. She folded. Unable to pretend that she was all right any longer, she gave herself up to the big heavy sobs that shook her body.

She was terrified of being sent back to Rainbow House, of being sent back and having to face Shaun James again after what he did to her.

She wanted her mother.

She wanted to go back in time to when none of this had ever happened.

Letting Davey wrap his arms around her, Georgie properly sobbed, her rare show of emotion setting Marnie off too.

Davey pulled them both in for a hug.

'Here, don't cry,' he said, trying to lighten the sombre mood. 'My hot chocolate ain't that bad, I promise.'

The girls were clinging to him; holding him tightly as if for dear life. They were both freezing cold, shaking, sobbing uncontrollably. He looked over towards Mandy, his heart breaking in two for the pair of them.

Mandy shrugged. Feeling useless, like a spare part, as she watched the scene unfold before her eyes. She didn't have a clue what to say or do. She couldn't make sense of any of it. How had it all come to this? It was crazy. Josie shouldn't have been locked up; she should be here with her kids. This was just madness.

'Come on now, girls. I can't have you two crying like this; you're going to set me off in a minute,' Davey said, trying his hardest to comfort them. 'And trust me, you don't want to see that, because it's not a pretty sight. There'll be snot and tears everywhere.'

They gave Davey a small smile.

'Come on, let's go and get you both a nice hot drink, yeah? We can have a little chat, yeah?'

The girls nodded.

Taking their hands, Davey walked towards the bedroom door, shooting a look of apology back towards Mandy.

Laying her head back against the pillow she stared up at the ceiling wondering what she could do. The girls must have really been distressed if they'd both felt that they had no other option but to run away, and Mandy, knowing Josie the way she did, knew she wouldn't want the girls to be separated from each other. That would break her heart.

There was only so much that she and Davey could say and do to help, though. They didn't have any leverage over what the authorities decided for the girls. That was the long and short of it.

Mandy screwed her mouth up, thoughtfully. There was one person though, who might be able to do something. It was a gamble, but right now, it was the only hope the two girls had.

Reaching down to her handbag beside the bed, Mandy rummaged around for her phone. She had to at least try to make things right for them; it was the least she could do for Josie.

Tapping in the number, she just hoped that she was making the right decision.

CHAPTER THIRTY-NINE

'Can you believe the cheek of that young one, speaking to me like that? She's the spit of her mother, isn't she? Josie was always such a crass, vile woman. It's no wonder those kids have turned out the way that they have.' Mary Sheelan shook her head in disgust. Still smarting from the way Georgie Parker had just humiliated her in front of the entire pub, she couldn't help herself, she was chomping at the bit. Determined to save face as she sat there slagging Josie and her two daughters off to anyone who would listen.

Unfortunately that meant Rita Gregory had been lumbered with her as no one else wanted to give her the time of day. Serving behind the bar, she couldn't just up and move away like some of the other locals.

'Did you see the state of them? Like feral animals, the pair of them.'

Rita Gregory yawned exaggeratedly, the woman was boring her something stupid; though, the way Mary was knocking back her pints of Strongbow, Rita would be surprised if the woman was capable of picking up her glass, let alone the hint.

Mary continued with her constant rambling, convinced now that the child had been lying. The police hadn't made a mistake. Mary would have heard by now.

The child had called her bluff. Cheeky little madam.

'The only good thing, I suppose, is the fact that the woman is locked away. I mean, those kids are probably damaged beyond repair as it is. You can't blame them, can you? Having a mother like that dragging them up. Josie was always a wrongun, opening her legs for anyone willing to slip her a few quid, but a murderer…' She gave an exaggerated shiver. 'It makes my skin crawl. That could have been me you know!'

Mary stared at Rita for added effect, willing the barmaid to ask her to elaborate. When Rita didn't Mary continued, regardless.

'The amount of times that Josie started her drunken brawls with me. I should have known the woman wasn't right in the head. She'd pick a fight in an empty room that one. She clearly had anger issues. I mean, most of the time I didn't even do anything to goad her. Just kept myself to myself, minding my own business. Just think, the wrong place, the wrong time and I could have been beaten to death with a hammer too.'

Rita Gregory rolled her eyes at this. Mary Sheelan, keeping herself to herself. Who was the woman trying to kid? Normally, Mary would have taken herself off home by now, but she was still lingering around the bar like a bad smell, and Rita knew why. The woman was dying to see if Georgie Parker was going to make another appearance.

It wouldn't surprise Rita one bit if Mary went for the girl. She hadn't taken kindly to being shown up like that.

In the meantime, Rita was having to execute the patience of a saint, listening to the woman, seeing as no one else was listening to her now.

'You know what, I'm going to give the police a call and find out what's going on. Those two young ones shouldn't be walking around here late at night. Did you see them: both half naked and soaked through with the rain? It ain't right is it?' Rummaging around inside her handbag for the mobile phone that her son had brought her for Christmas, she said, 'It's my duty to ensure that the police know their whereabouts.'

Mary wasn't fooling Rita; Mary didn't give two craps about the children's welfare. The woman just wanted to cause drama.

'Maybe you should just keep out of it,' Rita said, trying to stop Mary from doing something that she might later regret. 'They've gone up to see Davey. I'm sure that he'll be sorting it all out as we speak.'

Rita wasn't sure why the girls had come here either, or where they should be right now, but one thing she did know for sure was that if Mary started poking her nose in, the woman was just going to make things ten times worse for everyone involved. The girls especially.

'Keep out of it? After the way that gobby little madam just spoke to me. Not a chance!' Showing her true colours once more, Mary was having none of it. 'The police will probably send a social worker down here to fetch them.'

Holding her phone in her hand, she was making a big song and dance about it all. Sensing people around shifting about uncomfortably in their seats, some of them getting up to leave, Mary still didn't realise that the atmosphere in the room around her had changed like the flick of the switch.

Good. Let them leave. She didn't care. She was only speaking the truth. If people didn't like it tough luck.

'Someone needs to teach that young Georgie some bloody manners. Forget about a children's home; the kid needs locking up in a youth detention centre. She needs some discipline.'

'Is that so?'

Mary Sheelan didn't even need to turn around. She could tell by the reaction of everyone around her that it was Delray Anderton who was standing behind her.

She was so drunk, so busy sitting here slagging Josie and her girls off, that she hadn't realised the real reason that people were looking at her funny.

Sensing trouble, they were getting up and leaving. Knowing that Mary had dug herself a hole big enough to be buried in and, knowing her luck, that was exactly what Delray was going to do.

Josie Parker worked for Delray; no matter what she'd done, the woman was still under Delray's protection – or at least she had been – and the man wouldn't take too kindly to anyone slagging off one of his girls.

'Drink up, ladies and gents. The pub's closed.' Delray raised his voice, though he didn't need to. Just the sight of him standing behind Mary Sheelan with a face on him like thunder had given him everyone's undivided attention.

'Well, Delray. How are you?' Mary gulped, praying to God that the man hadn't heard her entire conversation. Though she could see by the look on his face that he had.

People were disappearing. Leaving their drinks behind, they were all scurrying out of the pub.

Selfish bastards.

'You done?' Delray glared at her.

'Yes, Delray. I'm just off home.' Unsure if Delray was asking about her conversation or her half-empty glass, Mary nodded. Either way, yes, she was done. She just wished to God she'd kept her big mouth shut.

Delray held his hand out.

Mary looked down at it confused.

'Your phone,' he demanded.

Passing it to him with shaking hands, Mary watched as Delray dropped the phone down on to the floor, before he began stamping on it with his huge size twelve boots.

The phone was smashed into a hundred pieces. Ruined beyond repair.

'Sometimes, Mary, contrary to the crappy adverts you see on telly, it ain't good to talk. Do you get me!'

Mary nodded obediently.

'Keep that big trap of yours shut, do you understand? You didn't see the girls; you haven't heard anything about the girls…'

The last thing Mary wanted was the likes of Delray Anderton on her back.

She felt sick now. All the cider she'd knocked back tonight threatened to show itself once again. She gulped the bile in the back of her throat.

Looking down at the shattered phone, she wondered if she was next.

Delray nodded towards the main door.

'Go on, then. Fuck off. And if I hear that you've opened your mouth and so much as a peep has come out of it, it will be the last thing you do, do you understand, Mary?'

Again Mary nodded.

Delray waved the woman off.

He had more pressing matters that he needed to deal with tonight. Matters that didn't need an audience.

Aware that she was getting off lightly – very lightly indeed – Mary made a bolt for the pub door before Delray changed his mind.

As much as she was certain Josie Parker must have a few mental problems in order to have battered poor Trevor Pearson to death with a hammer, Josie had nothing on Delray Anderton. The man was a complete and utter nutcase, and Mary Sheelan, finally put in her place now, couldn't get out of the pub fast enough.

'Well, this looks nice and cosy, doesn't it?' Delay Anderton stepped into the kitchen, taking in the scene before him. Georgie and Marnie were sitting huddled in massive cardigans, their hands wrapped around mugs of hot chocolate. Davey and Mandy both sitting at the table opposite them. 'It's almost like one of those wholesome scenes from *The Waltons*.'

Delray had heard the girls giggling as he'd come up the stairs. Davey had obviously said something funny and the girls were both laughing.

None of them were laughing now though. They were all staring at him wondering what he was doing here.

'How can we help, Delray?' Davey asked warily, wondering why the man had thought it was okay to come upstairs into his home without being invited. He had no reason to be here. No reason at all.

Davey tried his hardest not to associate with the likes of Delray. The man was nothing but bad news.

Delray smirked. Looking over towards Mandy he raised his eyes.

'I take it you didn't tell your boyfriend here about our little phone call then, Mandy?'

She squirmed in her chair.

'You called Delray?' Davey looked at her, confusion written all over his face.

Mandy didn't answer. She didn't even have the good grace to look him in the eye.

The second Delray had stepped into the kitchen, as Mandy saw that twisted, crooked smirk of his, she knew she'd made a mistake of epic proportions. She'd thought she was doing the right thing earlier. Calling Delray. She'd somehow convinced herself that, in some way, she was actually doing the girls a favour too. Trying to find them a place where they could stay together. A place where they'd be looked after. But a small part of her had been selfish too. She didn't want Davey to get involved in all of this.

Now though, seeing the angry look on Davey's face, she realised that he already was, and he was not one bit happy that Mandy had just made things even more complicated by involving this man.

Staring down at her mug, she avoided eye contact. Guilt written all over her face.

Davey shook his head, annoyed that Mandy had taken it upon herself to involve someone else.

'I'd said I'd sort this, didn't I?' Davey looked at Delray and shrugged his shoulders. 'I think there's been some kind of misunderstanding; everything's under control here. I don't know why Mandy called you, but it's all sorted. Really.'

Davey couldn't stand Delray.

The man was nothing but scum. He made a living from forcing girls to work for him. Pimping them out as if their only purpose was to line his pockets. Davey had seen the damage that he'd done to Josie and Mandy over the years. Josie more so. Unable to cope with the lifestyle she led, looking after her girls single-handedly – she'd turned to drink and drugs.

The woman's behaviour had been spiralling out of control for months. Davey suspected that Josie had been back on the gear too. He'd wondered if heroin had played a part in her committing a murder. Ultimately, he knew Delray had been the root cause of it all.

There was no way he was going to hand these kids over to the man. Josie wouldn't want him to, he was convinced of that.

'I think you best leave.' He knew he was crossing the line speaking to Delray in such a short manner, but he was also letting Delray know that he wasn't a man to be easily intimidated.

He'd never caused Delray any issues in the past. In fact, Davey had always allowed Delray's girls to tout for business in his bar without so much as a word of trouble from him, mainly for the girls' sake, if anything. At least having them in the pub meant that they weren't out having to walk the streets. They could stay inside in the warm, and Davey could keep an eye on them.

He'd even sorted out the mess that Delray had made of his pub last week when Delray and Lenny had kicked Billy Stackhouse all around the place. Davey hadn't ever mentioned the broken furniture or the blood on the carpet; instead, he'd just sorted it all out himself.

Now in return all he asked for was a little bit of mutual respect.

This was Davey's home, and he wasn't going to let anyone just waltz in here and start poking their nose in his business. The girls had come to him. He was going to sort this out.

'Well, that's just it, Davey, everything isn't under control, is it? These two have done a runner from the kids' home, haven't they? They are going to have people looking for them.' Delray laughed as he pulled up a chair and sat down at the table. Leaving Davey in no doubt that he wasn't going anywhere.

'Now, are you two going to tell me what's been going on?' Delray stared at the girls.

Delray had to admit the news about Josie had floored him too. He knew Josie had been in a bad way, but murder?

Just like everyone else around here, he hadn't thought she was capable. Still, it just proved you never really knew, did you. She'd murdered a punter too… which only confirmed that Delray had been right to out the woman. He didn't want to be associated with any of that shit. Delray had far bigger fish to fry these days. Josie could rot for all he cared.

'What happened?' Delray looked at Georgie.

She looked down at the table. She couldn't speak; she didn't dare.

Seeing the obvious discomfort on the girl's face, Davey stepped in.

'I'm sure Georgie will tell us when she's good and ready. Let's not force them, eh?' Davey saw Georgie relax at his words, glad to have the attention back off of her.

'Oh, fuck me. You even sound like a bleeding social worker, Davey, no wonder they came to you, eh?' Delray laughed.

'I think you should leave,' Davey repeated looking at Delray; then turning to Mandy, beyond angry, he added: 'You should go too.'

'You don't understand, Davey, I was trying to help. Trying to do what's best for them…' Mandy said, heart sorry now for landing Davey with Delray.

She should have kept her nose out of it.

Delray, however, didn't move. Helping himself to a biscuit, he dunked it into Davey's hot chocolate. He could hear the seriousness in Davey's voice; he could see that the man was scared of him, but he was also standing up for himself too. Delray liked that. A man with a backbone. It made a change around these parts.

As refreshing as it was though, no one barked orders at him.

'I heard you, mate, and that's exactly what I am going to do, Davey-old-boy, don't you worry. Let's just let the girls finish up their hot chocolate before we leave, yeah?'

'Leave? They aren't going anywhere. Not with you.' Davey raised his voice now. 'Josie would have wanted me to help them. It's the least I can do for the girl.'

'Well, you see, Josie don't really get a say in the matter. She ain't going to be around for a while from what I heard.'

Delray was smug, and so he should be. He'd been racking his brains over whether he'd be able to try to gain custody of the girls via the authorities, and with his reputation and criminal record, the chances of that ever happening had been slim to none. Yet, here he was again: destiny had thrown him another lifeline. He hadn't needed to try to fight for the kids; the kids had come to him, albeit through Davey-boy.

'We want to stay here,' Georgie said, folding her arms across her chest.

Delray sat back in his chair. Sucking his teeth, he shook his head slowly. The last thing he wanted to do tonight was cause a scene, but he would if he needed to.

'I ain't going to tell you again, Davey. The girls are coming with me. Now drink up, girls.'

'No, they are staying.'

Marnie and Georgie stared from man to man, seeing the tension between them both, unsure who they should be listening to.

'Who the fucking hell do you think you are, eh?' Davey said, so angry now that he was prepared to take Delray on. No matter what the bloke said or did to him, Davey had a lot of time for Josie and her girls. He wanted to help them, and he'd do a damn sight better job than the likes of Delray Anderton.

The man was a scumbag, a criminal. He lived the kind of life that no young child should be any part of. Well, Davey wasn't going to just sit here and put up with the man trying to intimidate him. This was his home. The girls had come to him.

'Who do I think I am?' Delray roared with laughter. 'Are you going to tell him, or shall I?'

Mandy, sensing where this conversation was going, felt sick to her stomach. Tonight she'd opened up the biggest can of worms in calling Delray here. Looking across the table to Davey, then finally to Georgie and Marnie, her voice was barely audible.

'He's Marnie's father, Davey. Marnie, darling, Delray is your dad.'

CHAPTER FORTY

'Is this really your house? It looks like a hotel!' Marnie gasped out loud as the lift doors opened and she, Georgie and Delray all stepped inside the huge apartment's main front door, unable to believe her eyes; she had never been inside a house that looked this posh.

Shiny textured wallpaper, large mirrors. Every surface sparkled and gleamed.

Following Delray and her older sister, she felt the warmth of the thick, plush carpet envelop her feet as she walked. Gazing up at the impossibly high ceilings, she was mesmerised by all the glass-like beads of crystal that hung down from the light fittings.

'Fancy ain't it!' Delray said proudly, as he tossed his keys down on the mirrored console table in the hallway, and led the two girls through into his huge open-plan lounge and kitchen.

Sometimes he forgot how well he'd done for himself. Memories of growing up on the Aylesbury Estate, over in Lambeth, seemed like a lifetime ago now. Living in poverty back then had been the norm. Delray hadn't known anything else.

He'd always wanted more. Ever since he was a young boy. He despised the Aylesbury Estate and everything it stood for. A sink estate, set in a depressing cluster of concrete flats, surrounded by a maze of dingy alleyways and communal gardens that were rife with crime. Drug dealers, prostitutes, gangs. The dregs of society all clustered together and forgotten about. Most people Delray's age were lucky to make it out of the place alive, let alone make it out and achieve the kind of status that Delray had attained for himself.

Delray was one of the lucky ones. He'd clawed his way out of the gutter by all means necessary, and he meant any means. Whatever it took. Determined to make a decent life, he'd reinvented himself.

Even now he'd made it big time, he still wanted more.

'Your front room looks bigger than my whole school,' Marnie said. 'Listen to this. Hello. Helloooo. Helloooo.' Marnie giggled as her voice carried all the way through the apartment, echoing off its walls.

Delray couldn't help but laugh at the child. So young and innocent; the kid just said whatever came into her mind. Nothing was rehearsed, nothing pre-empted. Delray liked that about her; at least he knew where he stood. Unlike her older sister, Georgie, who, since Mandy's little outburst at the pub, had barely said two words.

It had been a shock to both of the girls, finding out that Delray was Marnie's father, he knew that. Fuck knows how he'd fallen in bed with Josie after all those years, but somehow Delray just had. Josie had been nothing more than a quick, convenient fuck when he'd needed one. Only, he'd gone and got the woman up the duff. Still, as far as he was concerned that was all down to Josie. She was their mother and if she'd decided to lie to the girls then that was down to her. All he was doing now was picking up the pieces.

The truth be told, Delray had never had any interest in Marnie, not really. When Josie had first told him that she was pregnant Delray had told Josie that he couldn't keep her. That she had to get rid. He'd even driven Josie down to the abortion clinic over in Romford. Forcing her to go through with it against her wishes, he'd had to physically walk her in through the main doors of reception and sit with her until the nurse called her through.

Only, typical Josie, she'd made a right song and bleeding dance. Crying and wailing like a banshee when it came to her turn to go through with the procedure, she told the nurses that she couldn't do it. She'd become so hysterical that the medical staff had refused to carry out the operation, insisting that Josie needed more time to decide. That she needed to be certain.

So, Josie had won. She'd got to keep her baby.

Convinced that she'd been trying to trap him, Delray had refused point-blank to offer any form of support. He'd told her that if she had the baby, it was her responsibility and hers alone. Just because she'd had his kid it didn't mean that the woman would catch a free ride. In fact, because she'd gone ahead and had his kid, she'd actually had it harder over the years than most of the others.

Delray had wanted to ensure that he kept her on her toes, kept her from thinking that she could ever try to take the piss out of him and, to her credit, Josie hadn't asked for a single thing from him over the years. She'd earned her own keep, and paid Delray every week for his protection, just like all the other women did. She didn't get so much as one ounce of special treatment.

'Wow, look, Georgie, can you see the boats?' Running over towards the huge window that spanned the entire length of the apartment, Marnie pressed her face up against the cool glass and stared out into the dark night sky. Her eyes drinking in the twinkling lights of London that reflected on the river.

Georgie joined her.

'London looks beautiful like this doesn't it, Georgie?'

Both of them were mesmerised, standing side by side as they admired the breathtakingly stunning view of London, lit up in all its colourful glory. Georgie's eyes followed the spray of lights that twinkled all along the river's edge. The brightly lit buildings; the vast Lambeth Bridge; the boats dotted about on the Thames.

It was hard to believe that they were only a few minutes away from home. From their house in Brixton. This place felt like a million miles away. Like a lifetime away.

A whole new world; one that Georgie was petrified of.

She thought of her mother then. Standing in the bedroom doorway. Trevor's lifeless body at her feet, splayed out on the floor. The hammer embedded in his skull.

All that blood. That brain matter.

Georgie squeezed her eyes shut as if to blot the image from her mind, grateful when Marnie's voice broke her thoughts.

'Do you live here in this big house all by yourself, Delray?'

'Marnie. Don't be so nosey,' Georgie warned as she stood awkwardly in the middle of the room, feeling suddenly very out of her comfort zone.

'It's all right. She's just curious. Nothing wrong with being inquisitive,' Delray said as he went to the fridge and poured himself and the girls a glass of fresh orange juice.

'Sometimes my mate, Lenny, stays here, but he's gone away for a few days. I have a girlfriend though. Her name's Javine. She's in bed at the moment. She loves her beauty sleep. Maybe you girls can meet her tomorrow?'

Delray hadn't expected to have the girls here so soon. He'd thought he had a few more days yet, maybe even a week or so, if he went via the official route of getting access to them.

As it was, they were here almost of their own doing. It was a right touch. Now he had to pull his finger out if he had any hope of getting Javine to play ball: pull out all the stops tomorrow morning. Try to get the girl to come around to his way of thinking; hopefully, before the girls woke up. If this plan of his was going to work, he needed Javine back onside.

'Why don't you sit down, girls, make yourself at home,' Delray said as he placed a glass of orange juice down on the coffee table in front of them.

Georgie, glad of the distraction, led her sister over to the sofa, where they both sat down. Excited at her new surroundings, Marnie couldn't sit still. Spinning around on the chair, she was taking it all in.

'Woah! Your telly's as big as a cinema!' she said, running her hand across the smooth, soft leather sofa. She glanced up at the gigantic television and did a double take. 'Are you rich?'

She was positive that Delray was. She'd seen inside the fridge when he'd taken the orange juice out of it. The last time Marnie had seen that much food in one place had been when she'd gone to the supermarket.

'I wouldn't say rich, not yet, anyway, but I do all right.' Delray was being modest now. Georgie and Marnie were acting like this was a palace; compared to the shit tip that they'd lived in with their mother, Delray guessed that's exactly what this place must be like.

'What do you think, Georgie?' Delray asked. 'You like it?'

'Your place ain't none of my business.' Georgie shrugged.

Delray smiled.

The kid was the spit of Josie. All attitude and raised eyebrows.

Georgie wrinkled her nose. None of this impressed her, not really.

Expensive things, fancy decorations. Seeing how Delray lived only made her angrier.

Georgie had spent her life watching her mother scrimp and save for everything. Half the time, they hadn't even been able to afford a loaf of bread. As much as Georgie had always hated her mother working – all the men, the sex noises – she knew that her mother had had to do all those things. She'd had to support her and Marnie. What had Delray ever done for them? Other than come around to the house and take money off her mother every week. It should have been the other way round. If Delray really was Marnie's father, then he should have been supporting their mother. Not living here in this apartment like a king, while they had all struggled. It made sense now why her mother had hated Delray so much. The few times he'd brought them presents over the years, instead of being grateful for them, Josie had resented them, and rightly so.

'You okay?' Delray asked noting how pale she looked, her eyes watery.

Georgie nodded. The truth was, her head was spinning.

She couldn't believe that her mother had kept the truth from them both all of this time. She couldn't believe that all this time, all these years, Delray was Marnie's father all along. Lurking in the background, watching her sister; at least, from afar.

She was angry with her mother right now, but she hated Delray Anderton even more.

Georgie had her suspicions all along that she and Marnie didn't share the same father, but she also knew that they had both spent a lifetime fantasising about the day their dads finally came back to look for them. She'd spent so many years blaming her mum, assuming that their mother had been the one to scare her father off. Her job, or her mouth, or a combination of the two. There was always something. Georgie had imagined that her father would be someone rich and famous, and he'd come back because he realised what a mistake he'd made leaving his daughter behind. He'd say how he couldn't live without them. Even Josie. That he missed them all dreadfully.

What an idiot she'd been.

If Delray was Marnie's father, she didn't hold out much hope now for whoever had fathered her.

'Come on, let's get you two off to bed. It's gone one a.m.; you both must be knackered. 'We'll sort everything out properly tomorrow.' Leading the girls over to the bedroom at the opposite end of the apartment, Delray hoped that they'd have a lie in.

Opening the oak double doors, he stepped aside to let the girls walk in first.

'You girls are going to have to share, is that okay?' he said, guessing rightly that the huge queen-size bed would swamp the girls anyway.

'We always share a bed at home,' Marnie said quickly, her eyes flickering to Georgie as she prayed her sister wouldn't embarrass her and mention the amount of accidents that she sometimes had.

Georgie didn't say a word.

Instead, she just looked around the room, eyeing the beautiful decorated interior. The soft, comfy bed, lined with so many pillows that Georgie could barely see the headboard. Across the bottom of the bed was a huge grey fur throw.

It all looked so suddenly warm and inviting. All Georgie wanted to do right now was curl up and go to sleep. To escape from her living nightmare.

They'd been through hell and back the past few days.

'Here, new pyjamas.' He grinned as he grabbed a couple of his baggy T-shirts out of his wardrobe and threw them down on the bed.

Georgie sat down on the edge of the bed, waiting for Delray to leave so she and Marnie could get changed.

'Do you think we'll get in trouble when they notice that we're gone?'

Delray shrugged; he didn't seem too worried.

'How can you get in trouble? You ain't done nothing wrong. You shouldn't be in a children's home. First thing tomorrow morning, we'll call up your social worker and we'll get this shit sorted, okay? Let's face it, they ain't going to argue with me, are they?' Delray gave Georgie a small smile. 'I'm Marnie's dad.'

Georgie shrugged.

But he wasn't her dad, was he?

Still, they were here now, so they may as well make the most of it. Tonight they would get a good night's sleep. The first opportunity they got, though, she and Marnie were getting out of here.

CHAPTER FORTY-ONE

'You all right, babe?' Delray said as he drew back the bedroom curtains, and took in the spectacular view of Javine Turner's naked body sprawled out across the bed in all her glory.

There was no denying how stunning the girl was. It didn't matter how many times Delray fucked her, he still couldn't seem to get enough of her. It was just a shame that she had the personality of a soggy teabag and a brain to match.

He'd say one thing for the girl, though, Javine had been a tough one to break, and for once in his life Delray was pleased that the girl had a stronger spirit than he'd given her credit for.

Especially now.

'I've brought you some breakfast, Javine.'

Delray shot her his most angelic smile, enjoying the suspicious look that spread across Javine's face as she stared up at him.

Aware that he didn't have long before Georgie and Marnie woke up, Delray needed to work his magic – and fast. If his plan was to work out then he needed to get Javine back onside and out of the apartment this morning, pronto.

'Come on, then, sit yourself up. Don't be all shy. I've made you the works. Scrambled eggs, brown toast. And a lovely cold glass of orange juice to wash it all down with.'

Javine sat up obediently, pushing herself back against the headboard as she wondered what Delray was up to now. She didn't have the energy for another of the man's sick, twisted games. She eyed him warily as she waited for the punchline.

Instead, Delray just placed the tray down gently on the bed next to her, pretending that he didn't notice the girl flinch as his hand brushed against hers. He could see the way Javine was scanning the tray, wondering if this was some kind of a trick.

'Don't look so worried. It's breakfast, nothing more,' Delray said as if he could read the girl's mind. It was hilarious really, he thought. The way that with just a few words, a few actions, he could fuck with someone's head like this. He should do this more often. Play mind games. Hot one minute, freezing cold the next. It worked a treat, it seemed. 'I just thought you might be hungry.'

Javine nodded – hating herself for being so weak.

She wished that she was strong enough to refuse Delray's offer of food. That she was brave enough to launch the tray back at him, to tell him to shove it up his arse – sideways.

But she was so hungry that her stomach hurt.

She hadn't eaten since yesterday morning when Delray and Lenny had finally brought her in a sandwich. They'd teased her with it. They'd both taken great delight in tormenting her with the fact that she was starving as they made her perform for the privilege of eating it. They'd degraded her first. Taken it in turns on her then finally they had given her the food as her reward.

Delray remembered it too. He could see the fear in her eyes; reading her thoughts he knew that she thought he was going to repeat the previous day's torment.

Fear was good. It meant that he was still in control here.

He had to try to make this right now. Try to convince Javine that he had made the biggest mistake of his life by treating her the way that he had.

Resting his head in his hands now, as he sat on the edge of the bed, Delray's body started visibly shaking.

He was crying? She was sure of it.

Staring at the man in horror, Javine wondered what on earth was going on.

She didn't dare speak though.

Instead she stared down at the food in front of her; she sat in complete silence. Her mouth watering, but her body so frozen with fear that she couldn't move.

Delray spoke first.

'I'm so sorry, Javine.' Through his tears, his words were almost inaudible. Javine thought she'd misheard at first, but then he repeated himself. 'I'm sorry for everything, babe. I don't know what's got into me this past week. The way I've treated you; the things I've done to you. I fucked up…'

Javine bit her lip.

Fucked up? That's what he was calling it. Imprisoning her in his apartment. Raping her, humiliating her.

Still she held her tongue, too stunned to speak.

'You're a good girl, you know that? I think I've been around so many wronguns in my time that I just had you down as the same. I thought you were just using me for my money, for my name. I thought that you were just another bird out for what you could get. It was Lenny, Javine. He kept putting ideas in my head. Telling me all this bad shit about you. He'd given me some dodgy pills too. You know, just for the buzz. Only, the drugs fucked with my head 'en all. Made me even more paranoid. Made me start doubting everyone around me.'

Delray shook his head.

'Lenny's a cunt, Javine. I see that now. I don't know why but he took a real dislike to you. He tried to get in-between us. Tried to poison me against you, and the bastard succeeded, didn't he?'

Delray bit his hand now, as if stifling his emotions.

'Jesus, Javine, how could I have done what I did to you. You're the best thing that's ever happened to me. I'm a fucking fool.'

Delray looked at her. Staring into her big doe eyes. Even after spending a week locked away in here, her hair unwashed, her lips dry, chapped, she was still stunning-looking. He felt a stir in his loins as he looked at her, noting the rawness of how scared she was.

The combination turned him on.

'I know it means fuck all to you now, Javine, but I've thrown Lenny out. I packed his stuff up myself, personally, and made him leave.'

Javine stared at Delray wide-eyed. She didn't know what to say, what to think. Her head was all over the place, and she was still in doubt as to whether or not this was just another one of Delray's headfucks. For a second, she questioned his mental stability. Wondering if perhaps he was a little bit crazy. That would explain the sudden Jekyll and Hyde change in the man's personality. Why he'd gone from treating her worse than an animal to now acting like he'd had some kind of an epiphany.

Seeing the doubt in Javine's eyes, Delray knew that the girl still wasn't convinced, but that was okay, because he hadn't played his trump card yet.

Reaching out, he held her hand; he felt her stiffen at the feel of his touch.

Cautious, wary.

'I understand if you can't forgive me, Javine. God knows, I don't even think I can forgive myself for what I have done to you. I just wanted to say that I'm sorry. I need to make this right. Have your breakfast. I'll run you a shower before I drop you back off home, okay?'

Javine felt her heart lurch at his words.

Shaking her head, as if to un-jumble what she'd just heard, she held her breath for a few seconds before daring to speak.

'Home? You're going to let me leave?' She could hear the slither of hope in her voice as she waited for Delray to take back everything he'd just said, to laugh in her face.

Delray didn't do any of those things.

He simply sat there looking at her, his eyes sad, his body language like a man defeated.

'Yes. Now come on. Eat up.' Willing her to pick up her cutlery and eat the food that he'd brought.

He meant it?

Not wanting to antagonise him, Javine did what he wanted. Picking up her fork, she ate a mouthful of the scrambled egg. As hungry as she had been a minute ago, she couldn't eat at all now. Her mouth was dry; her throat felt tight, restricted.

She didn't have a clue what was going on.

Forcing the mouthful of food down into her stomach, she kept her eyes fixed on Delray as she tried to work out what his motive was.

'I want you to have something too.' Delray spoke softly, rubbing Javine's hair, stroking it down one side of her face. He was looking intently at her. Trying so hard to convince her that he was genuine. He was counting on her ignorance. Counting on her greed for this lifestyle.

'I understand if you don't want it, babe, but I just wanted to show you that I really mean it. I'm really sorry. I want to make things up to you.'

Delray pulled out the small red box from his pocket and placed it on the tray next to the plate of food.

Javine almost choked on her food then. Her heart was hammering.

She already knew what was inside.

She recognised the packaging.

'Go on, have a look,' Delray said, as he watched Javine open the box, her fingers trembling.

A huge sparkling engagement ring from Selfridges: the one she'd sent him a picture of whilst she'd been shopping.

He'd thought that Javine was a demanding, money-grabbing little bitch at the time, sending him endless demands as if she was some kind of rare commodity. Turns out, Javine had given Delray that extra carrot that he needed to dangle.

'Look, I don't expect you to give me another chance,' he said.

He put on the tears now. Squeezing out as many as he could, faking his upset.

His hand back on the ring box, snapping it shut. Ready to snatch it away. 'I'm such an idiot. I must be, 'eh? To lose a girl like you. 'Course you ain't going to want this now. What am I even thinking?' he said sadly.

Getting up from the bed, he held out his hand for Javine.

'Come here.'

Again, Javine did as she was told.

Delray led her out to the main lounge. To the large picture on the wall behind the bar.

Removing the print, he showed her the safe.

This was the bit that he thought was genius.

This was the bit that would seal the deal, Delray was sure.

If she didn't stay because she was naive enough to believe he had repented, he was sure she would when she realised what else there was to gain.

'This is how much I trust you, Javine; how much I want you to know I'm sorry. I'm the only one that knows the code for the safe. Not even Lenny has a clue. Here, you put this inside for me while you have think about what you want to do.'

Javine took the engagement box from Delray.

'Type in: 773482; type it in.'

Javine did as she was told, and the safe popped open. She looked at him nervously, wondering what to do next.

'Go on,' he said, encouraging her to open the door. 'Put the ring in there, and if you feel like you want it you know the code now, you can help yourself.'

Opening the safe door, Javine almost gasped out loud as she saw the piles of money inside. Stacks and stacks of the stuff, all aligned in neat little bundles. She placed the ring down and closed the door.

Delray could see it in Javine's face. Her mind was whirling; the cogs spinning rapidly in amongst the sawdust of the girl's brain.

He had her, he was sure of it.

She faltered.

Delray did seem different suddenly. Sincere.

What if it had been Lenny all along?

'Okay, I'll give you one more chance, Delray,' Javine said still warily. 'But I have conditions.'

'Anything you say, Javine. Anything,' he said, trying to hide his smile.

'I want my own room. Your room. You can move into that tiny box room, or Lenny's room.'

'You got it.' Delray nodded.

It wasn't much to ask in the scheme of things.

'And I want you to promise me that that bastard Lenny will never come anywhere near me ever again.'

'Consider it already done, babe. He's gone. I promise. You'll never have to see him again.'

Javine nodded. Glad that Delray had accepted her terms.

He stepped forward and kissed her gently on the forehead.

'Now you go and get that shower, babe. From here on out, you're my queen and I'm going to treat you as such. In fact, do you know what, you get yourself dressed, babe; I'm going to book you into that swanky beauty salon over in Marylebone. Treat you to a day of pampering, just as you deserve.'

Catching the small smile, Delray was pleased that Javine looked genuinely happy about that.

Watching as she walked from the room, Delray smiled to himself. Javine Turner was every bit the girl that he'd been hoping she'd be. After everything he had done to her, she was still going to stick around. That alone told him everything he needed to know about her. She was only here for one thing: his money.

A true whore through and through.

Well, for now, she'd have her uses but, when this was all done, Delray was going to see that Javine earned back every last penny he'd ever given her. Javine Turner thought she was being clever, but she still hadn't learnt her lesson and that made her the dumbest bitch of them all.

CHAPTER FORTY-TWO

'Shut the fuck up!' Ashleen Jacobs growled as she pulled the duvet up over her head to try to drown out the noise. Thoroughly pissed off at being woken up yet again by Javine's two mangy little mutts downstairs as they continued to bark the house down, Ashleen was close to losing her rag.

Glancing at the clock, she winced. It had gone midday. She'd slept in. The little ratbags would be starving by now; no wonder they were yapping.

Annoyed that she was going to have to get out of bed and take them both for a walk so that they could do their business, she knew what would be awaiting her: a kitchen floor covered in dog shit and puddles of piss, if the last few days were anything to go by.

Yanking back the bedcovers, Ashleen sat up and started pulling on her clothes. Delray had taken the complete piss out of her, lumping her with Javine's two flea bags like this. Ashleen wouldn't mind as much, but Delray hadn't even sorted her out any extra money for dog food. He'd just expected Ashleen to sort it all out. So far, he hadn't answered any of her text messages or calls either, and Ashleen knew when to leave well alone. If she pushed too hard, Delray would lose it with her.

Storming down the stairs to try to stop the dogs from making such a racket, Ashleen pushed open the kitchen door and stared in despair as the two little dogs ran at her, tails wagging to show their happiness that they had finally got her attention.

Though it seemed the dogs hadn't waited for her to get up before they'd eaten. They'd ripped out the entire contents of her bin: rubbish and packets strewn all over the kitchen floor. Covering her nose with her hand Ashleen tried to block out the putrid smell, but it had already hit her, causing acidic bile to rise in the back of her throat. Already suffering from the mother of all hangovers after going out last night, she was feeling queasy as it was. The last thing she needed was to have to clean all this up too. 'Jesus Christ. Dolce and Gabbana. What have you done?'

They'd eaten all the leftover curry that she'd scraped into the bin last night and half a punnet of mouldy grapes that she'd thrown away too.

By the looks of it, the food had played havoc with their stomachs as the two dogs had been shitting through the eye of a needle, proceeding to crap all over the kitchen floor. Ashleen grimaced at the trail of diarrhoea, her eyes following the dogs' pooey little footprints that they'd walked in a zig-zagged trail all around the kitchen floor.

'Oh my God, please tell me you haven't?' Screeching, Ashleen walked over towards the breakfast bar, and picked up the half-eaten shoe. Covered in dog saliva, she eyed the big jagged chunk missing from the leather.

'My Jimmy's! They cost me £600,' she cried. 'You horrible little bastards.'

Throwing the shoe back down on the floor, Ashleen fought the urge to cry.

'That is it!' she cried. 'You are going. I've had a-fucking-nuff!'

Picking up her phone, she dialled Delray's number. So annoyed now, that she no longer cared that she was pissing him off by calling him.

He was pissing her off by not answering, and these dogs were pissing her off by basically ruining her entire life.

She was surprised when Delray picked up.

Explaining that she couldn't look after the dogs any more, Ashleen couldn't hide her astonishment as Delray actually sounded fine about it. Happy almost.

He told her to bring the dogs straight over.

Shaking her head, confused, Ashleen wasn't going to argue.

Slipping her feet into her trainers, ignoring her pounding head, Ashleen grabbed the dog's leads. Shooting a fleeting glance at herself in the hallway mirror she didn't care that she looked like shit warmed up. All she cared about was getting rid of these mutts out of her house once and for all.

'Right, you two, move it.' Ashleen spoke through gritted teeth as the dogs jumped around excitedly and she led them out the front door.

At least outside Ashleen could breathe again. Taking a few long deep breaths, she couldn't shake her bad mood.

Reaching Brixton High Street she had half a mind to turn around and, instead of heading over to the Albert Embankment, she thought about taking the two little ratdogs down to the RSCPA and telling them that she'd found them wandering the streets. Make out they were strays.

That would teach the little bastards for eating her favourite shoes.

Instead she was going to hand deliver these little furballs personally to Delray, and have great pleasure in the knowledge that it would be Delray's plush apartment that they'd be tearing up. His floors they would be shitting all over. See how he liked it for a change.

Tugging at the dog's leads, Ashleen felt a little bit happier now. Once she'd dropped the dogs off, they'd no longer be her problem.

The quicker she ditched these two mutts, the quicker she could crawl home to her bed and deal with her hangover properly. This time in peace.

CHAPTER FORTY-THREE

Sitting at the manicure station at Beauty Within salon in Marylebone, Javine Turner watched in amazement as the beauty therapists almost fell over themselves to ensure that she was given five-star treatment.

She was Delray Anderton's girl. His fiancée.

They'd surrounded her now. The small group of beauticians all huddled around her, admiring the huge rock that adorned her engagement finger.

She could see the look in their eyes.

The envy, the jealousy.

The way they wondered how Javine had been able to bag herself someone as wealthy and notorious as Delray.

'Wow, that is one of the most beautiful rings I've ever seen. It must have cost your fiancée an absolute fortune.' Tilting Javine's finger so that the diamond sparkled under the manicure lamp, Trina Woods tried to hide the surprise in her voice.

Delray Anderton settling down? Marriage? Trina knew Delray. Better than most people around here did. The man wasn't the type to settle down and get married. He was a player. The man was known for having a different woman for every night of the week, and the only ones that ever stuck around were the ones he had working for him.

'I know; I'm so lucky, aren't I?' Javine said forcing a smile.

Trina smiled back. She wasn't sure about this Javine. She certainly looked the part. She was beautiful, of course, but that was standard with Delray's girls these days. Even dressed down, with no make-up, Javine looked like she could have stepped out from the pages of a high fashion magazine. Delray always went for that model-type look. There was just something about Javine's mannerisms that didn't fit the bill though, and Trina couldn't put her finger on exactly what it was. She didn't seem like the usual bimbo; maybe that was it.

But there was something else too.

Considering the girl had just bagged one of London's most sought-after, eligible bachelors, she wasn't exactly cartwheeling around the salon with excitement, like Trina would have expected a girl to do. In fact, come to think of it, she had barely even cracked a smile. Not a genuine one, at least.

Most of the girls that had been through these doors over the years had been nothing but airheads.

All of them had been exactly like Javine looks-wise, but full of big ideas about what their futures held. About how Delray was going to help them to change their lives and make some real money.

Most times, Trina had struggled to get her head around the mentality of them all. It baffled her how deluded these girls could be. I mean, come on, beauty therapists got a bad rep for being a bit thick and ditzy but these girls were in a class all on their own. It was as if they had fallen under some kind of spell. They all hung on to Delray's every word, and believed everything that the man told them. Trina didn't know how Delray did it, she really didn't, but whatever he was doing, he was clearly doing something right.

Javine, though, didn't seem to be under any spell. It was like there was something going on behind those dark mysterious eyes of hers.

She sat there sipping the champagne that Trina had poured her, and nodding and smiling in all the right places but, apart from that, the girl seemed so distracted she almost seemed stand-offish.

Trina wasn't getting anything out of this one today. It was a shame because not only did Trina like to hear what Delray's girls said about him – whether they adored him, and couldn't sing his praises high enough, or whether they told Trina how he'd mistreated them; how they asked her to help them get away – but Trina had been counting on her 'extra bonus' from Delray for reporting back to him what the girl said.

Javine wasn't saying anything; she seemed closed off.

Trina couldn't help but feel disappointed; she quite enjoyed being able to help Delray out if she could. He knew full well that discretion was Trina's middle name. The stories some of the girls had confided in her over the years, before they realised that Delray had her in his pocket. Unlike most beauty salons, whatever Trina heard inside of these four walls didn't go any further. Unless, of course, she was reporting back directly to Delray, in which case he always made sure that she was given an extra 'gift' for her loyalty to him.

He'd done right by Trina over the years. Supplying her with enough business over the years with all the girls he had on his books – and a little 'extra' revenue on top for her discretion –that Trina had managed to buy the salon outright.

It was early yet. Delray had Javine booked in for the full works today. Trina still had time to do a bit of digging.

'Well, Delray must be smitten with you!' Trina said, making small talk. She hoped that showering Javine with compliments might soften her up a bit. 'And I can see why, an'all. You're stunning. So, go on then, tell me. How did Delray propose?'

'Oh, you know, he cooked me a surprise meal. Three courses. Then just after dessert, he got down on one knee and asked me to marry him.'

'Wow, that sounds so romantic.' Trina eyed the girl. She could tell a well-rehearsed story when she heard one. For some unknown reason, Javine was lying.

For starters, Delray didn't cook, and for seconds the man didn't possess a single romantic bone in his body. Something was going on here, and Trina had a feeling that she might never get to the bottom of it either.

'Ahh, he must be a big softie deep down. He just keeps it hidden well,' she said, hoping the girl missed her sarcasm. 'Ahh, it's a shame he couldn't come in with you today; you could have both had a lovely full body massage in our double treatment room,' Trina said cautiously, digging to find out why she was spending her first official day as a fiancée on her tod when Mr Casanova had just proposed to the girl.

'Oh I know, he was gutted that he couldn't come in with me, but he just has so much work on right now. Someone's gotta pay the bills.' Javine smiled.

Trina was starting to get on her nerves.

The girl was asking far too many questions and, right now, Javine couldn't even be arsed with the pretence.

When Delray had told her that he was booking her in for a spa day, Javine had been looking forward to it purely because she needed a few hours away from the apartment, away from Delray. She needed to get her head straight.

'Well, he's got a very lavish wedding to pay out for now, hasn't he?' Trina continued to babble on, oblivious to Javine's mood. Then spotting Javine's champagne flute looking low she grabbed the bottle and topped it up. 'How about another chocolate, babe?'

'Oh no, I've got to watch my figure now.' Javine rolled her eyes up, and then said playfully: 'Bridezilla.'

The truth was, Javine couldn't stomach another single thing. Not even the champagne was taking the edge off her anxiety, which had rocketed this past week.

'Right, I'm going to go and set the room up ready for your massage. You sit back and relax. I bet you're floating on cloud nine, aren't you!'

Javine smiled once more, glad of some time on her own. She'd forced her smiles so much today that her jaw ached, but not half as much as her head.

Today had been a complete and utter mind fuck. Waking up to find Delray so apologetic for the way he'd treated her. Then the ring; his proposal. He was offering everything that she wanted. The plush apartment; the glamorous lifestyle.

Everything she'd ever dreamed of. Or, at least, so he said.

Javine didn't believe any of it – not for one single second.

Gulping back the rest of her champagne she prayed that the numbing effect of the alcohol would start kicking in soon. She thought about something her grandma used to say: 'The eyes are the window to the soul.' Javine had looked into Delray's eyes this week; she'd seen inside his soul and all that had stared back at her was a very dark place indeed.

She'd figured Trina out from the off. The girl was far too nosy. She was another one on Delray's payroll, Javine was certain of it.

For now, though, Javine was happy to play along. To feed the girl with nothing but nice things, making sure it all went back to Delray so the man was thrown completely off the scent.

Delray Anderton was still playing games with her, she was certain of that. What the man hadn't anticipated though, was that Javine was playing them right back. He could keep all his money. His fancy apartment. His extravagant gifts. After what

Delray and Lenny had put her through this week, there was only one thing that Javine wanted now, and that was revenge.

Delray had tried to break her.

Well, two could play at that game.

Stepping out of the salon, Javine took a deep breath of fresh air and smiled to herself.

It was amazing how a day of being pampered could make her feel like her old self again.

She felt like a million dollars. Her hair was tousled into long, voluminous curls, her nails shaped and coloured to perfection, and she'd even had her make-up airbrushed on.

Spotting Delray waiting for her, Javine sauntered over to the car. Opening the door, she slipped into the passenger seat.

'Fuck me, Javine, you look amazing, girl.' Delray grinned.

'Thank you. I so needed that. That Trina is lovely. Think she gave me way too much champers though; I emptied the bottle. God, I don't half feel tipsy,' Javine said, making out that her and Trina had got on like a house on fire.

Delray was lapping it up. That had been exactly what he'd been hoping to hear. Good old Trina; the girl was on the ball when it came to keeping him happy. She'd followed his instructions to a T.

'I've got another surprise waiting for you at home, babe!'

Unable to keep his hands off the girl, he leant over and gave Javine a long lingering kiss on the lips.

'Uh, uh!' Javine wagged her finger at him. 'I told you, it's all on my terms now. You still have a lot of making up to do.'

'Oh, don't you worry about that. I intend to, babe.'

Pulling up at the apartment a few minutes later, Delray ran around to the passenger side and opened the door for Javine, before leading her up to his apartment.

Holding out his hands as they finally reached the top floor and the lift doors opened, he encouraged her to step out first. Opening the front door of the apartment, he nodded at her to go inside.

'Go on then,' he said with a smile, letting Javine go first.

Unsure what to expect she raised her perfectly drawn eyebrows before stepping into the hallway.

Within seconds, two small dogs came bounding towards her.

'Dolce! Gabbana!' she shrieked with joy. The first genuine bit of happiness she'd felt in a long time at the sight of seeing her little babies jumping up and down with excitement, yapping loudly at the sight of their owner

'Oh my God, Delray. You got my dogs for me!'

Delray grinned.

'I can't believe it. Thank you so much!'

Javine knelt down on the floor and picked the dogs up. Hugging them tightly to her, she began crying with joy. She'd missed her little babies so much.

'Oh, I love you, Dolce and Gabbana. Did you miss your mummy-girl? I missed you too! Yes, I did.' Javine was kissing the two little doggies now. Rubbing their fur, she was overjoyed at how happy they seemed to see her. The feeling was definitely mutual.

'Thank you, Delray. I know how much of a sacrifice this is to you.' Standing up, Javine gave Delray a small kiss on the cheek to show her appreciation.

First the engagement ring, now the dogs.

Fucking hell, he really was pulling out all the stops.

'I meant what I said to you this morning, Javine. I want to show you how sorry I really am. How committed I am.' Shrugging modestly, Delray averted his eyes to the floor. His voice thick with emotion. 'I know it will take time for you to believe me.'

'I do believe you,' Javine said, holding on to the memories of the previous week. If she hadn't endured the hellish abuse from

Delray and his sidekick Lenny herself, she wouldn't have even believed it now.

Delray was acting so odd. The polar opposite of the man he'd been last week. She didn't have a clue what he was playing at, but he was definitely playing.

'There's something else too. Someone else I'd like you to meet. Two people, actually,' Delray said cryptically as he led Javine around the corner to where the two girls were sitting waiting on the couch. Just as he'd told them to before he'd rushed out to pick Javine up from the salon.

The girls looked nervous. Delray had told them that he wanted to surprise his new girlfriend by introducing them to her.

'Oh wow.' Javine was surprised all right. Staring at the two girls, a flicker of confusion spread across her face. She recognised the younger one. 'Aren't they Josie Parker's kids?' she asked. Curious as to what the two girls were doing in Delray's flat, and what they had to do with her.

'Yep. This is Georgie and Marnie.' Delray grinned as all three girls eyed each other warily.

'Only Marnie isn't just Josie's kid. She's mine too. Marnie is my daughter.'

CHAPTER FORTY-FOUR

'I've got to go out, babe.' Delray hugged Javine to him, breathing in her heady perfume.

She seemed a lot happier now she'd spent the day at Trina's salon, much more relaxed.

Trina had reported back to him too, letting him know that Javine seemed genuinely besotted with him; she hadn't bad-mouthed him once.

That was something, Delray thought. The girl was clearly intending to stick around.

Getting the dogs back here for her had been the icing on the cake. Personally, he couldn't fucking stand the stinky little bastards but, as long as they stayed the fuck away from his furniture, and didn't crap anywhere, then for now they could stay.

Fingers crossed it wouldn't be for too long anyway. Once Javine was dealt with, he'd be dealing with her little furballs too.

'You all right to keep an eye on the girls for me, babe? I got a couple of things I need to do tonight. You know, a bit of business. I wouldn't ask you, it's only, well, it's nice, isn't it – this? You, me and the girls. It's a bit like being a family.'

'I suppose.' Javine shrugged. She wasn't sure that she could cope with playing stepmum to a child that was only five years younger than she was herself.

She was still in shock to be honest. She and Josie Parker hated one another, and Javine had always wondered what type of a hold the woman had over Delray. She'd always wondered why Delray had kept the woman on. I mean, compared to most of the girls that worked for him, Josie was nothing but an old, fat has-been.

Now, though, it all made sense.

She was the mother of his kid.

Though what Delray had ever seen in the woman was beyond Javine's comprehension.

She wasn't really into kids, and playing mummies, but she could see that Delray was trying to include her and, for now, she figured, what harm could it do to go along with it all?

Though she was convinced the older child, Georgie, hated her guts.

Javine had been trying. Really, she had. Asking them both questions about their favourite TV programmes, and what food they liked to eat, but so far all she'd come up against was a wall of silence.

Marnie, remembering Javine from the little run-in that she'd had with the girl's mother in the shop a few weeks ago, had ignored her completely, and insisted on running around the apartment winding the dogs up as she screeched loudly and chased them and the older child. And Georgie, having clearly been filled in on the encounter, had done nothing but throw Javine filthy looks every five seconds.

The atmosphere in the apartment had been stony to say the least.

'I don't think they like me, Delray,' she said now honestly, her voice just a whisper; she didn't want the girls to overhear.

'Oh behave.' Delray laughed. 'Look at you. How could they not like you? Give them a chance, babe, they've been through so much the last few days. They just need a bit of time, yeah?'

Javine nodded in agreement. Maybe Delray was right. Of course the past few days must have affected them. Even she couldn't get her head around what Delray had told her. Josie had murdered one of her punters in cold blood. Bludgeoned the man to death with a hammer in front of both of the girls. She couldn't imagine what it would have been like to witness something so horrific. Javine had always known that something wasn't right with the woman, but murder?

'Tell you what, I've got just the idea. Why don't you do a makeover or something on Georgie? Do her nails and her hair, let her put some of your clobber on. She's almost as tall as you!' Delray said, trying to sound like this wasn't all pre-planned. 'She's the one you need to try to keep sweet. Marnie will warm to anyone.' Delray shrugged. 'At least it will give you something to do while I'm out. Tell you what, I'll sort out a sitter for tonight. When I get back me and you can go to Liberties; we'll get a couple of bottle of champers in to help us celebrate our engagement properly? Make it official.'

'That would be lovely.' Javine smiled, though she wasn't sure she was really up for going to the club with Delray just yet. But she knew she was going to have to just go along with it.

'Good.' Delray grinned. 'I can't just let you sit at home all night when you look this sexy. I wanna show you off.'

Javine couldn't help but smile at that.

'If you hear the phone or the intercom, don't answer it, okay? There's been some kids hanging around outside, making nuisances of themselves,' Delray lied. He hadn't bothered calling Children's Services about having the girls.

People would still be out looking for them. Delray couldn't chance anyone coming in and taking them away from him now. Not when he'd worked so hard on the deal that was on the table for him. By rights, here was the last place the Old Bill would probably look. There was no reason why the girls would be here; no one knew of their whereabouts and the very few people that did – Davey, Mandy, Mary Sheelan – had all been warned what would happen if anyone opened their mouths.

Grabbing his keys from the side, he planted a kiss on Javine's cheek.

'See you in a few hours, babe. Have fun, yeah!'

Javine smiled.

Fun? It wasn't the first word that sprang to her mind at the thought of spending the next couple of hours with a pair of stroppy kids that acted like they both hated her guts.

'Of course!' Javine said, determined to at least try.

How hard could babysitting possibly be?

'Do you fancy playing a game?' Javine said to Marnie. 'We can play I Spy, or Truth or Dare?'

Marnie shook her head, sulkily. 'I don't want to play games, I just wanna watch my programmes.' Moving her head to the side, Marnie looked deliberately past Javine so that she could see the TV screen again.

Javine sighed.

Well, at least she'd tried.

So far, Georgie and Marnie just weren't interested in anything that she suggested. She tried to remind herself what Delray had told her about the girls having gone through so much the past couple of days. About how she should give them a bit of time to settle in, to get their heads straight, but she just couldn't help thinking that they just didn't like her.

Georgie had barely spoken two words to her all evening. Every now and again, Javine had caught the child watching her. Looking at her curiously.

'Oh bugger.' Feeling her false eyelash coming loose over her right eye, Javine marched over to the mirror. The mass of thick black lashes had come loose. She tried to squeeze the line of fake lashes back, but they wouldn't stay in place now.

Grabbing her make-up bag, she drew a line of glue along the lash band before blowing on the adhesive to make it slightly tacky, then she stuck it back on to her own lashes.

'Voila,' she said to herself, pleased that they were back on again.

'What's that?'

'These?' Javine turned, surprised that not only had Georgie finally opened her mouth to talk, the girl was actually directing a question at her. 'They are fake lashes.'

Georgie eyed them curiously. Suddenly taking an interest in something.

'You stick them on to make your eyelashes look longer.' Javine fluttered her perfect lashes at Georgie as if to demonstrate.

'They look nice.'

Javine smiled. Then remembering what Delray had said about trying to bond with Georgie, trying to clear the air, she added, trying to keep her tone casual: 'You want me to put some on you?' She knew if she pushed it Georgie would just shrug her off. That was the beauty of communicating with a stroppy teenager, Javine wasn't far off one herself.

Georgie looked at the make-up bag, then back to Javine's beautifully made-up eyes, and nodded. She was bored anyway. Marnie was watching baby programmes and hogging the dogs.

'Tell you what. How about you let me give you a makeover?' Javine said, excited that Georgie was finally acknowledging her presence; she was determined to try to get through to the girl. Javine had no idea how long the girls would be sticking around, but as long as they were here, they may as well at least try to get on.

'Okay then.'

Javine beamed at that. Grabbing her make-up bag, she began lining up all her products before pulling out a chair at the dining table for Georgie to come and sit on.

She started with the girl's foundation.

'You've already got beautiful skin,' Javine said as she brushed the make-up evenly across Georgie's cheekbones. She blended it along the girl's jawline with a sponge.

'And your eyes are so pretty.'

'They're like my mum's,' Georgie said, her body suddenly tensing at the mention of her mother.

Aware of the sore subject, Javine didn't push the conversation. Instead she began drawing on a perfectly straight line of eyeliner across the top of each of Georgie's eyelids, before going through the same process with the fake lashes as she'd done to herself just minutes earlier.

Georgie waited patiently as Javine used pots and tubes of God knows what until finally she beamed.

'Okay, you want to look?'

Georgie nodded, unable to wait a second longer. She was dying to see the end result.

'Actually, hang on…' Javine giggled, eyeing Georgie's figure. The girl was tall and slim, apart from being flat-chested; Delray had been right again: Georgie's shape was very similar to hers.

'How about before you get to see yourself, we dress you up a bit too. You can borrow one of my dresses?'

'Okay,' Georgie agreed. Feeling a bit shy now, though she was really starting to get into the whole dress-up routine.

She actually felt like she was having fun for a change. Enjoying the rare opportunity of spending time on herself.

She was always keeping an eye on Marnie, or running errands for her mum. It felt good to do something for herself.

'What size shoe are you?'

'I'm a size four.'

'Damn, I'm a size five.' Then wrinkling her nose she added: 'That's okay; we'll stuff them with a bit of toilet paper in the toes. Come on.'

The two girls were enjoying themselves now.

Laughing and giggling as Javine pulled out some dresses for Georgie to try on, she was looking forward to seeing Delray's face when he got home.

Georgie Parker looked stunning.

Javine had done a blinding job.

CHAPTER FORTY-FIVE

Hearing the microwave ping, Mandy padded across her kitchen half-heartedly, and peeled the film lid off her ready meal, before giving it a stir and putting it back in for another few minutes.

This is what her life had come to, she thought sadly. A soggy, plastic bowl of slop on a Saturday night, all on her tod. She shook her head, feeling well and truly sorry for herself this evening, but she knew it was all her own doing. Davey was beyond pissed off with her, and rightly so. Even she didn't know what she'd been thinking to have called Delray Anderton of all people, but she'd just panicked. Seeing the girls turn up like that; seeing them both looking so lost and scared.

Josie wouldn't have wanted the girls to be abandoned to some horrible old children's home or fostered out to God Knows Who. She certainly wouldn't want the girls to be separated. Georgie and Marnie were all each other had now.

As much as Josie despised Delray most of the time for the way he treated her, she was certain that Josie would only want what was best for them both and, right now, Mandy thought that was Delray. She would have taken them in herself if she could have, but how would she have been able to help them? Here in her one-bedroom flat, she didn't have a pot to piss in for herself, let alone able to feed and care for two children.

She'd acted on impulse. Why should Delray Anderton wander around London like a dog with two bollocks, with money to burn, yet these two children had nothing?

As far as Mandy was concerned the man owed Josie big time, and it was about time he took responsibility for his child. He was Marnie's father after all.

She'd known about it for years, Josie had confided in her when she'd first found out she was pregnant. She'd told Mandy that she was going to have the baby, despite the fact that Delray wanted no part in its life, and that's exactly what her friend had done.

Tough as old boots and determined for her child, Josie had held her head up high, and brought up her children on her own, without a single penny from anyone else. The fact that she handed over half her money to Delray every week for his protection often made Mandy's blood boil but, like Josie always said, it was the only way she could guarantee a regular income and still have Delray's protection.

It was the only way she could survive.

It was about time he made an effort for Marnie. Georgie too, it was the least he could do for Josie.

When Mandy had rung him to tell him about the girls being at Davey's she never in her right mind thought that he'd agree to step up to the plate and do his bit for them. She'd half expected him to laugh down the phone at her, or tell her to sling her hook before hanging up.

She wished he had now, the amount of trouble it had caused her.

She'd been just as surprised as Davey had been when Delray had turned up at the pub fifteen minutes later.

Davey had been so angry that she hadn't discussed it with him, that she'd made the call behind his back. Delray Anderton was a fucking lunatic, a pimp, a criminal. How the hell would the girls have a better life? He was right, of course he was, but she'd realised that all too late. Now Davey was refusing to take her calls.

She'd been trying to ring him all day, desperate to explain, to talk to the man. But Davey was as stubborn as an ox.

She shouldn't have got involved; she should have just let Davey deal with them like he said he would. He would have rung Children's Services first thing in the morning and the girls would have been back in care. Instead, Delray had taken the kids himself, and Mandy had felt on edge ever since.

Police and Children's Services would be looking for the girls. There would be a search party for them. Two young runaways. Especially with the murder case splashed over the front of the newspapers. The media would be having a field day with it all. She was expecting a knock at her door any minute. People would start asking her questions. She would have to lie. She'd have to tell them that she didn't know anything, that she hadn't seen them. Delray had made that perfectly clear. He'd threatened Davey. Humiliated the man in front of them all. That was the hardest bit for Mandy to swallow. Davey didn't deserve that. He was a kind man, with good intentions. He'd only been trying to help. The whole thing was just one big mess.

Hearing the microwave ping once more, Mandy took the black plastic tray out and stared down at the congealed sauce and the nuked bits of pasta.

Her appetite had well and truly gone now. Lifting up the dustbin lid, she threw it inside. Pouring herself another glass of Chardonnay, she slumped down at the table and lit up a fag; she thought about Josie. Guilt flooding her.

She still couldn't process what had happened. Unable to get her head around the fact that her friend was in prison – for murder.

It was like, suddenly, the world had gone mad.

Josie. Her Josie.

Fuck me, the woman had a wicked temper on her at times, but murder?

Josie hadn't really been herself now for a while, but Mandy thought that she was getting better. She'd told her that she was clean, that she'd stopped the drugs. She was drunk, yes. They'd had a right skinful that night when they'd been out together, but not enough for Josie to hop in a taxi and then go home and turn into a hammer-wielding psycho.

That's what the newspapers were trying to paint her as.

CRACK ADDICT HAMMER HORROR ATTACK.

Nothing about the fact that Josie was clean now. They'd painted her out to be some kind of monster. Implying that a life of prostitution had made her hate all men. That she was mentally unstable.

Mandy hadn't been able to even read the damn thing. It was all lies. All such horrible lies. She knew her friend better than anyone, and she knew for certain that something must have happened that night to make Josie flip the way she had. Trevor must have done something to provoke the attack.

Georgie!

Mandy remembered then.

That night, when she and Josie had been out. Josie had been at it with that college student, and Mandy had taken a call from Georgie. Georgie had been crying, saying that Josie needed to get home. She couldn't remember what else had been said.

Mandy shook her head. Her memory vague. She'd had too much to drink too, and the call had been cut off. Something had happened though, something really bad, Mandy was certain of it. Shit! How could she have forgotten something so vital.

Taking a big glug of her wine to calm her nerves, she tried to recall exactly what Georgie had said, but she couldn't think straight. The past few days had all been such a blur.

She wished to God now that she'd gone home with Josie that night. That she'd made sure that Josie and the kids were all right. Instead she'd stayed out, hoping to get her leg-over with Davey.

Josie Parker a murderer? No chance. As fiery as her friend could be, she wasn't a cold-blooded murderer.

Mandy knew without a shadow of a doubt. She knew the woman better than anyone else.

The police had said that it was a domestic. They suspected that she'd consumed a lethal cocktail of drink and drugs and she had lost control. A psychotic episode, she'd overheard one officer say.

Mandy was certain that wasn't the case.

Josie was clean. The toxicology reports would show that, she was sure of it.

The doorbell chiming dragged Mandy away from her thoughts.

The police? Her heart started hammering as she rehearsed the story in her head. She hadn't seen Georgie and Marnie since they'd been taken into police custody. She didn't have a clue where either of them were. She didn't know anything.

Or maybe it was Davey?

Maybe he'd finally calmed down and had come around to talk to her.

Anxious now, she tucked her hair behind her ear, taking a quick glance at herself in the hallway mirror as she passed. She wished to God that she'd worn something else tonight to slob out in. She looked ridiculous. A lacy cerise pink camisole and a pair of ill-fitting tracksuit bottoms that had faded to a dirty grey colour; but she hadn't been expecting company and there was sod all she could do about it now.

Opening the front door, Mandy felt the disappointment ripple through her as Delray Anderton barged his way past her.

'Hello to you too,' she spat, shutting the door behind him and following him into her lounge.

'You don't need to come round here checking up on me, Delray. I told you I wouldn't say shit to anyone about the girls and I haven't. I swear.'

'I ain't checking up on you. I know you ain't stupid enough to go running your mouth any more than you already have.' Delray looked Mandy up and down then with distaste. 'Fuck me you look rough as arseholes. I take it you and lover boy had a tiff after I left?'

'He won't even answer my calls,' Mandy said sadly. Though why the fuck she was telling Delray this, she had no idea. The man didn't have an ounce of sympathy in his entire body.

'Maybe he's had a better offer?' Delray said sarcastically. Enjoying winding Mandy up.

Mandy tugged at her tatty camisole top, feeling self-conscious.

'Has something happened to the girls? Where are they?' she asked.

'I've left them with my bird for a bit, while I sort out a bit of business.'

Mandy eyed the man warily, knowing full well what was coming.

'I need a favour.'

She knew it.

'I need someone to sit with the kids for a bit. I've made plans tonight that I can't get out of… And seeing as you ain't doing jack shit tonight, by the looks of it, except for sitting on your arse staring at your telly, I figured you could give me a hand.'

Mandy pursed her lips. Delray wasn't asking her, he was telling her. She didn't have a say in the matter. It galled her that he'd only had the kids for one day, and already he was trying to palm the poor buggers off on her. She was so annoyed now. Delray was still a master at shirking his responsibilities. Still getting someone else to do the hard work for him. Mandy had a good mind to tell the man to sling his hook. Only, she knew that would go down like a tonne of shit. Besides, she couldn't stop thinking about Georgie and that phone call now.

The girl knew what had happened that night. She'd been there. She'd seen it.

If Mandy could get Georgie alone for bit, maybe she could get to the bottom of what really happened with Josie and Trevor.

It was a long shot, she knew; whatever did happen in that house had traumatised the girls deeply but, right now, Georgie didn't have too many people around her that she could trust. Maybe somehow talking to Mandy would help?

'I'll get changed,' she said.

Delray sneered. 'Thank God for that! It might be dark out there, but it ain't quite Halloween just yet. Don't want to be scaring any of the locals, do you? The state of you, like!'

Walking from the room, Mandy shook her head. Delray Anderton was pushing his luck, but as she was acutely aware, the bloke probably knew that already.

As the lift doors pinged open and Mandy followed Delray into the apartment, she couldn't help but be impressed by the look of the place.

Delray had done more than all right for himself. She'd heard the rumours. Delray had over twenty girls on his books now. All bringing him in a fortune. They weren't just your average girl either. They were like an army of supermodels. All of them working their arses off under his so-called protection in his brothels and his 'escort agency', which cost them just over half their wages for the privilege. And this is what all their money had paid for. Some of Mandy's money too. Not that she'd been raking in a fortune for some time now.

'Fuck me, this is like something out of a film,' she said, to no one in particular.

If Josie wasn't already inside for murder, she would have been once she saw this place and how Delray had been living it up while she'd been struggling her arse off in that dive of a flat of hers back at the estate.

'Javine?' Delray called out. He spotted Marnie on the sofa, cuddled up with the dogs as she watched the TV.

'Hello Auntie Mandy.' Marnie grinned, glad that Delray was back now. 'Javine and Georgie are in the bedroom doing makeovers. I'm sooooo bored.'

Marnie rolled her eyes dramatically.

'Right little character that one, ain't she. A tonic.' Delray chuckled. 'She must get it from me. Her sister ain't said a word. She's like her mother. An attitude problem and a gob on her to match.'

Mandy gave a small nod. She couldn't argue with that. That was Georgie all right.

'Javine?'

Delray sat on the arm of the chair, glaring at the pesky mutts as they started jumping all over him. Fighting the urge to kick the smelly fuckers across the room.

'Get down.' He shooed them off the couch; ignoring them, he grinned as Javine strutted out of the bedroom.

Ready for their night out, she'd changed into a tiny red dress. She looked sensational.

'You look stunning, babe.' Delray beamed. 'Where's Georgie?'

Javine looked at Delray, then Mandy and tried to suppress her excitement.

'We've been dressing up and doing make-up,' she said, sounding every bit the seventeen years that Delray now knew that she was. 'You wanna see?'

Humouring her, Delray nodded.

'Come on, Georgie. Come out!' Javine clapped her hands, full of enthusiasm as the bedroom door opened and Georgie stepped out.

Delray nearly fell off his chair.

Mandy's mouth was so wide open her jaw was almost touching her boobs, and that was no mean feat these days either seeing as they were almost down past her belly button.

Georgie was unrecognisable.

Javine had curled the girl's long dark hair and made her face up perfectly. Dark smokey eyes lined with thick dark lashes. A nude pink mouth.

She was wearing one of Javine's dresses too.

A hot pink mini-dress that shimmered under the lights.

'She looks at least twenty, doesn't she?' Javine said, admiring her handiwork.

Surprisingly, she and Georgie had really hit it off. They'd spent the past hour laughing and joking, and Javine found herself really liking the girl.

'Wow, you look beautiful.' Marnie smiled as she gazed over at her sister. 'Can I have my make-up done too, Javine?'

Javine nodded.

'We can do yours tomorrow, okay? I'm going out tonight.'

Marnie nodded, excited that tomorrow she was going to be made to look beautiful like her sister.

'What do you think?' Javine said, feeling almost proud of her creation. It had helped that Georgie was naturally very pretty anyway; all Javine had done was bring out all her best features.

'Georgie, you look beautiful.' Delray shook his head. 'You'd definitely get into the club; you and Javine, you look like best mates.'

Delray grinned, seeing the look that Georgie shot Javine. He knew it. Georgie had warmed to the girl. A bit of TLC and attention and Georgie was a pushover. Knowing full well he'd sown the seed now, Delray shrugged.

'Probably wouldn't be your thing though, Georgie. Dancing the night away with Javine, having a laugh. Nice little club it is too. They have a wicked DJ doing his set tonight...'

Javine narrowed her eyes at Delray's suggestion. Georgie might look older than her years, but she was twelve.

'She can't go to a nightclub. She's much too young,' Mandy said, butting in. Looking Javine up and down in distaste, determined to stay loyal to Josie. Mandy couldn't help but notice that the girl had dressed Georgie up just like her. A little clone. 'Your mother would do her nut if she could see the state of you, all done up like a dog's dinner,' she said, shaking her head.

Someone had to give the girl a dose of reality. She didn't look pretty; she looked cheap and tarty.

'Leave her here with me, Delray. She's too young for clubs.'

Hearing that her mother wouldn't approve of her going to the club was like a red flag to a bull to Georgie, still reeling from her mother's actions. For all of this mess. For Delray being Marnie's dad. Georgie could think of nothing she'd rather do than piss off her mother.

'I want to go,' she said.

Mandy shook her head, but Georgie wasn't asking her.

Instead, she looked at Delray.

'Can I?'

Delray tried to repress his smirk. Once again everything was falling into place with the minimum effort from him. It was as if it was meant to be.

'Oh I dunno, Georgie. I don't mind, but I said me and Javine would go out. We're celebrating our engagement.'

Mandy stared at Delray as if the bloke had had a lobotomy. Unsure if she'd just heard right. Delray was going to marry this bimbo? Fucking hell, as if the last few days couldn't have got any stranger.

'Javine?' Delray said, putting the pressure on her now. He knew she'd crumble; she wouldn't be able to help herself.

Javine looked at Georgie, apprehensive about the whole idea, but she knew she couldn't refuse the girl. Not after everything she'd been through. They'd been getting on so well this evening too. Georgie had really opened up to her. The kid was sweet. There was no harm in her having a bit of fun for one night after everything she'd been through; she deserved that, at least.

'It's fine with me. We'll have a right laugh,' Javine said, catching Georgie actually smiling.

'Though you better stick some more loo roll in those shoes, babe. If you think they are hard to walk in, you wait until I get you on that dance floor for a little boogie.'

CHAPTER FORTY-SIX

Georgie Parker was in her element.

She couldn't believe that she was in a nightclub.

If her mum found out she would do her nut. In a way that only made the whole night even better.

Looking around in awe she tried to take it all in.

The loud thumping music; the glare of all the colourful strobe lights. The fancy cocktails and podium dancers. The place was packed with people too. Everyone looking dolled up and glamorous and, thanks to Javine doing her hair and make-up and lending her some clothes, for once Georgie actually felt like she fitted in.

No one here was staring at her, or judging her. No one here knew anything about who she was or where she came from and, most importantly, no one cared. This was the kind of place that would have normally intimidated Georgie, especially being so young, but somehow, being here with Javine, Georgie didn't feel any of that.

She was far too busy having fun.

She felt part of something exciting for once. This whole new world that she hadn't even known was out there and she was determined to make the most of it.

Twirling around on the dance floor, she giggled as she showed Javine some of her finest dance moves. The ones that her and Marnie did some nights at home when the radio was on.

Javine tilted her head back and laughed as Georgie pranced about in front of her, doing her rendition of the running man and not caring who saw her. The girl was such a tonic. Javine hadn't laughed like this for ages. She was genuinely having fun. Tonight had been just what Georgie needed. A night off from everything and a chance to be herself again. From the little Georgie had told her about her mother this evening, Javine could tell that Georgie had a lot of anger towards the woman. For doing what she had done. For ruining all their lives.

Javine knew exactly how Georgie felt. She had felt the same about her own mother. She'd been through similar: let down in the worst possible way by the one person who she had loved and trusted. Javine was feeling protective of the young girl, and she could tell that Georgie had taken a genuine liking to her. Who'd have thought after their steely introduction that they would have become such good friends?

'Ahh I think I'm going to go and sit down for a bit; I feel a bit funny,' Georgie said, hoping that Javine would come with her. The idea of going back to the VIP booth and sitting with Delray and his frumpy old business associates didn't really appeal to her. She'd spent most of the night on the dance floor for that very reason.

'I ain't surprised that you need to sit down, you've probably knackered yourself with those moves.' Javine grinned; then seeing Georgie looking a bit peaky, she added: 'Are you okay, babe? You look a little off colour.'

Georgie nodded, not wanting to admit that she was starting to feel light-headed, dizzy; she didn't want to tell Javine in case she came across like a silly little kid. She was just going to have to front it out. Have a seat for a few minutes and a drink of her lemonade. Like Javine had said, she'd probably knackered herself out.

'You go and sit down, babe. I'm just going to go and have a quick wee, then I'll go and grab you a glass of water, okay,' Javine said, not convinced that Georgie really was okay.

The girl had gone very pale all of a sudden.

Making her way back to the table, there was no sign of Delray now and most of the other men had moved away from the booth too – standing in clusters around the VIP bar, or they'd gone off to the dance floor, or outside for a cigarette.

Sitting down at the table, Georgie took a sip of her lemonade. It had been sitting there for a while now and gone flat. Georgie could taste a strange bitterness to it.

It was alcohol, she realised. Delray had bought it for her; she'd been drinking it all night. He was letting her drink? That must be why she felt a bit queasy. The alcohol had gone to her head. She wasn't feeling sick; she was feeling drunk.

Plonking the glass back down on the table, she nearly missed and dropped it over the edge. She could barely see straight. She felt like she was having a panic attack. The club felt suddenly claustrophobic.

Scanning across the dance floor, through the hordes of people standing around in groups, draped over chairs, she looked for Javine. She wanted to go home. The music blaring loud; the base thudding through her. She suddenly felt like she might throw up.

'How are you doing tonight?' Georgie looked up to see the older man from earlier. His strong Middle Eastern accent making him almost hard to understand.

She knew he was one of Delray's contacts.

The one that had been watching her all night.

She'd told Javine that he'd been making her feel funny, creeping her out, and Javine had agreed with her and told her to make sure she stayed away from him.

Only, now he was here, sitting beside her in the booth, and Georgie felt too nauseous to go anywhere.

All she could do was pray that Javine hurried up so that she wouldn't be stuck with the man for too long, but looking around the club, Javine was nowhere to be seen.

'Can I get you another drink?' the man said, moving in closer, resting his hand on Georgie's thigh.

Georgie froze.

She could feel his fingers caressing her skin; she could see how intensely he was looking at her.

But she couldn't move.

'Have you seen Delray?' Georgie said, hoping the mention of her being here with Delray would be warning enough.

The man shook his head.

'You look like you've had too much alcohol,' he said. 'I think you need some fresh air.'

'I'm fine,' she said. Though she was feeling worse now.

'Let me take you to Delray. Maybe he needs to take you home?'

Georgie nodded.

Allowing the man to put his arm around her shoulder as he guided her through the thick flurry of people, Georgie felt like she was floating.

The noise, the heat, the drink. It was all too much for her.

She could barely walk straight. Barely speak.

She just wanted to get back to the apartment and see her sister.

She wanted to go to sleep.

'Are we going outside?' Georgie asked as she saw the man nod his head at the club's bouncers. He made some kind of comment about young girls who couldn't hold their drink.

'Is that where Delray is?'

The man didn't answer her question, but instead he just told her to watch her step as he led her out the main doors.

The cold air instantly hit Georgie once they were outside. It intensified how drunk she felt.

She was trying to keep her head up, to keep her focus but she was feeling really odd now. Her head suddenly too heavy for her shoulders. Watery bile in the back of her throat.

Her feet scraped against the uneven gravel beneath her as she walked, struggling to keep her balance. The man pulled her in tighter. Trying to keep her upright.

They were making their way towards a car at the back of a car park.

A fancy-looking black Mercedes.

Maybe Delray was in there?

Georgie could feel the man put his hand over the top of her head. He helped her duck down as he guided her carefully into the back of the Mercedes, before clambering in beside her.

It was nice and warm inside, but the smell of the leather interior mixed with the heady vanilla aroma of the car air freshener made Georgie feel even worse.

Trying for the door handle, she needed to get out. She needed some air.

But the doors were locked now.

Yanking at the handles, they wouldn't budge.

She was trapped here, alone, with this man.

That's when she realised they'd never been looking for Delray at all.

Pushing her way through the people standing around the bar, Javine asked the bartender for a glass of water, before turning back and looking out across the other side of the club to the booth they'd all been sitting in earlier.

Smiling, she could see Georgie sitting waiting for her. Sipping her lemonade, looking anxious as she waited for Javine to join her.

Javine really liked the kid. She was a nice girl; way too young and innocent to be in a place like this though.

Still, she guessed that was Delray's business.

She was just glad that she was here to keep an eye on her. Especially seeing as Delray was typically nowhere to be seen. Javine recognised a few faces that were standing behind where Georgie was sitting at the VIP bar: the rowdy group of Delray's friends that had been sitting with them earlier.

Javine eyed one of the older men in the group. A Middle Eastern man by the name of Hamza Nagi.

She didn't know what the score was with him, but she knew that Delray was practically falling over himself tonight in order to please the man. Plying Hamza and his men with an endless supply of Cristal jeroboams, the men had been like leeches, drinking the stuff like it was water.

Javine had taken an instant dislike to Hamza.

There was something about the man.

Georgie had noticed it too. She'd said how the man had kept staring at her, how he made her feel uncomfortable. To be fair, he wasn't the only man looking at Georgie so lustfully.

The girl had got herself an awful lot of male attention tonight.

She looked sexy, and the fact that she was clearly underage hadn't seemed to put the men off. In fact, Javine thought sadly, it had only added to Georgie's appeal.

Seeing Hamza walking over to where Georgie was sitting, Javine grabbed the glass ready to go back to her rescue, and save her from having to endure a conversation with the old perv.

Turning, she spotted Delray.

He was laughing and joking with some man next to him.

Someone familiar, Javine realised, as the man turned just enough that Javine could recognise his face.

It was Lenny.

Deep in a conversation together, Delray was smiling and talking animatedly. Tapping his friend on the arm, they certainly didn't look like two people who had recently fallen out. In fact, they looked like the best of friends.

Squeezing in behind a large group of men standing next to them, Javine kept her face to the bar so that if she was seen she could pretend she was waiting to be served. She edged a little closer so that she could make out what they were saying over the rest of the voices and music around her.

'You were right, Len, she was hanging off my every word.' Delray was laughing. 'Lapping it up.'

They were talking about her. She knew it.

'Wait till it dawns on her that she's fallen for it for a second time. Silly bint.'

Lenny laughed and handed Delray an envelope.

'Ashleen couldn't find Javine's passport so we just got both of the girls new ones made up. They're quality copies, Delray. They look spot on.'

Delray nodded; looking pleased that tonight was all coming together without a hitch.

'There's a couple of Mercs parked out the back in the car park,' he said. 'We'll give the girls a few more drinks then we'll make our way out there. Tell them that we're going to an after-party or something.' He put the documents into the inside pocket of his jacket. 'Then we'll just wave our friend Hamza off. By the time the girls realise that there ain't no after-party and that we've fucked off, there'll be jack shit they can do about it. They'll be Hamza and his men's problems then.'

Javine couldn't believe what she was hearing.

Delray was talking about her and Georgie. He was planning on leaving them both with Hamza? He'd had fake passports made up specially?

She felt physically sick now, stunned.

Javine had been playing the long game, biding her time; she'd been waiting for her perfect opportunity to get her revenge on him. Only, it seemed that her time had run out.

He'd been setting her up. Even tonight, suggesting the makeover for Georgie. He'd manipulated them into thinking it had been their idea. When this had been Delray's plan all along.

He'd set her up. Set Georgie up.

They were both in real danger.

She needed to get Georgie, and they both needed to get the fuck out of here.

Turning back to the booth, Javine couldn't see Georgie. The seat she'd been sitting in was empty. Javine scanned the faces nearby. Hamza wasn't there either. She looked around the club, frantic now. The main bar; the dance floor.

Georgie wasn't here.

The car park?

She had an awful feeling in the pit of her stomach that Georgie was in danger.

She just prayed that she was somehow wrong.

Fearing the worst, Javine kicked off her shoes and made her way to the club's main stairs. Running as fast as she could.

CHAPTER FORTY-SEVEN

The man was sitting so close to her that it felt like he was almost on top of her, the huge bulk of him making her feel fenced in, claustrophobic.

Georgie was suddenly feeling very frightened of that fact they were alone out here. No one knew where she was. No one gave two shits.

She felt stupid. Stupid and scared.

'It's okay, Georgie,' Hamza said, taking no time in getting himself acquainted with the girl. He stroked her thighs with his rough, calloused hands, as she tried to move away from him.

'I thought we could just have a little fun tonight. You'd like to have some fun, right?'

Georgie was looking around the car, trying not to make it obvious she was wondering if she could make it into the front seat, if maybe she could try to get out of one of those doors. Or perhaps a window, even.

But she knew it was pointless.

Hamza had the keys. He'd locked them both in. There was no escaping.

'How old are you, Georgie?'

'I'm twelve,' she said, her voice suddenly sounding even younger.

The man smiled. Closing his eyes and taking a deep breath as if he was savouring her words, like music to his ears.

'Delray will be looking for me,' Georgie said, hoping the tactic of mentioning Delray's name would be enough to deter him from trying to hurt her.

It wasn't.

Mirthlessly, the man just laughed. Shaking his head. He said he couldn't help but admire the young girl's spirit.

'Delray won't be looking for you,' he said with certainty.

Georgie nodded. 'He will be; he'll be looking for me. You better let me out. He'll get mad.'

'He's not going to help you, darling. Trust me. He was the one that gave you to me.'

The man was hurting her now. Kneading at her skin roughly with his hands, pinching her flesh between his fingers.

His hand scooping beneath the hem of her dress, as he tried to push it up higher.

Georgie yanked it down.

'Delray said you were feisty.' He grinned.

Smiling, surprised at the young girl's strength, her fight only added to his fun. He wasn't going to let her lack of enthusiasm deter him. In fact he quiet liked a bit of rough and tumble every now and again. It made a nice change from the obedient little bitches whose services he normally hired at the weekends.

Tugging at the material once more Hamza tried to yank the dress up over Georgie's head; only, Georgie was using all her strength to tug it back down again.

She felt exposed, frightened, as he tried to move on top of her. His fat sweaty body in-between her legs, trying to force them apart.

Georgie refused to let him touch her, to hurt her.

He was too strong for her though. With the added advantage that he was completely sober.

She didn't stand a chance.

He was on top of her now. Pinning her body down to the back seat.

Georgie couldn't move to get the man off of her.

She could barely squirm.

'That's it,' he said, practically salivating over the child beneath him as she finally lay still. 'Play nice, Georgie. I only want to have a look at you; I'm not going to hurt you.'

He was tugging at her dress again. Pulling it up, exposing her body.

The image of Shaun and what he'd done to her flashed in her mind. She wasn't ever going to allow that to happen to her again. Georgie started to scream. Projecting her voice as loud as she could, she prayed that someone would hear her cries.

The man brought his hand down. Determined to silence the child, to cover her mouth.

Just as Georgie had hoped he would.

This was her only chance.

Latching on to the man's plump sweaty hands, Georgie sunk her teeth firmly into his skin. Wildly now, she shook her head, making sure that her bite was having maximum impact as she tore at his flesh. She could taste blood, could feel a chunk of the man's flesh coming away in her mouth.

The man was screaming. Throwing himself back wildly, grabbing at his injured hand as he tried to calm himself, as the pain tore through him.

Georgie took her chance and made a grab for the key fob.

Reaching for the door handle, she managed to wriggle her way out from underneath Hamza and out of the car. Out on to the cold wet ground of the car park.

Scrambling to her feet, ready to run, the man leapt out from the back of the car and grabbed at her leg, causing her to fall back down on to the ground.

'You vicious little bitch.'

He pulled her back into the car, forcefully; angry that the girl had bitten him.

Georgie struggled with everything that she had, but the man was just too strong for her. She couldn't escape him. She couldn't get away.

He had her. He was going to hurt her.

A noise from behind her caught her off guard. It caught the man off guard too. The sound of a glass smashing against something hard. Shards of glass raining down all around her. A cold, icy spray.

Hamza slumped forwards, unconscious. Blood pouring out of the cut on his head.

Georgie looked up and saw Javine standing there, the remnants of a champagne bottle that she'd picked up from the holder in the back of the car in her hand. Blood was trickling down her wrist. Georgie went to say something, but Javine silenced her.

'We don't have time to talk. We need to leave. *Now.*' Grabbing Georgie by the hand, she pulled her up on to her feet. 'Come on, Georgie.'

The urgency in Javine's words told Georgie all she needed to know. They weren't out of trouble yet. But she didn't understand why. The man was out cold. He couldn't hurt her.

Javine had saved her.

But Javine didn't seem too convinced that she had. Pulling at the younger girl's shoes, Javine yanked them from Georgie's feet.

'We're going to have to run, Georgie. We need to get the fuck out of here. We need to get Marnie away from Delray's right now. You're not safe.'

CHAPTER FORTY-EIGHT

'Good evening, Miss.'

Ignoring the concierge as she ran past the apartment's front desk, Javine Turner frantically pressed the button next to the silver metal doors. Staring up at the numbers she willed the lift to hurry the hell up.

'Come on,' she said, as the doors finally opened and she pulled Georgie into the lift alongside her, wrapping her arm around the girl as they made their way up to the top floor.

'Is he dead?'

Javine shook her head regretfully.

It was the first thing that Georgie had said to her since they'd run away from the club.

Javine had knocked Hamza out, he had a nasty gash on his head too, but the man had still been breathing when they left. Unfortunately.

'We didn't do anything bad, Georgie. It was self-defence. What that man tried to do to you was wrong, really wrong. You're going to be okay now. We just need to get your sister and get out of here.' Javine knew that they wouldn't have long before Delray noticed that they were missing, or one of Hamza's men found him out in the car park.

Once they put two and two together, this would be the first place they looked for them.

Delray on his own was bad enough, but Hamza's men would be out for blood.

She needed to warn Mandy, and to get Georgie and Marnie the fuck out of here, pronto.

They didn't have long. Maybe ten minutes, if they were lucky.

Javine still couldn't believe what had almost happened tonight. What Delray had been planning. The idea of what that fucking pervert had almost done to Georgie, of what he was intending to do with them both, sickened Javine to her core. These poor, traumatised kids had already been through so much. They'd trusted Delray and, all the while, he'd been planning to do something so despicable that even Javine couldn't get her head around it.

'Quick, come on.' Reaching the top floor, Javine led Georgie out of the lift, bashing her fists against the apartment door as hard as she could.

'Mandy, open up. It's me, Javine!'

'All right, all right!'

Mandy had barely had time to prise her arse off the sofa and Javine was already hammering the door down. 'Keep your hair on. You're going to break the bloody thing down in a minute. Have you not heard of having a bit of patience?' Mandy scolded as she flung the door open and stepped aside, wondering what was so urgent that little miss fancy pants couldn't wait a few minutes for her to open the door, like any normal person.

'Me and Marnie were just snuggling up to watch *The Wizard of*— Oh My God! What's happened?' Mandy said stopping dead in her tracks as she took in the state Georgie was in.

The girl had left here a couple of hours ago looking like a supermodel. Now, her dress was all torn, and she had smudges of black mascara streaked across her face. She'd clearly been crying.

'Have you been in a fight?' Mandy asked, confused to see Georgie in such a bad way. She searched behind the two girls and realised they were on their own.

Seeing Georgie standing in the doorway crying, Marnie ran to her sister, wrapping her arms around her. She hated to see her sister crying.

'It's okay, Georgie. I'll mind you, please don't cry.'

Javine looked at the two sisters with sadness. Shaking her head once more. This was all such a mess.

'Where's Delray? Why have you two come back on your own? What's happened?'

'I haven't got time to explain, Mandy. Just get Marnie. We're leaving,' Javine said, pushing her way past her.

'What do you mean "we're leaving"?' Mandy said, watching the girl as she rushed about the place, grabbing some bags from the cloakroom and shoving items of clothing inside.

'I need to get something for the girls to wear,' Javine said, running into the bedroom, and pulling open one of the wardrobe doors.

Coming back into the room, she slung a cardigan over to Mandy.

'Put this around Georgie. She's freezing. It's probably a bit of shock.'

Mandy did as she was told. Then, taking the other jumper Javine had left on the sofa, she put it on Marnie.

'Trust me when I say that we need to get the fuck out of here, and fast. The girls aren't safe here.'

Sensing Javine's urgency, Mandy ushered the girls towards the door.

She didn't have a clue what the hell had gone on tonight, but she knew that it must be something really bad.

Especially if Delray was behind it all.

'Marnie. I'm going to need you to mind the dogs for me, okay?' Javine said.

Marnie nodded at Javine, only happy to help. Javine's little dogs were her two new favourite animals. She watched as Javine scooped them both up and placed them inside the holdall before looping the strap over Marnie's shoulder tightly.

'You got them?'

Marnie nodded, holding the bag to her for dear life.

'Right, are we ready?' Mandy said, putting her arms around the girls as she led them out into the main hallway and pressed the lift button.

'Hold on, I'll be two minutes.' Grabbing the last holdall, Javine ran back into Delray's office.

Remembering the money.

It had all been part of his little mind games: showing her the safe, telling her that he trusted her. He must have thought she was really thick to fall for his bullshit. Javine hadn't believed a word of it. She knew now that Delray didn't give two fucks about her. Why would he? He didn't even care about his own blood. The only thing that Delray cared about were material things. This apartment, his fancy clothes, his car.

Money.

The only way she'd ever come close to hurting him would be to hit him where it really hurt. Right in his pocket.

After tonight she was going to have to get as far away from here as possible. He'd kill her for scuppering his plans. For wrecking his big 'deal'.

Well, fuck him. The man owed her big time.

Keying in the code, Javine's heart started to pound as she heard the loud beep, then the safe's door sprang open.

Opening the holdall, she wasted no time, swiping the piles of money straight inside with one swift motion.

Her fingers touched something hard and cold at the back. She leant her arm back inside, standing on her tip-toes so that she could reach it.

'Javine. Come on.'

Bingo, she got it.

Looking down, Javine held Delray's gun tightly in her hand. It wouldn't hurt to have an extra bit of security she figured, as she placed it inside her coat pocket.

Just about to leave, she remembered one more thing.

Her engagement ring.

Twisting it off her finger, she slung it inside the safe. Delray Anderton could take it back. She was taking his gun and his money, but she wouldn't be taking the ring. It meant nothing to her. Nothing to him. Besides, at least when he did see that she'd cleared him out, he couldn't really claim she took everything.

Not such a money-grabber after all, hey?!

Javine ran now. Out to where Mandy and the kids were standing by the lift, waiting for her…

Just as the lift door sprung open and Delray Anderton stepped out in front of them all.

'And where the fuck do you all think you're running off to in such a hurry?' Delray said stepping into the hallway, a thunderous look on his face as he stared at Javine and Mandy. Incredulous that these two bitches thought they could just do a runner.

Delray eyed the blood that had splattered all down Javine's legs, and he shook his head despondently.

'You do know that you're a fucking dead girl walking now, Javine, don't you?' he sneered.

He'd already seen the state of Hamza Nagi. The bloke had been properly fucked up. This divvy bitch in front of him had beaten the man around the head with a bottle of his own finest champagne and left him to bleed out on the floor of the club's car park. Hamza was on his way to see a private doctor as they spoke. He was bleeding heavily, but he'd live. Unlike Javine, when the man eventually got hold of her. Delray hadn't been able to apologise enough. He'd offered to find Javine himself and personally deliver the girl to him. All fees waived, of course.

Only by the looks of it, Javine had no intention of sticking around. The brain-dead cow didn't realise that she wouldn't be going anywhere. She'd well and truly signed her fate now.

Delray was beyond angry.

Up until now, Delray had executed his deal with Hamza Nagi to perfect precision. Tonight had been set to be what Delray had only hoped would be the first of many.

Javine had chosen to fuck it all for him, in epic proportions.

'Ohh, Javine, Javine. You have no idea, do you?' he sneered. 'If you think me and Lenny were ruthless cunts, you haven't seen anything yet. Hamza Nagi is a fucking lunatic. The man gets off on torturing birds like you, even more so seeing as you almost caved his fucking head in.'

Delray looked at Georgie then.

The girl looked a mess. Her hair all matted against her scalp. Her make-up all smudged.

He screwed his mouth up.

He'd guessed the score already.

Hamza Nagi had been greedy tonight. That had been the real flaw in Delray's plan. Hamza had taken Georgie before the deal had been properly sealed. There was a code of procedure that should have been followed. Handshakes that should have been made on the official handover of 'the goods'.

'Turns out you ain't so much like your mum as I first thought,' Delray said nastily. By the state of her, the kid must have put up a good fight. He knew that.

Georgie didn't speak. She couldn't. Biting her lip, she fought back her tears.

All she could feel was a white hot rage burning inside of her.

'We don't like you. You're horrible,' Marnie said, picking up the tension around her, the fact that Delray was being mean to her sister.

Delray laughed.

'Well that, Marnie, to you especially, is tough shit.'

Bored of the melodramatics, Delray needed to get a move on. Hamza's men were waiting. Tonight could still be salvaged.

There was unfinished business.

'Get her back in the apartment now and stay put until I say so, do you hear me?' Pointing at Marnie, Delray instructed Mandy to move.

Then he looked at Javine and Georgie.

'You two are coming with me. Get your arses in gear.'

'Delray, please. They're just kids. Leave them be,' Mandy said, knowing that *leaving them be* was no longer an option. It had gone way beyond that now.

She felt genuinely scared for the girls. They were in real danger. They all were. There would be no coming back from this tonight.

In all her years, Mandy had seen many sides of Delray, but this was far scarier than anything she'd encountered.

Delray was unhinged.

'I said, fucking move!' Bellowing now, Delray marched towards Mandy and grabbed a chunk of her hair. Dragging her along the corridor, ignoring her screams of pain, he shoved her inside the doorway of the apartment.

'You,' he said looking at Marnie. 'Move it too!'

Holding the bag with the two dogs in it, still petrified, Marnie ran past Delray seeking comfort in her Auntie Mandy.

'Right, you two. Let's go.' Shouting his orders, Delray grabbed hold of Georgie by the arm and led her into the lift. 'Mr Nagi is waiting. You've both got some serious making-up to do.'

'We're not going anywhere,' Javine said, her voice resolute.

'You what?' Delray turned to laugh at the girl's delusional choice of words – only to be stopped in his tracks.

Javine was standing in front of him, pointing a gun directly at him.

His gun, he realised.

The bitch had been in his safe.

'Oh, have a fucking laugh.' He sneered, hoping the girl was just calling his bluff. The resolute look on her face told him otherwise. 'Calm down, Javine. Let's not get fucking hasty,' Delray said, reading the look on Javine's face. The anger that flashed in her eyes. There was no doubt in Delray's mind that the girl would shoot him. She was more than capable of causing murders this one; he'd seen the state she'd made of Hamza.

'Let go of her,' Javine said, keeping her arm steady. Her finger hovering over the trigger, she indicated to Georgie to move away from the man.

Delray did as he was told, and held his hands up, hoping to buy himself some extra time.

'All right, Javine, for fuck's sake. Put the gun down, yeah. Before you do something you really regret.'

'Regret?' Javine spat. 'I'll tell you about regret, shall I?'

'Mandy, take the girls downstairs. Wait for me, okay,' Javine said, her eyes not once leaving Delray's.

Mandy nodded, feeling bad for fleeing at the first opportunity, but her only priority was the two girls. Mandy needed to get them out of here to make sure they were safe.

As the doors opened, Mandy ushered the girls into the lift, then she looked at Javine, her conscience eating her up.

Javine might be a stuck-up little cow, but she wasn't much more than a kid herself. Gun or no gun, she was no match for Delray. One wrong move, one slip and Delray would annihilate her for doing all of this tonight. Mandy couldn't just leave her.

'Are you coming, Javine?'

Javine shook her head. Resolute.

'I'll meet you downstairs.'

As the lift doors closed, Mandy nodded silently, praying that Javine knew what she was doing.

'Javine this is stupid,' Delray said. He was trying to talk the girl down, but going by the determined look on her face he knew that wasn't going to be an easy task.

'There's no need for all this bullshit. It's just got out of hand. How about we cut a deal? How about I let you leave, huh? I'll tell Hamza that you weren't here, that you must have got away. He'll be pissed, but I'm sure he'll get over it eventually,' Delray said, hoping that he could appeal to Javine's softer side.

He just needed her to lower the gun.

Just lose her focus for a few seconds and then he would sort this shit out once and for all.

Only, Javine didn't look like she was about to lose focus anytime soon.

'It's win-win. I tell him you got away, and that way you get to leave and I get to not have one of my own bullets lodged in my skull.'

Javine shook her head again. 'I don't want you to tell him that I got away.'

'Why not?' Delray raised his eyebrows, thinking he must be missing something. He was giving her a get-out-of-jail card here, yet Javine didn't seem to want it.

'Because I want to stay here and kill you, that's why,' she said.

He could see she meant it too. Every word of it.

Aware of everything he'd done to the girl, his plans for her tonight. There wasn't any getting out of this. Unless he could get the gun off her.

'You tried to destroy me, Delray. But you didn't do it. You couldn't do it,' Javine said, her eyes transfixed on Delray. 'After everything you did to me, you really think that I was stupid enough to stick around? That I'd fall for all your bullshit? Getting engaged? After what you put me through?'

Delray shrugged.

'Well that's just it, Javine, you did stick around, didn't you? You stayed, and do you know why you stayed, because you're a greedy little whore.' Delray wanted to rile her up a bit, get her so vexed with him that she'd forget about the fact that she had a gun pointed at his head. 'You just wanted all of this. This place, the kudos, my money!'

Holding his arms out, gesturing at the wealth all around him, Delray laughed now.

'Only, girls like you don't deserve any of this, Javine. Girls like you don't work nearly fucking hard enough for all of this. You think you can just lie on your back and it's yours, like it's your God-given right?' Delray spat. 'That ain't how things work. Put the gun down, Javine. This is fucking stupid. If you were going to shoot me, you would have done it by now.'

'Well that's where you're wrong, Delray,' Javine said as she saw his bravado slowly fading. 'I didn't shoot you because I didn't want to put Georgie and Marnie through the trauma of seeing someone have their brains blown out over the wall behind them,' Javine sneered.

Delray was scared now. He was hiding it well, but his sudden silence gave him away.

'You might not care about Georgie and Marnie, but I do, and those girls have been through enough these past few days to last them a lifetime. No thanks to you and that mother of theirs.'

Javine was thinking of her own mother too now.

All those painful memories that she'd buried so deep.

The woman hadn't given two shits about her as a child.

All she'd cared about was making her fortune. Even if it meant that she had to pimp her own kid out. The woman had been just like Delray: they were two of a kind.

She didn't even realise that she'd pulled the trigger until the loud gunshot rang out, making her jump.

She stared at Delray with pure fascination as his face twisted into a warped look of pain and shock.

Blood spurted out from the bullet hole in his chest.

Shooting again, Javine aimed at his stomach.

Delray flopped to the floor then, lifeless, like a rag doll, as Javine stood over him.

Watching him die.

Smiling down at him as he took his last strangled breath.

One bullet for him, and one for her mother. The one that had got away.

She was done now.

No one else would ever hurt her again. She'd make sure of that.

Tucking the gun back inside her pocket, Javine grabbed the holdall containing Delray's money from the floor behind her, and pressed the button for the lift.

Delray had underestimated her.

Granted, she was broken in places, but broken people were the most dangerous of all.

CHAPTER FORTY-NINE

'Do you fancy another slice of toast and chocolate spread, Marnie?' Tania Moore asked as she sat down at the kitchen table opposite her husband and checked the time.

Rose would be here soon to pick Marnie up for her counselling session. Both the girls were having EMDR: a type of counselling technique used for treating post-traumatic stress syndrome.

'Oh no, one slice is more than enough, isn't it, Marnie?' Carl winked at the child and Marnie giggled. 'She's not a little greedy guts, are you, Marnie?'

Marnie giggled and shook her head.

'I mean, it's not like we snuck any more toast and chocolate spread while you were upstairs getting ready and ate it up really quickly before you came down and caught us, is it, Marnie?'

Again Marnie shook her head, trying her hardest not to giggle.

'One slice, huh?' Tania smiled playing along. 'That's an awful lot of chocolate around your mouth, madam, for just one slice.'

Marnie grinned at Carl. Hearing him snigger she couldn't contain herself any longer, bursting out laughing.

'Okay, we had two slices each. Didn't we, Carl?'

Carl held his hands up good-naturedly.

'You caught us!'

Smiling, Tania poured herself a cup of tea and sipped it while she observed Marnie.

She was glad that she was settling in. Three weeks ago when she'd arrived here it had been a very different story. Marnie had seemed withdrawn, shy. After everything that Tania and Carl had been told about the child's circumstances they could see that she was very damaged. Her sister, Georgie, too. Tania had a feeling that they'd turned a corner now though. Marnie hadn't wet the bed for three days in a row. Her bedding had been bone dry.

Even this morning, with another counselling session hanging over her, she didn't seem fractious or agitated at all. In fact, this morning was the happiest Tania had ever seen the child.

'Right, me and Georgie are off now, Mum! See you later, Dad!'

Stepping around the table, already dressed in her coat and shoes, Hollie gave her mother and father a kiss on the cheek. 'See you later titch!' Hollie said, ruffling Marnie's hair fondly.

Tania eyed her daughter curiously.

She was another person the girls seemed to have a positive impact on. Ever since Georgie had moved in, she and Hollie had become inseparable. Constantly locked away inside Hollie's bedroom, laughing and giggling.

Tania normally had to treat getting out the door to school like a military operation, forcing her out of the bed and nagging her to eat her breakfast and brush her hair, but lately Hollie had motivated herself. Up and dressed early, Georgie and Hollie couldn't get out the door quick enough. Tania smiled to herself. It was nice that Hollie and Georgie had become such good friends.

'See you later, Marnie.' Standing in the doorway behind her, Georgie blew Marnie a kiss.

Marnie pretended to catch it and put it in her pocket.

Then Carl pretended to grab it back out. The giggling persisted.

'You're going to get to school awfully early, girls. You haven't even had any breakfast,' Tania said, wondering what the girls were up to that they needed to leave the house an hour before school started when it was only a five-minute walk.

'Don't worry, Mum!' Hollie rolled her eyes, used to her mum's constant fretting. 'We'll get something at the canteen. We're meeting our friends there, aren't we, Georgie?'

Georgie nodded.

She hated lying to Tania, especially after the woman was so nice to her. She felt bad.

'Okay, well, make sure you do.' Tania looked at Georgie. 'Don't forget I'm picking you up at lunchtime today for your visit.'

Tania gave her a wry smile as Georgie nodded again.

Tania could have kicked herself for her wording. Of course the girl wasn't going to forget. Today was going to be the first time since her mother had been arrested that Georgie would see her.

She expected, if anything, the visit would be playing heavily on the girl's mind, not that she'd ever know with Georgie. Georgie was very closed off and, as Tania knew from experience, these things took time.

She wasn't as outgoing as Marnie: she held back a little.

The only person she really seemed to get along with and trust was Hollie and, for now, that was something at least.

She'd get there in the end with the rest of it, Tania had no doubt. Between her and Carl looking out for the girls, and Rose Feltham ensuring that they had the best counsellors and support available to them, they were all determined to try to make Georgie and Marnie happy again.

'See you later then, girls.'

'See you later!' the girls chorused back as they slammed the front door behind them.

Carl Moore sat back and gave Tania a look. Aware that Marnie was sitting here, they were communicating in their special code. Tania shrugged.

'It's just friends.'

Carl pursed his lips not so sure.

'Uh, uh!' Marnie said knowingly as she scooped her finger along the chocolate spread that smudged across her plate, and then sucked her finger. Tania and Carl were rubbish at not letting her know what they were really taking about. 'You do know that "friends" really means "boys", don't you?' Marnie said innocently. Her eyes wide; her face all serious.

'I overheard them last night. They are meeting Freddy and Harry, the twins. Hollie said she's got a crush on Freddy, but she thinks Freddy likes Georgie. Georgie says she doesn't want a boyfriend though, so she said Hollie can have him. But Hollie said that she doesn't want a boyfriend either. They just pretend they do because they like the boys carrying their bags for them all the time, and fetching them their lunch trays. They said it makes all the other girls jealous of them.'

Tania looked at Carl, both of them stifling their laughs.

'I don't know how they think that boys make them look really cool, though. Boys are just smelly,' Marnie said matter-of-factly before pushing her plate aside now that she'd finished licking up the chocolate.

Tania couldn't help but laugh at Marnie's tone. Carl shook his head, unable to keep a straight face either.

'Our regular little spy!' Then for good measure he screwed up his nose. 'Er, hang on, does that mean that I'm just a smelly boy then?'

'No, you're not. You're a man,' Marnie reasoned, seeing the pretend hurt on Carl's face. Then she saw Tania wink at her before she wafted her hand in front of her nose, getting in with the fun. 'So that makes you extra, extra smelly,' Marnie concluded, before she fell about laughing once again.

CHAPTER FIFTY

'Face this wall, please. Stand still and don't pat the dog,' the prison officer instructed as the passive drug dog carried out its search on Georgie.

Sniffing at her legs, it quickly circled around her before moving on to Tania who was standing at Georgie's side.

Satisfied that the two visitors weren't concealing anything illegal on their person, the prison officer led them through to the main visitor's room.

'Place your finger on the scanner pad.'

Shaking now, Georgie held her hand still. Hearing a bleep, the prison officer nodded curtly at the girl and allowed them through the secure door that led into the main visitor's room.

'You can go through now.'

Georgie was shaking. She knew visiting her mum in prison was going to be a scary experience, but she hadn't factored in for the fact that she would have to be patted down and searched. That she'd have her fingerprints scanned. A dog sniffing around her. The entire process felt like it had taken ages. The guards hadn't been overly friendly either. Most of them cold and abrupt.

By the time Georgie stepped through into the visiting room, with Tania following closely behind her, she felt like she was a criminal herself.

Georgie spotted her mother straight away. That bright blonde mop of hair. She was sitting half way across the hall, at a table underneath the window.

'Georgie, darling,' Josie said as Georgie and Tania approached her. Wrapping her arms briefly around her daughter, Josie couldn't stop her tears from falling as she hugged the girl to her. 'It feels like I haven't seen you in for ever, Georgie. I missed you so much.'

Sitting down opposite her mother, she was overcome with emotion. Georgie couldn't help but cry then too.

It had only been a few weeks, yet, already, her mother looked so much older.

Void of make-up; bags under her eyes.

She hadn't lost that sparkle in her eyes though.

'And you must be Tania?' Josie smiled warmly at the woman. 'Thank you for taking such good care of my girls.'

Tania nodded. Unnerved by the woman's politeness. This wasn't the Josie she'd been anticipating. In fact, she hadn't known what to expect at all.

'How you doing, Georgie darling?' Josie said sitting opposite her child now. Trying to coax her into talking. She knew that this was hard. Coming into prison like this, seeing her locked away.

'How's your sister doing?'

Georgie nodded. 'She's good, Mum.' A tear rolled down her cheek and landed on the table between them both.

Georgie wiped it away with her finger.

'I know it's hard, Georgie. Don't cry, babe. We're going to get through this. All of us.'

'How about I go and grab us all a cup of tea?' Tania suggested, deciding to make herself scarce for a few minutes so that Josie and Georgie could talk.

'That would be nice, thanks,' Josie said appreciatively, before watching the woman walk across the visitor's room to the tea bar.

She looked at Georgie then; her heart had been yearning for her beautiful daughter. Josie had been dreaming of this moment. Craving for the chance to see her girls.

Now Georgie was here, sitting just across the table from her, but the girl seemed cold. Distant. A few feet felt like a thousand miles.

'She seems nice,' Josie said, genuinely. Glad that Children's Services had managed to get her children's foster family right.

She'd spoken to Georgie and Marnie a couple of times on the phone before today, and they both seemed happy where they'd been placed. That was some comfort to her, at least.

'She is nice, Mum.' Georgie said. 'Her and Carl. They have a daughter my age too. Hollie. They're just a normal family. We never had that, did we? A normal family?'

'No, love, I guess we didn't.' Josie shook her head, ashamed of herself for everything she'd put the girls through. She had so many regrets, so much remorse.

She spent the long days in here thinking about every moment, every incident. Torturing herself with guilt and shame.

She blamed herself for Trevor.

For letting him into their home, near her children. It had all been her fault. That was a heavy cross to bear.

'How could you have not told us about Delray, Mum?' Georgie said, still angry at her for so many things. Her head was spinning. There was so much to say, so much to ask, but Georgie didn't even know where to begin with it all.

'I just wanted to protect you both. He didn't want to know, Georgie. He had no interest in Marnie. How could I tell a little girl that… that her father didn't give a shit about her?' Josie shook her head. 'You were both mine. No one else's. From the minute you were both born, you were only ever mine.'

Looking down at the table, she was truly sorry that the girls had found out the way that they had. She wished more than ever she had been there, been able to explain.

She still couldn't believe that Delray was dead. That Javine Turner had killed him before doing a runner.

Josie had spoken to Mandy on the phone, and her friend had filled her in on everything that had happened. It was a shock, but after what Mandy had told her that Delray had done to Georgie, Josie hoped the man rotted in hell.

'I know that it didn't feel like I was always a good mum to you both, Georgie, God knows I've had my problems, but I should never have put you both through the things that I did. The job, the drugs, all of it. I'm more sorry than you'll ever know.'

Georgie stayed quiet. She needed to hear this more than anything. She needed to try to understand.

'I just want you and your sister to know that the two of you are my life. You are my reason for breathing. I failed you both, Georgie, and you have every right to hate me, but I want you to know that I will do anything now to make it better.'

'Then tell them the truth,' Georgie said, looking at her mum, her eyes pleading with her.

Josie shook her head.

'That's the one thing I can't do, Georgie. You know I can't.'

'But Mum—'

'No, Georgie. Just leave it. I failed you both once, and I will never do that to you again. This is the best way, believe me. You mustn't say anything, Georgie.'

Georgie bit her lip. Not wanting to cry any more.

'Let me make this right. I need to make this right. I'm not letting you and your sister suffer any more. I owe you both this. Please Georgie, let me do this.'

Josie placed her hand on Georgie's. 'I ruined my life. I destroyed it, I know that. You two have everything ahead of you. I won't have that tainted.'

Georgie nodded. She knew that there would be no persuading her mother. Her mind was made up.

Tania was coming back to the table now, laden with drinks and some chocolate bars.

'Promise me, Georgie.'

Georgie looked up at her mother.

'I promise.'

CHAPTER FIFTY-ONE

'Remember, if at any time you want to stop, Marnie, you just tell Sally and she'll finish the session, okay?' Rose Feltham said, bending down on one knee so she was at Marnie's level.

'I'm going to be sitting just here. Just outside the door. Okay?'

Marnie nodded.

The child was doing really well considering all she had been through. Sally had made a real breakthrough the past couple of sessions. The signs were all there that Marnie had suffered a considerable amount of sexual abuse, but as yet it was as if the child was too young to even comprehend what had happened to her.

'She'll be just fine.' Sally King, the counsellor, assured Rose before she led Marnie into the room and closed the door behind her.

'Okay, so let's start from where we left off last week.' Sally said, getting herself comfortable on the chair opposite her young client. She'd already re-read over her notes from the previous session.

Marnie was suffering with Post-Traumatic Stress Disorder, and Sally, who had been informed of the child's background, could completely understand why.

Her challenge, however, was getting Marnie to reprocess what she had experienced so that she could work through the trauma. Night terrors, anxiety attacks. The classic signs of the body trying to make sense of traumatic events. Marnie's mind was already fighting to process and heal her past hurts. Sally just needed to help her to recognise all of this. To recognise her triggers. It was a slow process, though. Every time Sally mentioned Marnie's mother, Josie, or Trevor being murdered, Marnie just clammed up. The memory simply too painful for her to even think about. So Sally had decided to try Marnie with a course of Eye Movement Desensitisation and Reprocessing or EMDR, as it was more commonly known. A gentle technique that seemed to be working wonders for Marnie already.

They had begun to make real progress.

'Okay, are you ready?'

Sitting forward on the chair Marnie nodded. By now, she was used to what the sessions entailed, so she pressed her feet firmly on the floor, her hands relaxed on her thighs as she closed her eyes.

Sally King began the tapping process. Moving her hands up and down as she spoke, alternatively tapping on Marnie's knees.

'Okay, Marnie. So we're going to go back to the time that is most troubling you. Take a deep breath and tell me what you see.'

Marnie closed her eyes. Concentrating really hard she tried to picture that evening that she hadn't been able to shake from her mind.

Lying in bed, in her bedroom. She was back there.

I'm dreaming. I must be.

That's what they keep telling me. My mother and my sister.

That none of this is real. That it's just nightmares again.

'Where are you?'

'I'm at home, in my bedroom. I was asleep, but something woke me up. I'm scared. My heart is thumping hard.'

Tap, tap, tap.

'What are you doing now? What can you see?'

'I'm waiting for him to come. I can hear him. Walking along the landing. The sound of the handle twisting on my bedroom door.'

'Are you safe?' Sally asked softly.

'No, he's coming for me.' Marnie shook her head quickly, her movement firm.

'Who is coming for you, Marnie?'

'I thought it was Georgie. She hasn't come to bed yet. She's watching TV in the lounge.'

'Who is there, Marnie, can you tell me?'

Marnie was shaking now. Her small body trembling wildly, involuntarily, as she recounted what was happening.

'It's the Bogeyman,' Marnie said, crying, big fat tears cascading down her cheek. 'I've been a good girl. I did everything my mummy told me to do. I was good. I don't know why he's still come.'

'Take a big deep breath,' Sally said gently. 'You're safe here with me, Marnie. You are safe. No one can hurt you now.'

Marnie relaxed a little as Sally continued the tapping. Registering the fear on Marnie's face.

She had turned white with fear. Her eyebrows furrowing. Her eyes moving from left to right repeatedly as she tried to process what was happening to her.

It was hard to see the fear that the child was having to relive, but Sally knew that it was the only way to help her. She had to go through it.

'What are you doing now?'

'I'm running.' Marnie's voice sounded small, strained. Alien even to her own ears. A slight whisper laced with urgency.

She was there again. In the moment.

'My legs won't work, though. They feel like jelly. I'm trying to make them work but they are trembling so much, I can't make them stop. I'm on Georgie's bed. I don't know why. She's not there. She can't help me.'

Marnie winced.

Transfixed in the moment, Sally knew she had to try to guide her through.

'What's happening now, Marnie?'

Marnie shook her head, as if she was trying to change the image inside her mind: make it disappear.

Sally tapped once more.

'You are safe, Marnie. You are safe. Tell me what's happening.'

'I'm holding my breath. I can hear a funny noise. Banging. Then I realise that it's my heart thumping in my chest. The noise sounds like a drum in my ears.'

'What can you see?'

'I can see him.' Marnie was gulping at the air; gulping down short shallow bursts of air. So engrossed with what she was recalling that she'd forgotten to breathe.

'Breathe.' Sally reminded her. 'Take a slow deep breath. Remember, you are safe here. No one can hurt you now. Tell me where he is?'

Tap, tap, tap.

'He's standing in the doorway. He's watching me. He always does that. Creeps around at night when Mummy is sleeping.'

Marnie paused.

'I'm trying to hide from him. I've pulled the covers up over my head.'

'Does he find you, Marnie?'

Marnie clenched her fists.

Sally began tapping once more. Bringing the girl's eye movements back and forth, left and right. She repeated again.

'You are safe. No one can hurt you. I'm right here with you. You are safe. Does he find you?'

'Yes, he's lifted the covers from me. I try to open my mouth but nothing comes out. My voice has disappeared from me.'

'What's happening, Marnie? Can you tell me?'

'He's got me again. He's going to hurt me. Do those things to me that I don't like. He's going to hurt me.'

'What are you doing now?'

Marnie paused. Thinking really carefully.

'I'm hiding.'

Sally tried to visualise the scene. Marnie had said that she was in the bed. That 'the Bogeyman' had her. Now she was hiding?

'Where are you hiding?'

'I'm not sure. I think I'm hiding inside my body. I've made myself go really tiny. If I stay really still he won't be able to find me. He can only hurt my skin, but he can't hurt me. I won't let him.'

'What happens next?'

'I can hear Georgie. She's trying to help me. Trying to get into the room. But he's locked the door. He won't let her in. Then there's a banging sound. Really loud. He looks angry now that he has to stop hurted me.'

'Tell me what you see?'

'Georgie and Mummy.'

Sally shifts in her seat. Makes a note in the notebook next to her. Her eyes flicker to the clock again on the wall. They are almost out of time. She should stop. Take Marnie back to her safe place and end the session, but with the progress they are making today, Sally wants Marnie to continue working her way through it all. To make the breakthrough the child so desperately needs.

'What's Georgie doing?'

'They are shouting at him. They know that he hurted me now. They both look angry. Mummy is shouting, but she's crying too.'

'Can you tell me what happens next, Marnie? You're doing such a great job.'

'He pushes Georgie out of the way. He hurts her. She bangs her head on the wall. She's lying on the floor. He's going to hurt my mum too. He's shouting at her.'

'Then what happens, Marnie?'

Marnie is quiet now. Contemplating. Deep in thought.

Picturing the scene as if she was right there again.

'He's not angry any more.'

'Why isn't he angry. Marnie?'

'Because he's dead!'

Marnie stops talking again.

'Did you see what killed him, Marnie?'

Marnie nods again.

'It's a hammer. It's sticking out of his head. There is a lot of blood. It doesn't look very nice.'

'Is your mummy holding the hammer, Marnie?'

Marnie takes a deep breath then. Her eyes moving rapidly behind her eyelids as she recounts the scene.

There is blood everywhere, all up the wall; it's all over them too.

Splatters of blood streaking up the front of her nightdress; across her mother's face.

So much blood.

Mummy isn't holding the hammer. Neither is Georgie.

I am.

I look down at the hammer still gripped tightly in my hand.

All that blood. So much blood.

Mummy takes the hammer. Pulls it from my hand and won't let it go.

Now Marnie remembers what her mother told her, how she made the two girls promise not to tell.

How she made them both swear.

'Cross my heart and hope to die. Marnie, say it! You mustn't tell anyone the truth. You must tell them that I did it. Otherwise, they'll take you away. Promise me.'

'Cross my heart, Mummy.'

Marnie opens her eyes.

* * *

Back in the room, Marnie looks straight at Sally, her voice steady, controlled.

'Yes, my mummy was holding the hammer. She killed him. She killed the Bogeyman.'

CHAPTER FIFTY-TWO

Standing at the side of Delray's grave, Mandy stared down at the raised mound of earth, glad that no flowers had been laid.

Turns out the man wasn't as popular as he liked to think he was. His funeral was yesterday, but there was no way Mandy would have graced the man's funeral service with her presence. Not after what he'd tried to do with Georgie. The man was a monster. She couldn't wish his brutal murder on a more worthy person.

She'd read Javine all wrong. Despite what Josie had always thought of the girl, deep down, Javine had a kind heart. She'd done good, in the end, for all the right reasons. Mandy wished the girl well.

She doubted the police would ever catch up with her. It wasn't exactly a priority to them, finding someone who had ultimately done them such a huge favour. By killing the man, Javine had pretty much wrapped up the notorious Delray Anderton in a bow and given the man to the Old Bill as a gift. They probably threw themselves a fucking good knees-up to celebrate. Another piece of shit dealt with. Only, this time it was for good.

Feeling the rain start to fall, Mandy pulled her coat tightly around her, before looking down at the grave one last time.

'Goodbye, Delray,' she spat. 'I hope you rot in hell, mate!'

Mandy grinned to herself. She was glad to have done her bit. She'd promised Josie when she'd spoken to her on the phone that she would pay her last respects for the woman.

Though, as Josie had put it, Delray didn't deserve any respect. She just wanted Mandy to tell him on her behalf that she hoped he rotted for all eternity.

She was done now.

Turning on her heel, she made her way back towards where Davey was patiently hovering around by the cemetery's main gates.

The man was a saint.

He had thought she was mad wanting to come here today but, like always, he'd respected her wishes and even insisted on driving her down here.

Walking towards him, Mandy couldn't help but smile.

She'd finally got her break. They were making a go of it, the two of them, and Mandy was loving every minute of it. Working behind the bar, helping Davey run the pub.

Finally, she'd found her calling.

'You all right, Mand?' Davey said as Mandy stepped towards him. Wrapping his arm protectively around her shoulders, he kissed her tentatively on the lips. 'Come on, it's freezing out here. Let's get you home, yeah?'

'Home.'

Mandy nodded, unable to speak. The emotion caught in her throat. Then she grinned to herself and rolled her eyes.

She was turning into a right old soppy cow!

If only Josie could see her now!

It was still early days for her and Davey but, so far, Mandy had never felt happier.

They'd even spoken about seeing if they could foster the girls.

She still didn't know all the ins and outs of what had happened that night between Josie and Trevor, but Mandy didn't care. She knew her friend, and she knew that there was much more to it.

Maybe, one day, Josie would set her straight.

Until then, she'd promised Josie that she'd look out for Georgie and Marnie now. That she'd do everything in her power to make sure they were happy and safe, and it was a promise that Mandy intended to keep.

LETTER FROM CASEY KELLEHER

Thank you for taking the time to read *The Promise*. If you fancy leaving me a review, I'd really appreciate it. Not only is it great to have your feedback (I love reading each and every one of the reviews left), but adding a review can really help to gain the attention of new readers too. So if you would kind enough to leave a short, honest review, it would be very much appreciated!

I really enjoyed writing *The Promise*. Josie Parker was a great character to create. Flawed in many ways, not only was Josie a victim of her circumstances, but also of her many bad decisions, which eventually caught up with her. Ultimately, she meant well. She loved her two children Georgie and Marnie and in the end she tried her hardest to do right for them both in her own way. I really hope you enjoyed the story!

I'm currently working on the next book so if you'd like to stay in touch and find out about the next release, or you just want to drop by and say hello I'd love to hear from you!

If you'd like to keep up-to-date with all my latest releases, just sign up at the link below. Your email address will never be shared and you can unsubscribe at any time.

Casey x

www.bookouture.com/casey-kelleher

OfficialCaseyKelleher/

CaseyKelleher

www.caseykelleher.co.uk/

ACKNOWLEDGMENTS

To all my fantastic readers: Thank you so much for all your comments, messages and interaction on social media. You are the very reason I write, without you, none of this would have been possible. I love receiving your feedback and messages, so please do keep them coming!

Massive thanks to my editor Keshini Naidoo for her amazing editorial skills and advice. I love that you get my style of writing and how your ideas and input always seem to help pull everything together. It's a pleasure working alongside you.

Thanks to the lovely Kim Nash – Bookouture's very own Media Star! – for all your hard work, support and encouragement. You really are a star!

To the fabulous 'Blog-squad' – Noelle Holton, Katherine Everett, Shell Baker, Vicki Wilkinson, Book Addict Shaun, Sarah Hardy, Chelsea Humphrey, Celeste – Celeste loves books, to Deryl Easton who runs the Facebook Notrights book group, and to any of the many more fabulous bloggers out there (sorry if I haven't mentioned you all by name). You really do such an amazing job promoting us authors and I for one really appreciate all your support!

Thank you to all my lovely author friends I've met along the way (some whom have left me rather star struck). To all the Bookouture gang and to the Chickens on a Picnic Blanket crew... (Thanks to Ed James for that one!) Writing can feel like a very solitary career sometimes, and it's nice to know that I'm not alone on this sometimes insane journey.

Special thanks to Anne and Charlie Phesse of I Drive U Chauffeur Service for inviting me along to a charity event/book signing this year which they organised on behalf of Kent, Surrey & Sussex Air Ambulance. A brilliant day was had by all and Anne and Charlie managed to raise a fantastic £2563.00. Congratulations to Tania and Carl Moore and their daughter Hollie, who all won their names in this novel. As it was for charity, I wrote you all in as 'Goodies' ;-) I hope you enjoy it.

Thank you to Harriet Feltham for all your help on questions about social workers and Children's Services. I felt it fitting that beautiful little Rose Feltham played out her debut as a character in the book as a way of thanks. (If I had named the character after you we both know how I would not have been able to resist killing you off! x)

Special thanks to my brother Seán for always reading the very first copy of all my books and giving me his honest feedback. To Lucy my bestie for all your #FreeAgent work, and most importantly for the carrying of my gin at crime festivals, and to my sister Tara for proof-listening to the audiobook – sorry about all the swearing!

As always I would like to thank my parents, family and friends for all their ongoing encouragement and support.

Last but never least, to the most important people of all, Danny and my boys. My world. x